STEVENSON · ELLIS · WATTERS · ALLEN

LUMBERJANES

BEWARE THE KITTEN HOLY

Published by

BOOM! BOX™

Ross Richie ....Chairman & Founder
Jen Harned ....CFO
Matt Gagnon ....Editor-in-Chief
Filip Sablik ....President, Publishing & Marketing
Stephen Christy ....President, Development
Adam Yoelin ....Senior Vice President, Film
Lance Kreiter ....Vice President, Licensing & Merchandising
Bryce Carlson ....Vice President, Editorial & Creative Strategy
Hunter Gorinson ....Vice President, Business Development
Josh Hayes ....Vice President, Sales
Sierra Hahn ....Executive Editor
Eric Harburn ....Executive Editor
Ryan Matsunaga ....Director, Marketing
Stephanie Lazarski ....Director, Operations
Mette Norkjaer ....Director, Development
Elyse Strandberg ....Manager, Finance
Michelle Ankley ....Manager, Production Design
Cheryl Parker ....Manager, Human Resources
Breanna Sarpy ....Manager, Digital Marketing & Advertising
Rosalind Morehead ....Manager, Retail Sales

BOOM! BOX™

LUMBERJANES Volume One, October 2022. Published by BOOM! Box, a division of Boom Entertainment, Inc. Lumberjanes is ™ & © 2022 Shannon Watters, Grace Ellis, Noelle Stevenson & Brooklyn Allen. Originally published in single magazine form as LUMBERJANES No. 1-4. ™ & © 2014 Shannon Watters, Grace Ellis, Noelle Stevenson & Brooklyn Allen. All rights reserved. BOOM! Box™ and the BOOM! Box logo are trademarks of Boom Entertainment, Inc., registered in various countries and categories. All characters, events, and institutions depicted herein are fictional. Any similarity between any of the names, characters, persons, events, and/or institutions in this publication to actual names, characters, and persons, whether living or dead, events, and/or institutions is unintended and purely coincidental. BOOM! Box does not read or accept unsolicited submissions of ideas, stories, or artwork.

BOOM! Studios, 6920 Melrose Ave., Los Angeles, CA 90038. Printed in Canada. Fifteenth Printing.

ISBN: 978-1-60886-687-8, eISBN: 978-1-61398-358-4

Fried Pie Exclusive Cover
ISBN: 978-1-60886-880-3, e-ISBN 978-1-61398-551-9

THIS LUMBERJANES FIELD MANUAL BELONGS TO:

NAME: _____

TROOP: _____

DATE INVESTED: _____

FIELD MANUAL TABLE OF CONTENTS

LUMBERJANES
FIELD MANUAL

For the Intermediate Program

Tenth Edition • January 1984

Prepared for the

**Miss Qiunzella Thiskwin
Penniquiqul Thistle Crumpet's
CAMP FOR**  HARDCORE
LADY-TYPES

"Friendship to the Max!"

A MESSAGE FROM THE LUMBERJANES HIGH COUNCIL

miss Qiunzella Thiskwin
Penniquiqul Thistle Crumpet's
Camp for
HARDCORE LADY TYPES.
FRIENDSHIP to the MAX!

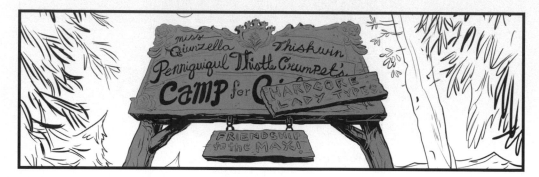

As young women, we were wild with the love of what the world had to offer—the trees, the birds, the wood-herbs and the live things that left their nightly tracks in the mud around our windows. We wanted to learn about them, to know the name of this or that wonderful bird, or brilliant flower. There were other things in the green and living world that had a binding charm for us, the almost unnatural call of curiosity to see what the world held. We wanted to learn to camp out, to live not only like the lady we were already growing up to be but to also learn tricks of winning comfort from the relentless wilderness.

It was then that we became Lumberjanes scouts, learning the joy of cutting wood with an axe, about the stars, the birds, the quadrupeds, the fish, the insects, the plants, telling their names; their hidden power or curious ways, about the camper's life the language of signs and even some of the secrets of the trail. It was at a Lumberjanes camp that we found our life's calling and the power of the tradition of helping young girls grow into the powerful ladies that they are.

Whether you are a dancer or a misfit, a career girl or the social elite, you have a place at this camp—no matter how different you feel. Being a Lumberjane is more than a short chapter in the continually growing pages of your life; it will show you the mysteries of life and the mysteries about yourself while still teaching you as much about the outdoor world that you wish to know. This handbook is meant to guide you on your path as a Lumberjane, as a friend, and as a human being. We hope it will show you a different side of life that will help guide you on your future journeys.

THE LUMBERJANES PLEDGE

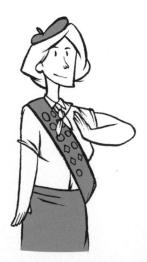

I solemnly swear to do my best
Every day, and in all that I do,
To be brave and strong,
To be truthful and compassionate,
To be interesting and interested,
To pay attention and question
The world around me,
To think of others first,
To always help and protect my friends,
[redacted]
And to make the world a better place
For Lumberjane scouts
And for everyone else.

THEN THERE'S A LINE ABOUT GOD, OR WHATEVER

BEWARE THE KITTEN HOLY

Written by
ND Stevenson
& Grace Ellis

Illustrated by
Gus Allen

Colors by
Maarta Laiho

Letters by
Aubrey Aiese

Cover by
ND Stevenson

Character Designs ....**ND Stevenson & Gus Allen**
Badge Designs .... **Kate Leth**
Lumberjanes Logo Design ....**Hannah Nance Partlow**
Designer...**Scott Newman**
Associate Editor......................................**Whitney Leopard**
Editor...**Dafna Pleban**

*Special thanks to **Kelsey Pate** for giving the Lumberjanes their name.*

Created by
Shannon Watters, Grace Ellis, ND Stevenson & Gus Allen

LUMBERJANES FIELD MANUAL

CHAPTER ONE

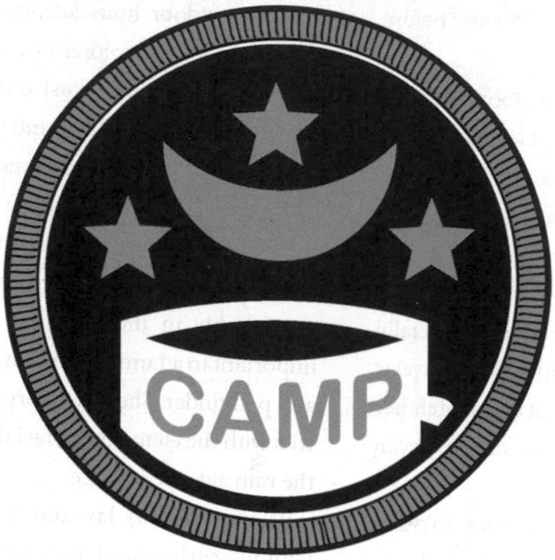
CAMP

Lumberjanes "Out-of-Doors" Program Field

UP ALL NIGHT BADGE

"Learn what goes bump in the night."

While nature is a great experience in the light of the sun, when majority of the living creatures are out and about, a true Lumberjane knows that there is even more to experience when the sun goes down. Curiosity and courage are especially important to a Lumberjane, she has an urge to get out and match her wits and fervor with the elements, to feel the cool crisp night air or possibly the rain in her face. To witness the hyper-natural power of lightning with the true darkness that a night with no moon can provide.

A Lumberjane knows about the experience and possible truths that can be found when the rest of the world is asleep. It is the urge to learn how to lay and follow trails, identify the healing abilities of the local fauna, how to walk great distances and run even farther, and how to work around the unnatural and supernatural forces that a Lumberjane is bound to confront. The *Up All Night* badge is the for Lumberjane that has already conquered the unknown in the daylight and is ready to explore the adventure of the night, ready to discover how to use all the ways of getting from one place to another. A Lumberjane is able to enjoy all of the known and unknown things that can be found in their world.

To obtain the *Up All Night* badge a Lumberjane must have enjoyed the sunset on a cool crisp afternoon with a group of cherished friends. She must have walked under the canvas of the stars and enjoyed their beauty while going where her curiosity takes her. She must have enjoyed the first wind of a new day with the moon above her head and without sleep, energetically explored the new possibility of viewing the world under a moon. And her final step to obtaining this particular badge, is she would have had to enjoy the sunset of the new day surrounded by her friends and ready to start

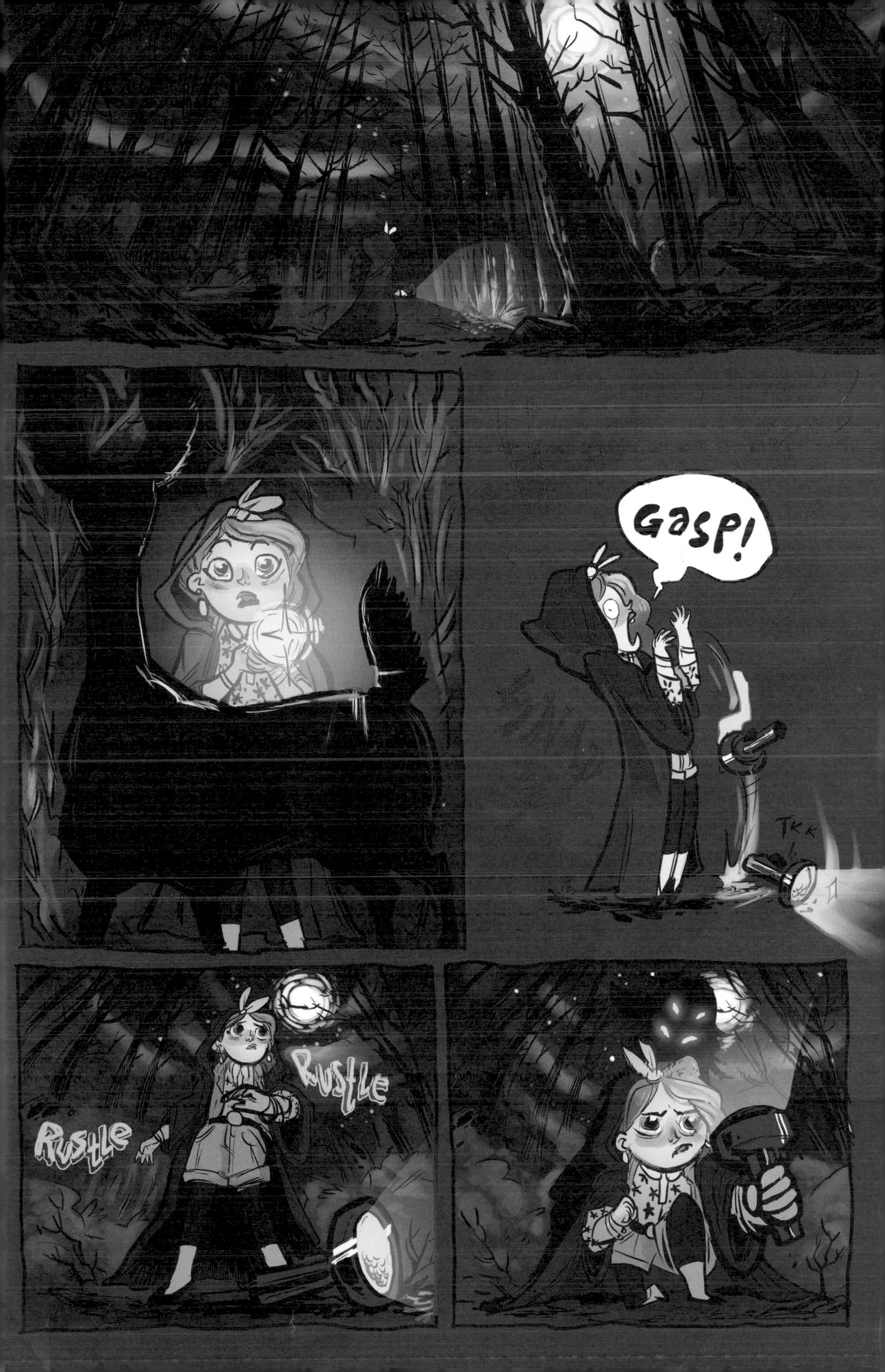
Gasp!
TKK
Rustle
Rustle

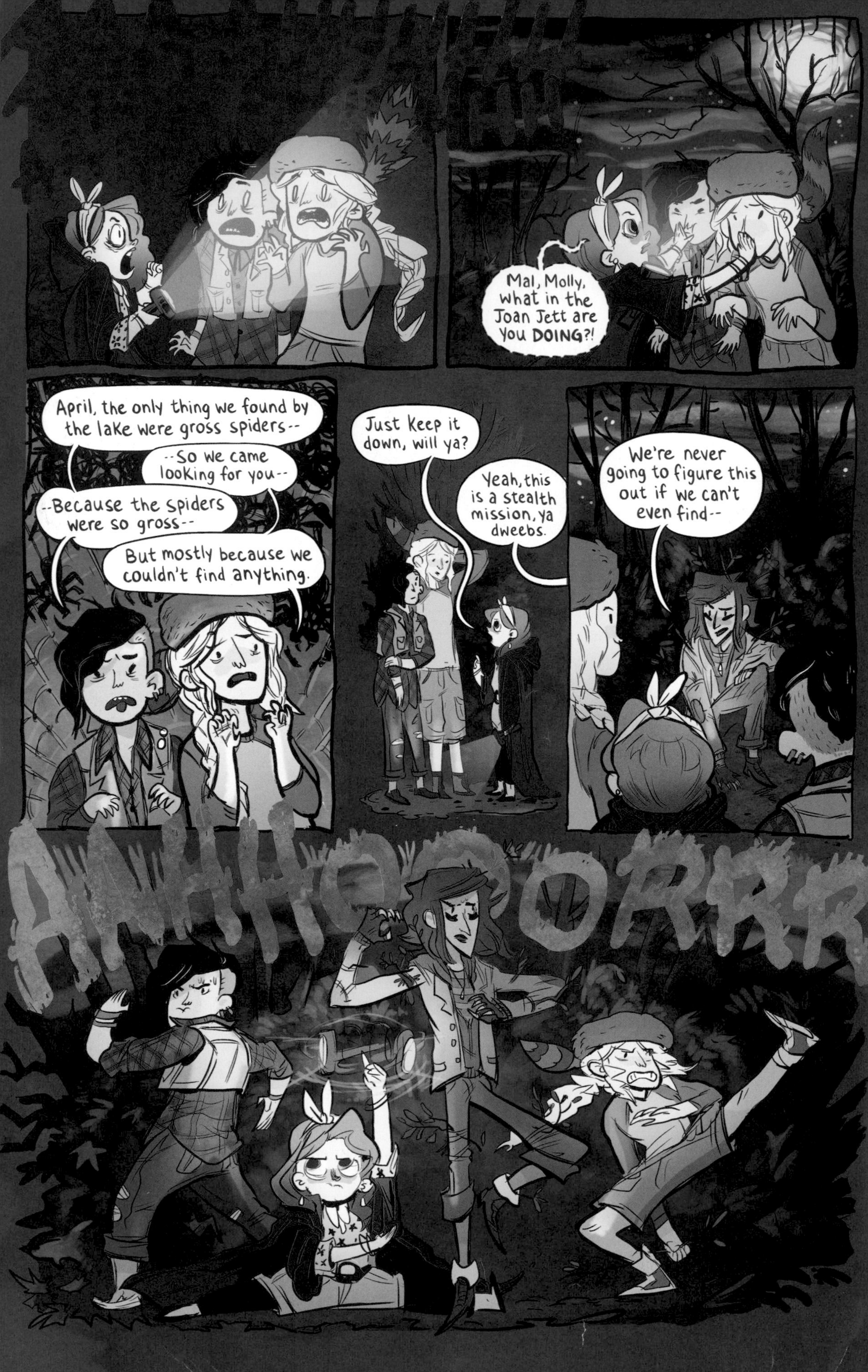
Mal, Molly, what in the Joan Jett are you DOING?!
April, the only thing we found by the lake were gross spiders--
--So we came looking for you--
--Because the spiders were so gross--
But mostly because we couldn't find anything.
Just keep it down, will ya?
Yeah, this is a stealth mission, ya dweebs.
We're never going to figure this out if we can't even find--
AAHHOOORRR

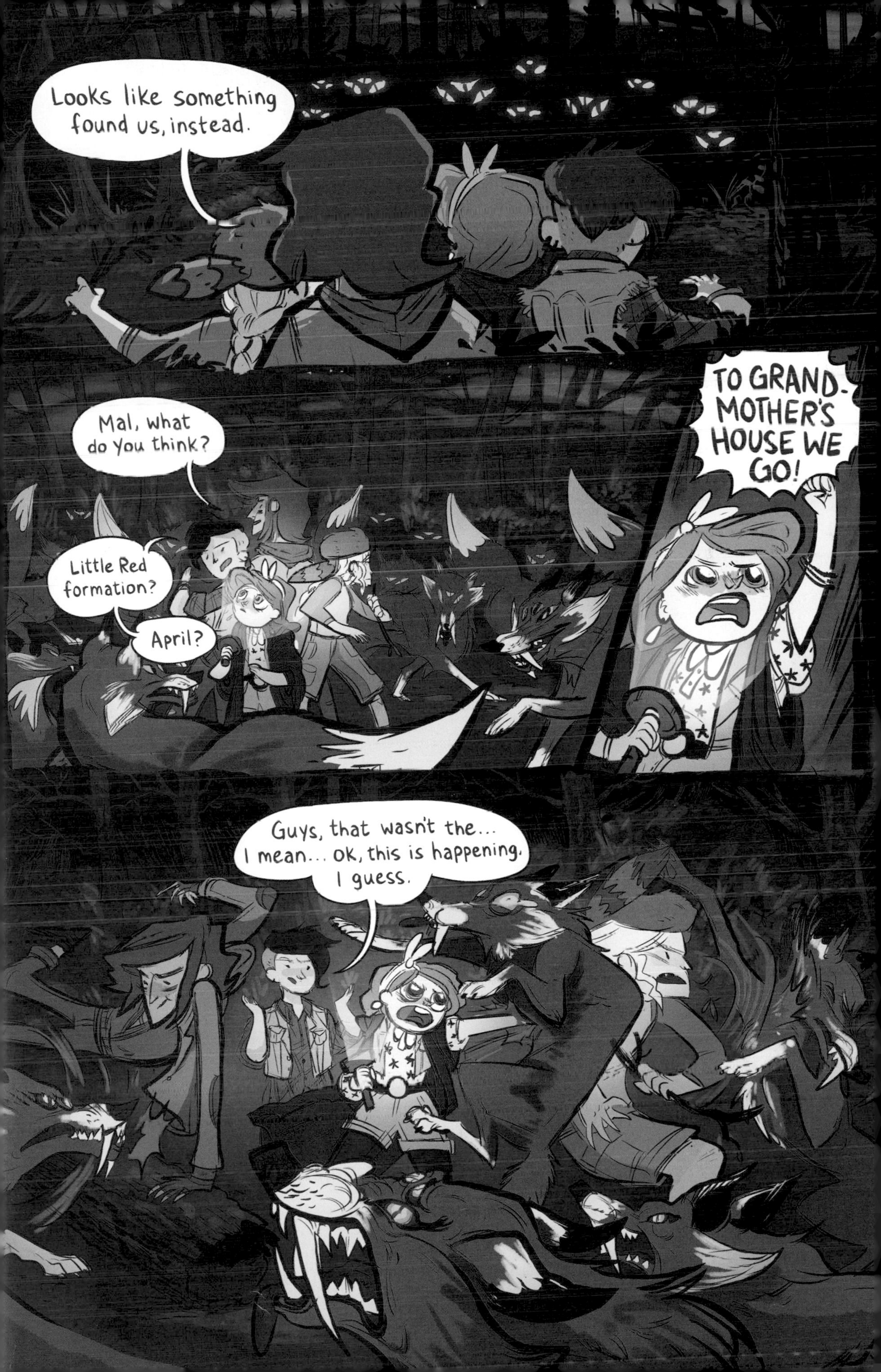
Looks like something found us, instead.
Mal, what do you think?
Little Red formation?
April?
TO GRAND-MOTHER'S HOUSE WE GO!
Guys, that wasn't the... I mean... OK, this is happening. I guess.

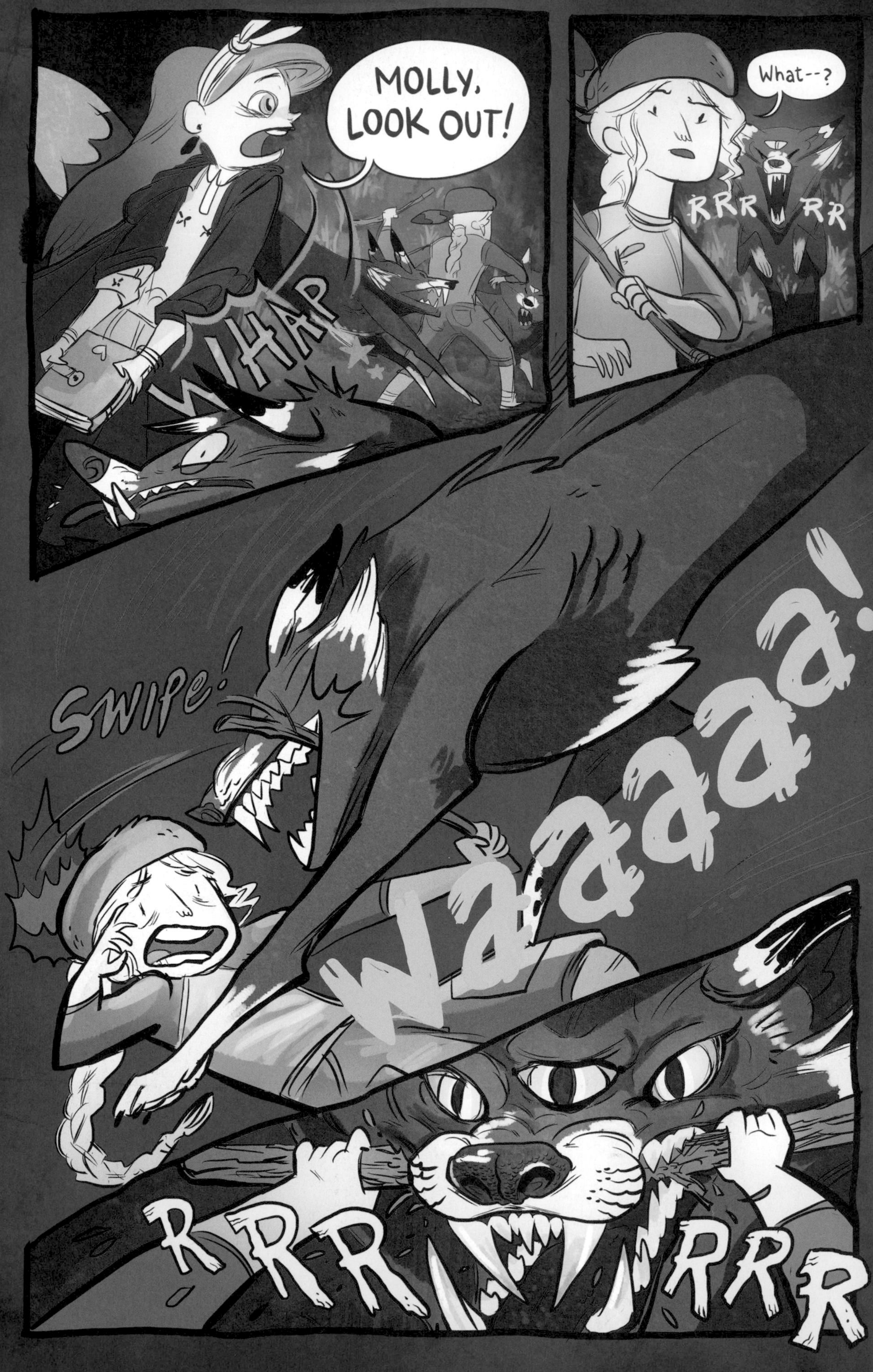
MOLLY, LOOK OUT!
WHAP
What--?
RRR RR
Swipe!
Waaaaa!
RRR RRRR

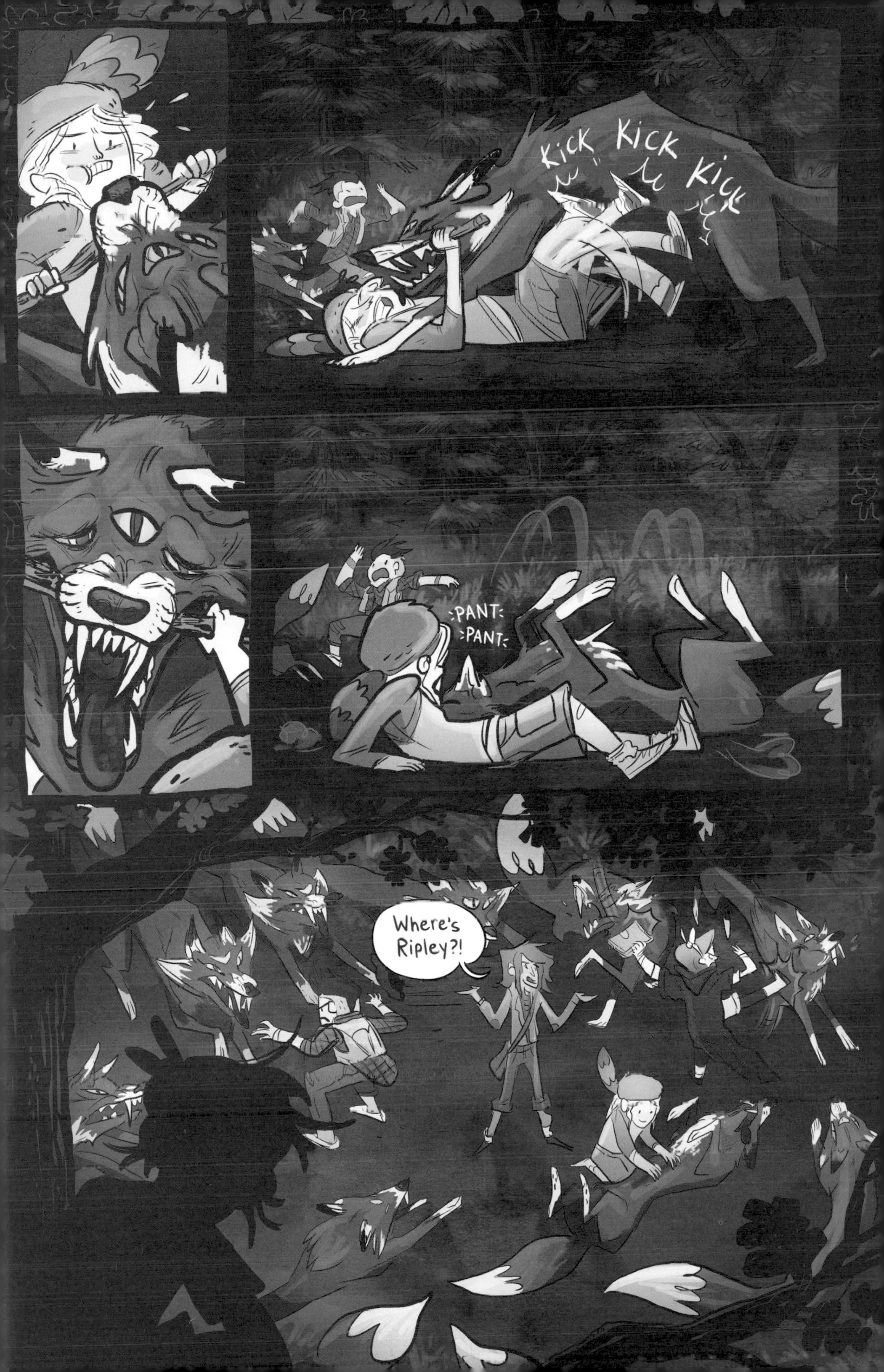
KICK KICK KICK
PANT
PANT
Where's Ripley?!

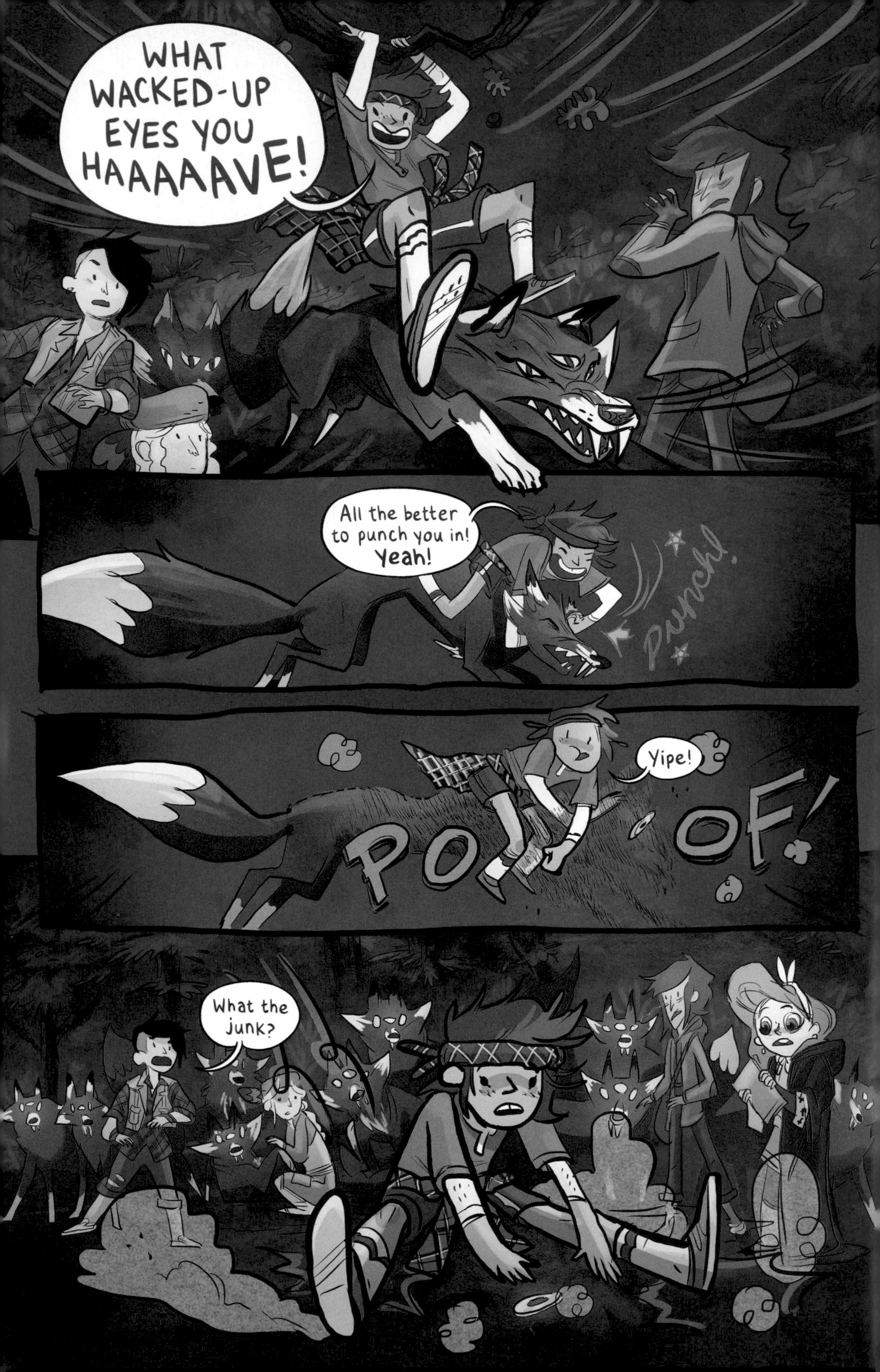
WHAT WACKED-UP EYES YOU HAAAAAVE!
All the better to punch you in! Yeah!
Punch!
Yipe!
POOF!
What the junk?

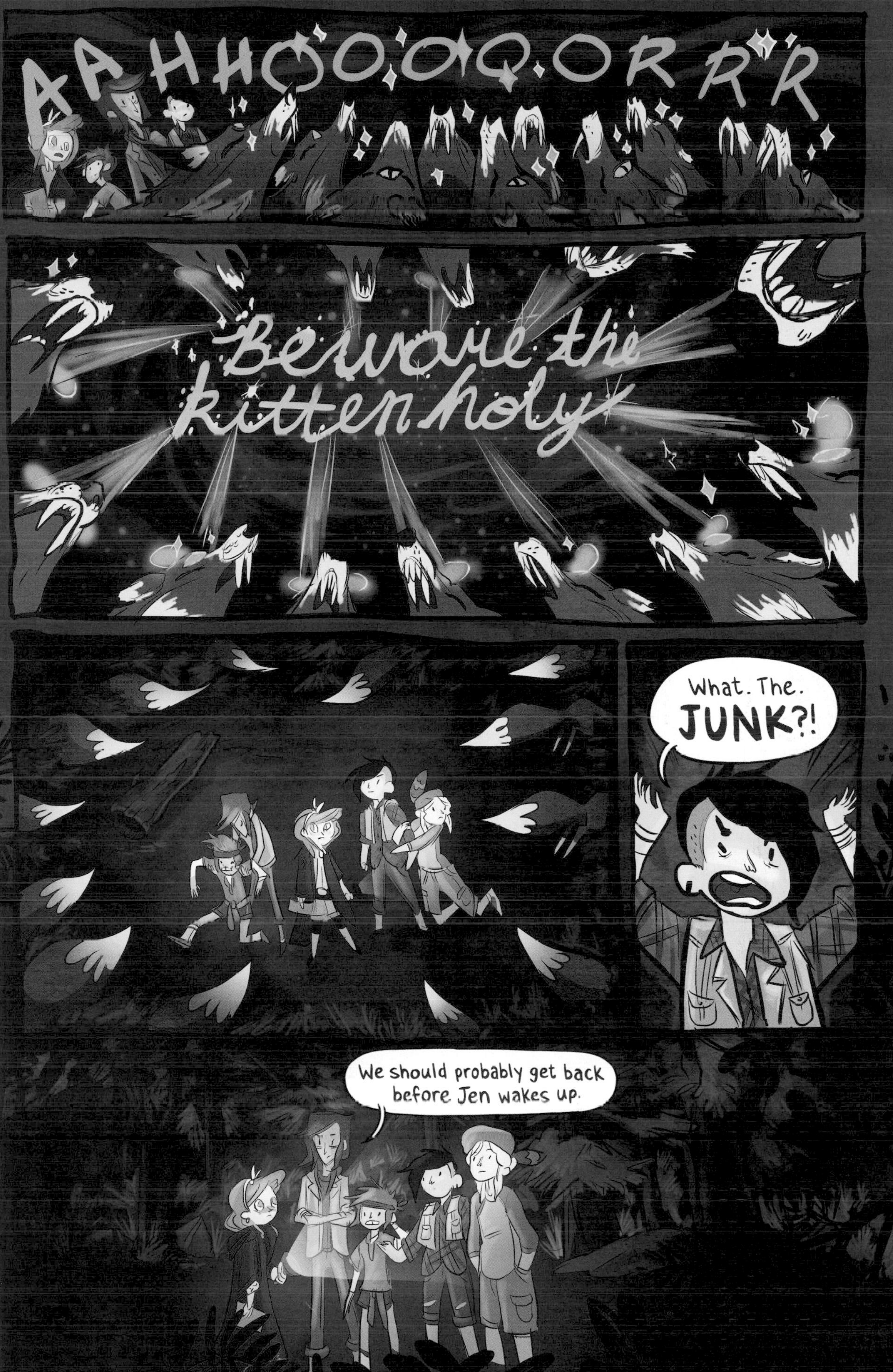
AAHHOOOOORRRR
Beware the kitten holy
What. The. JUNK?!
We should probably get back before Jen wakes up.

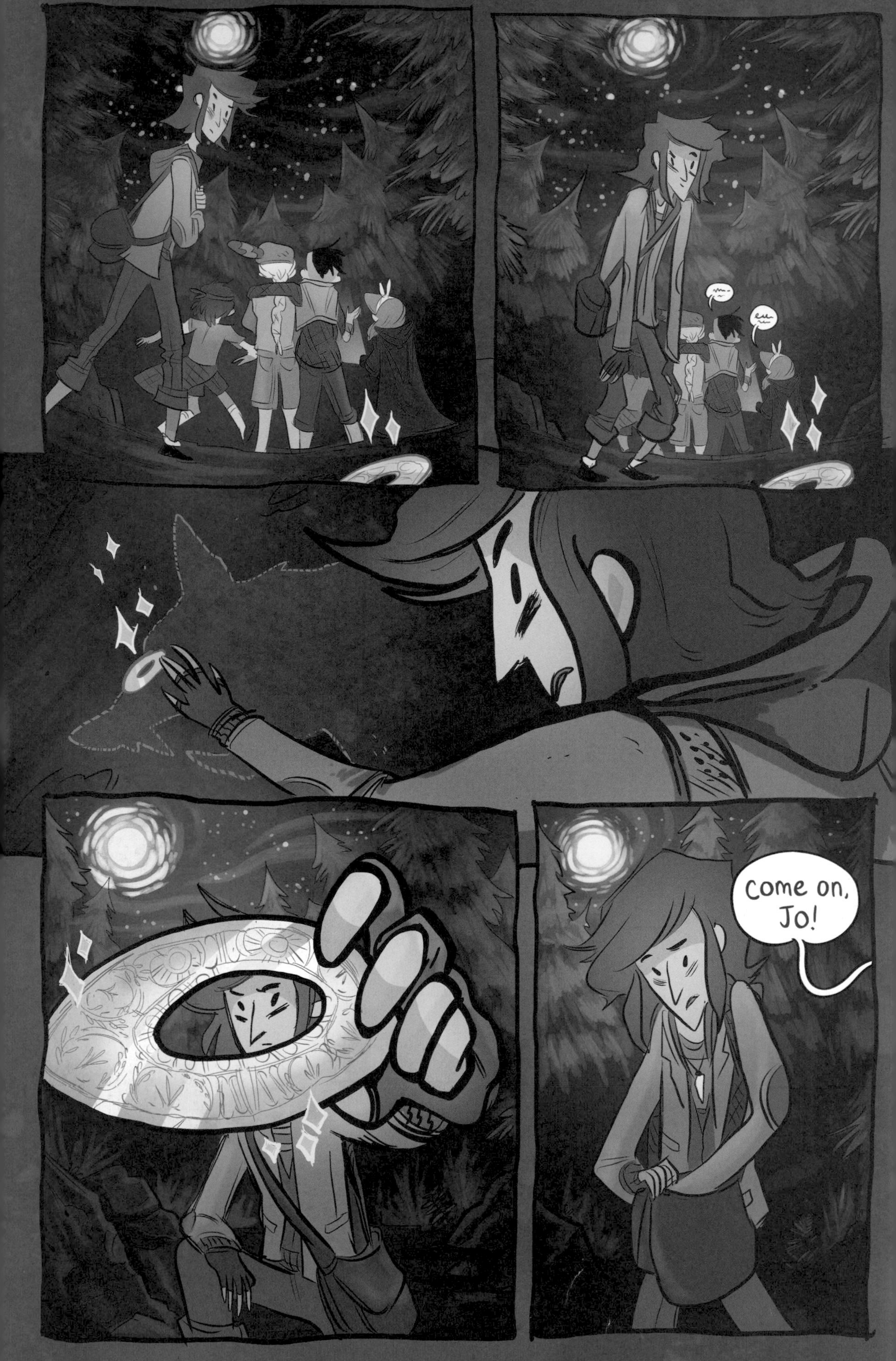
Come on, Jo!

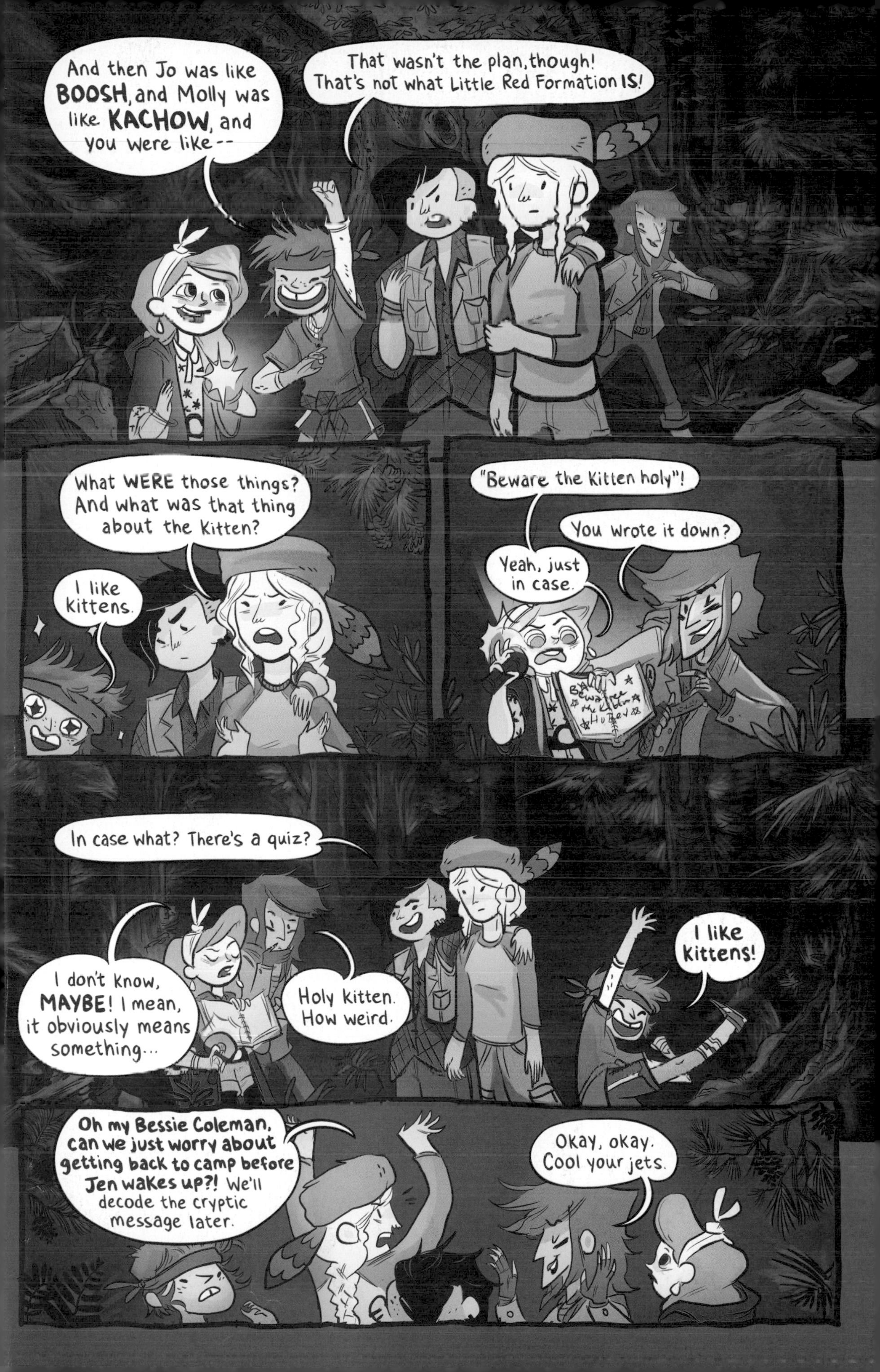

And then Jo was like BOOSH, and Molly was like KACHOW, and you were like--
That wasn't the plan, though! That's not what Little Red Formation IS!
What WERE those things? And what was that thing about the kitten?
I like kittens.
"Beware the Kitten holy"!
You wrote it down?
Yeah, just in case.
In case what? There's a quiz?
I don't know, MAYBE! I mean, it obviously means something...
Holy kitten. How weird.
I like kittens!
Oh my Bessie Coleman, can we just worry about getting back to camp before Jen wakes up?! We'll decode the cryptic message later.
Okay, okay. Cool your jets.

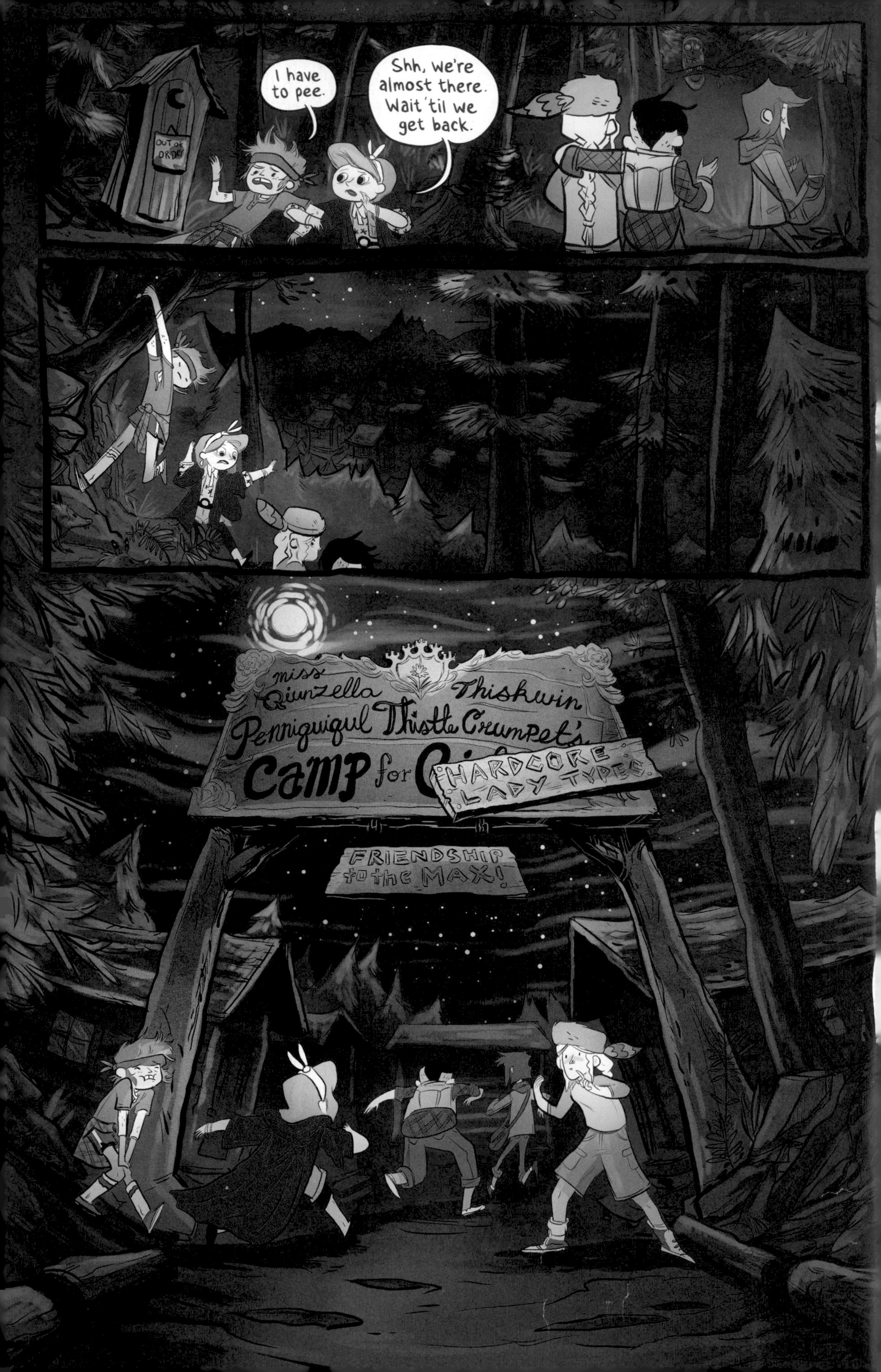

OUT OF ORDER
I have to pee.
Shh, we're almost there. Wait 'til we get back.
Miss Qiunzella Thiskwin Penniquiqul Thistle Crumpet's Camp for
HARDCORE LADY TYPES
FRIENDSHIP to the MAX!

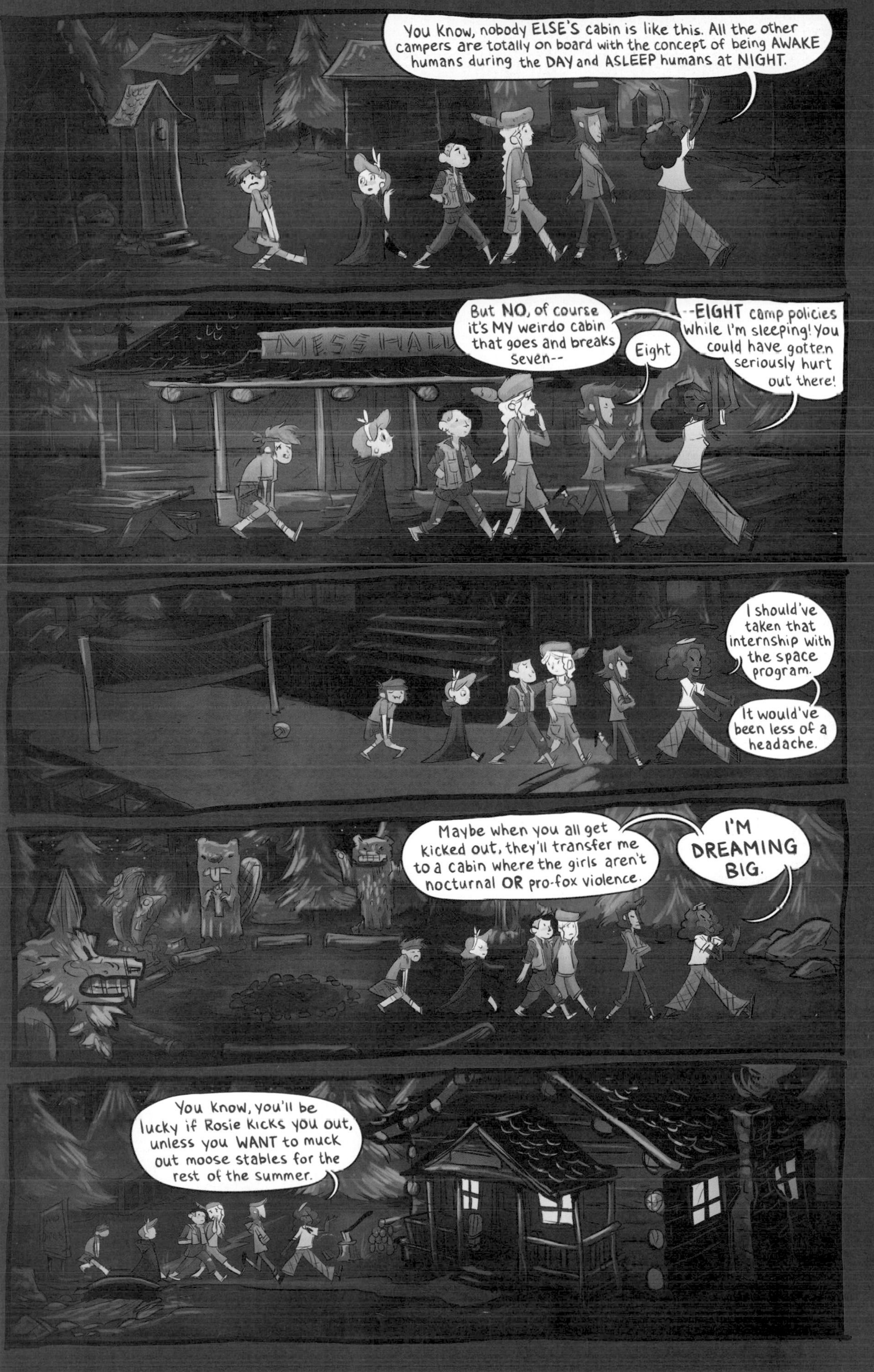
You know, nobody ELSE'S cabin is like this. All the other campers are totally on board with the concept of being AWAKE humans during the DAY and ASLEEP humans at NIGHT.
But NO, of course it's MY weirdo cabin that goes and breaks seven--
Eight
--EIGHT camp policies while I'm sleeping! You could have gotten seriously hurt out there!
MESS HALL
I should've taken that internship with the space program.
It would've been less of a headache.
Maybe when you all get kicked out, they'll transfer me to a cabin where the girls aren't nocturnal OR pro-fox violence.
I'M DREAMING BIG.
You know, you'll be lucky if Rosie kicks you out, unless you WANT to muck out moose stables for the rest of the summer.

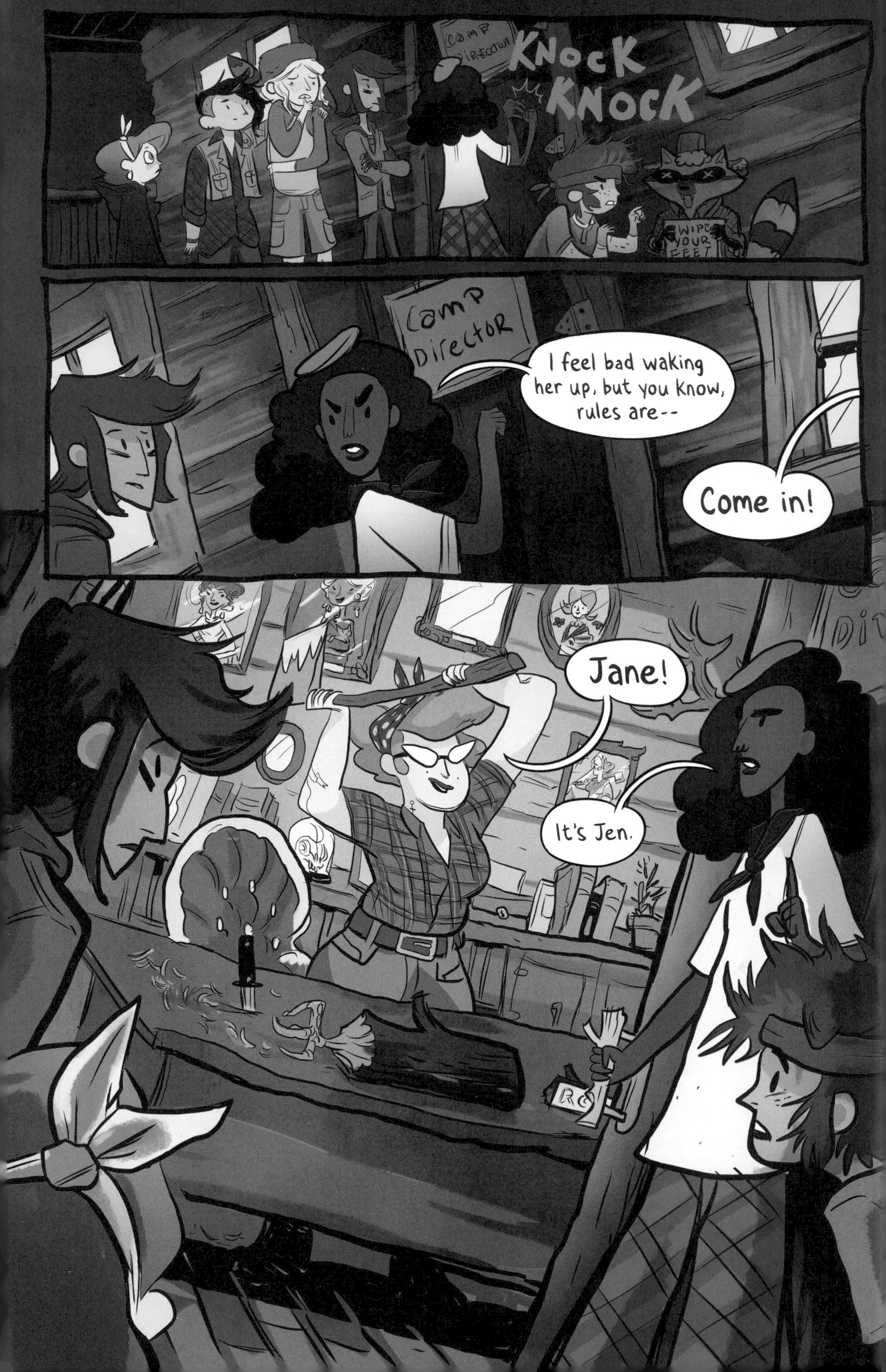

CAMP DIRECTOR
KNOCK KNOCK
WIPE YOUR FEET
CAMP DIRECTOR
I feel bad waking her up, but you know, rules are--
Come in!
Jane!
It's Jen.

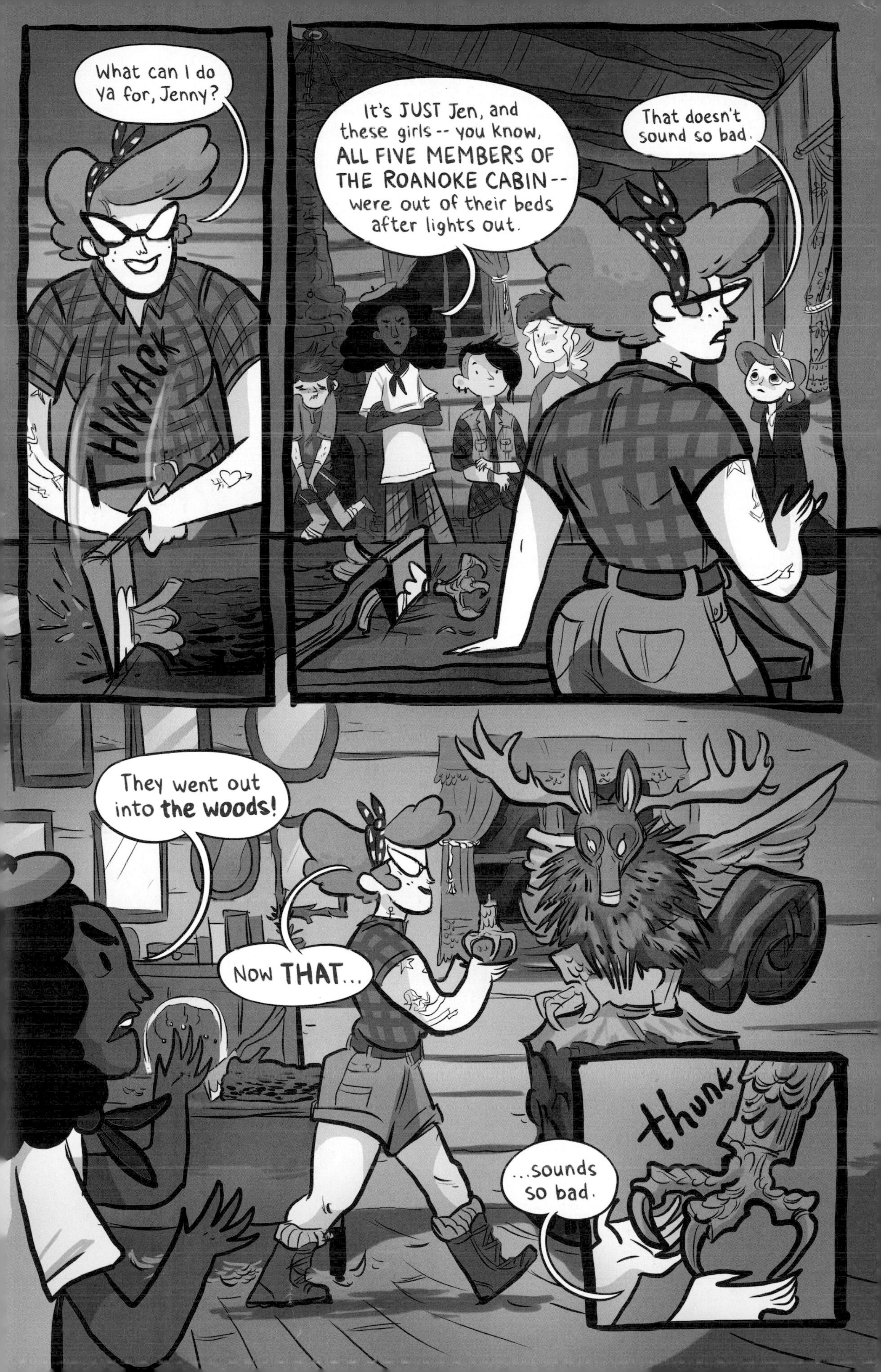

What can I do ya for, Jenny?
HWACK
It's JUST Jen, and these girls -- you know, ALL FIVE MEMBERS OF THE ROANOKE CABIN -- were out of their beds after lights out.
That doesn't sound so bad.
They went out into the woods!
Now THAT...
thunk
...sounds so bad.

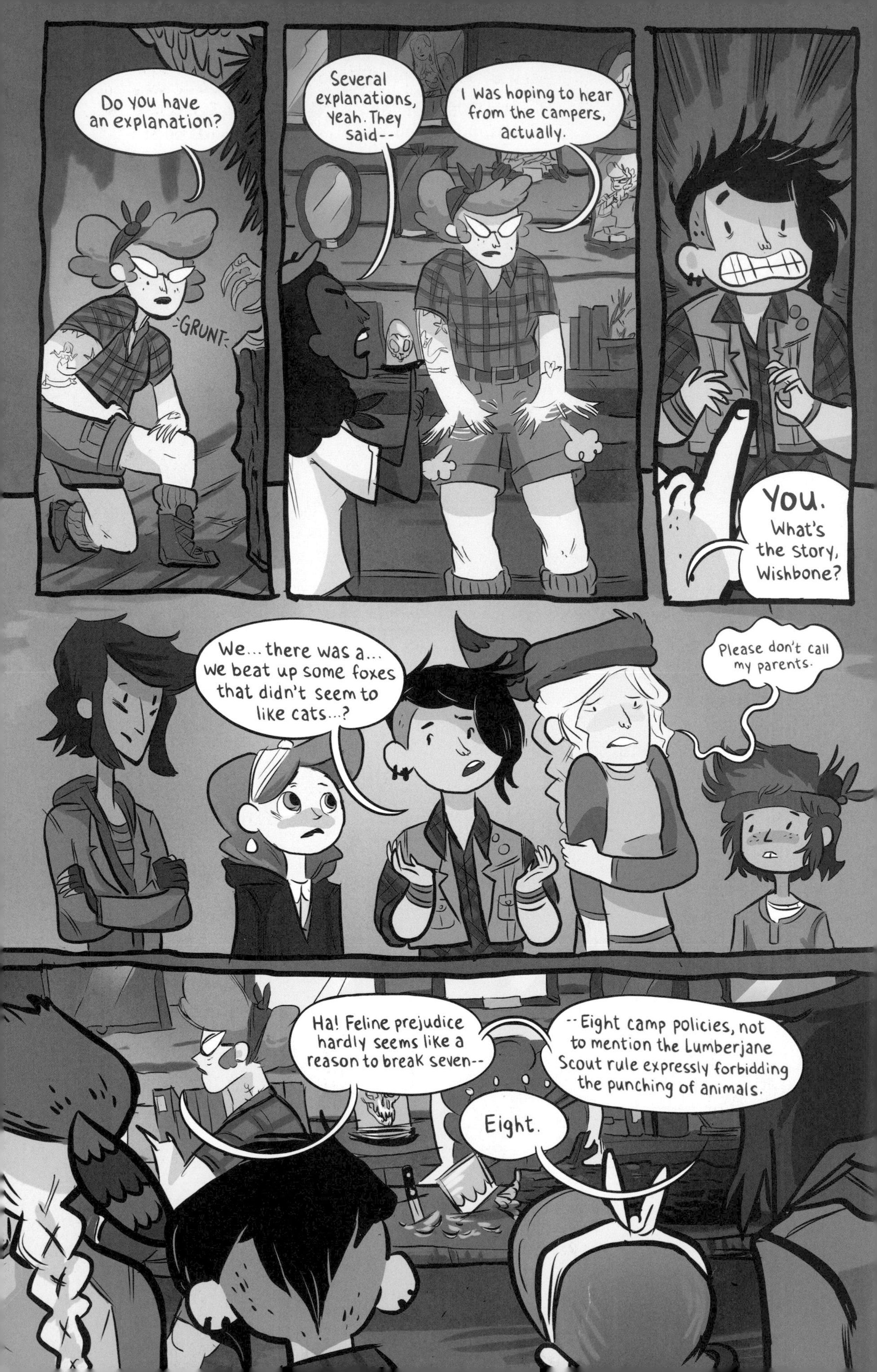
Do you have an explanation?
-GRUNT-
Several explanations, yeah. They said--
I was hoping to hear from the campers, actually.
YOU. What's the story, Wishbone?
We... there was a... we beat up some foxes that didn't seem to like cats...?
Please don't call my parents.
Ha! Feline prejudice hardly seems like a reason to break seven--
Eight.
--Eight camp policies, not to mention the Lumberjane Scout rule expressly forbidding the punching of animals.

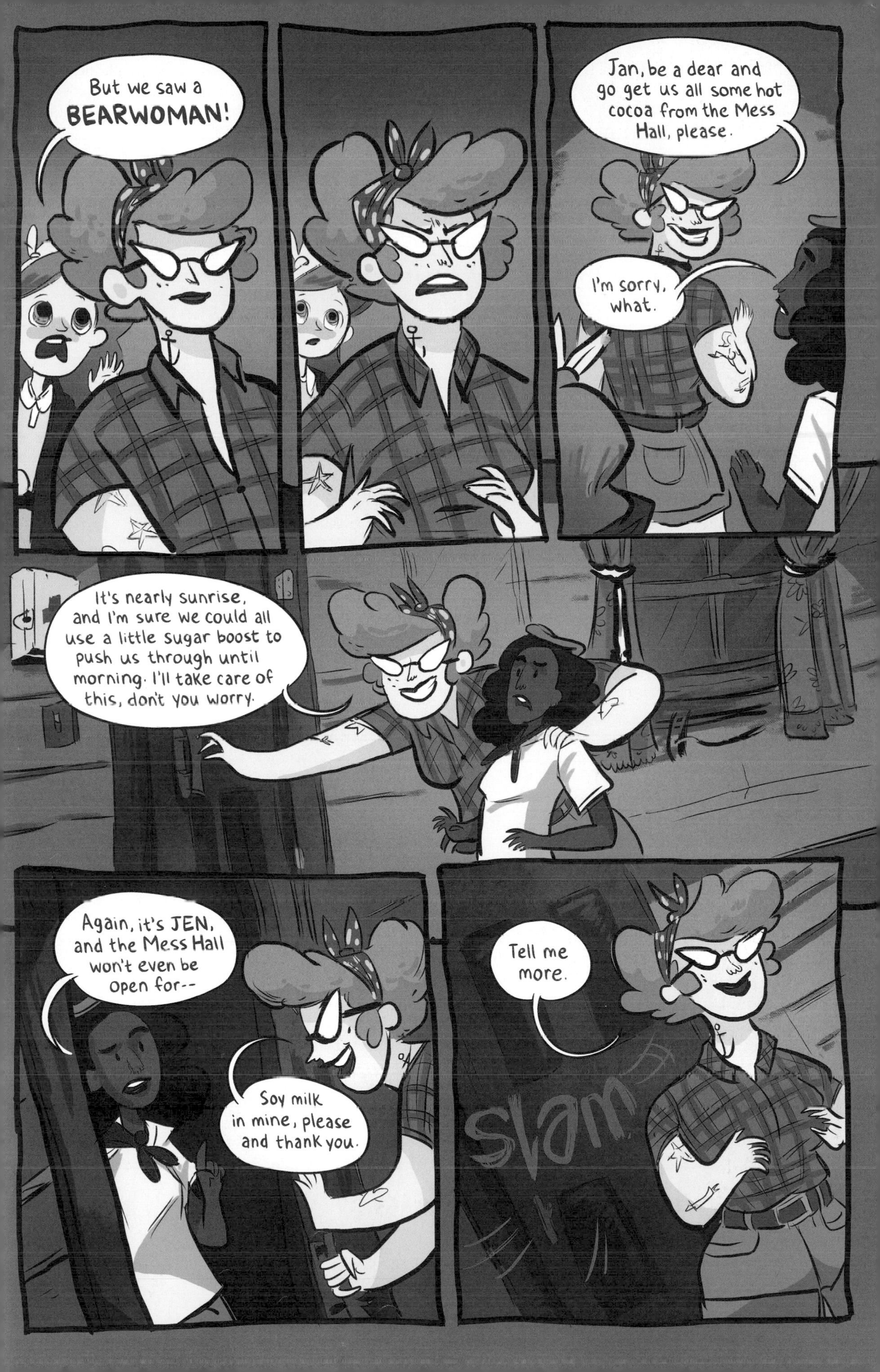
But we saw a BEARWOMAN!
Jan, be a dear and go get us all some hot cocoa from the Mess Hall, please.
I'm sorry, what.
It's nearly sunrise, and I'm sure we could all use a little sugar boost to push us through until morning. I'll take care of this, don't you worry.
Again, it's JEN, and the Mess Hall won't even be open for--
Soy milk in mine, please and thank you.
Tell me more.
slam

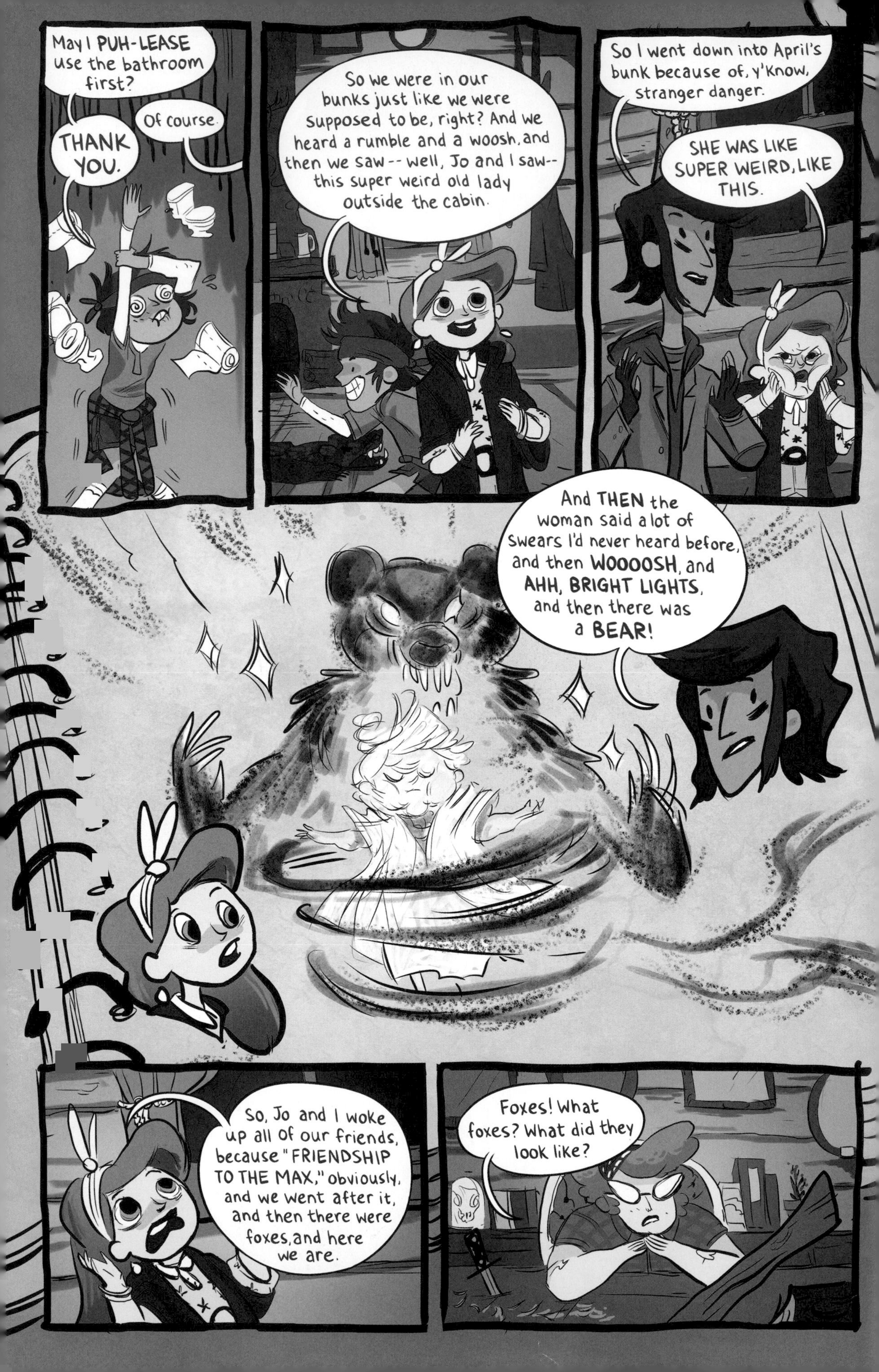
May I PUH-LEASE use the bathroom first?
Of course.
THANK YOU.
So we were in our bunks just like we were supposed to be, right? And we heard a rumble and a woosh, and then we saw -- well, Jo and I saw -- this super weird old lady outside the cabin.
So I went down into April's bunk because of, y'know, stranger danger.
SHE WAS LIKE SUPER WEIRD, LIKE THIS.
And THEN the woman said a lot of swears I'd never heard before, and then WOOOOSH, and AHH, BRIGHT LIGHTS, and then there was a BEAR!
So, Jo and I woke up all of our friends, because "FRIENDSHIP TO THE MAX," obviously, and we went after it, and then there were foxes, and here we are.
Foxes! What foxes? What did they look like?

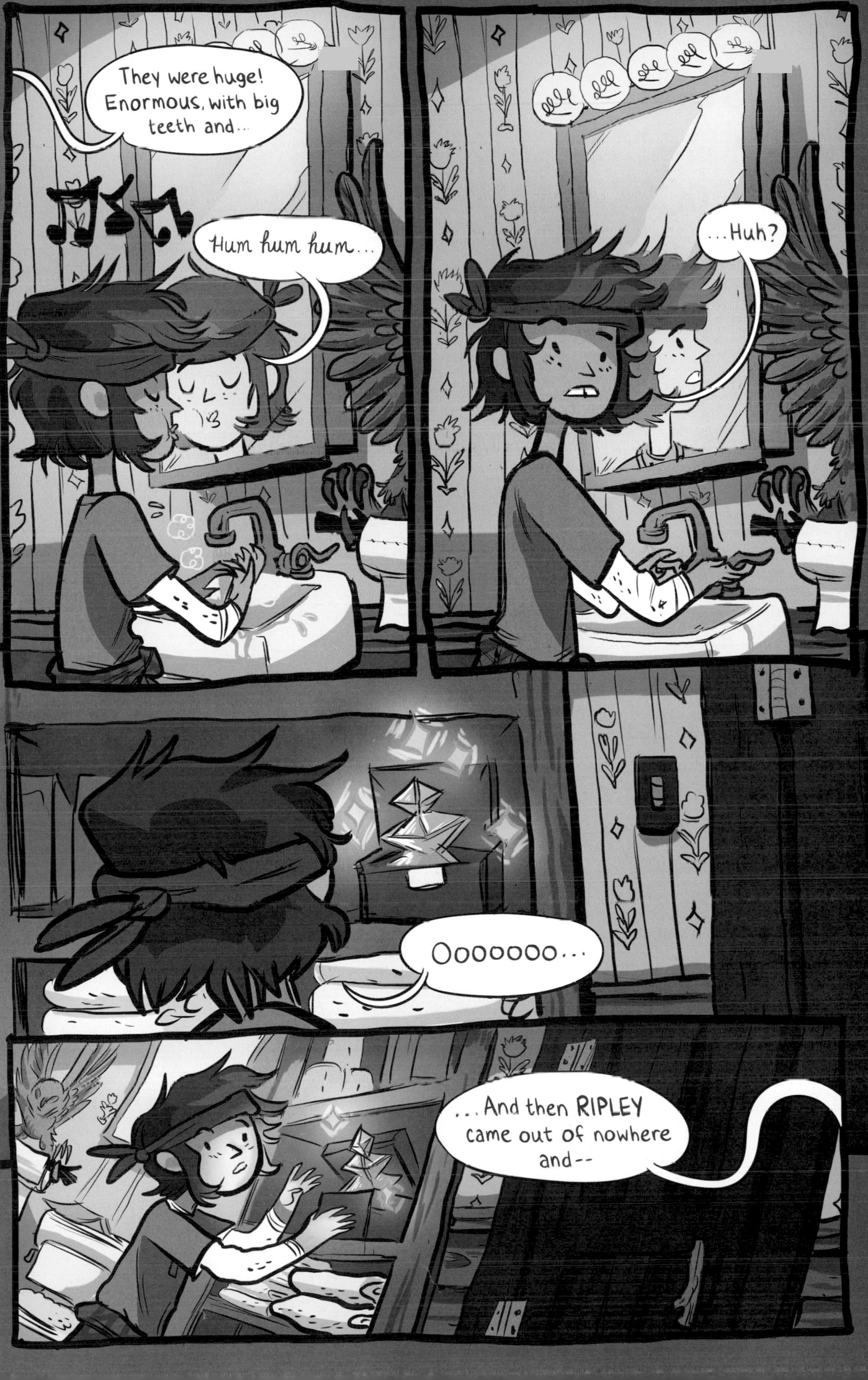
They were huge! Enormous, with big teeth and...
Hum hum hum...
...Huh?
Ooooooo...
...And then RIPLEY came out of nowhere and--

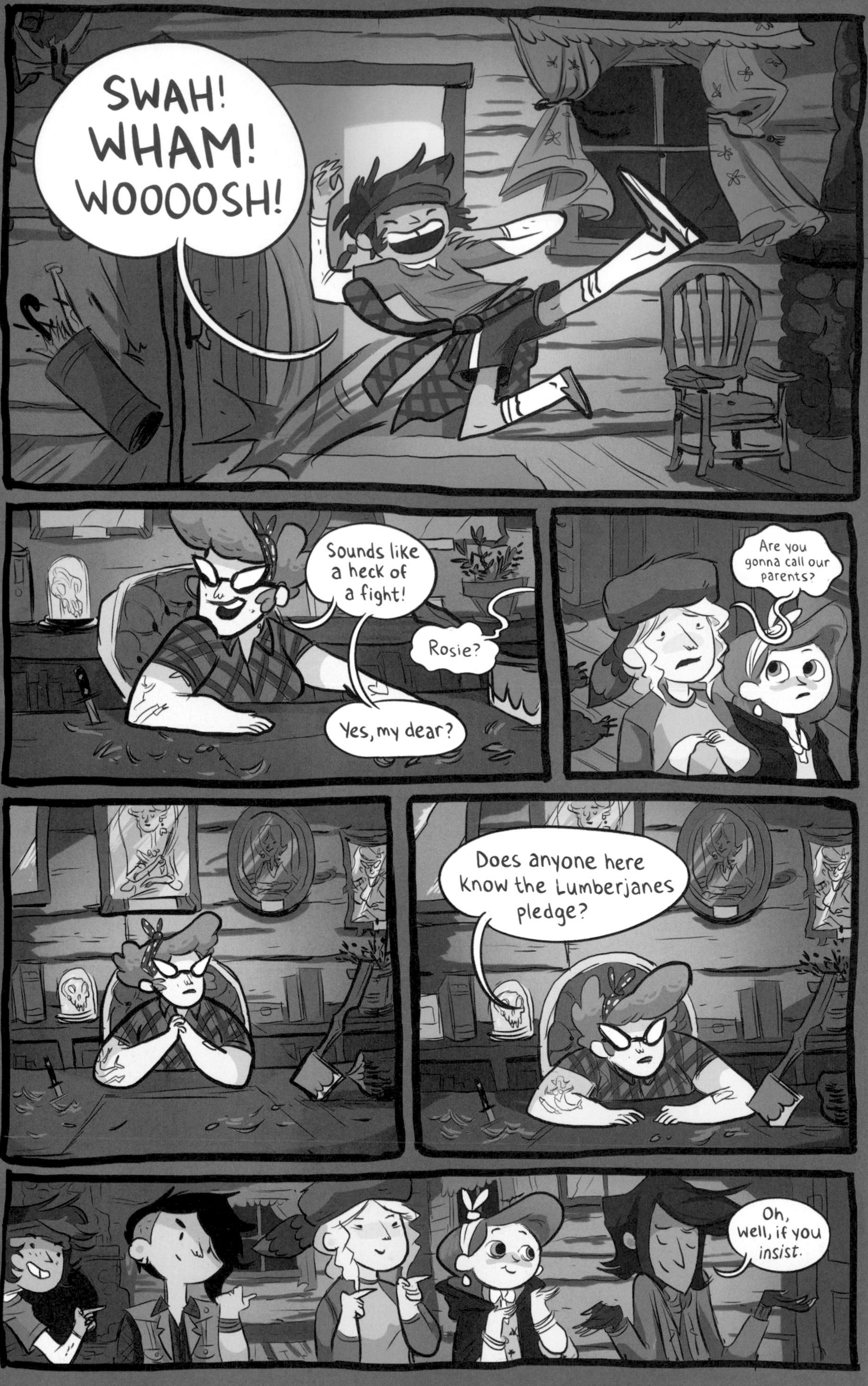
SWAH! WHAM! WOOOOSH!
Sounds like a heck of a fight!
Yes, my dear?
Rosie?
Are you gonna call our parents?
Does anyone here know the Lumberjanes pledge?
Oh, well, if you insist.

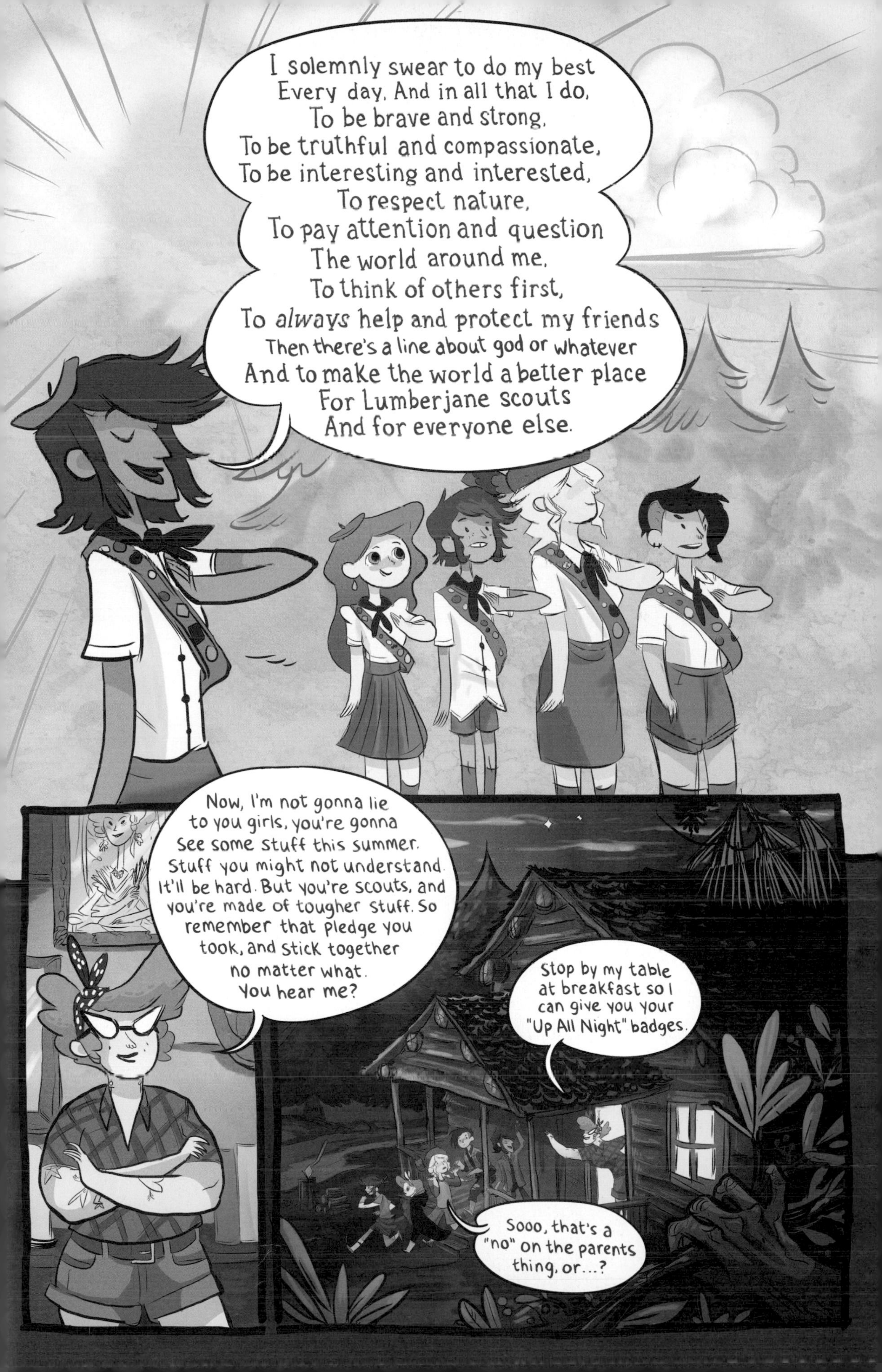
I solemnly swear to do my best Every day. And in all that I do, To be brave and strong, To be truthful and compassionate, To be interesting and interested, To respect nature, To pay attention and question The world around me, To think of others first, To *always* help and protect my friends Then there's a line about god or whatever And to make the world a better place For Lumberjane scouts And for everyone else.
Now, I'm not gonna lie to you girls, you're gonna see some stuff this summer. Stuff you might not understand. It'll be hard. But you're scouts, and you're made of tougher stuff. So remember that pledge you took, and stick together no matter what. You hear me?
Stop by my table at breakfast so I can give you your "Up All Night" badges.
Sooo, that's a "no" on the parents thing, or...?

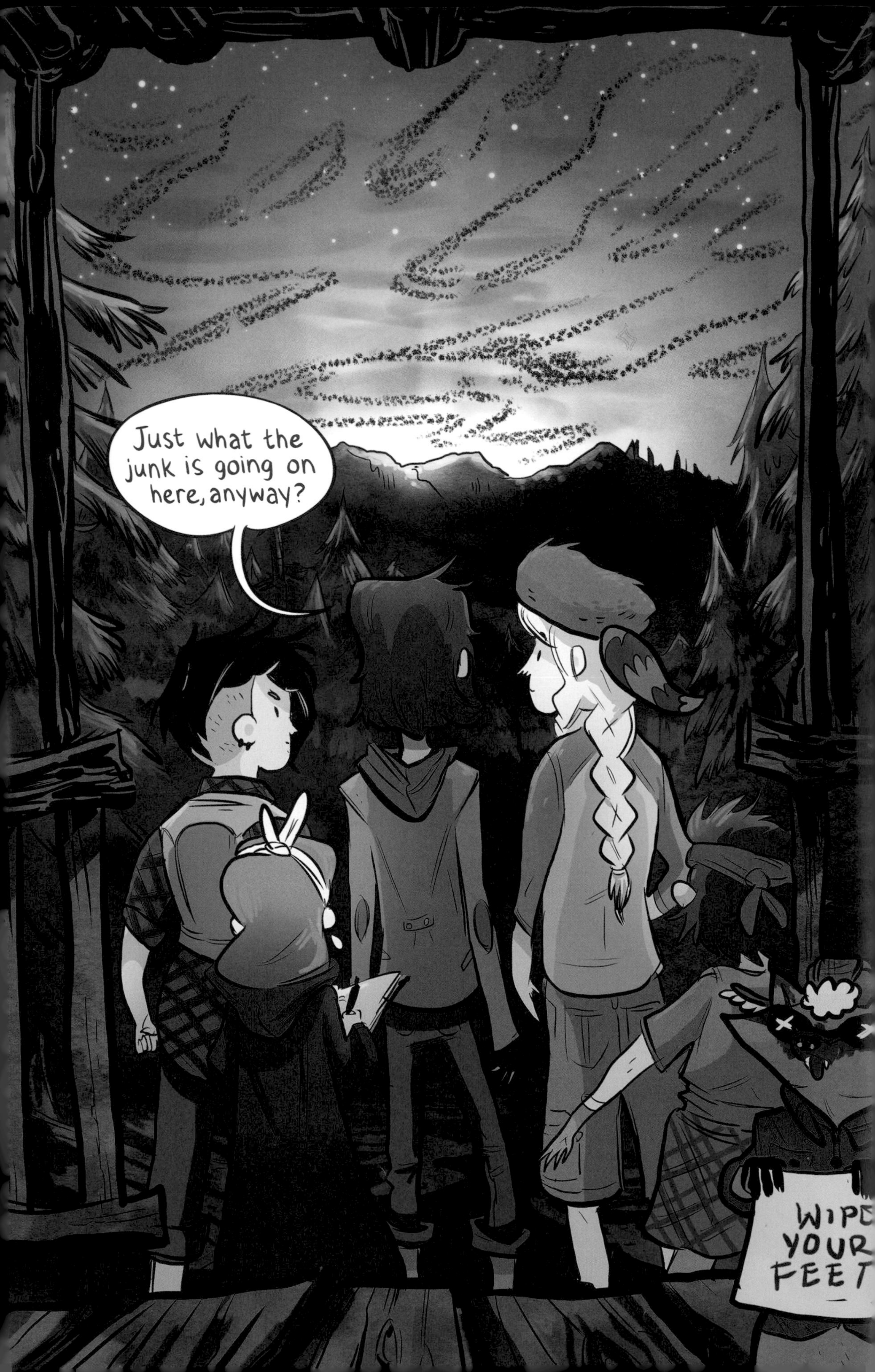
Just what the junk is going on here, anyway?
WIPE YOUR FEET

will co... ...E UNIFORM

The... ...hould be worn at camp

It hel... ...events when Lumberjanes

appearan... ...may also be worn at other

dress fo... ...ions. It should be worn as a

Further... ...the uniform dress with

Lumber... ...rrect shoes, and stocking or

to have...

part in... ...out grows her uniform or

Thiskw... ...her Lumberjane.

Hardc... ...a she has

have... ...her

them... ...her

LITTLE RED FORMATION!

ROANOKE CABIN

The...

yellow, short sl...

emb...

the w...

choose...

slacks,...

made o...

out-of-do...

green bere...

the colla...

Shoes ma...

heels, rou... ...ngs or

socks sho... ...h the shoes or wit...

the uniform. Ne... ...racelets, or other jewelry do...

belong with a Lumberjane uniform.

HOW TO WEAR THE UNIFORM

To look well in a uniform demands first of...

uniform be kept in good condition—clean...

pressed. See that the skirt is the right length for you...

height and build, that the belt is adjusted to your w...

that your shoes and stockings are in keeping with t...

uniform, that you watch your posture and carry yourself...

with dignity and grace. If the beret is removed indoors, ...helps to cre...

be sure that your hair is neat and kept in place with an ...in a group. ...

inconspicuous clip or ribbon. When you wear a ...active life th...

Lumberjane uniform you are identified as a member of ...another bond...

this organization and you should be doubly careful to ...future, and pr...

conduct yourself in a way that will show everyone that ...in order to b...

courtesy and thoughtfulness are part of being a ...Lumberjane pr...

Lumberjane. People are likely to judge a whole nation by ...Penniquiqul Thi... ...ore Lady

the selfishness of a few individuals, to criticize a whole ...Types, but m... ...es will wish to have one. They

family because of the misconduct of one member, and to ...can either bu... ...iform, or make it themselves from

feel unkindly toward an organization because of the ...materials available at the trading post.

JENNY, OUR CABIN LEADER!

LUMBERJANES FIELD MANUAL
CHAPTER TWO

Lumberjanes "Sports and Games" Program Field

NAVAL GAUGING BADGE

"Because drowning is a scary way to go."

Lumberjanes are considered to be girls who can find their way around any situation, whether it be an unsuspecting adventure in the great outdoors to the problem solving of every day matters. As a modern Lumberjane, you will be able to recognize the importance of naval abilities and how to navigate any stream. A Lumberjane will be able to find her way through any rapid, fall, or even quiet wilderness. Will understand the importance of safety and always be wary of the false sense of security that the wilderness can lull any unsuspecting person into, a Lumberjane will remain ready and able to adapt to whatever is thrown at her.

The *Naval Gauging* badge is a sense of pride for any Lumberjane, as she continues her journey through the daily trials that every Lumberjane must face. Not only will a Lumberjane learn how to forage in the wild, learn how to care for herself and her friends on the trail, be she will learn how to explore with a seeing and vigilant eye. She will make herself at home in the woods, and any future place she finds fitting for herself.

To obtain the *Naval Gauging* badge a Lumberjane must be able to tie rapidly six different knots. She will find herself well versed in rope work as it can be extremely important in her future adventure, she must know how to splice ropes, use a palm and needle, and fling a rope coil. A Lumberjane must be able to row, pole, scull, and steer a boat; also bring a boat properly alongside and make fast. She must know how to box the compass, read a chart, and show use of parallel rules and dividers. She must be able to state direction by the stars and sun, and be capable of swimming fifty yards with shoes and clothes on. She will know the importances of a life preserver, CPR, and the basic understanding of how to respond in emergency situations. She must understand

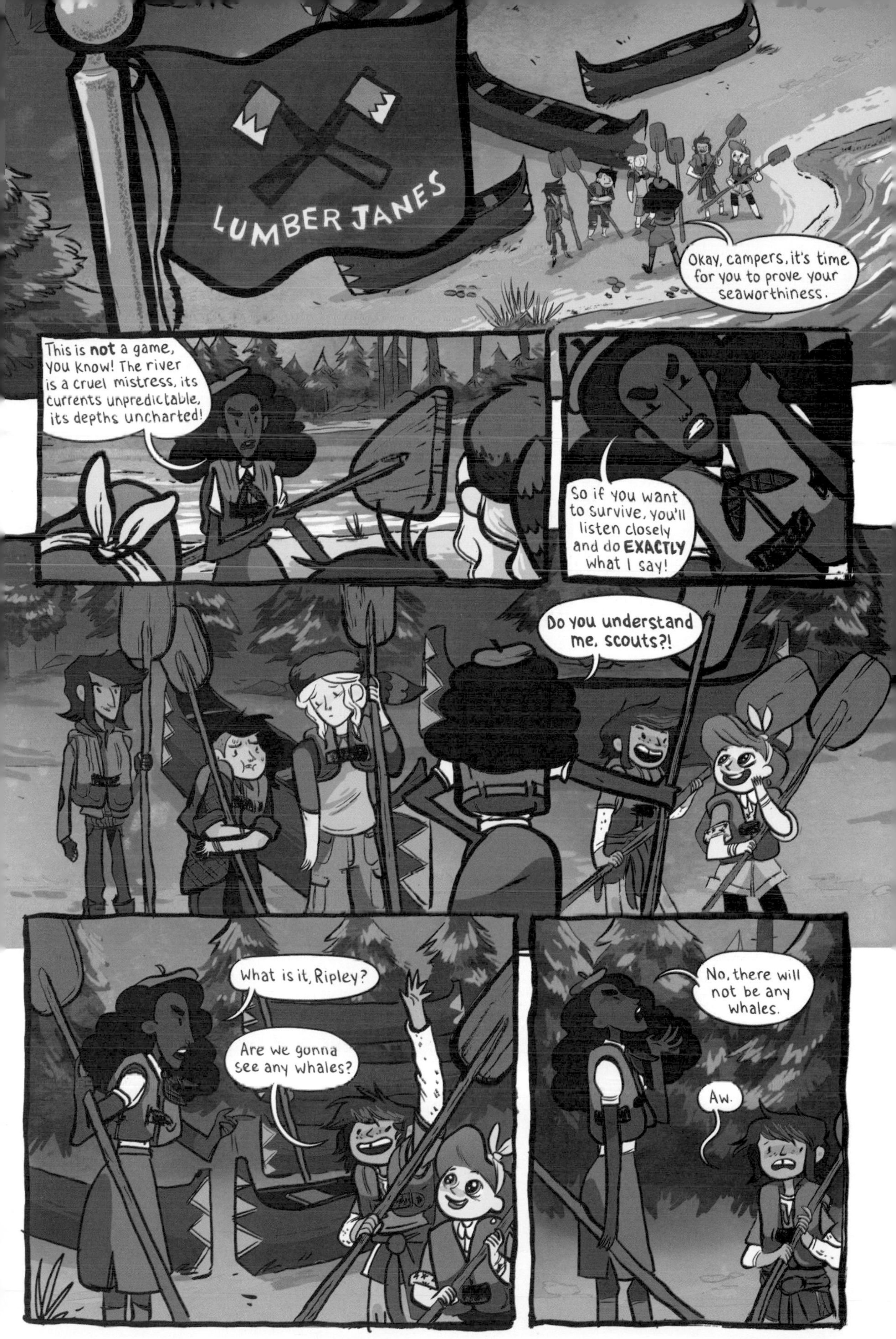
LUMBER JANES
Okay, campers, it's time for you to prove your seaworthiness.
This is **not** a game, you know! The river is a cruel mistress, its currents unpredictable, its depths uncharted!
So if you want to survive, you'll listen closely and do **EXACTLY** what I say!
Do you understand me, scouts?!
What is it, Ripley?
Are we gonna see any whales?
No, there will not be any whales.
Aw.

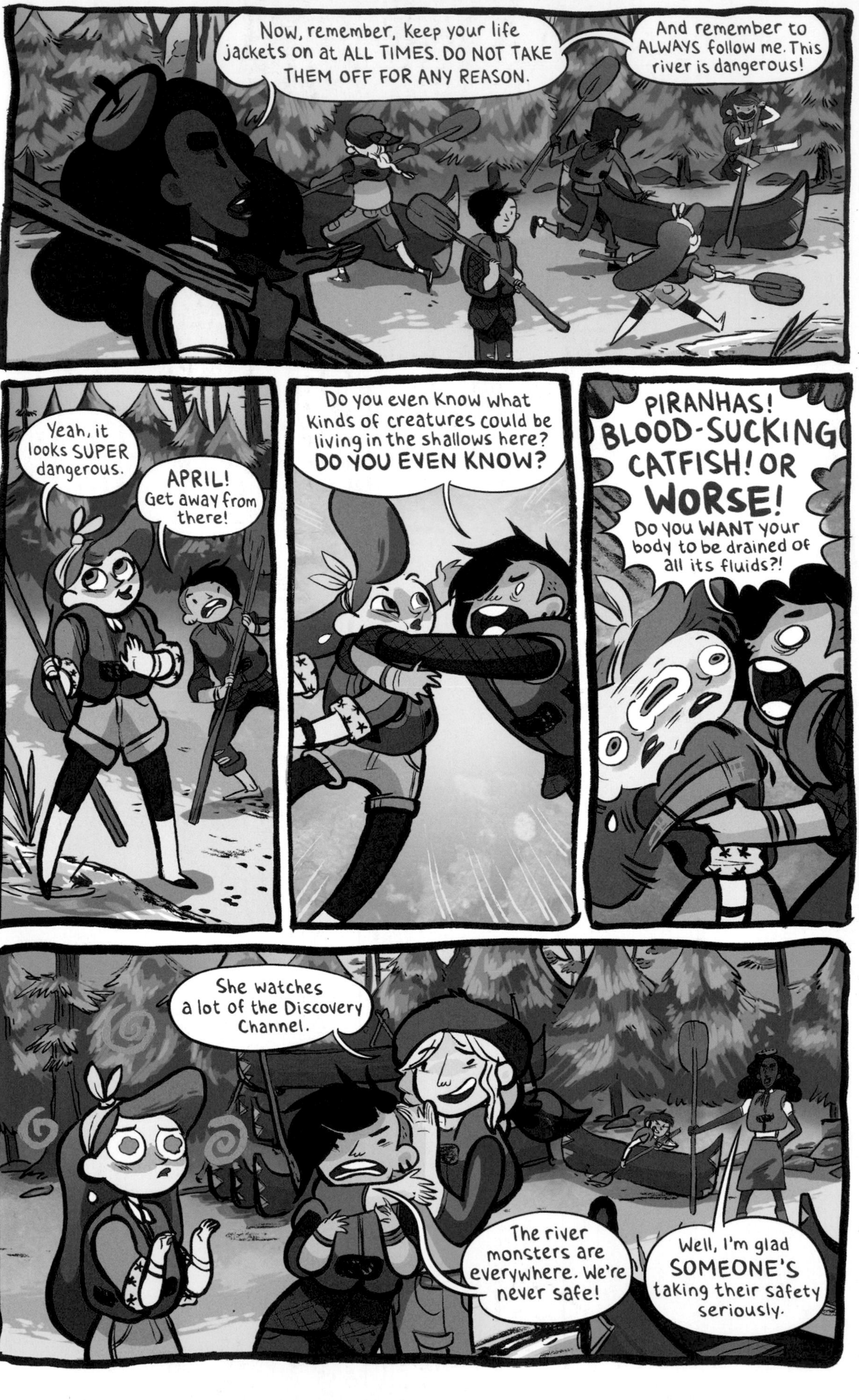
Now, remember, Keep your life jackets on at ALL TIMES. DO NOT TAKE THEM OFF FOR ANY REASON.
And remember to ALWAYS follow me. This river is dangerous!
Yeah, it looks SUPER dangerous.
APRIL! Get away from there!
Do you even know what kinds of creatures could be living in the shallows here? DO YOU EVEN KNOW?
PIRANHAS! BLOOD-SUCKING CATFISH! OR WORSE! Do you WANT your body to be drained of all its fluids?!
She watches a lot of the Discovery Channel.
The river monsters are everywhere. We're never safe!
Well, I'm glad SOMEONE'S taking their safety seriously.

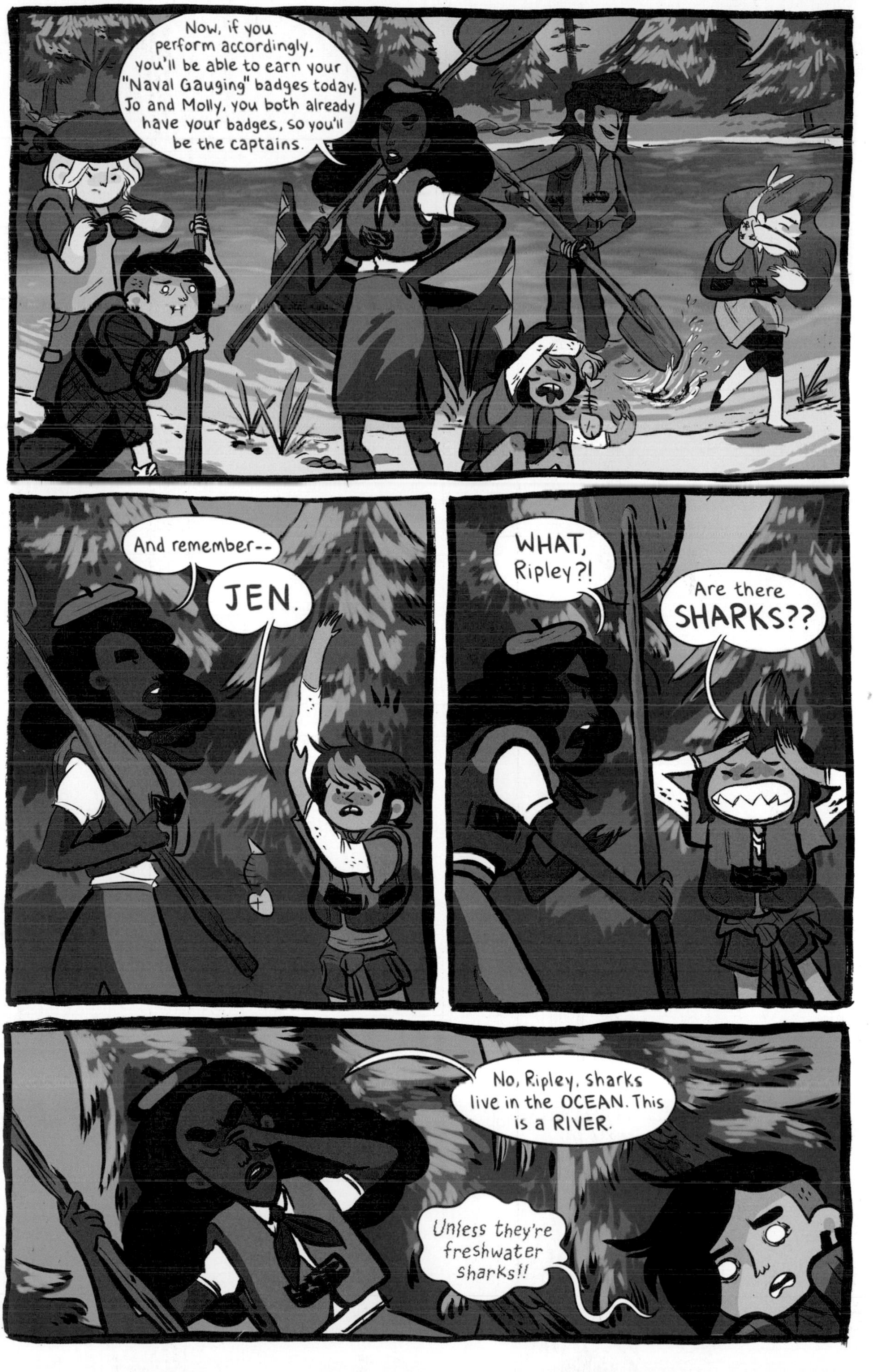
Now, if you perform accordingly, you'll be able to earn your "Naval Gauging" badges today. Jo and Molly, you both already have your badges, so you'll be the captains.
And remember--
JEN.
WHAT, Ripley?!
Are there SHARKS??
No, Ripley, sharks live in the OCEAN. This is a RIVER.
Unless they're freshwater sharks!!

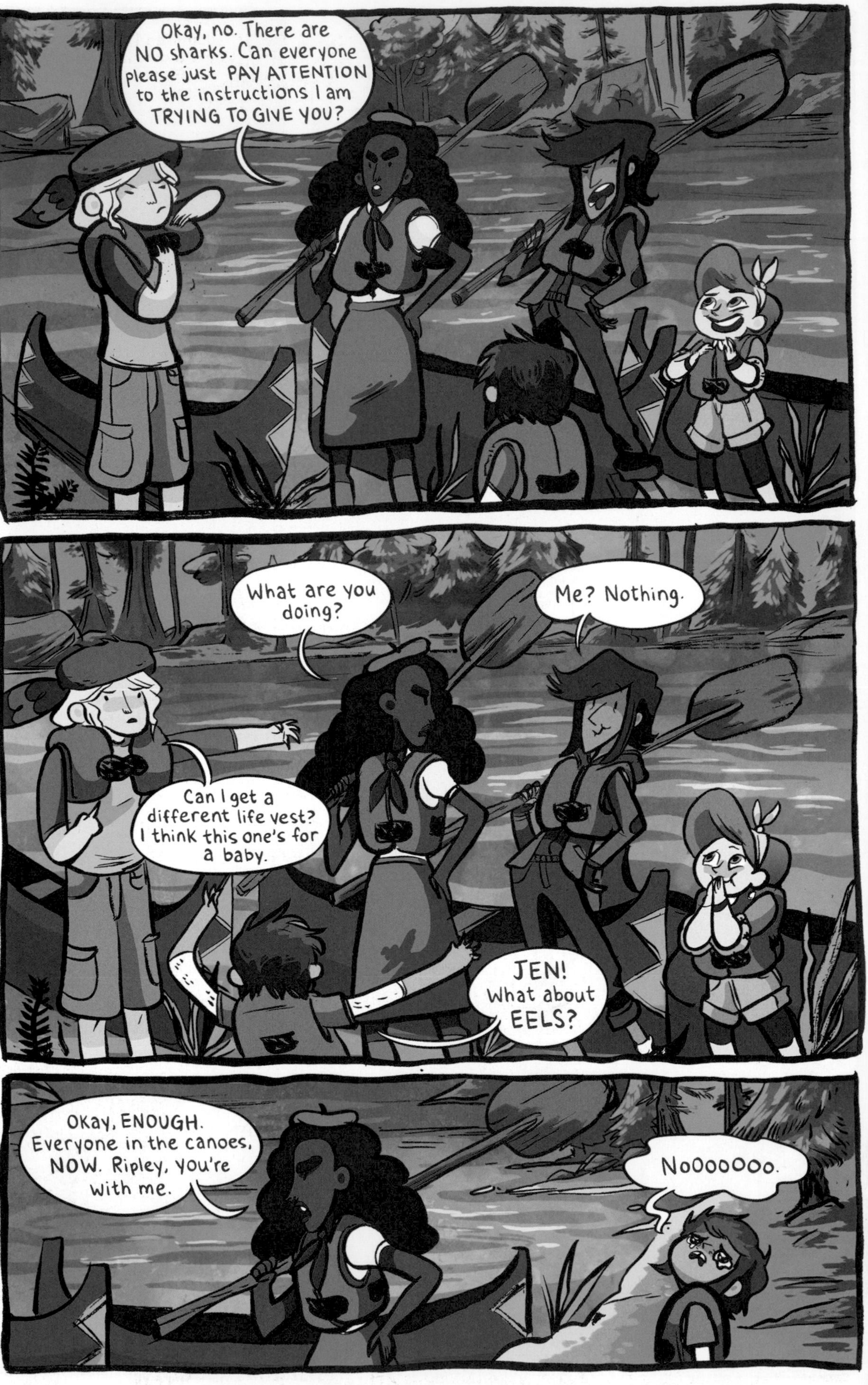
Okay, no. There are NO sharks. Can everyone please just PAY ATTENTION to the instructions I am TRYING TO GIVE YOU?
What are you doing?
Me? Nothing.
Can I get a different life vest? I think this one's for a baby.
JEN! What about EELS?
Okay, ENOUGH. Everyone in the canoes, NOW. Ripley, you're with me.
NoOooOOo.

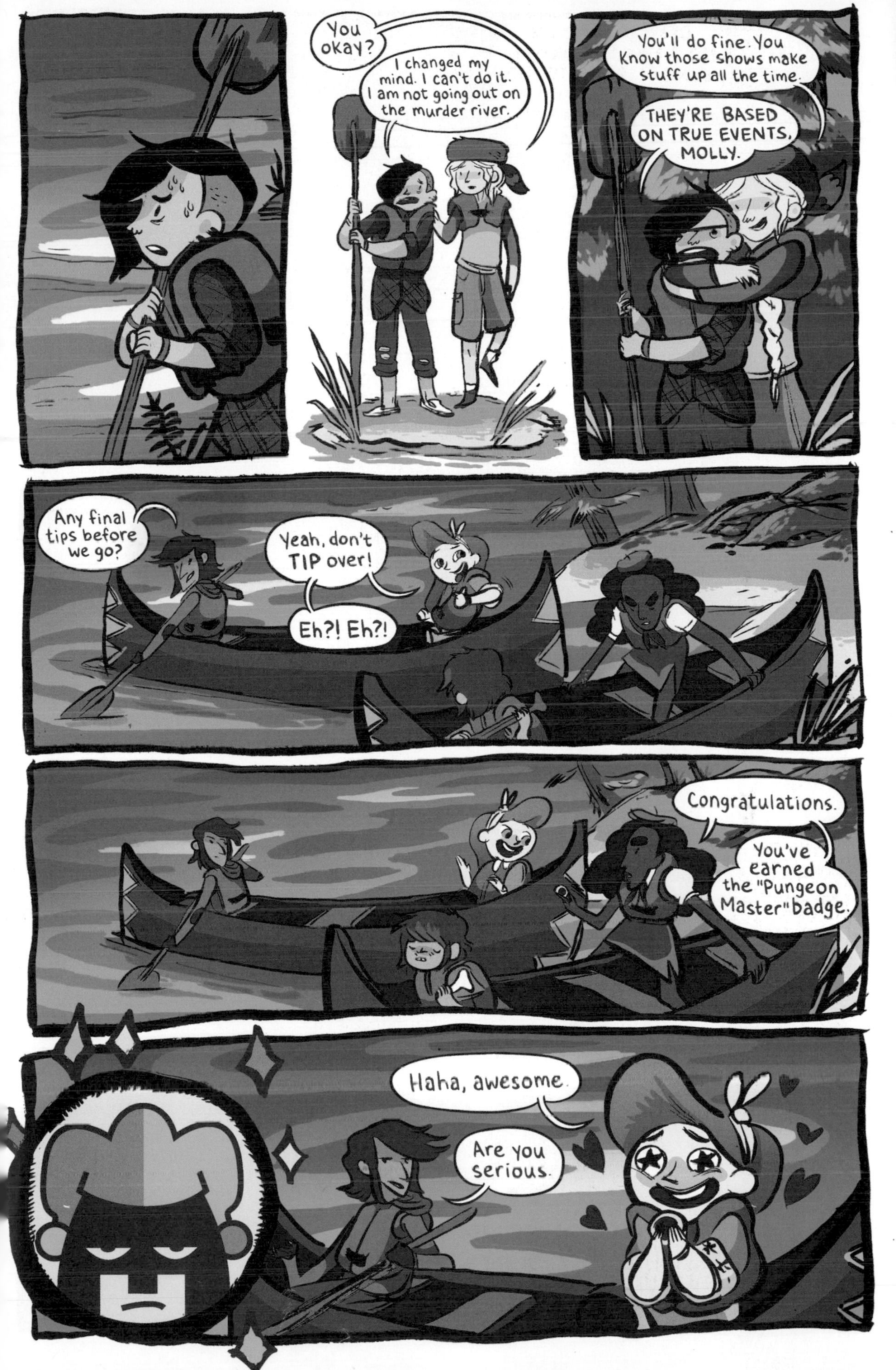
You okay?
I changed my mind. I can't do it. I am not going out on the murder river.
You'll do fine. You know those shows make stuff up all the time.
THEY'RE BASED ON TRUE EVENTS, MOLLY.
Any final tips before we go?
Yeah, don't TIP over!
Eh?! Eh?!
Congratulations.
You've earned the "Pungeon Master" badge.
Haha, awesome.
Are you serious.

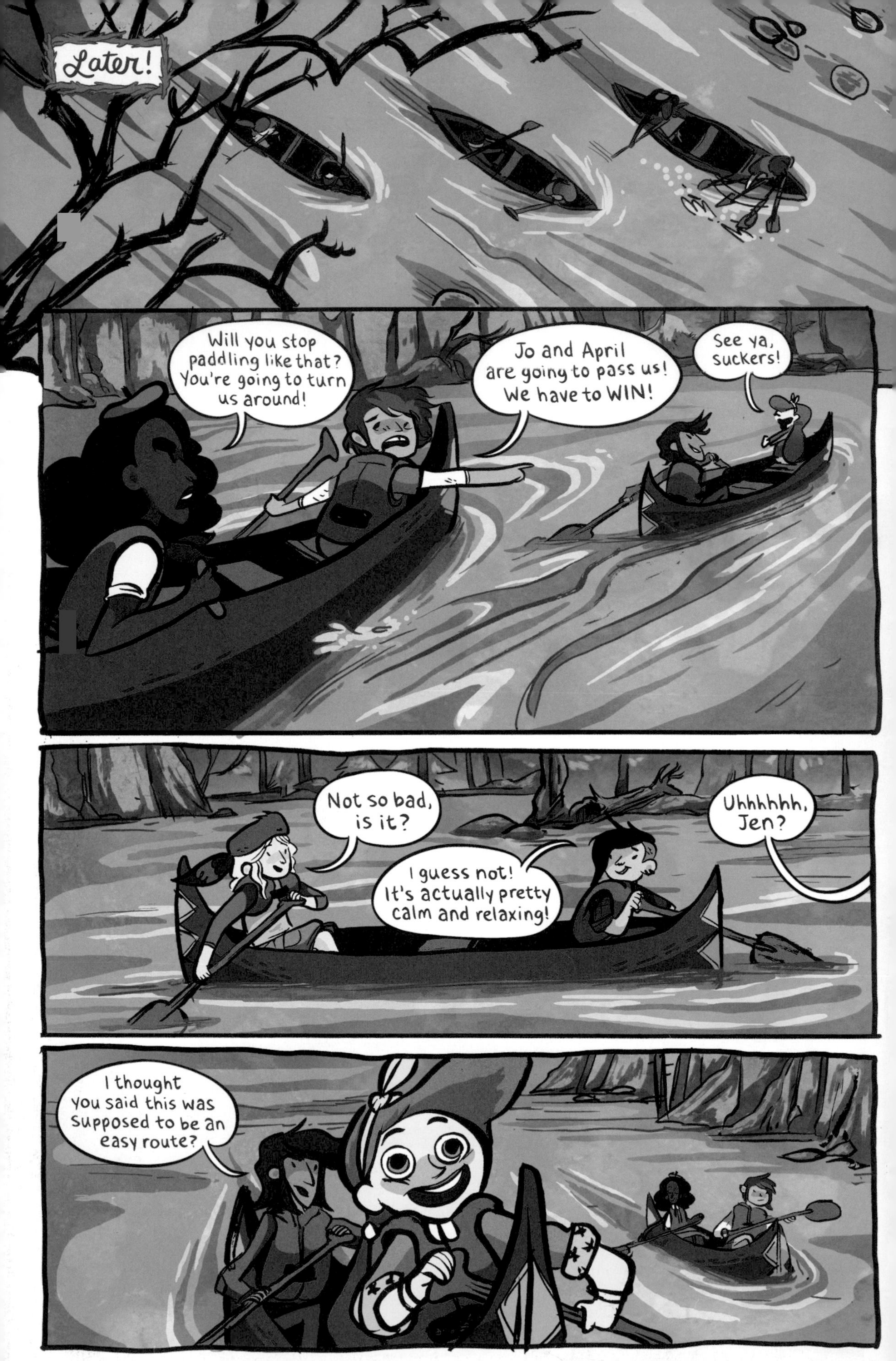
Later!
Will you stop paddling like that? You're going to turn us around!
Jo and April are going to pass us! We have to WIN!
See ya, suckers!
Not so bad, is it?
I guess not! It's actually pretty calm and relaxing!
Uhhhhhh, Jen?
I thought you said this was supposed to be an easy route?

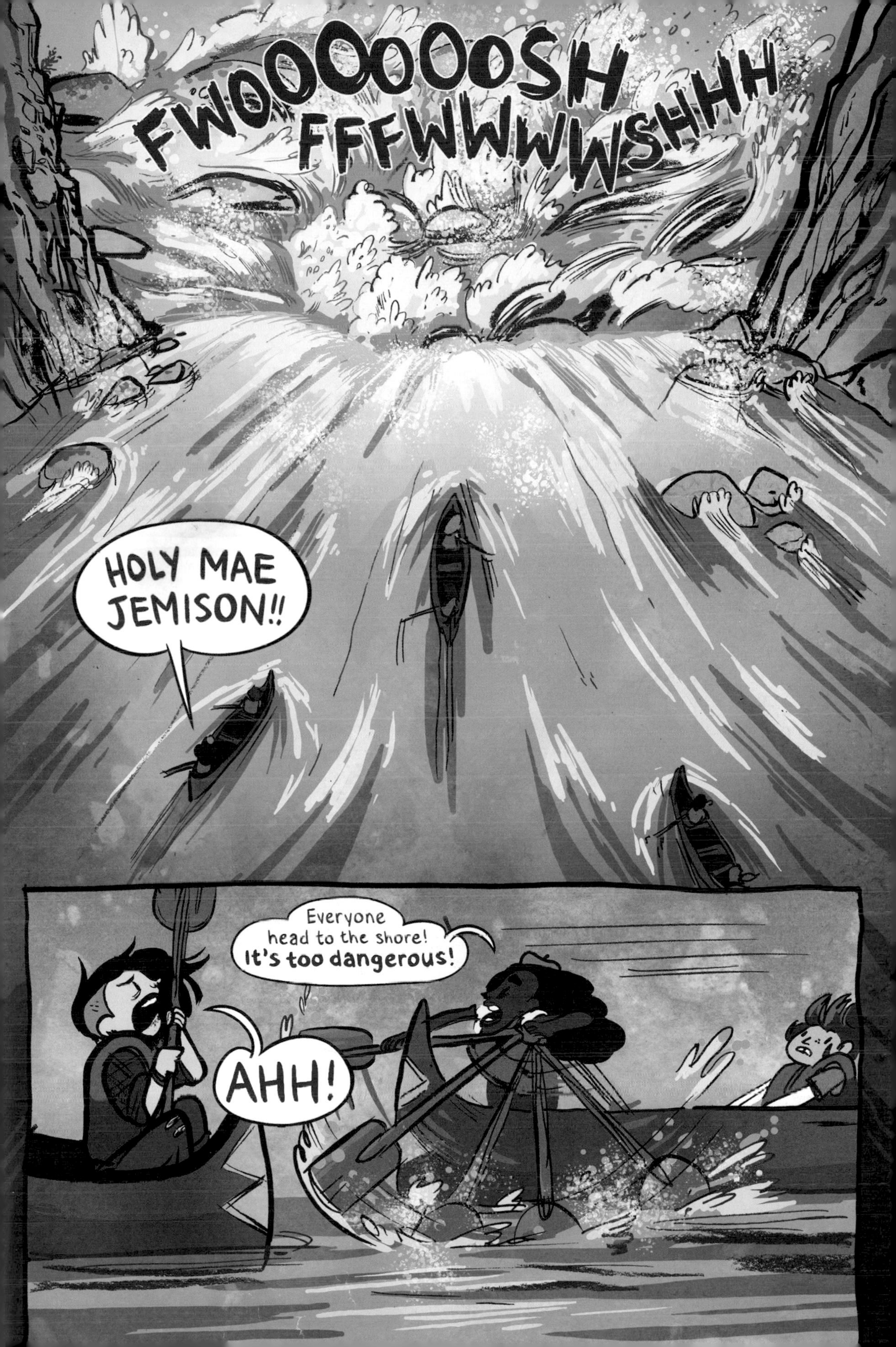
FWOOOOOOSH
FFFWWWWWSHHH
HOLY MAE JEMISON!!
Everyone head to the shore! It's too dangerous!
AHH!

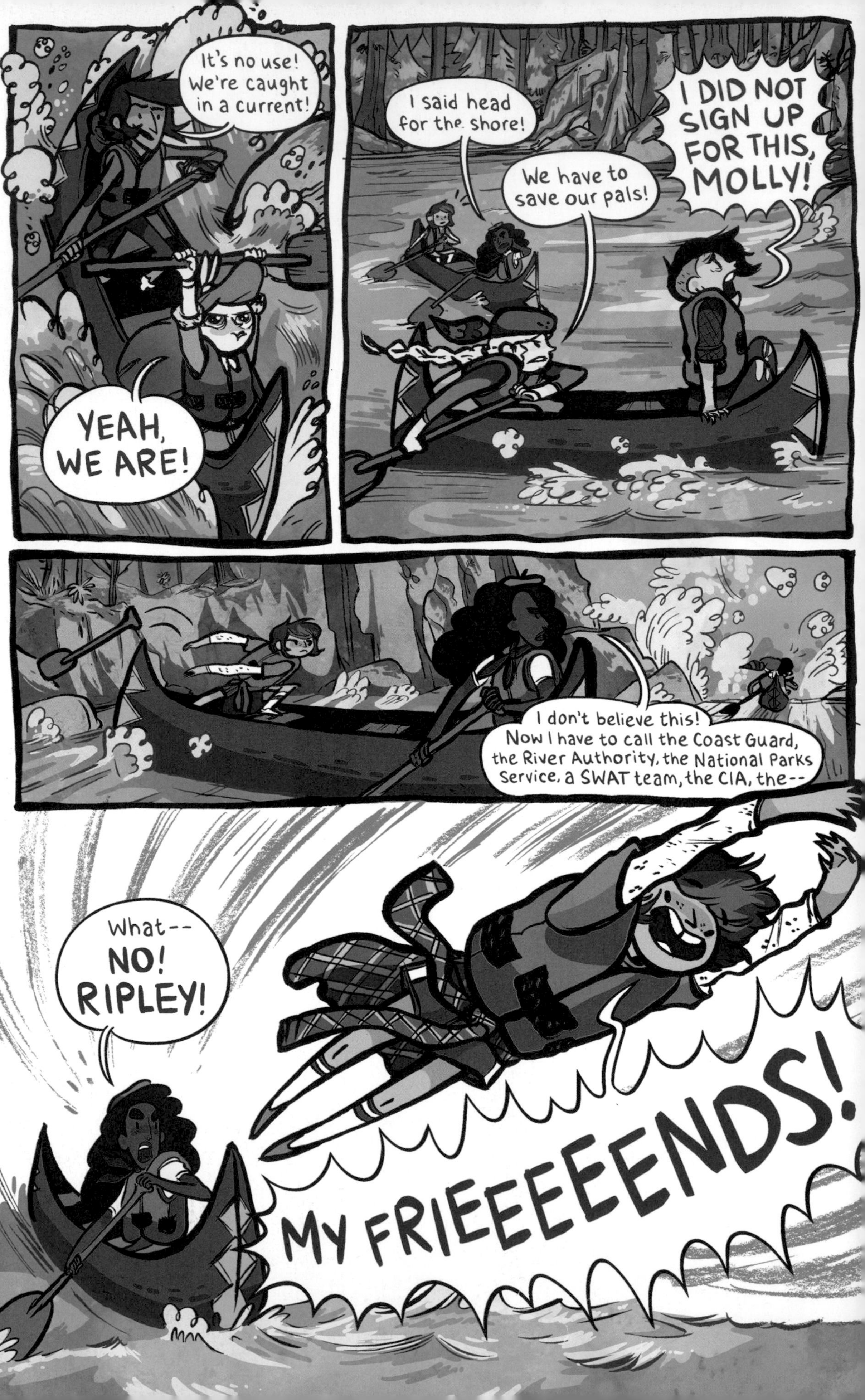

It's no use! We're caught in a current!
YEAH, WE ARE!
I said head for the shore!
We have to save our pals!
I DID NOT SIGN UP FOR THIS, MOLLY!
I don't believe this! Now I have to call the Coast Guard, the River Authority, the National Parks Service, a SWAT team, the CIA, the--
What-- NO! RIPLEY!
MY FRIEEEEEENDS!

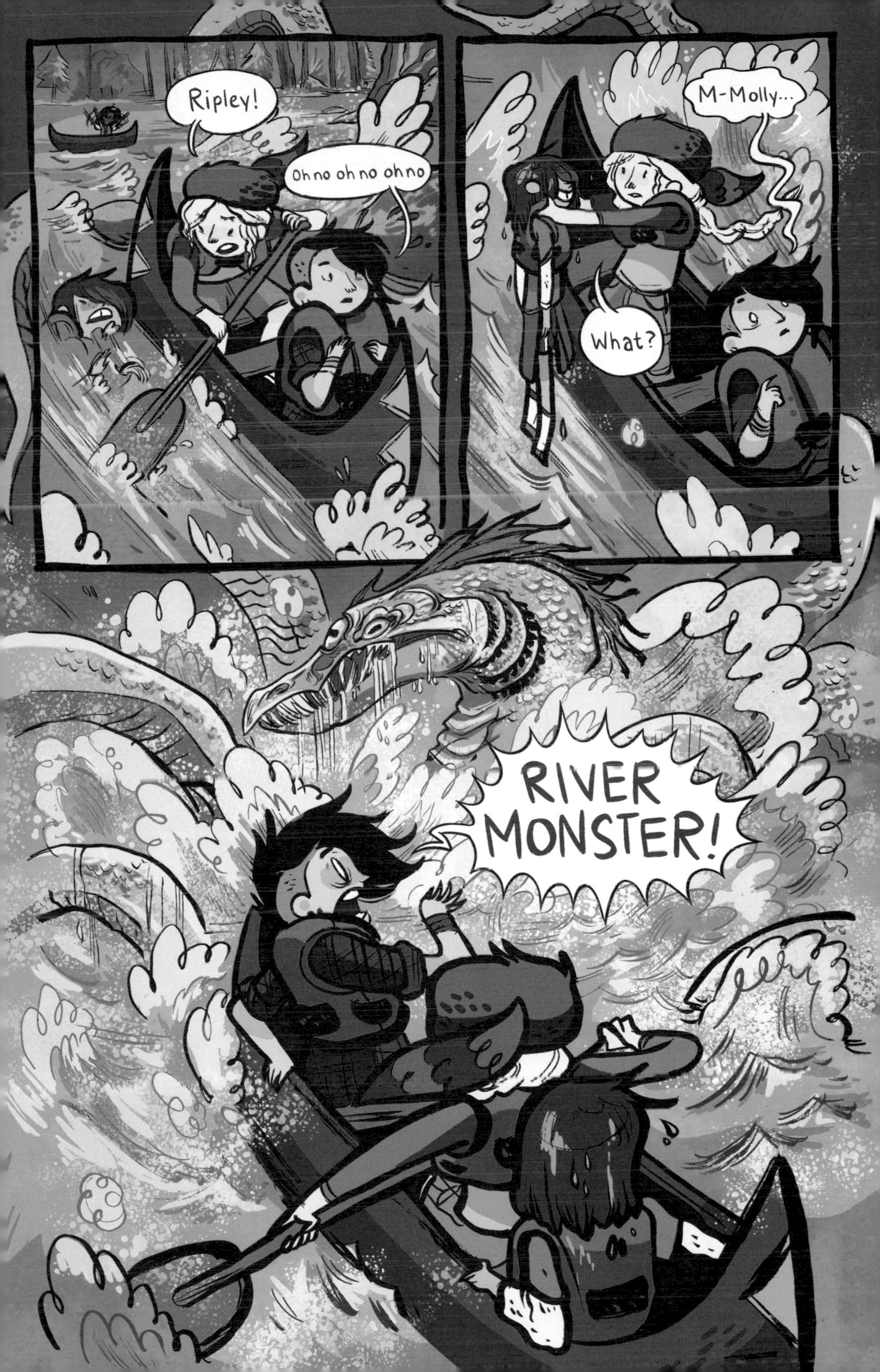
Ripley!
Oh no oh no oh no
M-Molly...
What?
RIVER MONSTER!

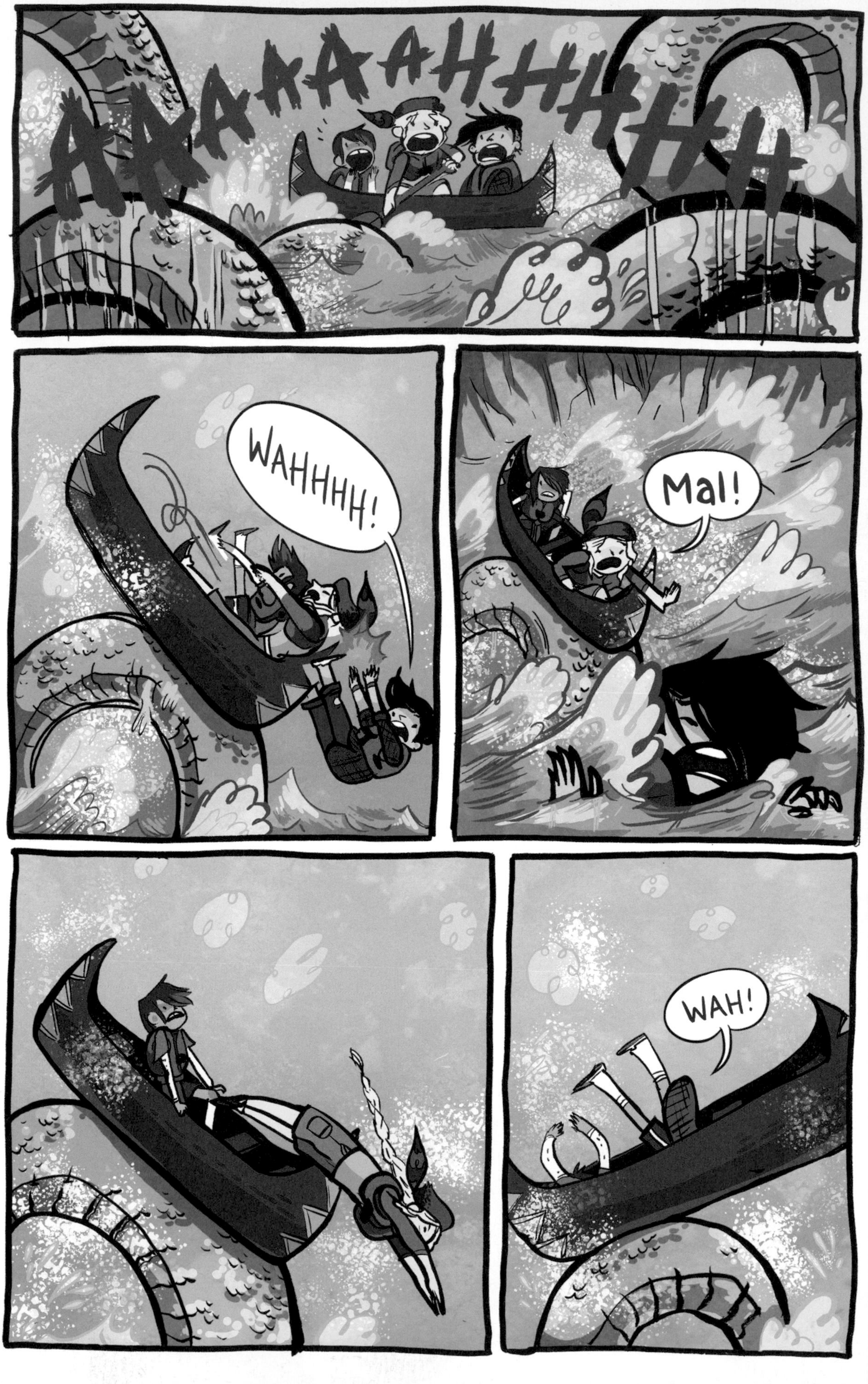
AAAAAAHHHHHHH
WAHHHHH!
Mal!
WAH!

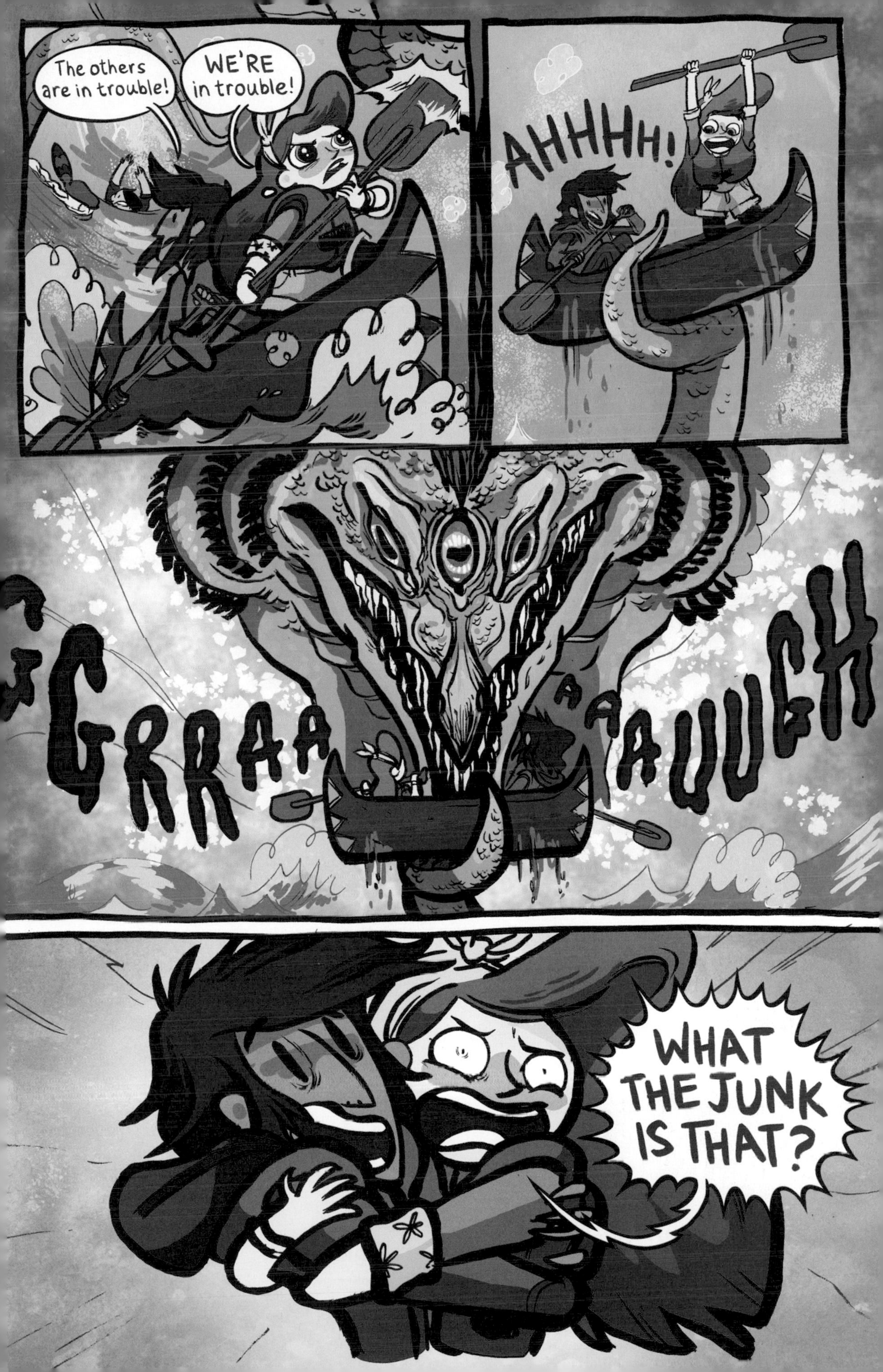

The others are in trouble!
WE'RE in trouble!
AHHHH!
GRRAAAAAAUUGH
WHAT THE JUNK IS THAT?

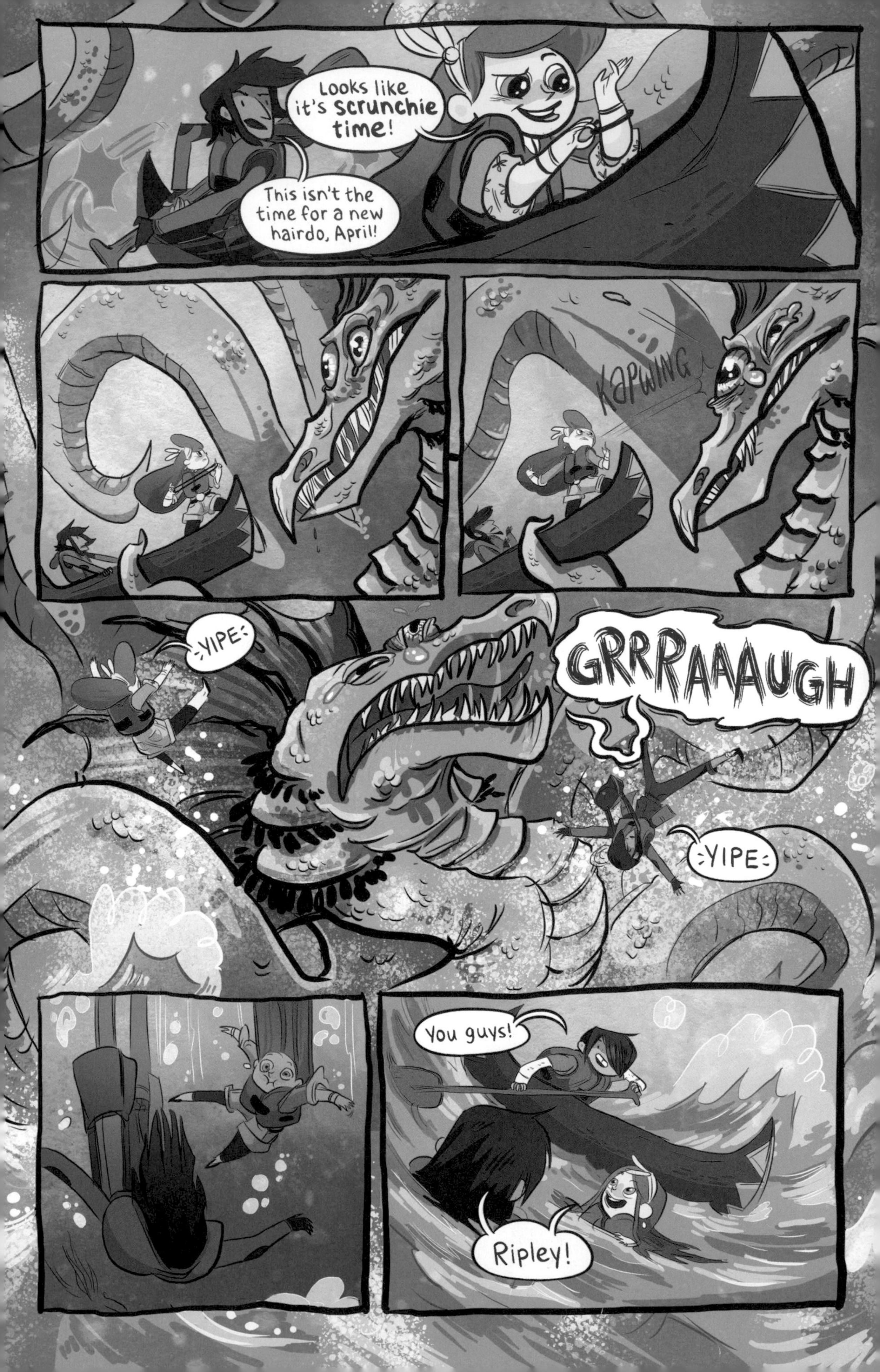
Looks like it's scrunchie time!
This isn't the time for a new hairdo, April!
KAPWING
YIPE
GRRRAAAUGH
YIPE
You guys!
Ripley!

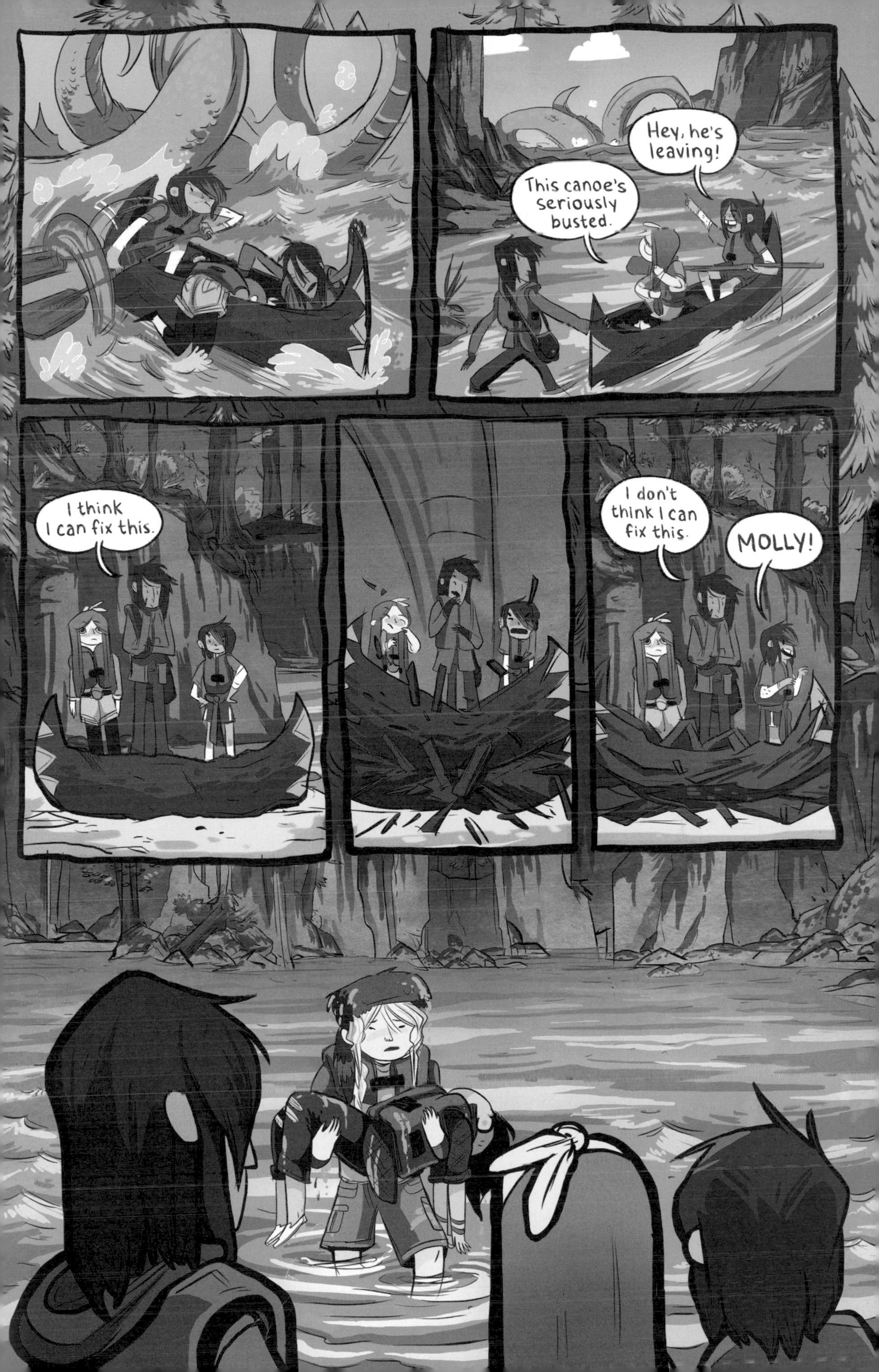
This canoe's seriously busted.
Hey, he's leaving!
I think I can fix this.
I don't think I can fix this.
MOLLY!

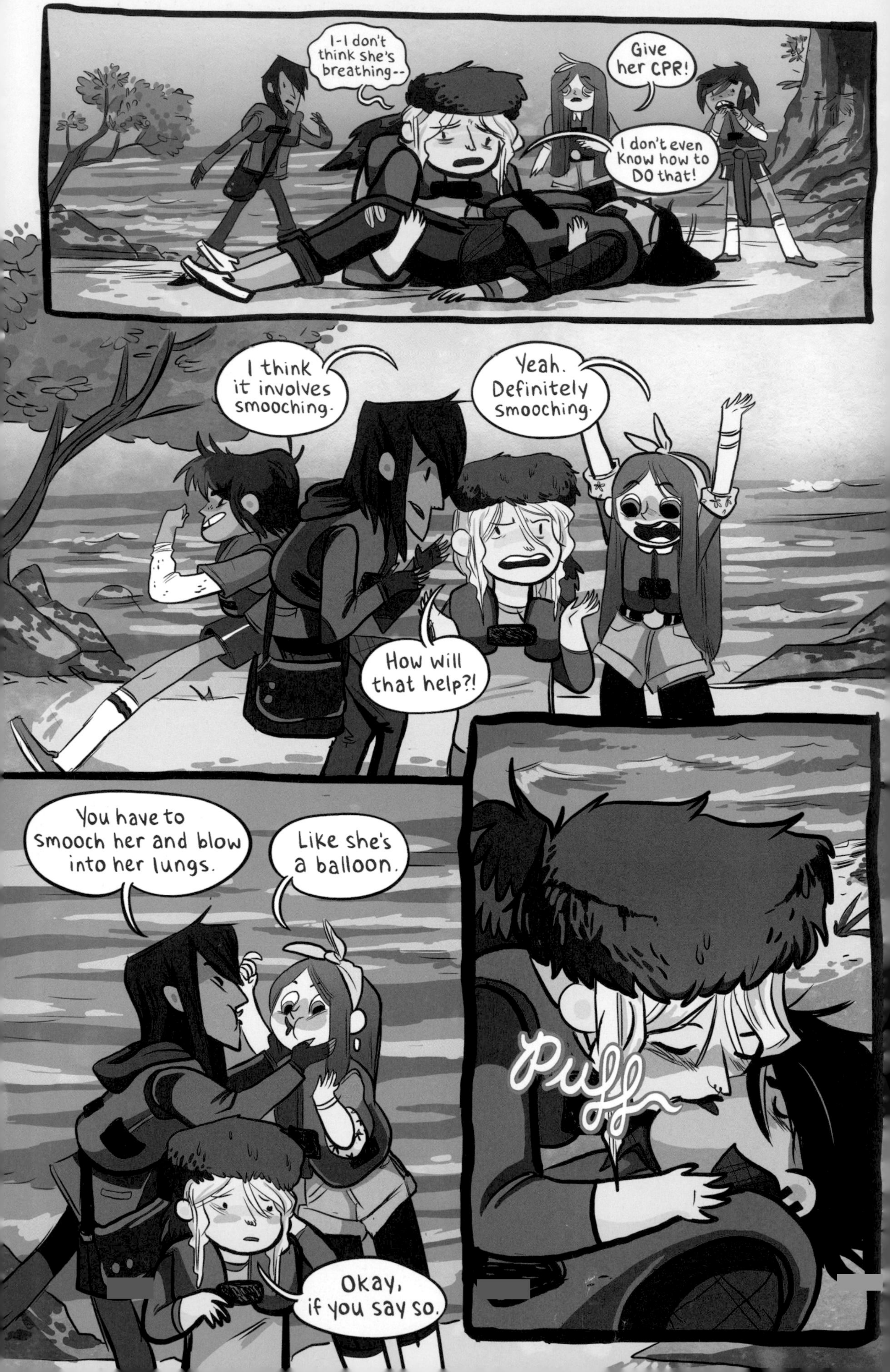
I-I don't think she's breathing--
Give her CPR!
I don't even know how to DO that!
I think it involves smooching.
Yeah. Definitely smooching.
How will that help?!
You have to smooch her and blow into her lungs.
Like she's a balloon.
Okay, if you say so.
PUFF

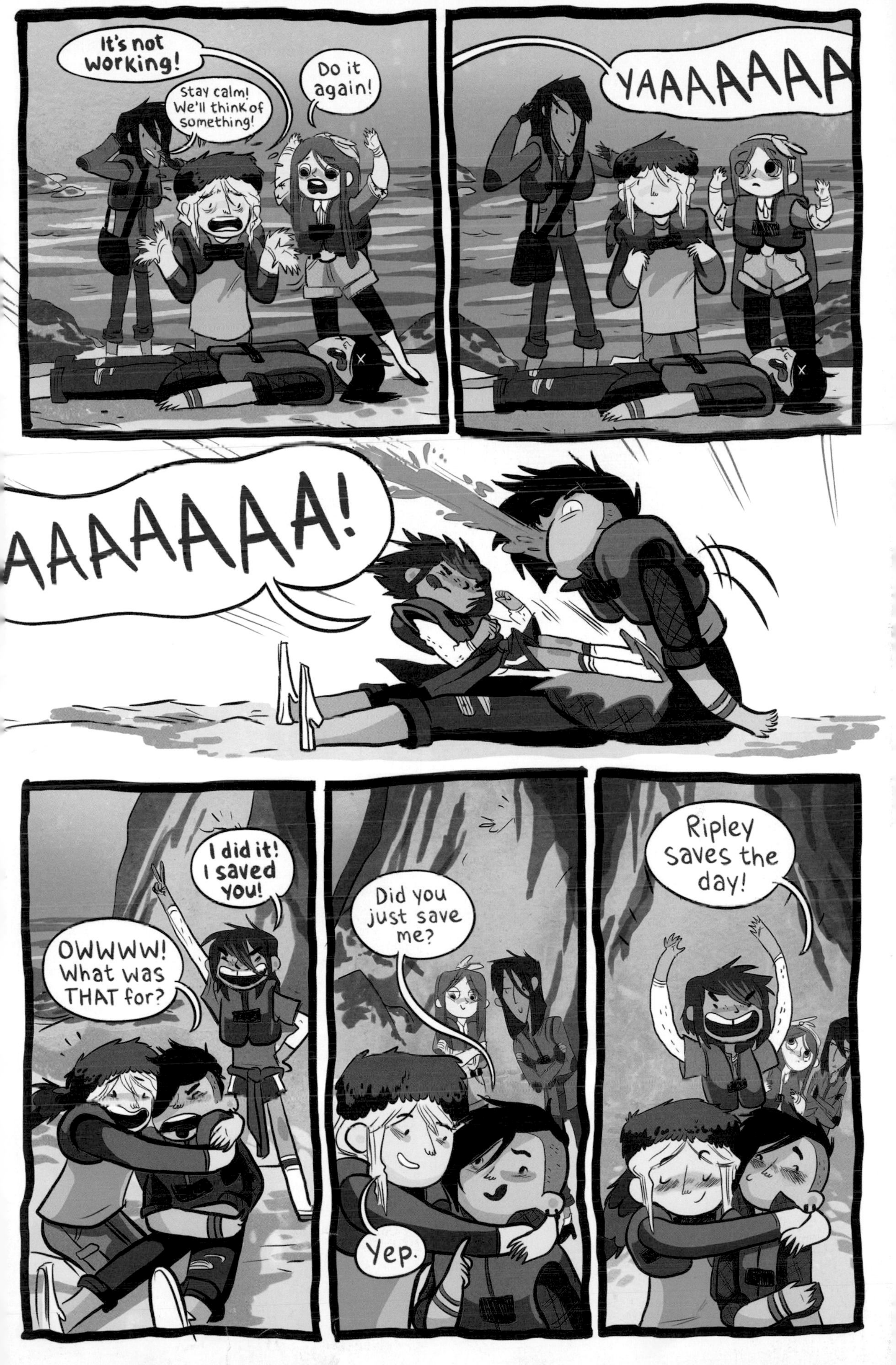
It's not working!
Stay calm! We'll think of something!
Do it again!
YAAAAAAA
AAAAAAA!
I did it! I saved you!
OWWWW! What was THAT for?
Did you just save me?
Yep.
Ripley saves the day!

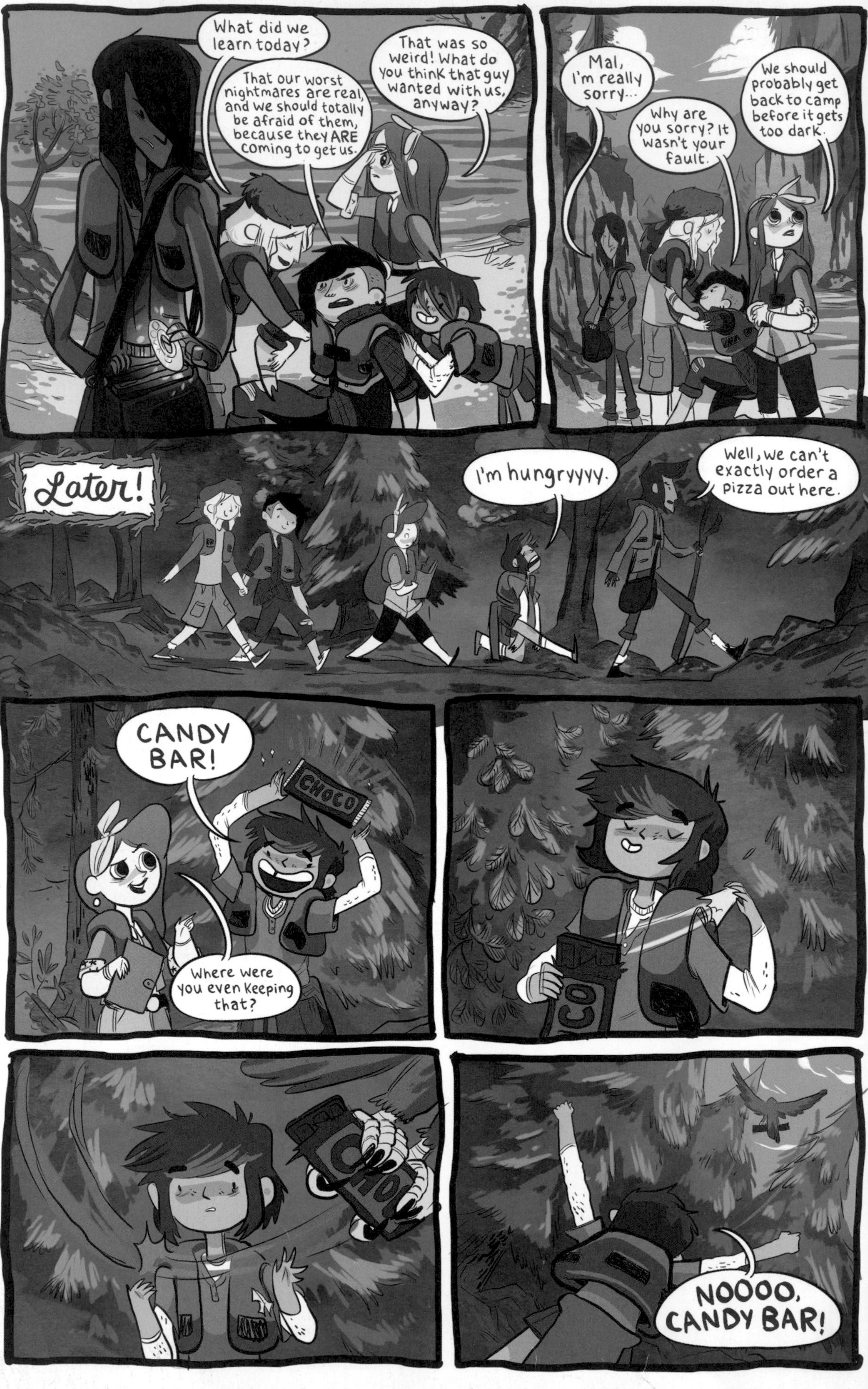
What did we learn today?
That our worst nightmares are real, and we should totally be afraid of them, because they ARE coming to get us.
That was so weird! What do you think that guy wanted with us, anyway?
Mal, I'm really sorry...
Why are you sorry? It wasn't your fault.
We should probably get back to camp before it gets too dark.
Later!
I'm hungryyyy.
Well, we can't exactly order a pizza out here.
CANDY BAR!
CHOCO
Where were you even keeping that?
NOOOO, CANDY BAR!

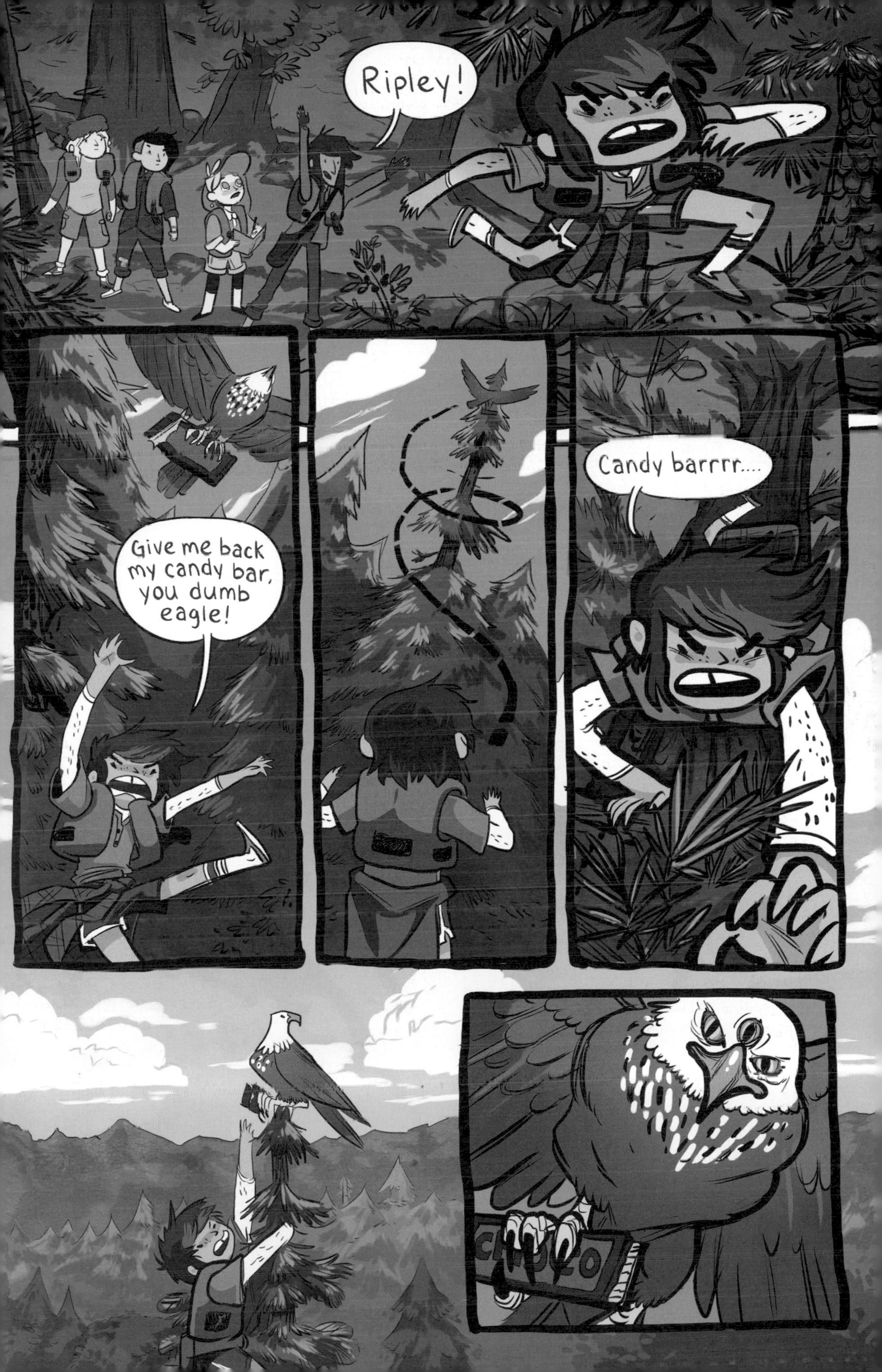
Ripley!
Give me back my candy bar, you dumb eagle!
Candy barrrr....

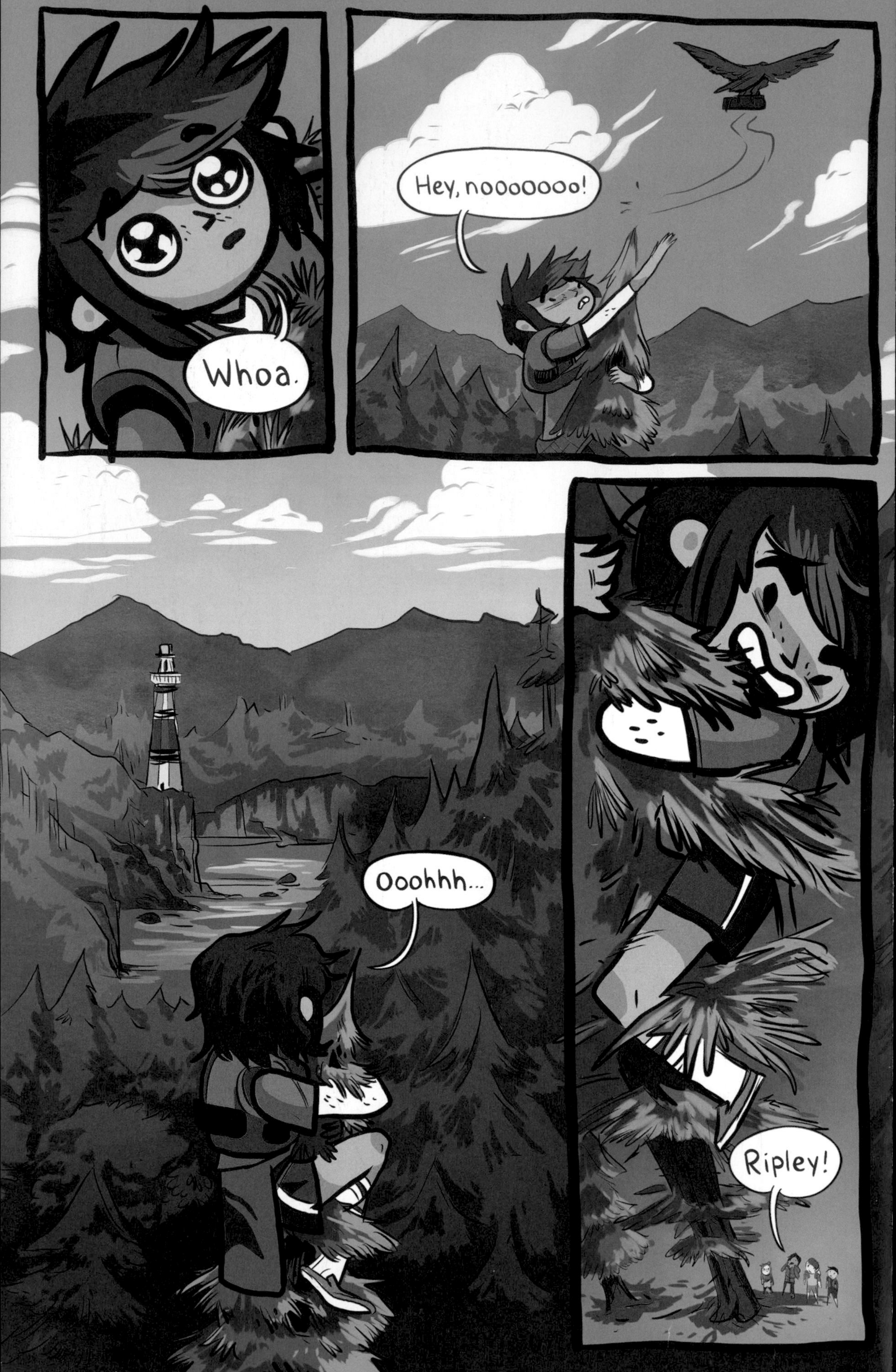
Whoa.
Hey, noooOooo!
Ooohhh...
Ripley!

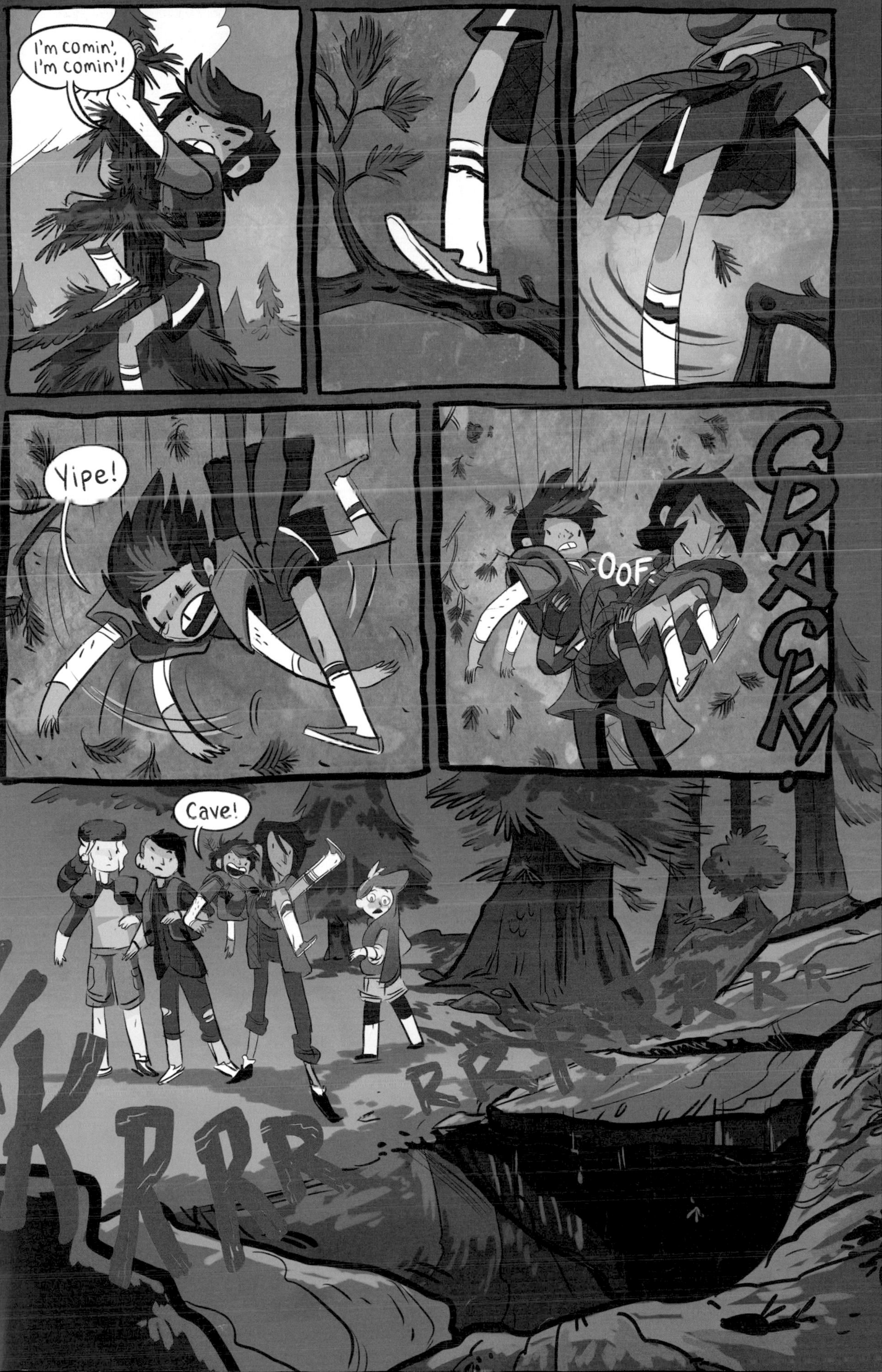

I'm comin', I'm comin'!
Yipe!
OOF
CRACK
Cave!
KRRR
RRRRRRR

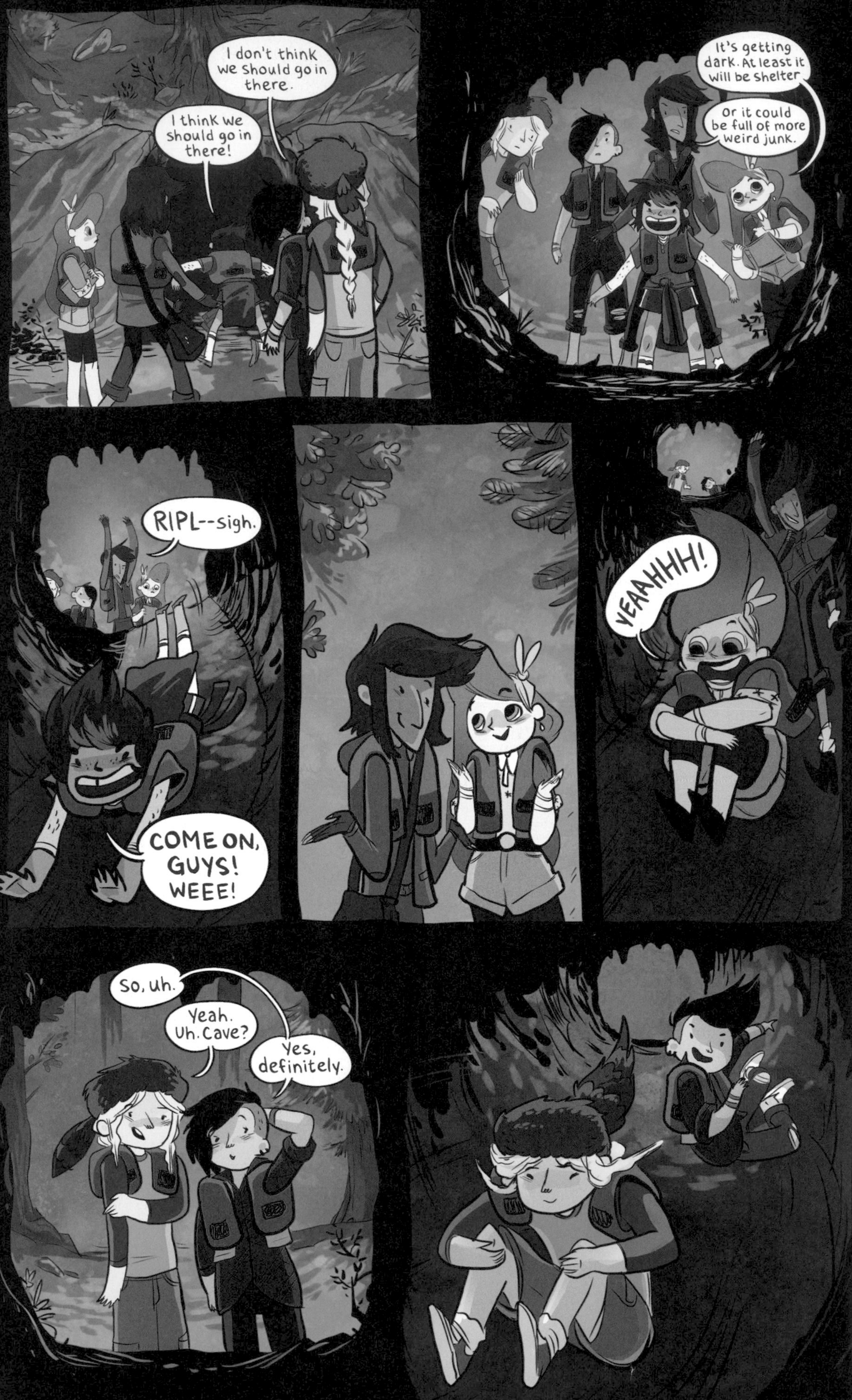

I think we should go in there!
I don't think we should go in there.
It's getting dark. At least it will be shelter
Or it could be full of more weird junk.
RIPL--sigh.
COME ON, GUYS! WEEE!
YEAAHHH!
So, uh.
Yeah. Uh. Cave?
Yes, definitely.

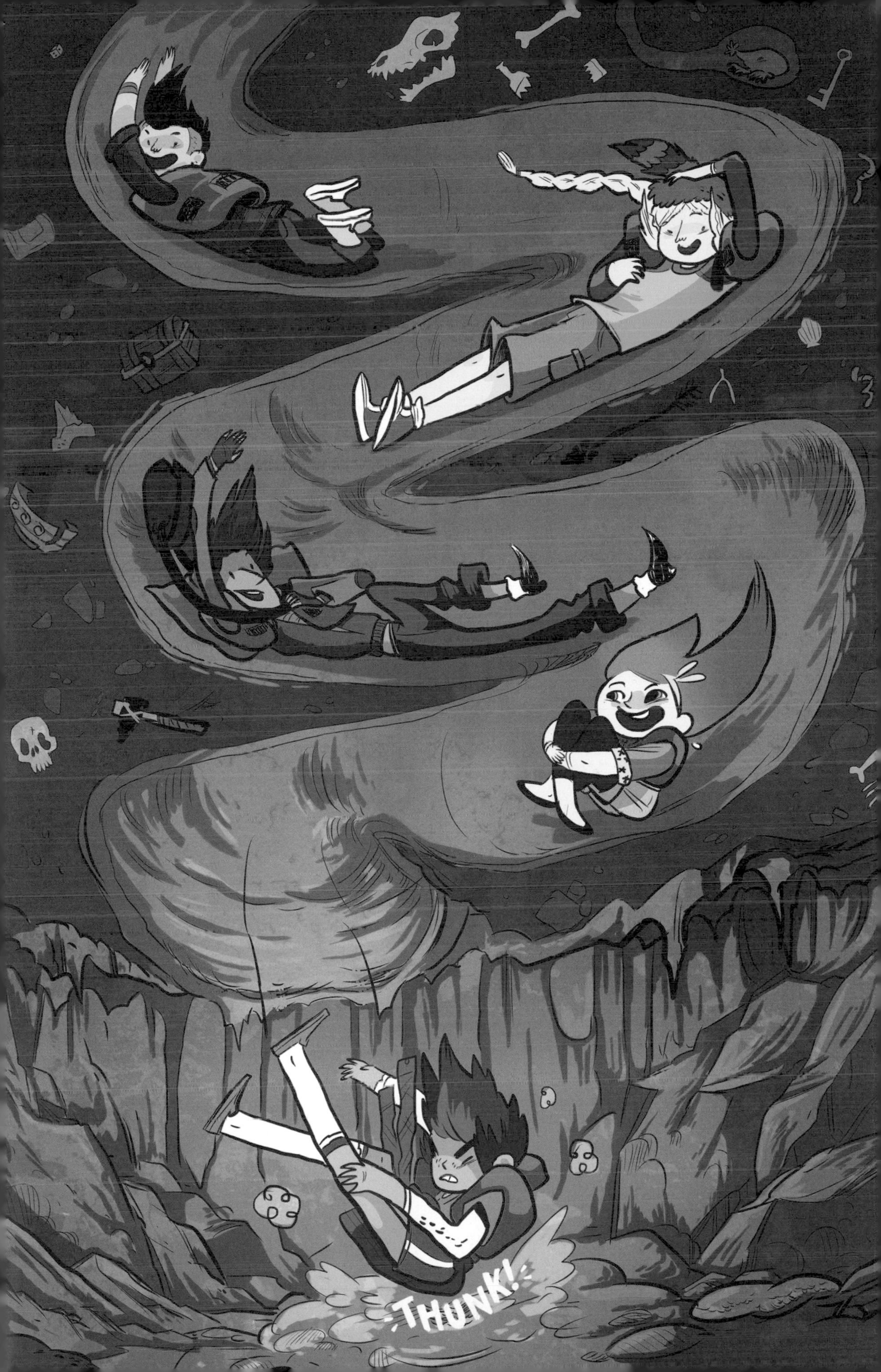
THUNK!

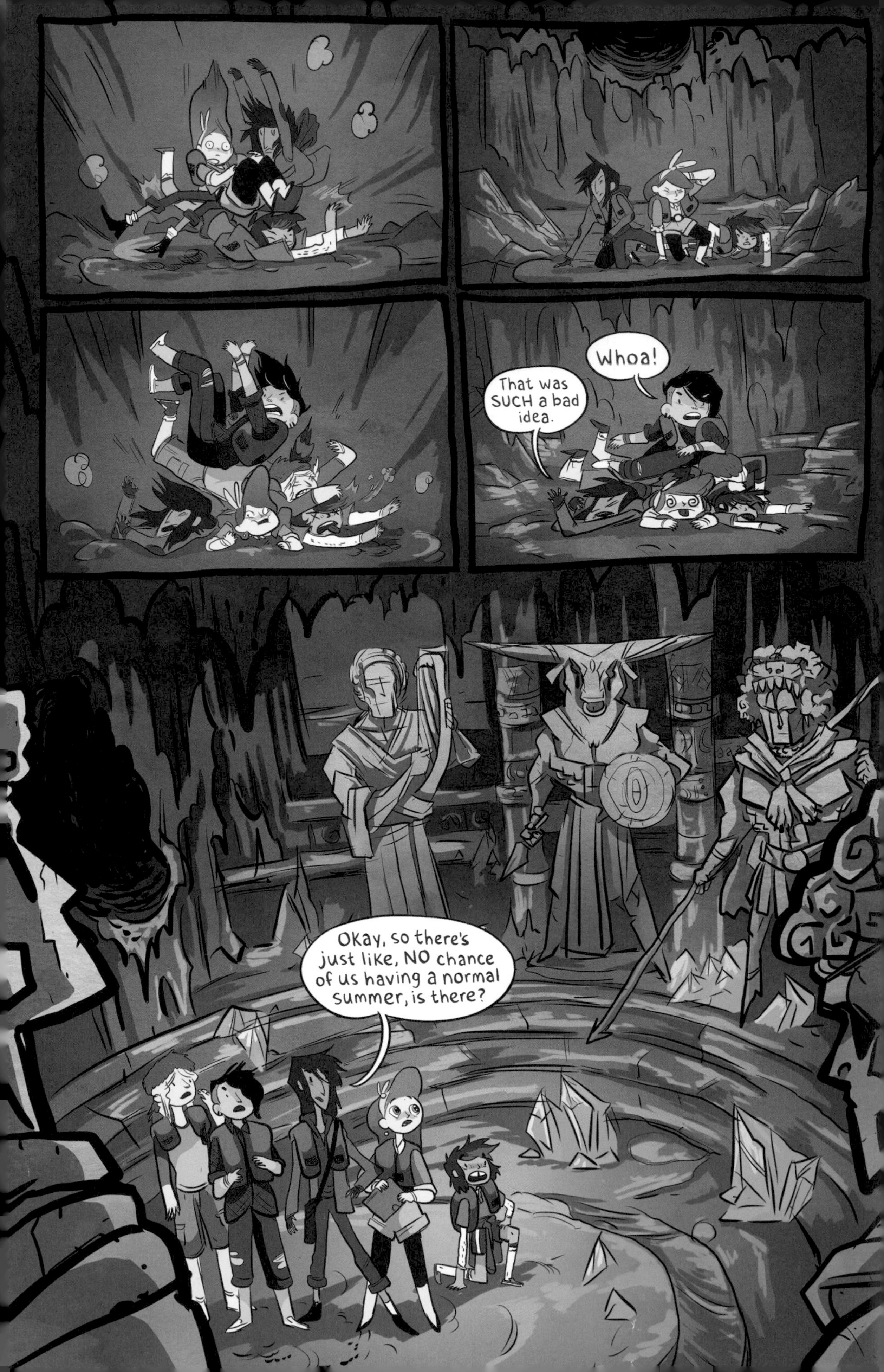
Whoa!
That was SUCH a bad idea.
Okay, so there's just like, NO chance of us having a normal summer, is there?

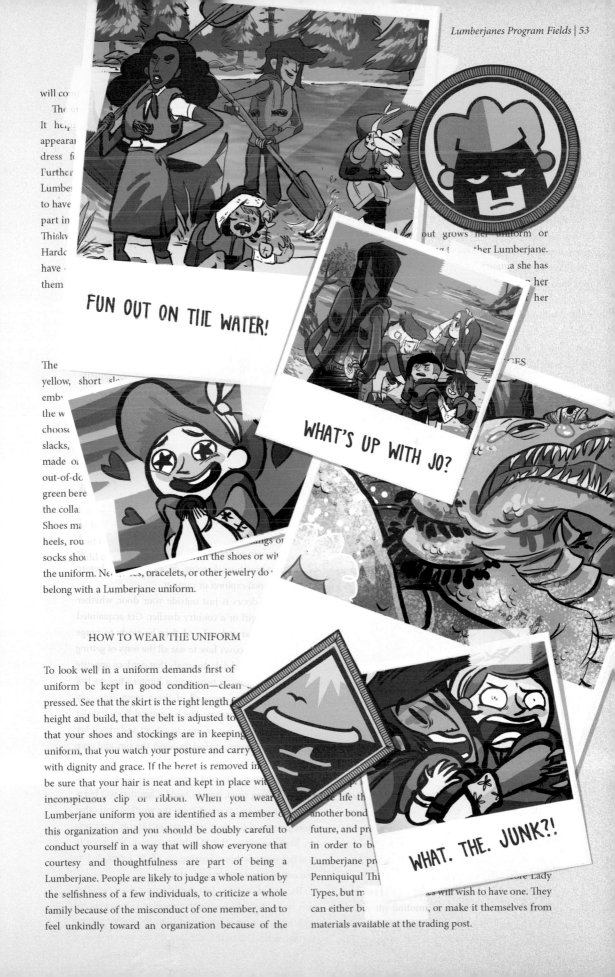

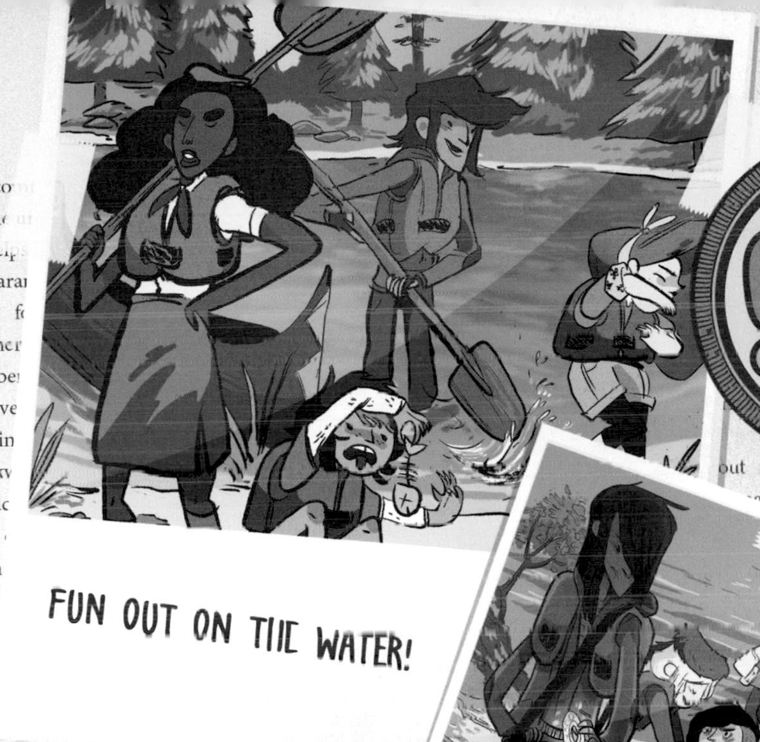
FUN OUT ON THE WATER!

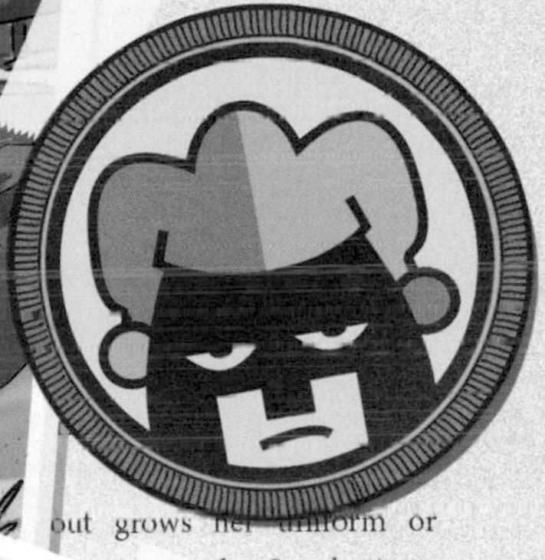

will co...

Th... It he... appeara... dress f... Further... Lumbe... to have... part in... Thiskv... Hardc... have... them

...out grows her uniform or ...g to another Lumberjane. ...insignia she has ... her ... her

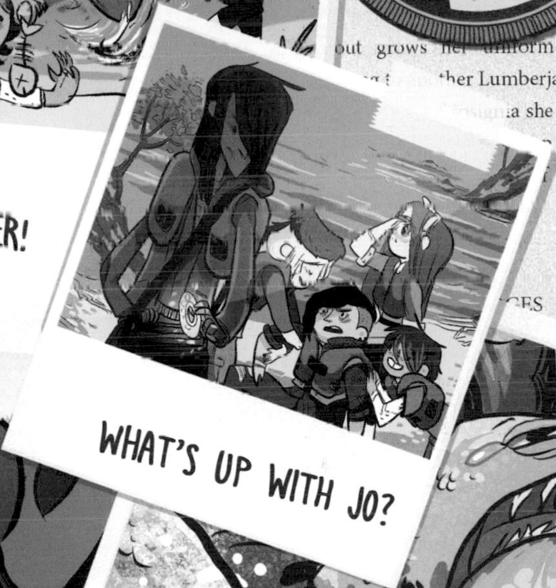
WHAT'S UP WITH JO?

...GES

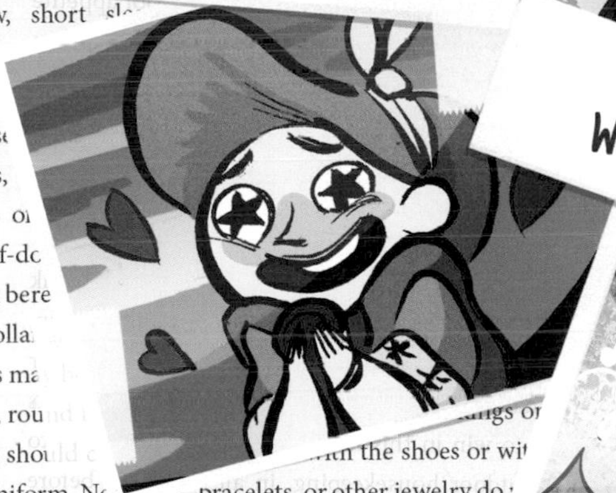

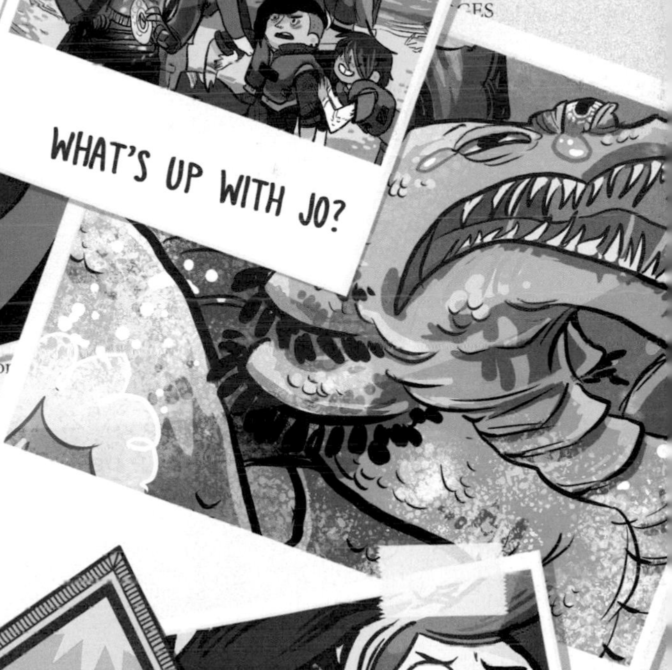

The... yellow, short sle... emb... the w... choose... slacks, ... made o... out-of-do... green bere... the colla... Shoes ma... heels, rou... ...ings or socks shou... with the shoes or wi... the uniform. Ne... es, bracelets, or other jewelry do... belong with a Lumberjane uniform.

HOW TO WEAR THE UNIFORM

To look well in a uniform demands first of ... uniform be kept in good condition—clean ... pressed. See that the skirt is the right length f... height and build, that the belt is adjusted to... that your shoes and stockings are in keeping... uniform, that you watch your posture and carry... with dignity and grace. If the beret is removed in... be sure that your hair is neat and kept in place wit... inconspicuous clip or ribbon. When you wear ... Lumberjane uniform you are identified as a member o... this organization and you should be doubly careful to conduct yourself in a way that will show everyone that courtesy and thoughtfulness are part of being a Lumberjane. People are likely to judge a whole nation by the selfishness of a few individuals, to criticize a whole family because of the misconduct of one member, and to feel unkindly toward an organization because of the

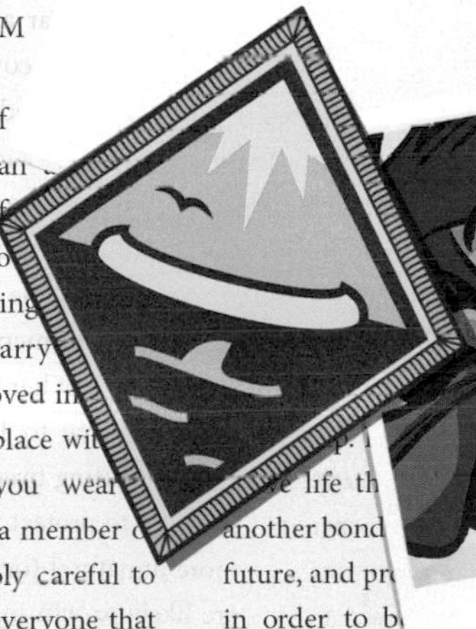

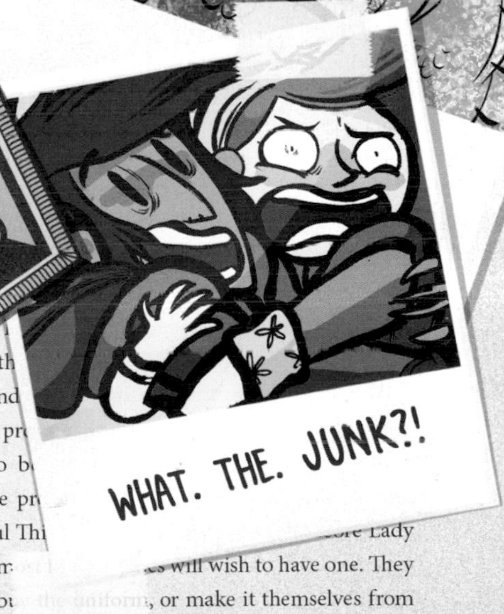
WHAT. THE. JUNK?!

...p. ... life th... another bond... future, and pr... in order to b... Lumberjane pr... Penniquiqul Thi... ...ore Lady Types, but m... ...es will wish to have one. They can either b... the uniform, or make it themselves from materials available at the trading post.

LUMBERJANES FIELD MANUAL
CHAPTER THREE

Lumberjanes "Mathematics and Science" Program Field

EVERYTHING UNDER THE SUM BADGE

"Math leads to a basic understanding of life."

While math is an important subject in schooling, a Lumberjane will learn the commonplace use in everyday situations from knowing the proper amount of kindling needed for a variety of fires to know the velocity needed to run in order to leap across a cliff and make it to the other side. A Lumberjane recognizes how basic understanding of equations can not only make the trials of the wilderness simpler but how furthering that knowledge will help them establish a firmer foothold in the adventure of their lifetime. The human experience can be boiled down to patterns and it is with this understanding that a Lumberjane sees her importance not only in the lives that she directly influences but those outside her circle.

To obtain the *Everything Under the Sum* badge, a Lumberjane must be able to map accurately and correctly from the country itself the main features of half a mile of road, with 440 yards each side to a scale of two feet to the mile, and afterward draw same map from memory. A Lumberjane must be able to measure the height of a tree, telegraph pole, and church steeple, describing method adopted. She must be able to measure the width of a river, estimate distance apart of two objects a known distance away and unapproachable. With this skill she will be able fully prepare for her adventure or task, but be able to set her friends up for success as they go on their journey together.

With an *Everything Under the Sum* badge, a Lumberjane will be able to measure a gradient, have a basic understand of theoretical mathematics and the basic of laws of physics, this will help give her a sure footing in her future career whether it be teaching the future generations or answering their patriotic call and going into the service of their country. While this badge may take some time to earn, every Lumberjane will be able to understand it's importance and, while working

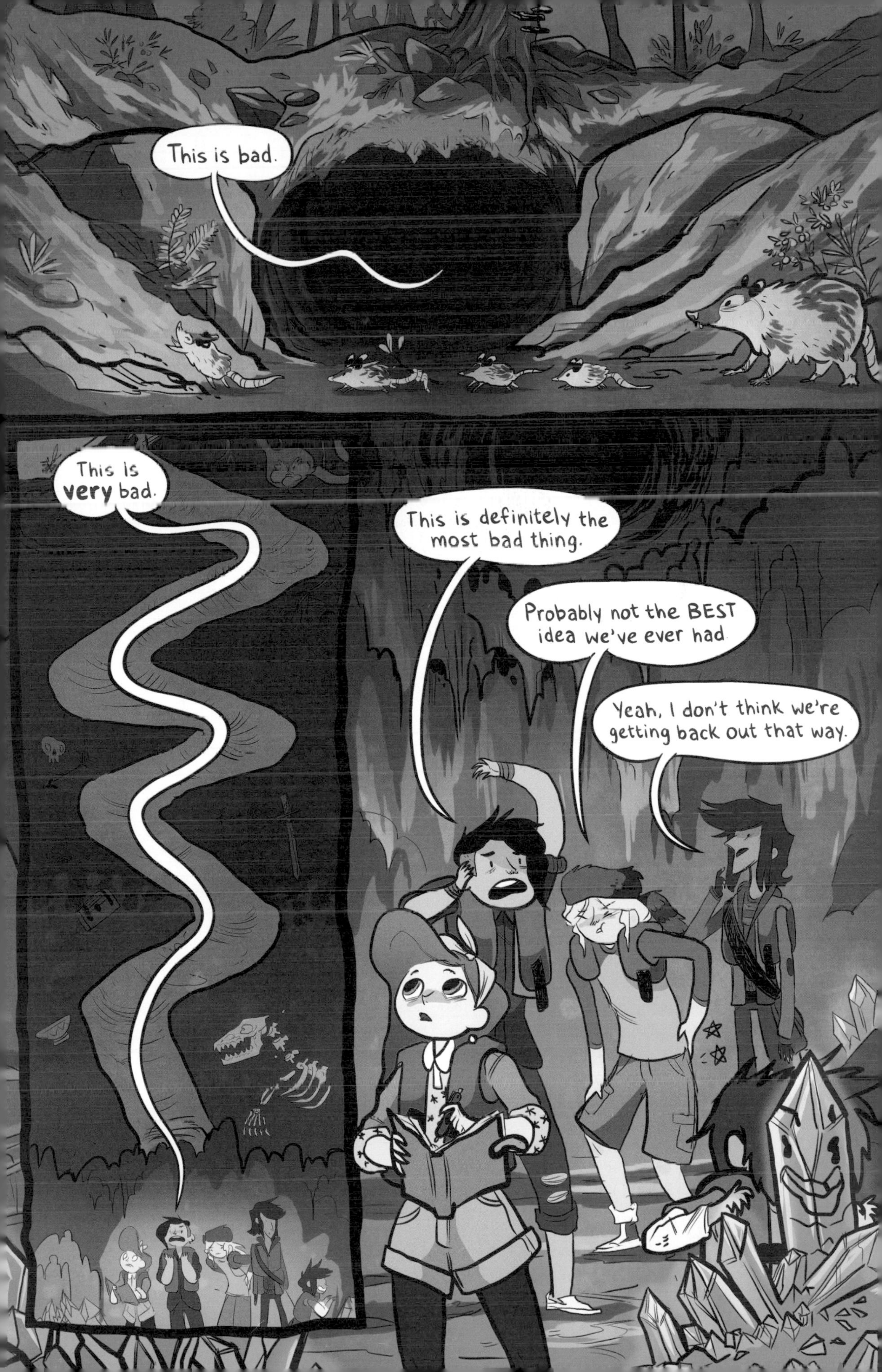
This is bad.
This is **very** bad.
This is definitely the most bad thing.
Probably not the BEST idea we've ever had.
Yeah, I don't think we're getting back out that way.

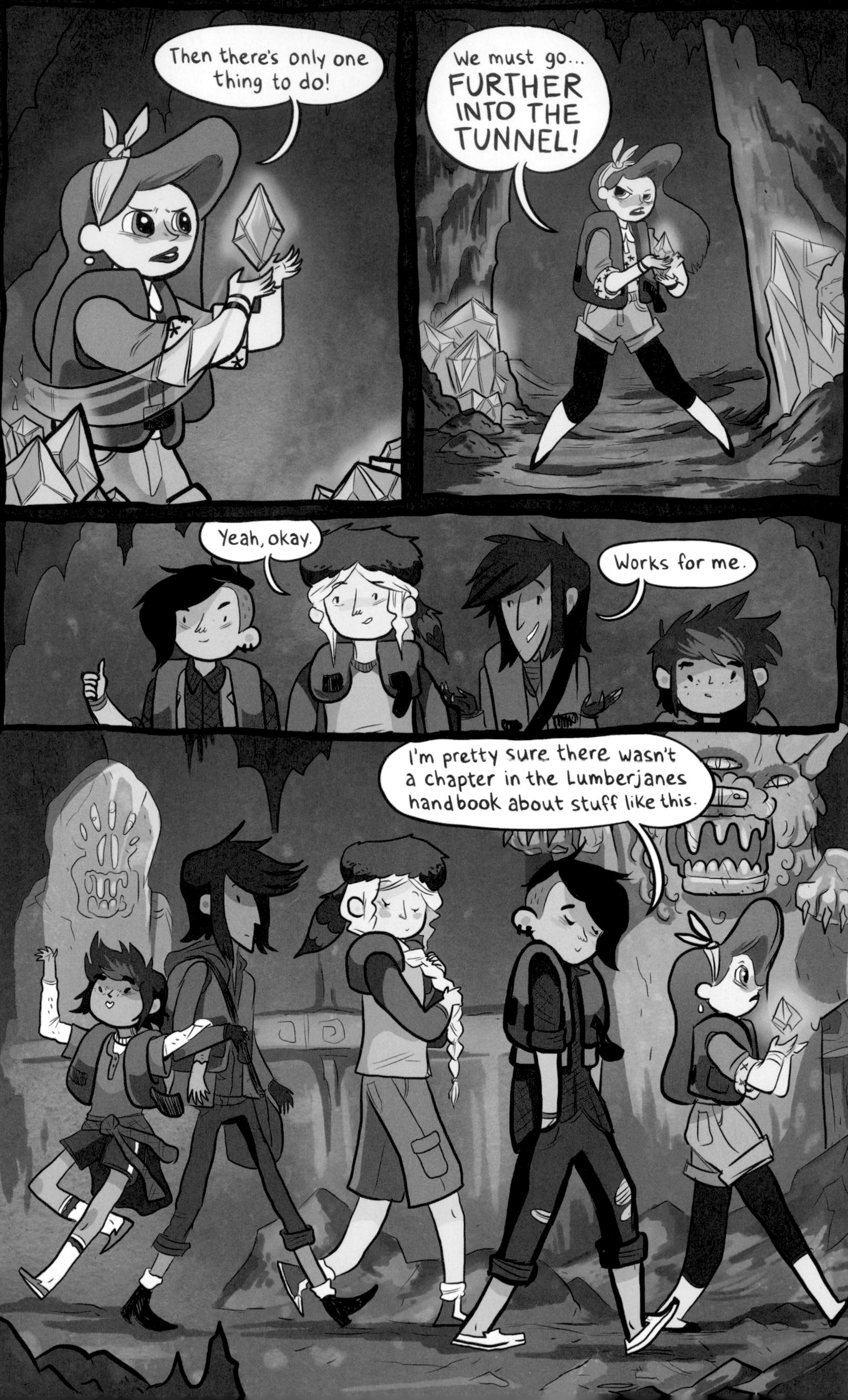

Then there's only one thing to do!
We must go... FURTHER INTO THE TUNNEL!
Yeah, okay.
Works for me.
I'm pretty sure there wasn't a chapter in the Lumberjanes handbook about stuff like this.

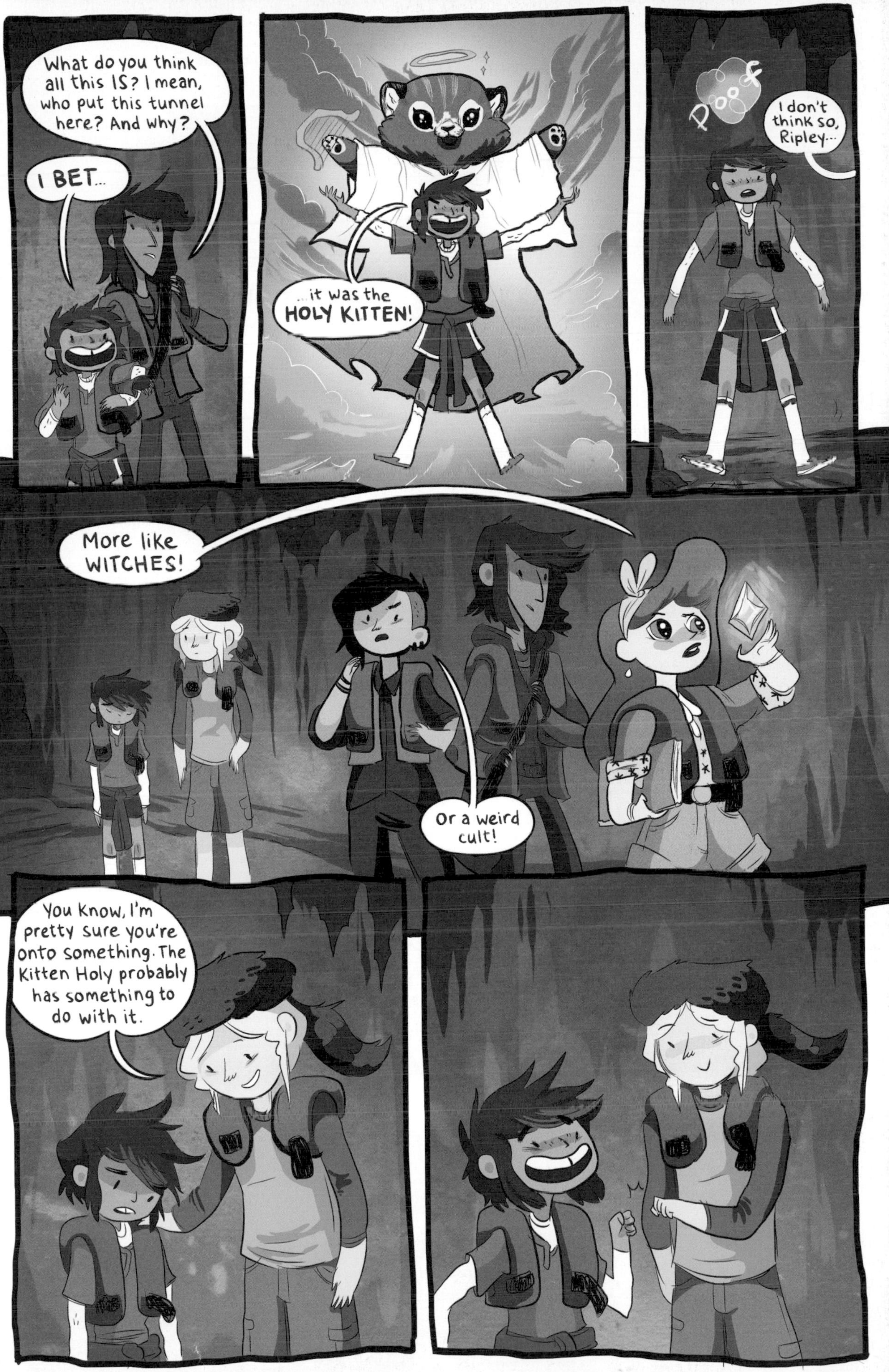

What do you think all this IS? I mean, who put this tunnel here? And why?
I BET...
...it was the HOLY KITTEN!
Poof
I don't think so, Ripley...
More like WITCHES!
Or a weird cult!
You know, I'm pretty sure you're onto something. The Kitten Holy probably has something to do with it.

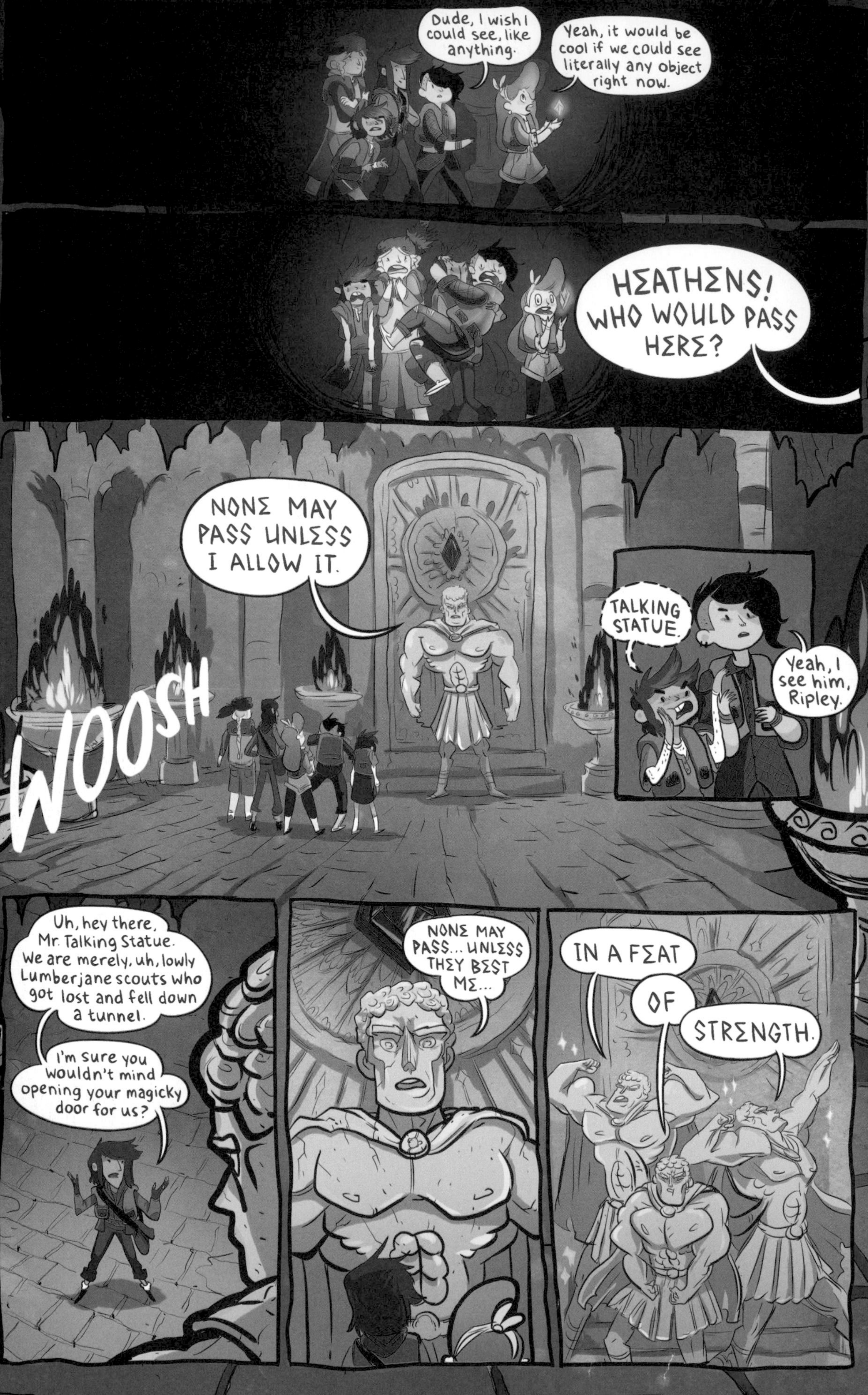
Dude, I wish I could see, like anything.
Yeah, it would be cool if we could see literally any object right now.
HEATHENS! WHO WOULD PASS HERE?
NONE MAY PASS UNLESS I ALLOW IT.
WOOSH
TALKING STATUE.
Yeah, I see him, Ripley.
Uh, hey there, Mr. Talking Statue. We are merely, uh, lowly Lumberjane scouts who got lost and fell down a tunnel.
I'm sure you wouldn't mind opening your magicky door for us?
NONE MAY PASS... UNLESS THEY BEST ME...
IN A FEAT
OF
STRENGTH.

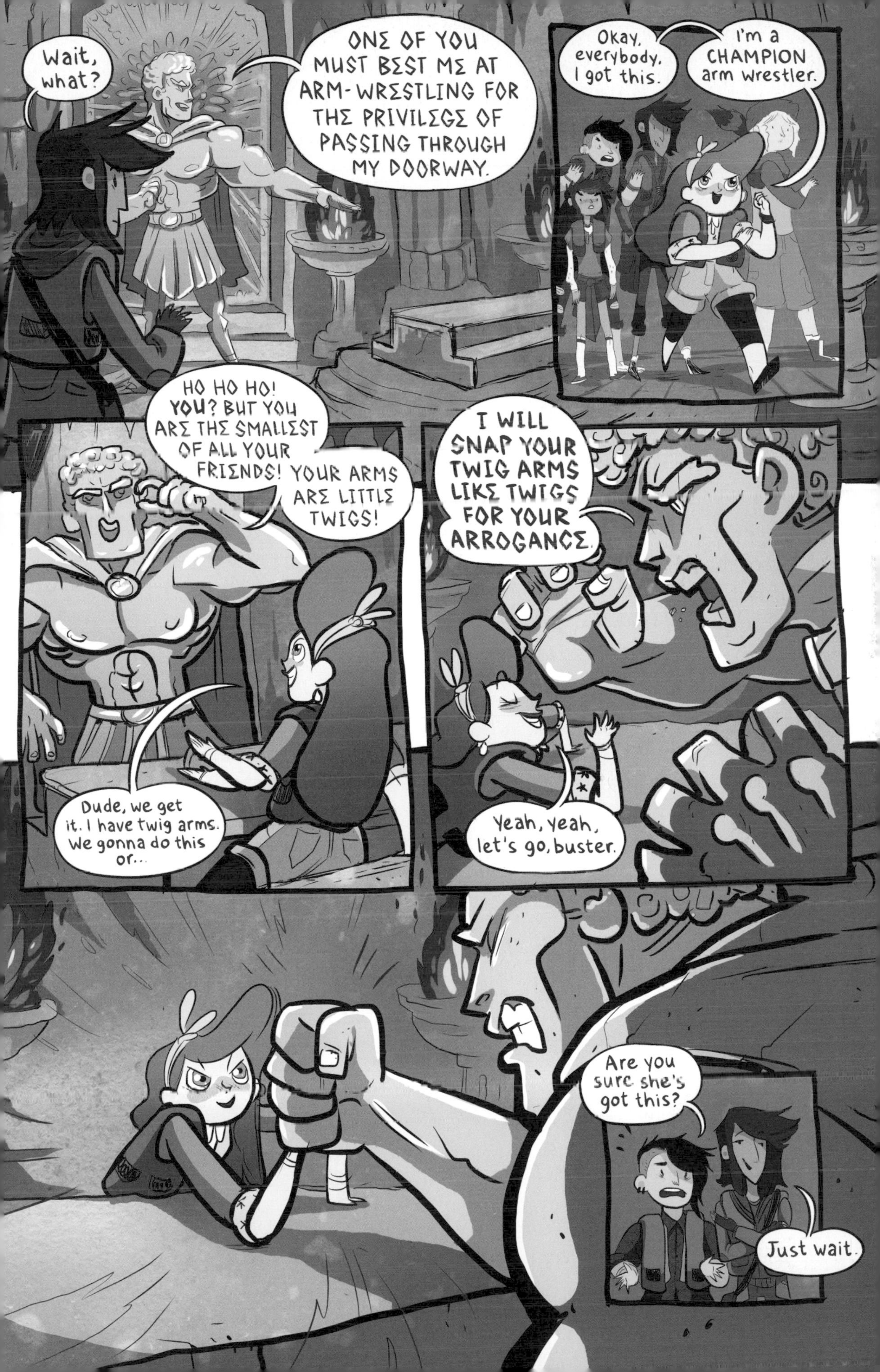
Wait, what?
ONE OF YOU MUST BEST ME AT ARM-WRESTLING FOR THE PRIVILEGE OF PASSING THROUGH MY DOORWAY.
Okay, everybody, I got this.
I'm a CHAMPION arm wrestler.
HO HO HO! YOU? BUT YOU ARE THE SMALLEST OF ALL YOUR FRIENDS!
YOUR ARMS ARE LITTLE TWIGS!
Dude, we get it. I have twig arms. We gonna do this or...
I WILL SNAP YOUR TWIG ARMS LIKE TWIGS FOR YOUR ARROGANCE.
Yeah, yeah, let's go, buster.
Are you sure she's got this?
Just wait.

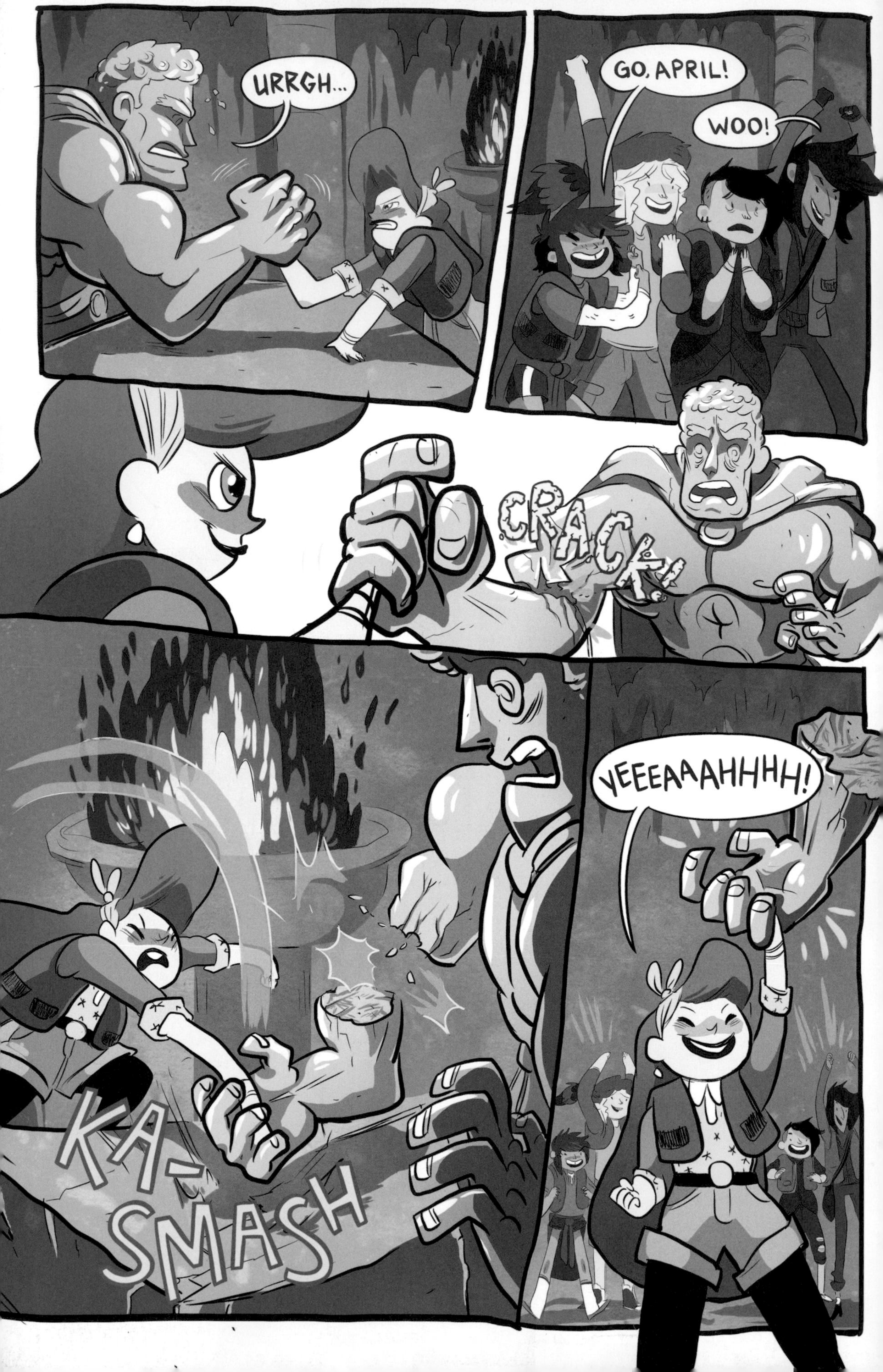
URRGH...
GO, APRIL!
WOO!
CRACK!
KA-SMASH
YEEEAAAHHHH!

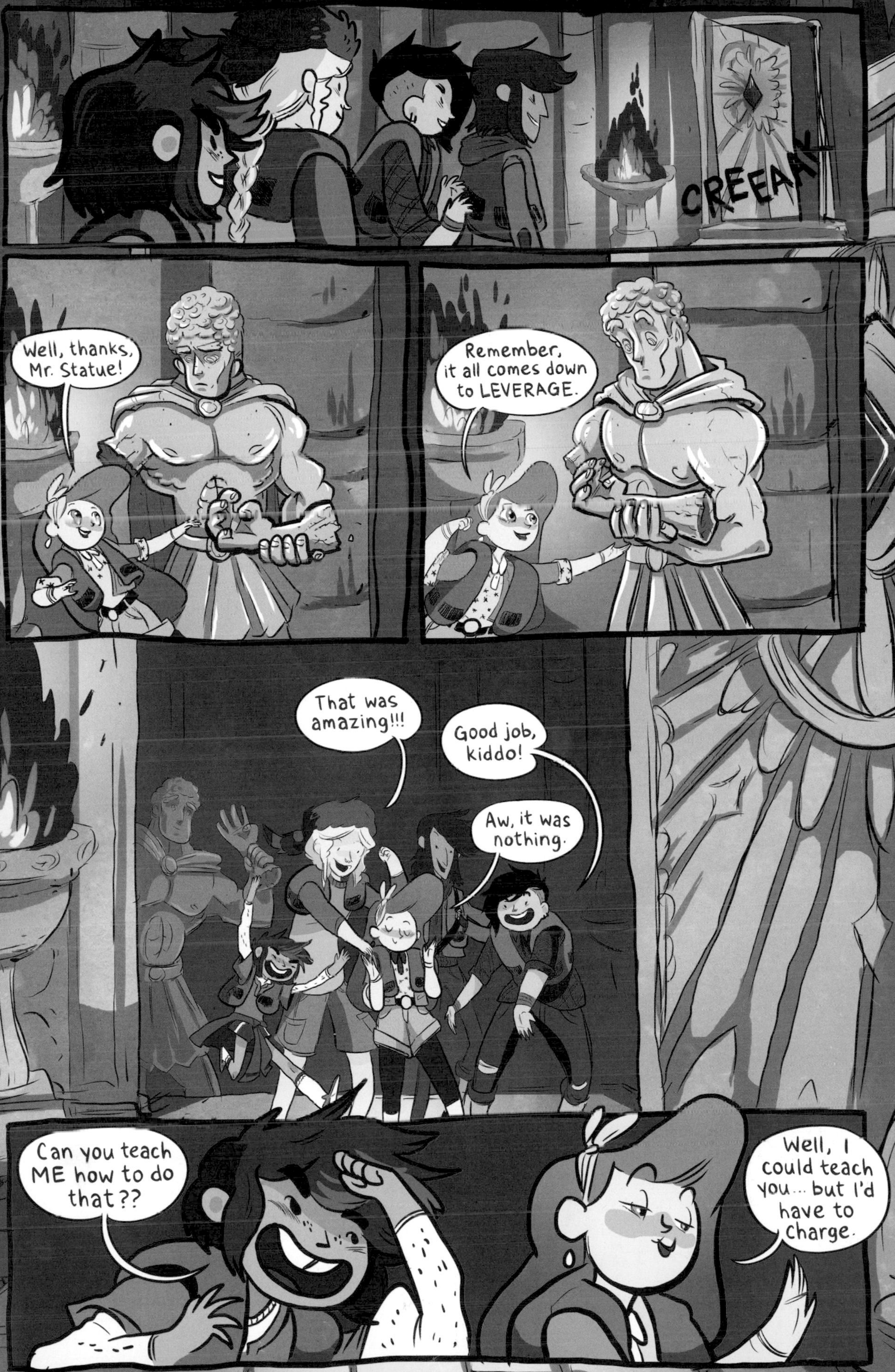
CREEAAK
Well, thanks, Mr. Statue!
Remember, it all comes down to LEVERAGE.
That was amazing!!!
Good job, kiddo!
Aw, it was nothing.
Can you teach ME how to do that??
Well, I could teach you... but I'd have to charge.

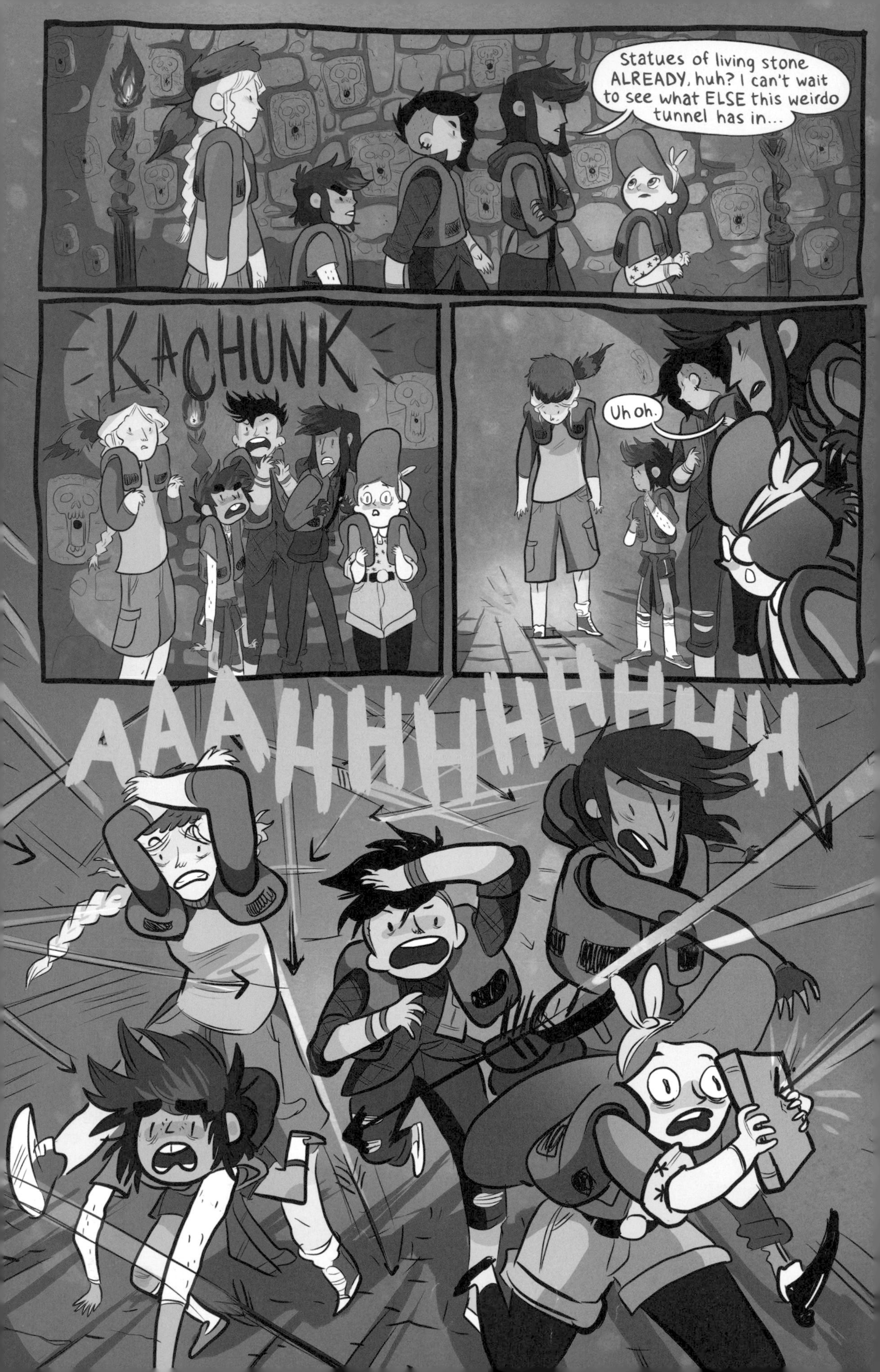
Statues of living stone ALREADY, huh? I can't wait to see what ELSE this weirdo tunnel has in...
KACHUNK
Uh oh.
AAAHHHHHHHH

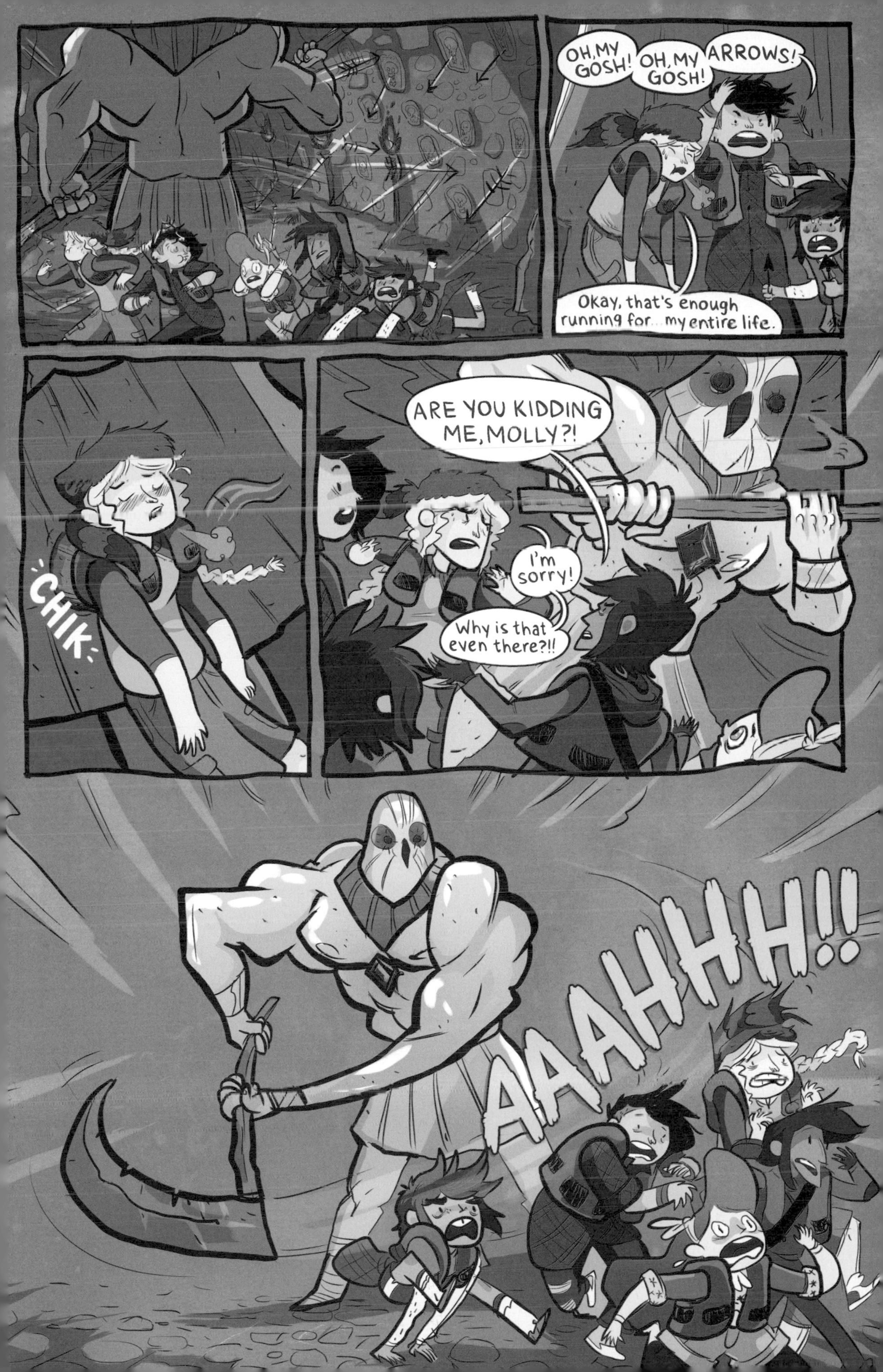
OH, MY GOSH!
OH, MY GOSH!
ARROWS!
Okay, that's enough running for... my entire life.
CHIK
ARE YOU KIDDING ME, MOLLY?!
I'm sorry!
Why is that even there?!!
AAAHHH!!

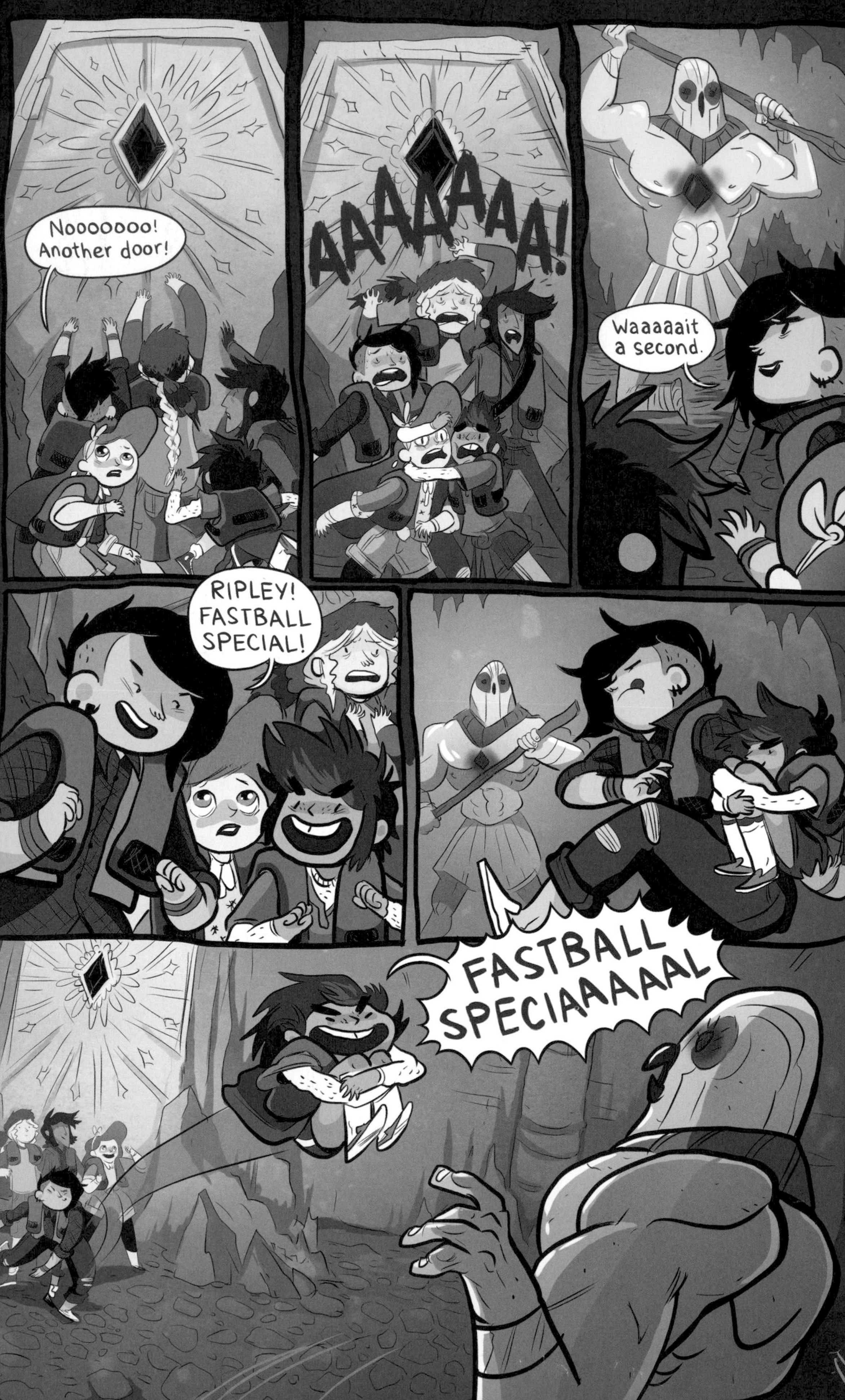
Noooooooo! Another door!
AAAAAAA!
Waaaaait a second.
RIPLEY! FASTBALL SPECIAL!
FASTBALL SPECIAAAAAL

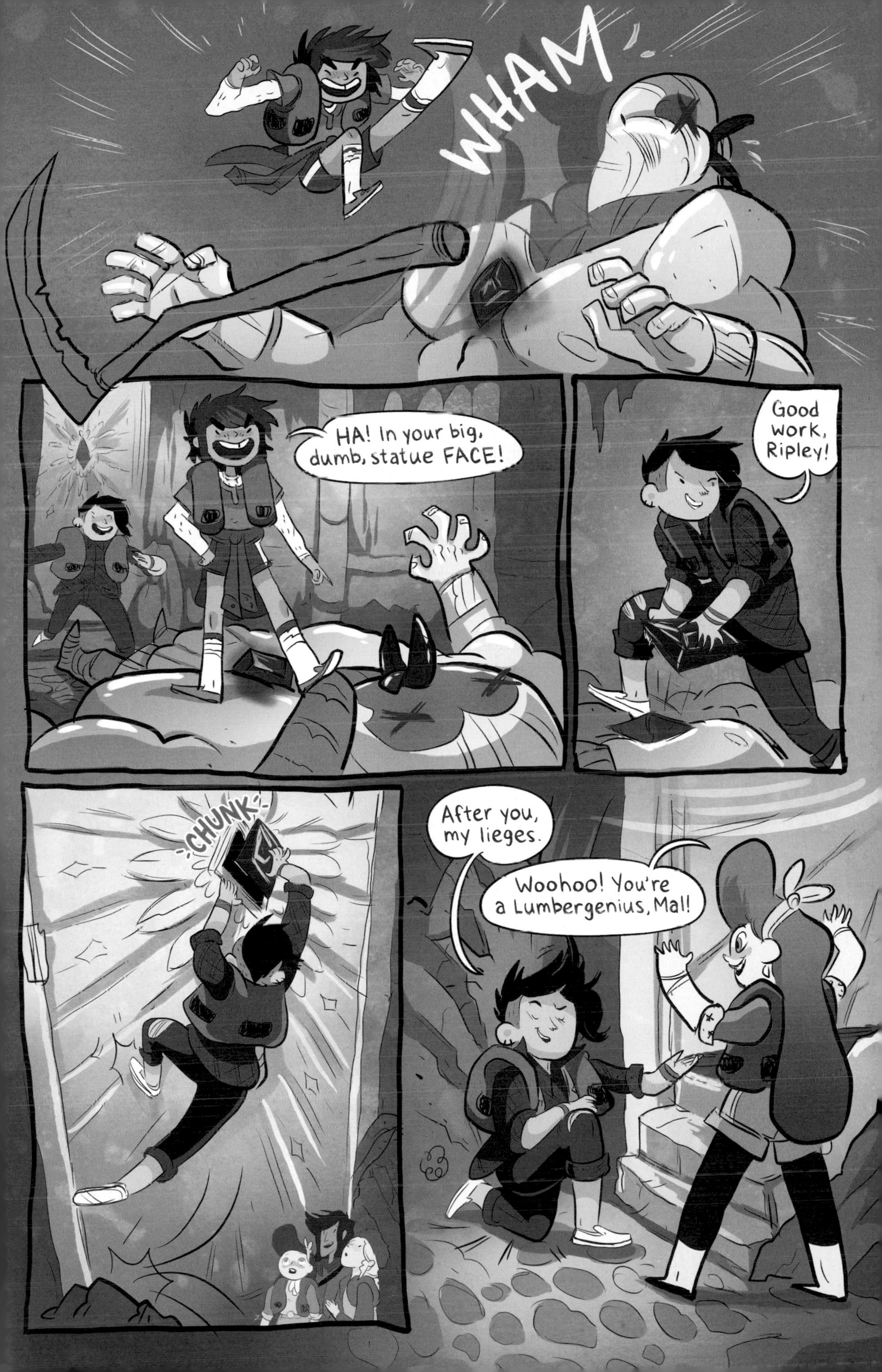
WHAM
HA! In your big, dumb, statue FACE!
Good work, Ripley!
CHUNK
After you, my lieges.
Woohoo! You're a Lumbergenius, Mal!

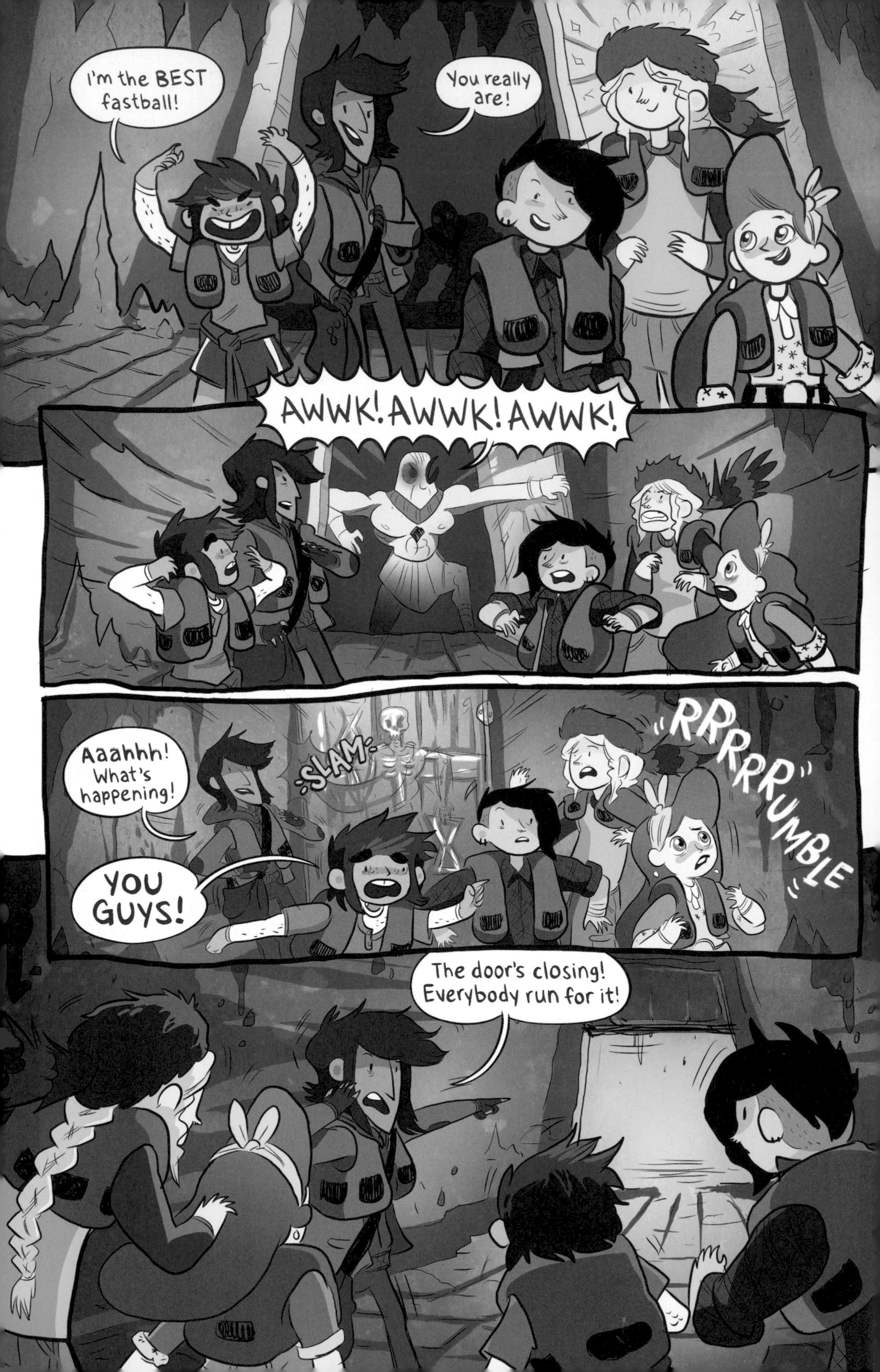
I'm the BEST fastball!
You really are!
AWWK! AWWK! AWWK!
Aaahhh! What's happening!
SLAM
RRRRRRUMBLE
YOU GUYS!
The door's closing! Everybody run for it!

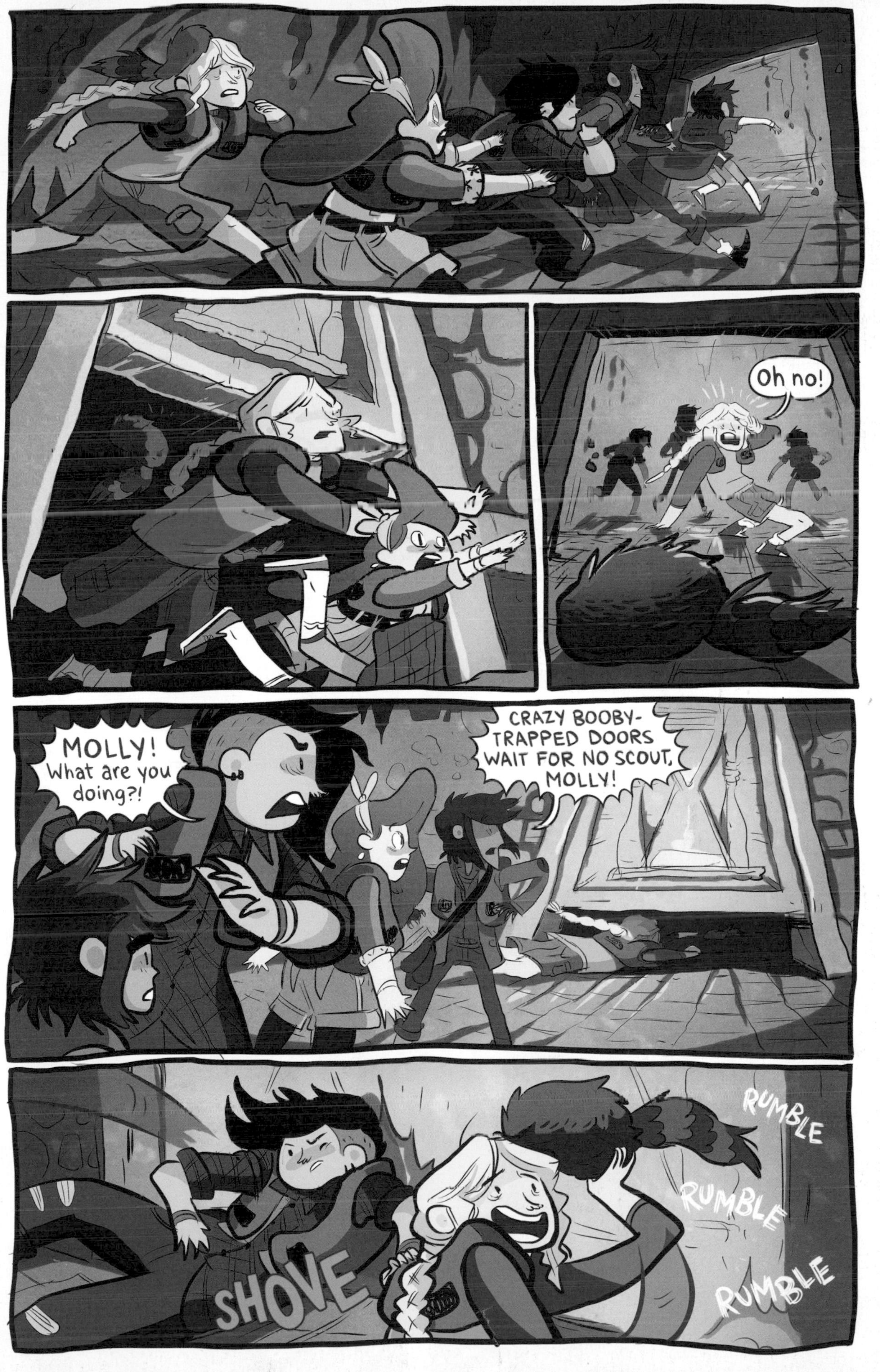
Oh no!
MOLLY! What are you doing?!
CRAZY BOOBY-TRAPPED DOORS WAIT FOR NO SCOUT, MOLLY!
SHOVE
RUMBLE
RUMBLE
RUMBLE

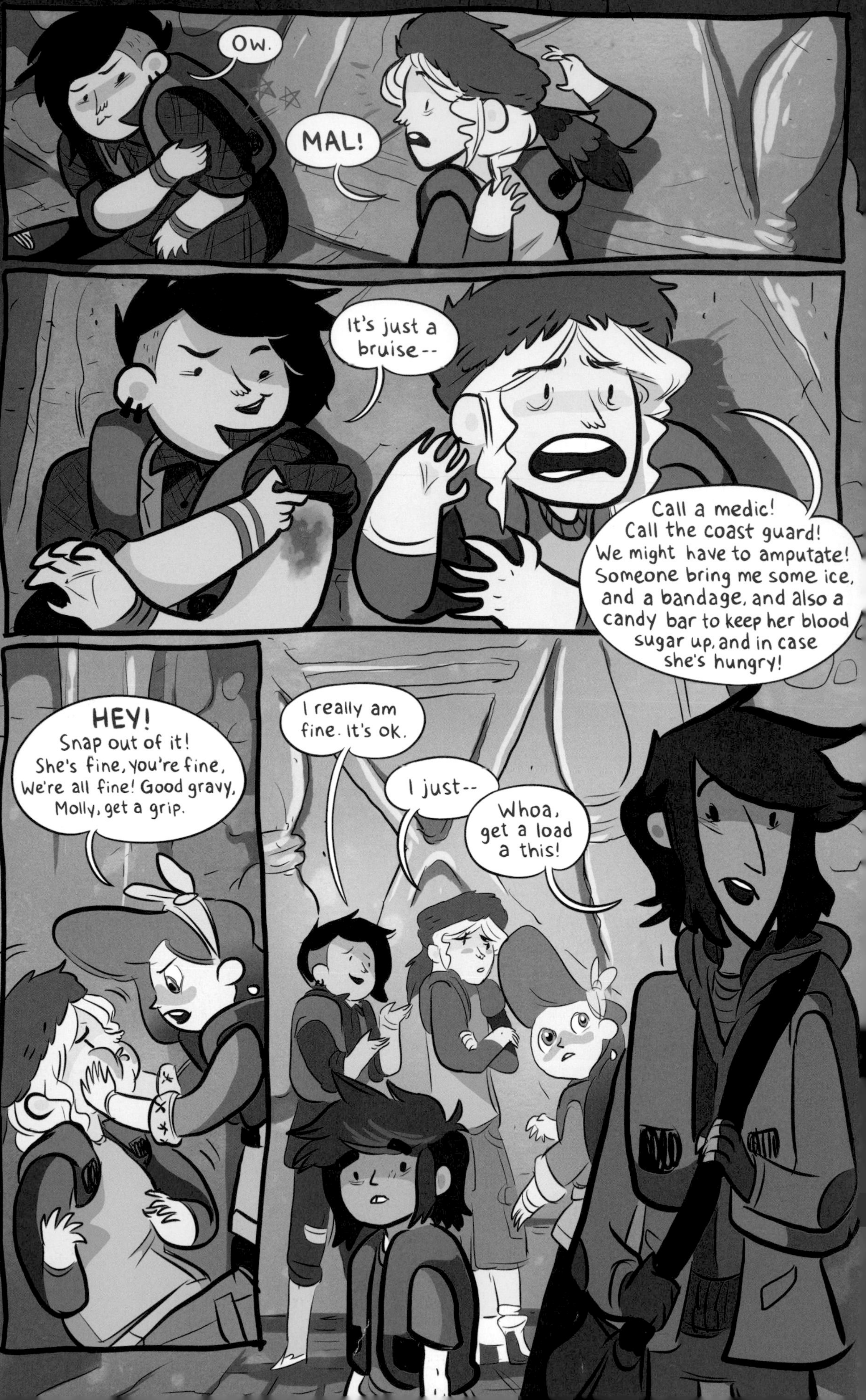
Ow.
MAL!
It's just a bruise--
Call a medic! Call the coast guard! We might have to amputate! Someone bring me some ice, and a bandage, and also a candy bar to keep her blood sugar up, and in case she's hungry!
HEY! Snap out of it! She's fine, you're fine, We're all fine! Good gravy, Molly, get a grip.
I really am fine. It's ok.
I just--
Whoa, get a load a this!

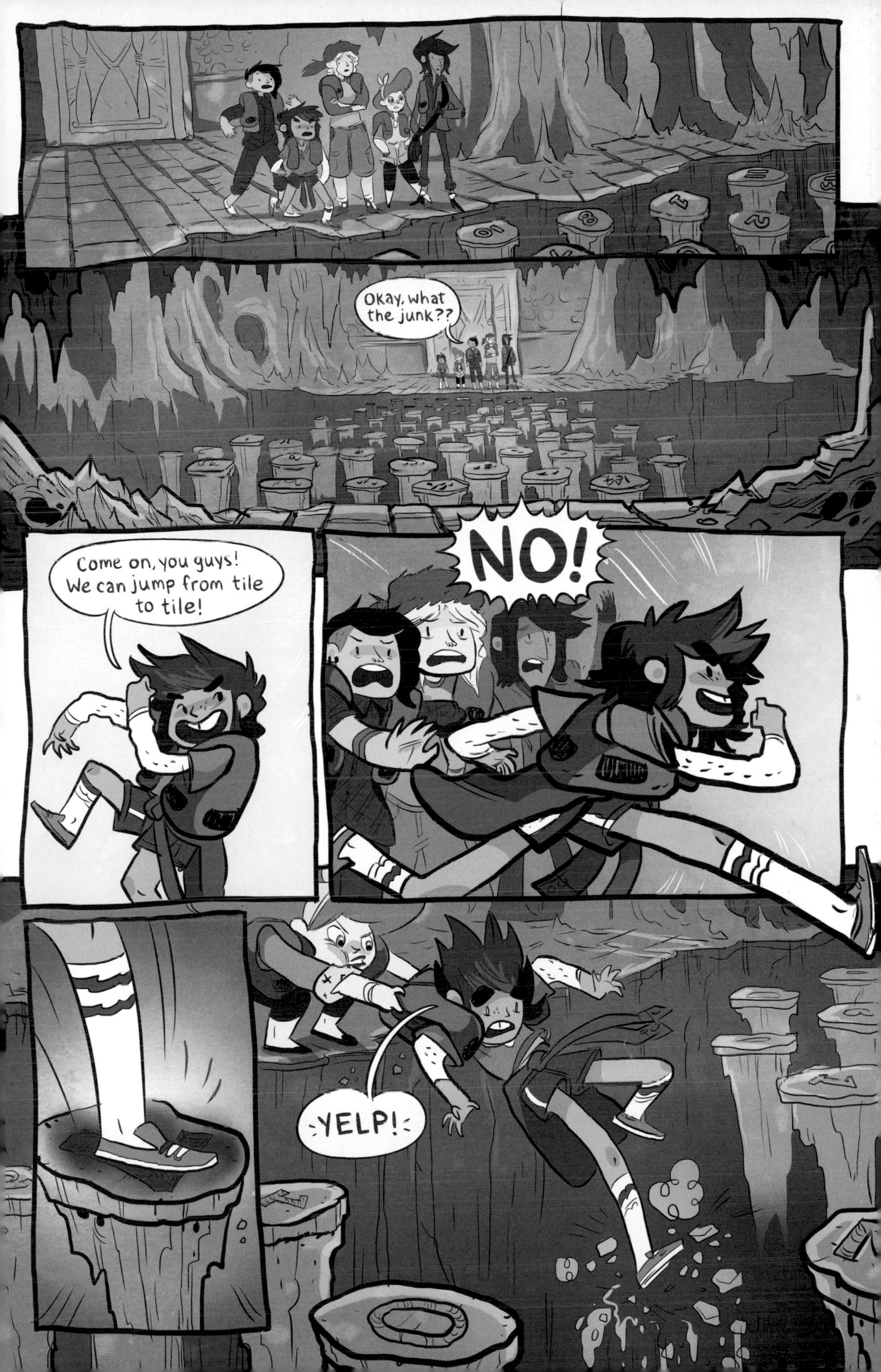

Okay, what the junk??
Come on, you guys! We can jump from tile to tile!
NO!
YELP!

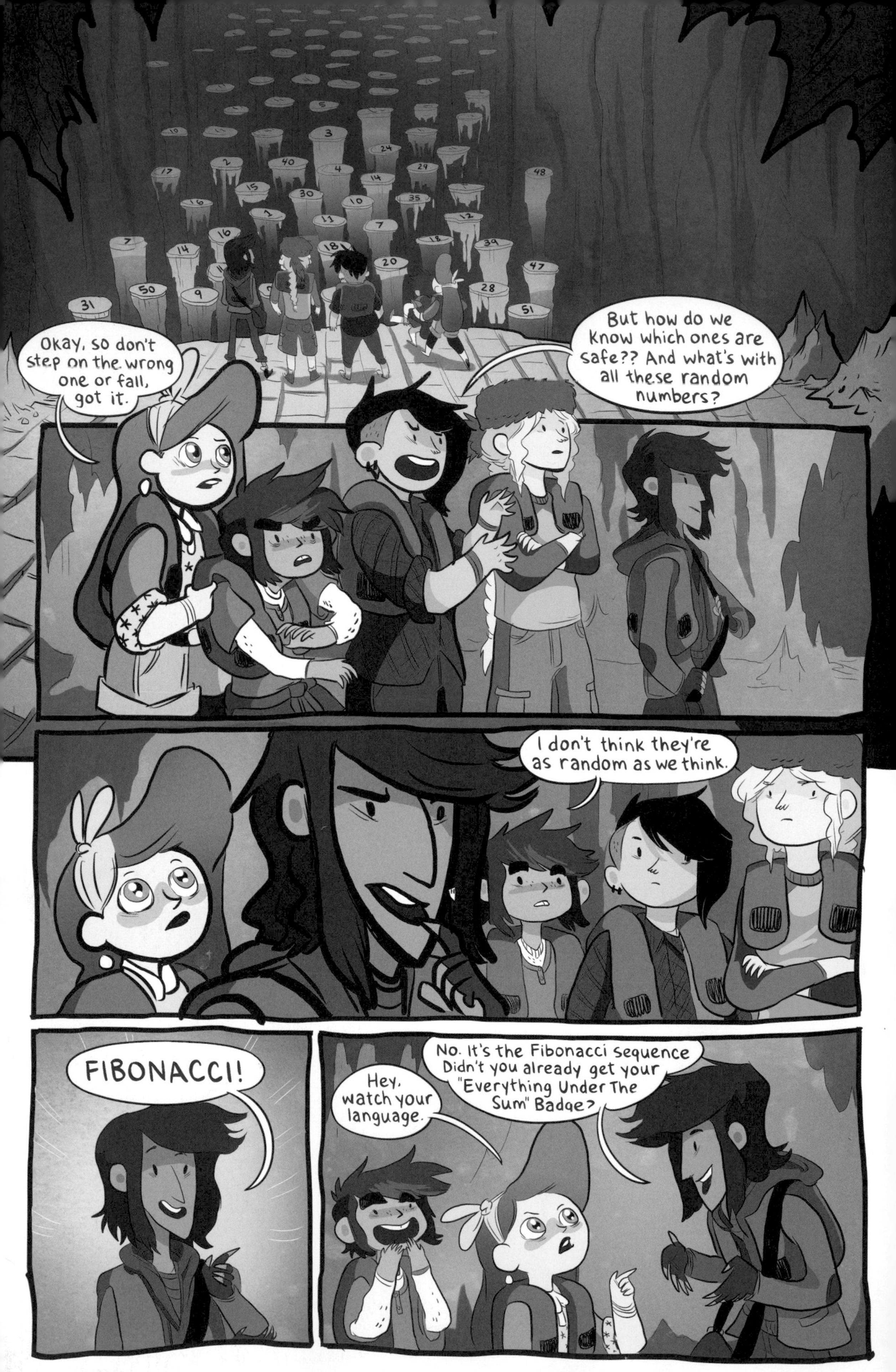
Okay, so don't step on the wrong one or fall, got it.
But how do we know which ones are safe?? And what's with all these random numbers?
I don't think they're as random as we think.
FIBONACCI!
Hey, watch your language.
No. It's the Fibonacci sequence Didn't you already get your "Everything Under The Sum" Badge?

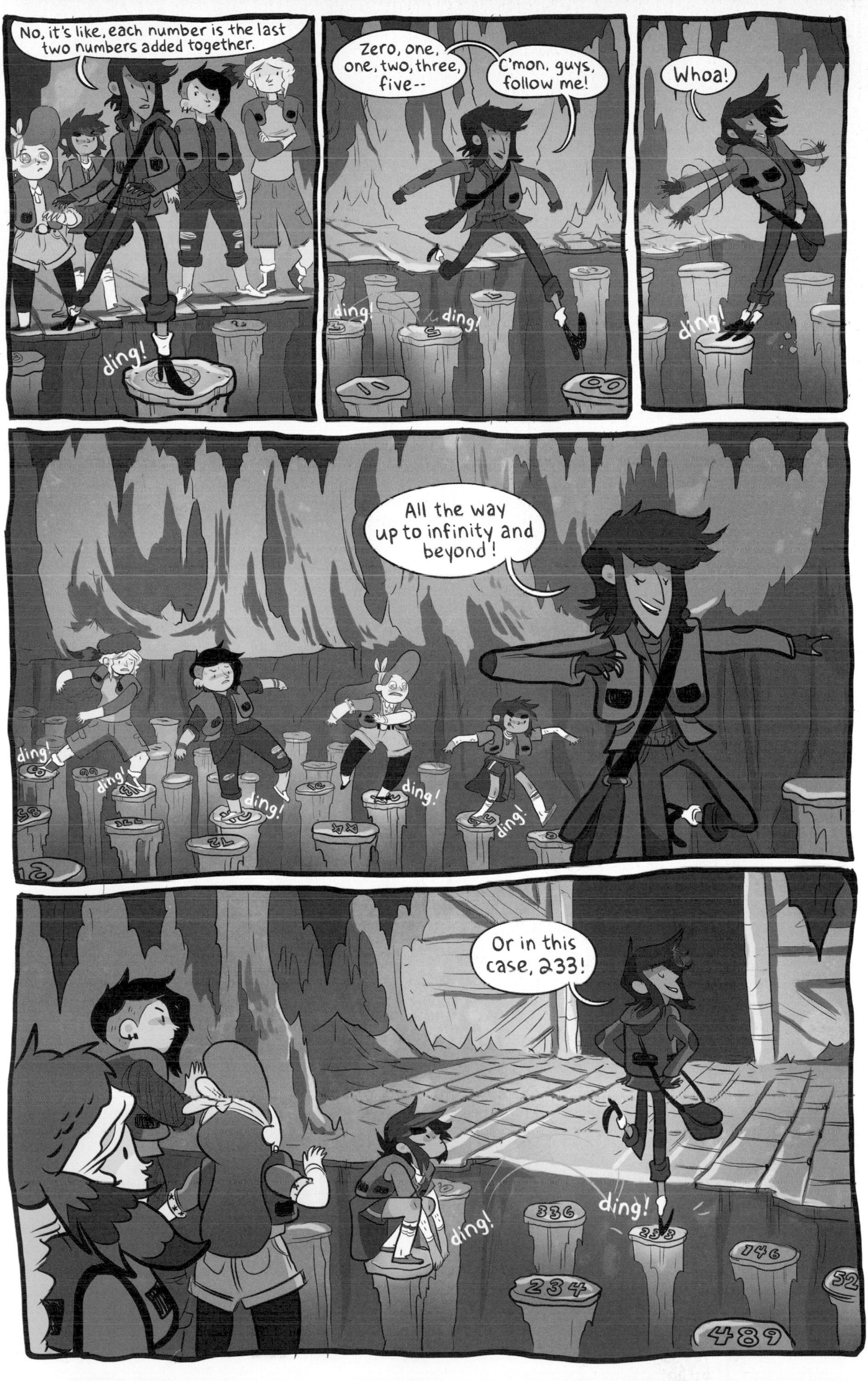
No, it's like, each number is the last two numbers added together.
ding!
Zero, one, one, two, three, five--
C'mon, guys, follow me!
ding!
ding!
Whoa!
ding!
All the way up to infinity and beyond!
ding!
ding!
ding!
ding!
ding!
Or in this case, 233!
336
ding!
ding!
234
146
52
489

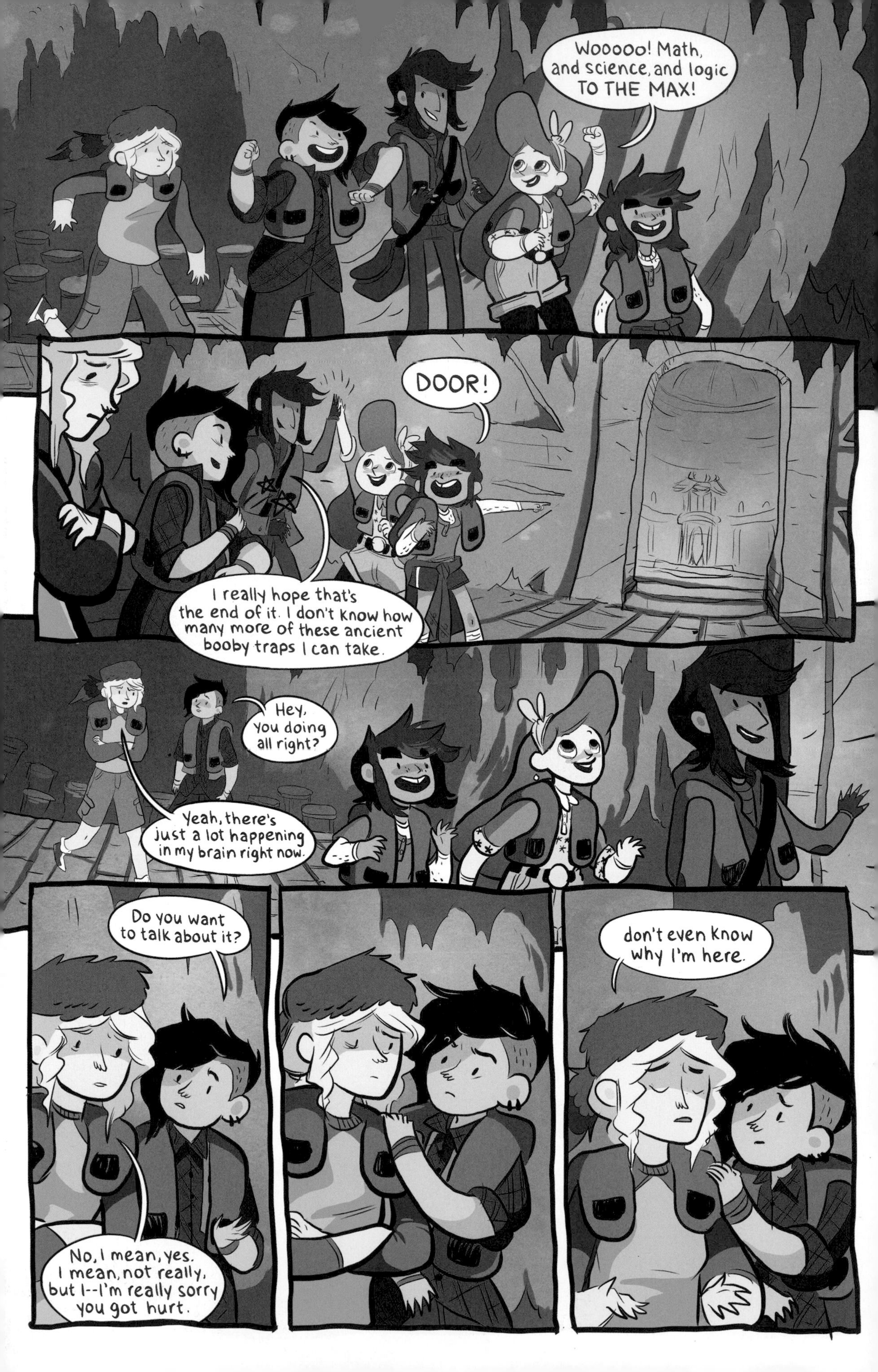
Wooooo! Math, and science, and logic TO THE MAX!
DOOR!
I really hope that's the end of it. I don't know how many more of these ancient booby traps I can take.
Hey, you doing all right?
Yeah, there's just a lot happening in my brain right now.
Do you want to talk about it?
No, I mean, yes. I mean, not really, but I--I'm really sorry you got hurt.
don't even know why I'm here.

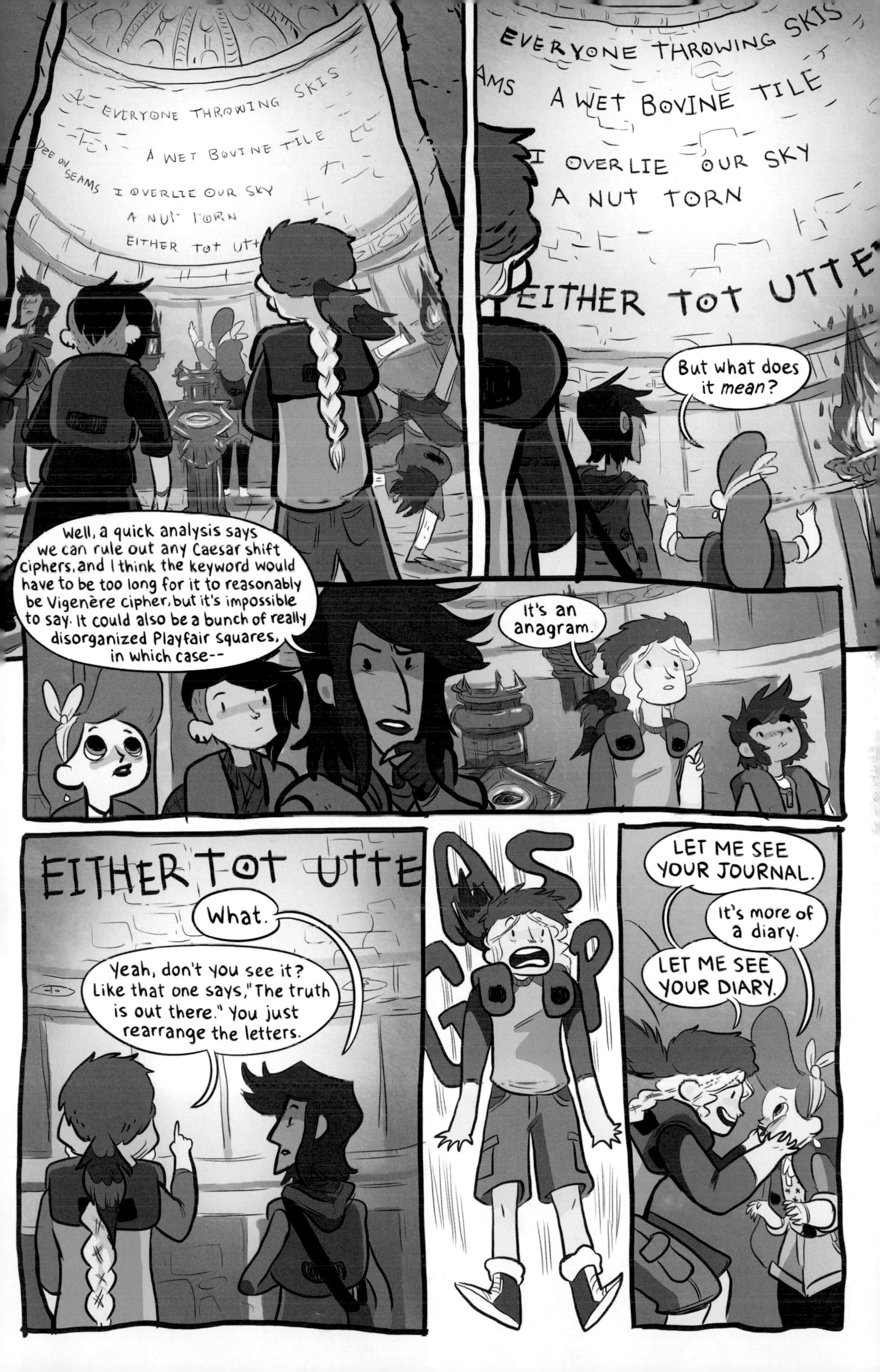
EVERYONE THROWING SKIS
A WET BOVINE TILE
I OVERLIE OUR SKY
A NUT TORN
EITHER TOT
EVERYONE THROWING SKIS
AMS
A WET BOVINE TILE
I OVERLIE OUR SKY
A NUT TORN
EITHER TOT UTTE
But what does it *mean*?
Well, a quick analysis says we can rule out any Caesar shift ciphers, and I think the keyword would have to be too long for it to reasonably be Vigenère cipher, but it's impossible to say. It could also be a bunch of really disorganized Playfair squares, in which case--
It's an anagram.
EITHER TOT UTTE
What.
Yeah, don't you see it? Like that one says, "The truth is out there." You just rearrange the letters.
GASP
LET ME SEE YOUR JOURNAL.
It's more of a diary.
LET ME SEE YOUR DIARY.

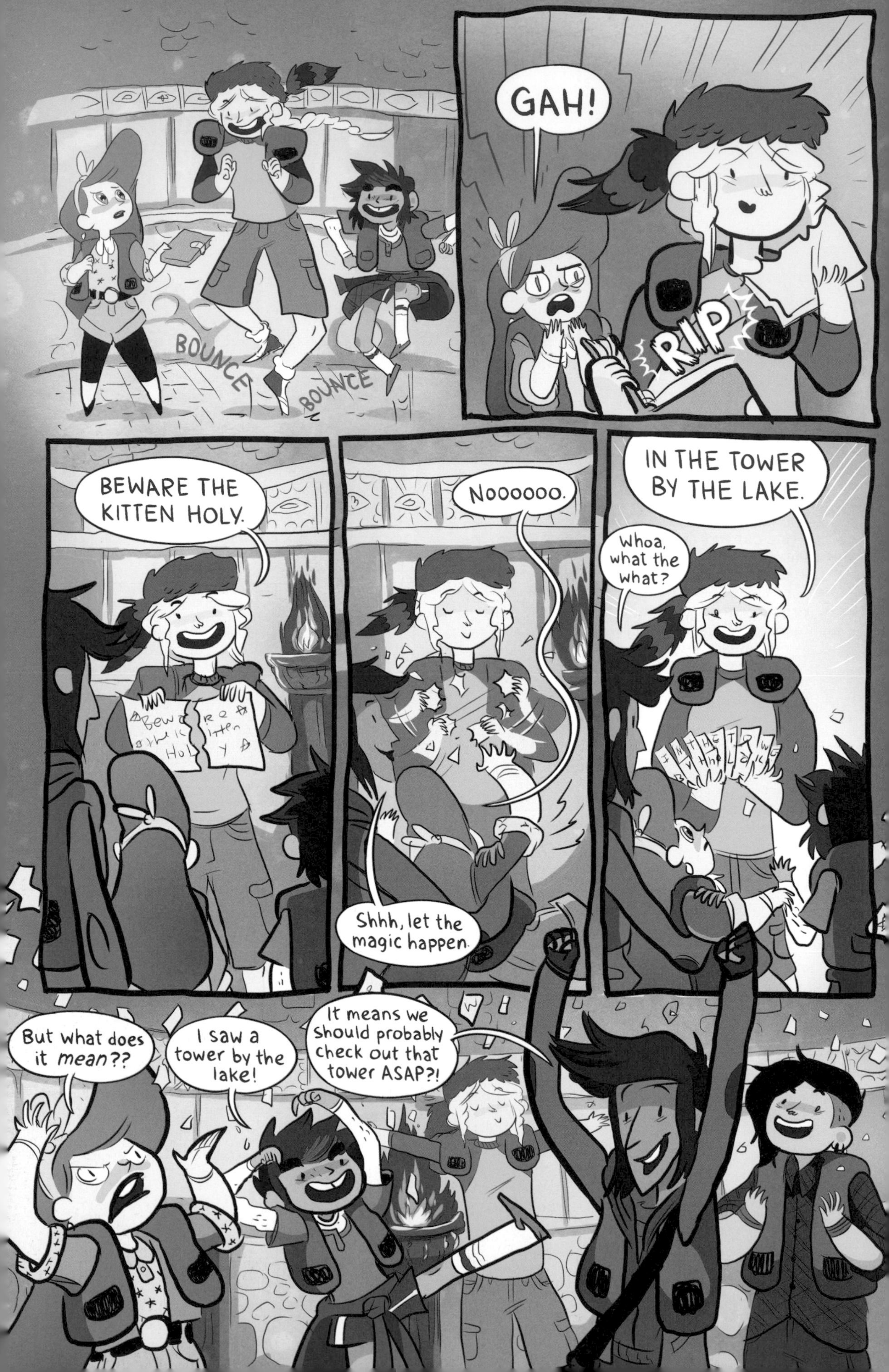

BOUNCE
BOUNCE
GAH!
RIP
BEWARE THE KITTEN HOLY.
Nooooooo.
Shhh, let the magic happen.
IN THE TOWER BY THE LAKE.
Whoa, what the what?
But what does it *mean*??
I saw a tower by the lake!
It means we should probably check out that tower ASAP?!

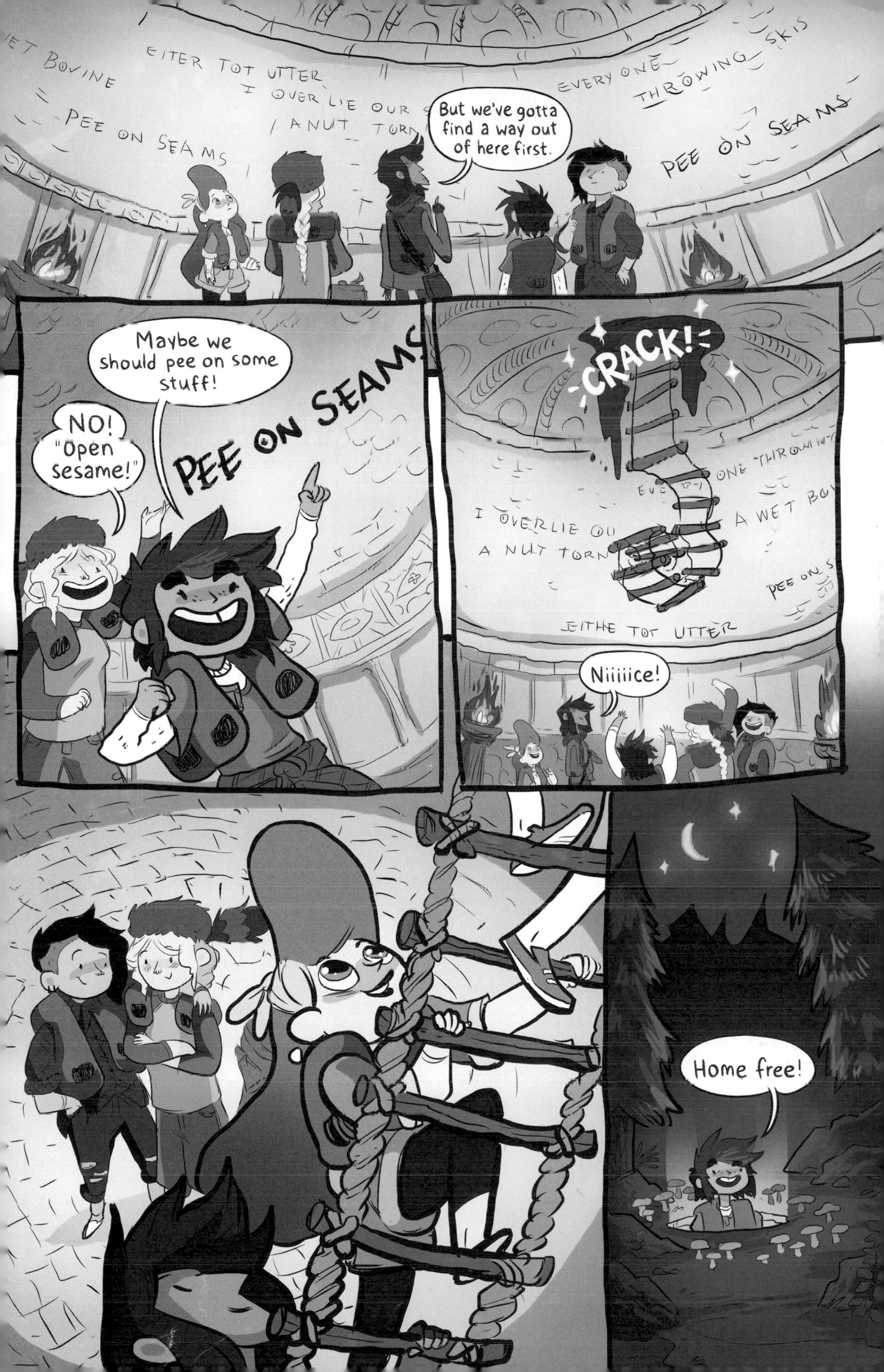

EITER TOT UTTER
I OVER LIE OUR
A NUT TORN
EVERY ONE
THROWING SKIS
PEE ON SEAMS
But we've gotta find a way out of here first.
PEE ON SEAMS
Maybe we should pee on some stuff!
NO! "Open sesame!"
PEE ON SEAMS
CRACK!
I OVERLIE OU
A NUT TORN
A WET BO
EITHE TOT UTTER
Niiiiice!
Home free!

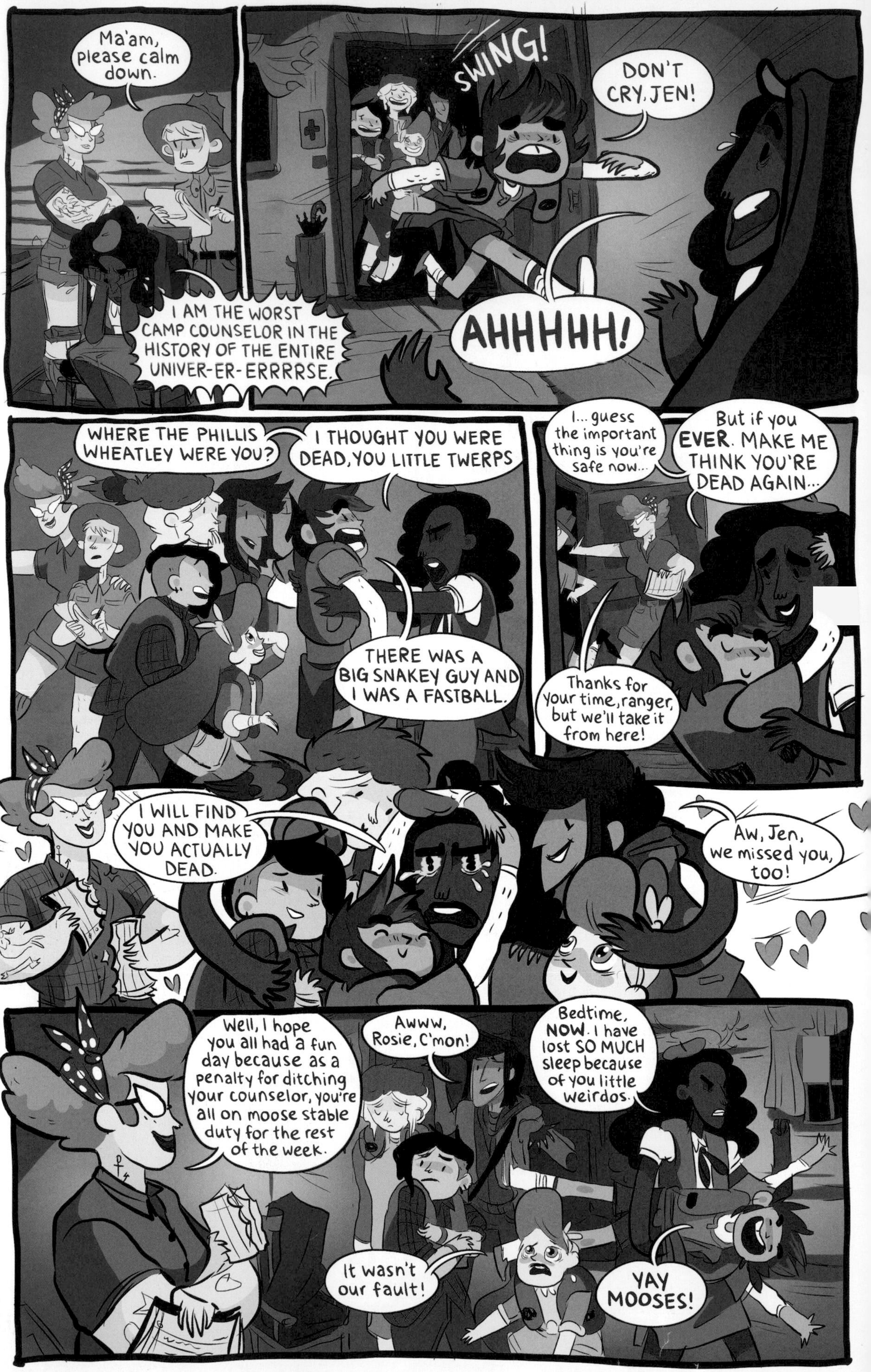
Ma'am, please calm down.
I AM THE WORST CAMP COUNSELOR IN THE HISTORY OF THE ENTIRE UNIVER-ER-ERRRRSE.
SWING!
DON'T CRY, JEN!
AHHHHH!
WHERE THE PHILLIS WHEATLEY WERE YOU?
I THOUGHT YOU WERE DEAD, YOU LITTLE TWERPS
THERE WAS A BIG SNAKEY GUY AND I WAS A FASTBALL.
I... guess the important thing is you're safe now...
But if you EVER. MAKE ME THINK YOU'RE DEAD AGAIN...
Thanks for your time, ranger, but we'll take it from here!
I WILL FIND YOU AND MAKE YOU ACTUALLY DEAD.
Aw, Jen, we missed you, too!
Well, I hope you all had a fun day because as a penalty for ditching your counselor, you're all on moose stable duty for the rest of the week.
Awww, Rosie, C'mon!
Bedtime, NOW. I have lost SO MUCH sleep because of you little weirdos.
It wasn't our fault!
YAY MOOSES!

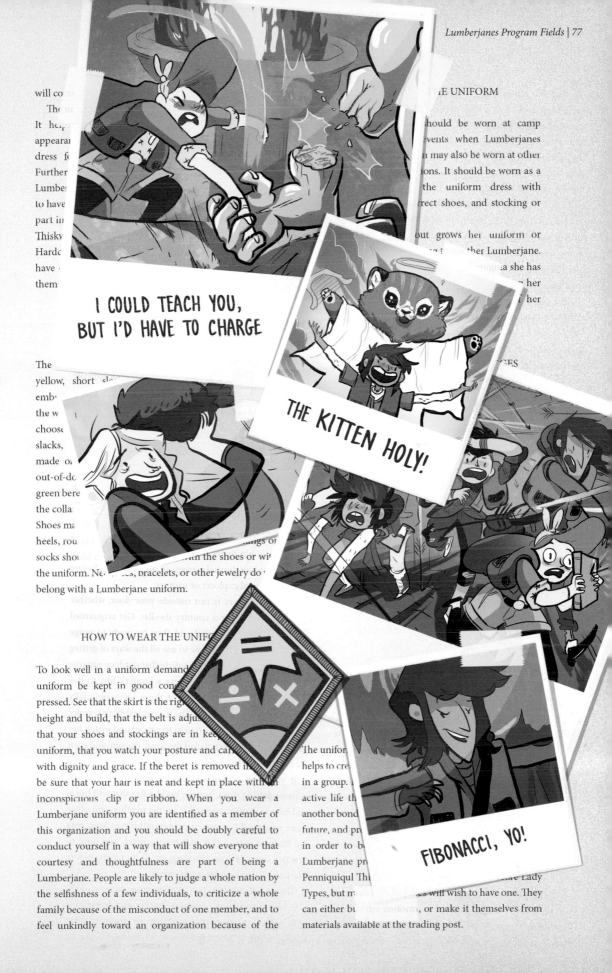

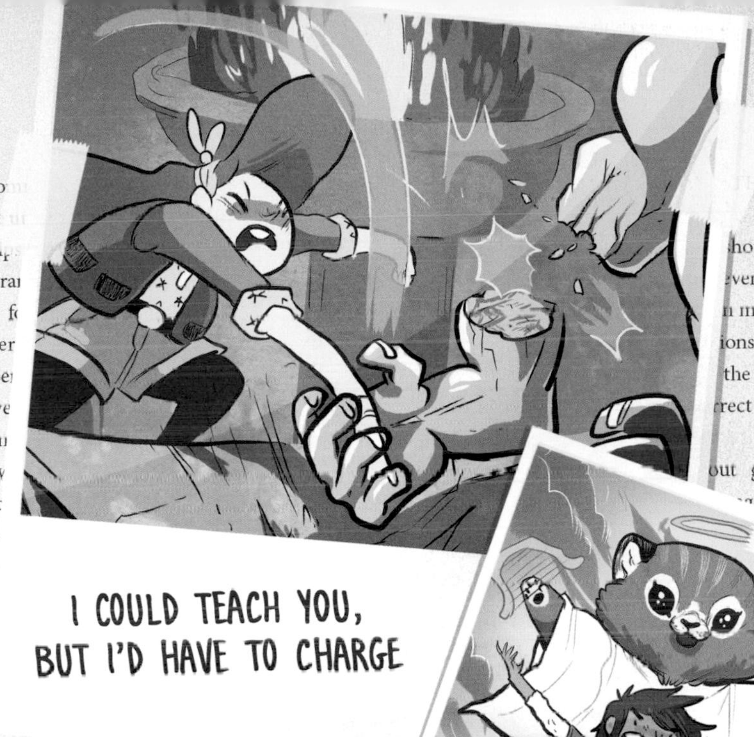
I COULD TEACH YOU,
BUT I'D HAVE TO CHARGE

will co

The u

It helps

appearan

dress fo

Further

Lumbe

to have

part in

Thiskv

Hardc

have

them

THE UNIFORM

should be worn at camp
events when Lumberjanes
may also be worn at other
ions. It should be worn as a
the uniform dress with
rrect shoes, and stocking or

out grows her uniform or
ther Lumberjane.
signia she has
her
her

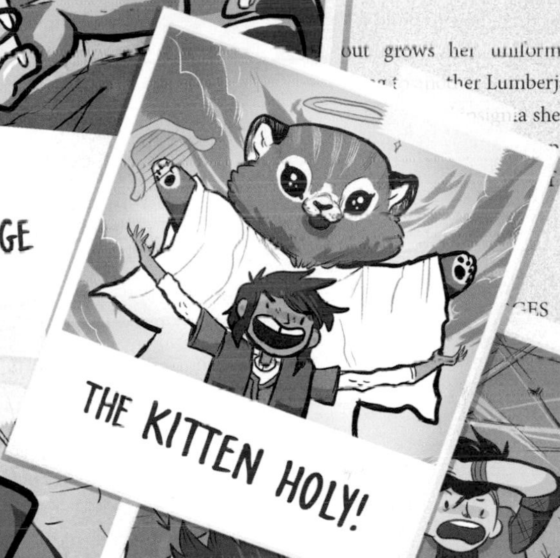
THE KITTEN HOLY!

GES

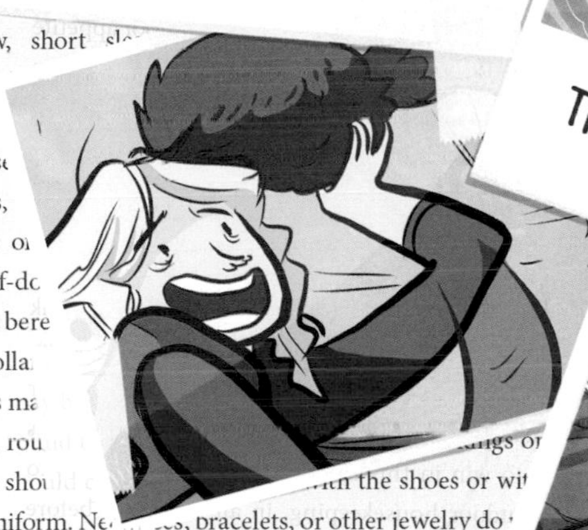

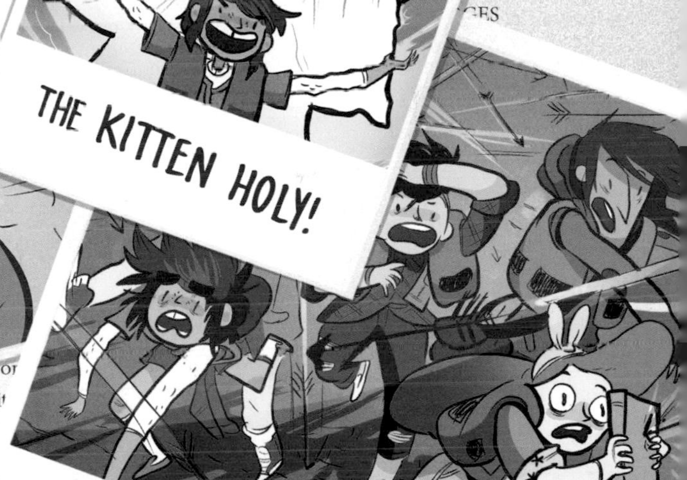

The
yellow, short sl
emb
the w
choose
slacks,
made o
out-of-do
green bere
the colla
Shoes ma
heels, rou … ings or
socks shou … with the shoes or wi
the uniform. Ne…es, bracelets, or other jewelry do
belong with a Lumberjane uniform.

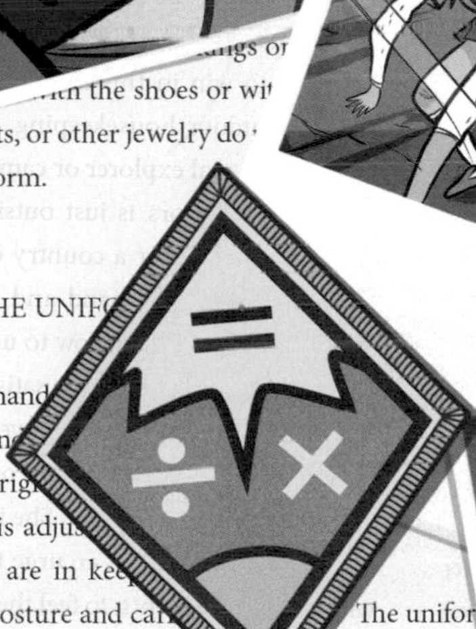

HOW TO WEAR THE UNIFO

To look well in a uniform demand
uniform be kept in good con
pressed. See that the skirt is the rig
height and build, that the belt is adjus
that your shoes and stockings are in kee
uniform, that you watch your posture and car
with dignity and grace. If the beret is removed i
be sure that your hair is neat and kept in place with an
inconspicuous clip or ribbon. When you wear a Lumberjane uniform you are identified as a member of this organization and you should be doubly careful to conduct yourself in a way that will show everyone that courtesy and thoughtfulness are part of being a Lumberjane. People are likely to judge a whole nation by the selfishness of a few individuals, to criticize a whole family because of the misconduct of one member, and to feel unkindly toward an organization because of the

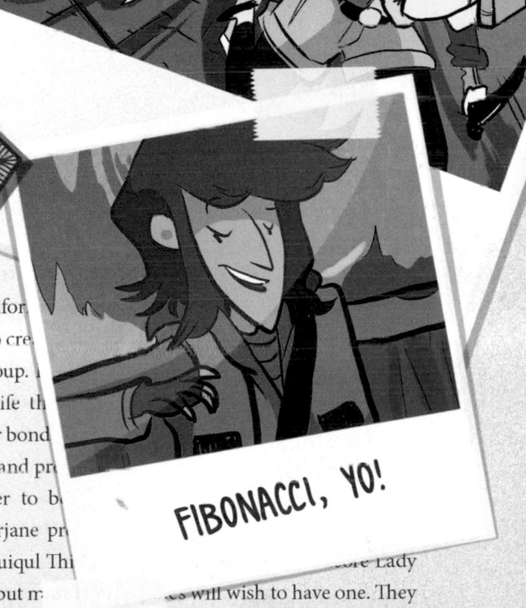
FIBONACCI, YO!

The unifor
helps to cre
in a group.
active life th
another bond
future, and pr
in order to b
Lumberjane pr
Penniquiqul Thi … ore Lady
Types, but m … es will wish to have one. They
can either bu … the uniform, or make it themselves from
materials available at the trading post.

LUMBERJANES FIELD MANUAL
CHAPTER FOUR

Lumberjanes "Sports and Games" Program Field

ROBYN HOOD BADGE

"A sharp eye shows sharp wit."

Hand and eye coordination is not only important for day-to-day activities, but can be instrumental in a Lumberjane's experience with nature. In these modern times the basic practices of what was once a right practice is seen more as a sport, but the Lumberjanes recognize the importance of not only the respect and care of their tools, but by training with their fellow Lumberjanes, they will learn to trust in not only each other, but in themselves and the skills the they already possess. It is important for a Lumberjane to know that she can rely upon herself in the great vastness of nature and that she will not be reliant on the machine manufactured tools of modern day but that with her own two hands she will be able to step forward into whatever life throws at her.

The skill of archery teaches every Lumberjane the importance of a good posture, the finesse needed when handling delicate instruments, the necessary upper arm strength and the poise of being able to take down prey from a great distance. Before a Lumberjane can earn her *Robyn Hood* badge, it is important for her to learn within the safety of the camp's archery range. She will be given the tools that she needs to succeed and with the support of her friends she will be able to hone her ability and gain the confidence she needs to send the arrow to it's target.

To obtain the *Robyn Hood* badge, a Lumberjane must first make a bow and arrow which will shoot a distance of one hundred feet with fair precision. It is an essential task that will let her learn about the benefits of putting time into a job to do it right. She must prove her knowledge of basic archery safety both in the range and outside. She must make a total score of 350 with 60 shots in one or two meets, using standard four-foot target at forty yards or three-foot target at thirty yards. She must be able to make a total score of 300 with 72 arrows, using standard

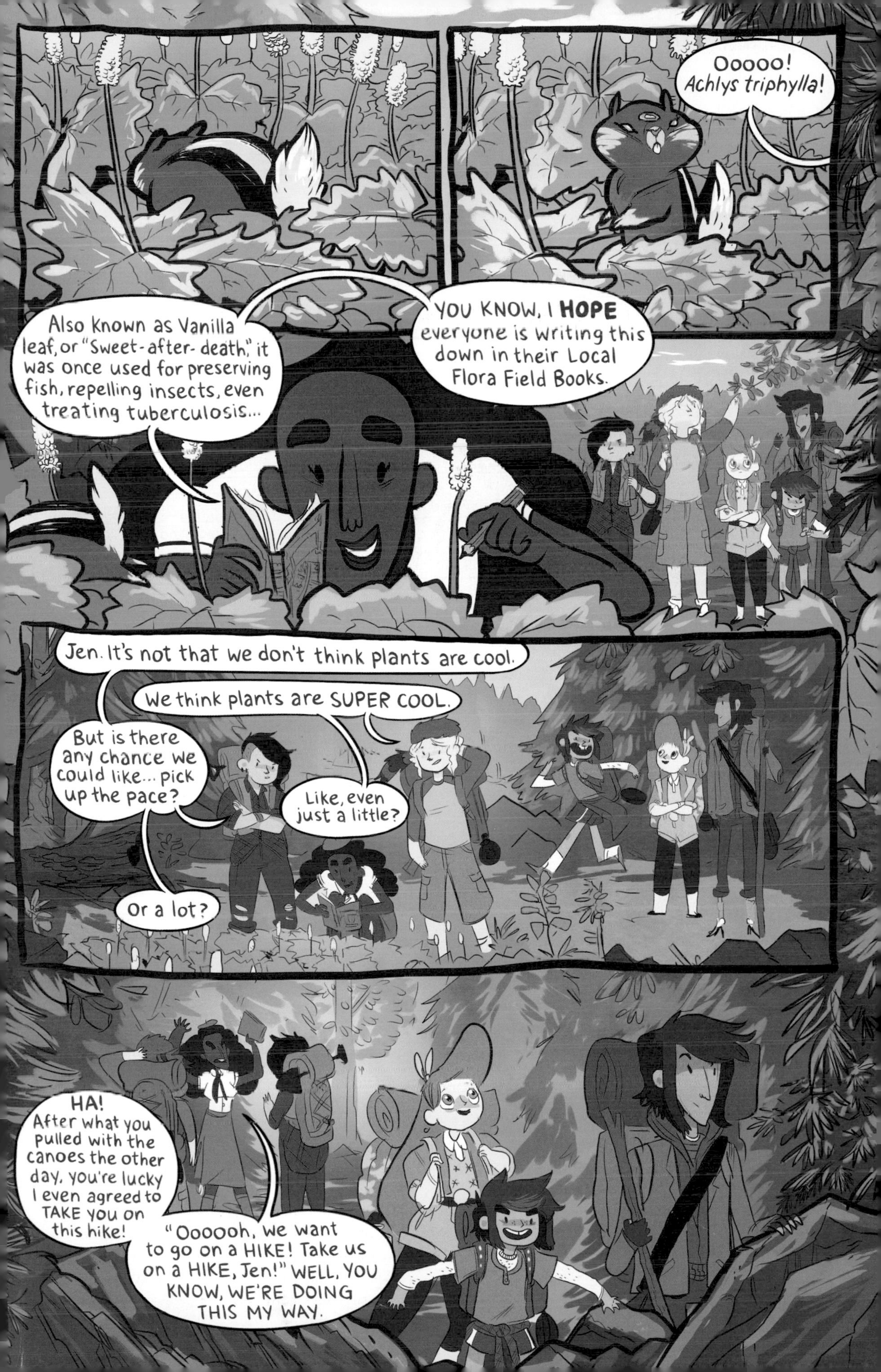
Ooooo! Achlys triphylla!
Also known as Vanilla leaf, or "Sweet-after-death," it was once used for preserving fish, repelling insects, even treating tuberculosis...
YOU KNOW, I **HOPE** everyone is writing this down in their Local Flora Field Books.
Jen. It's not that we don't think plants are cool.
We think plants are SUPER COOL.
But is there any chance we could like... pick up the pace?
Like, even just a little?
Or a lot?
HA! After what you pulled with the canoes the other day, you're lucky I even agreed to TAKE you on this hike!
"Oooooh, we want to go on a HIKE! Take us on a HIKE, Jen!" WELL, YOU KNOW, WE'RE DOING THIS MY WAY.

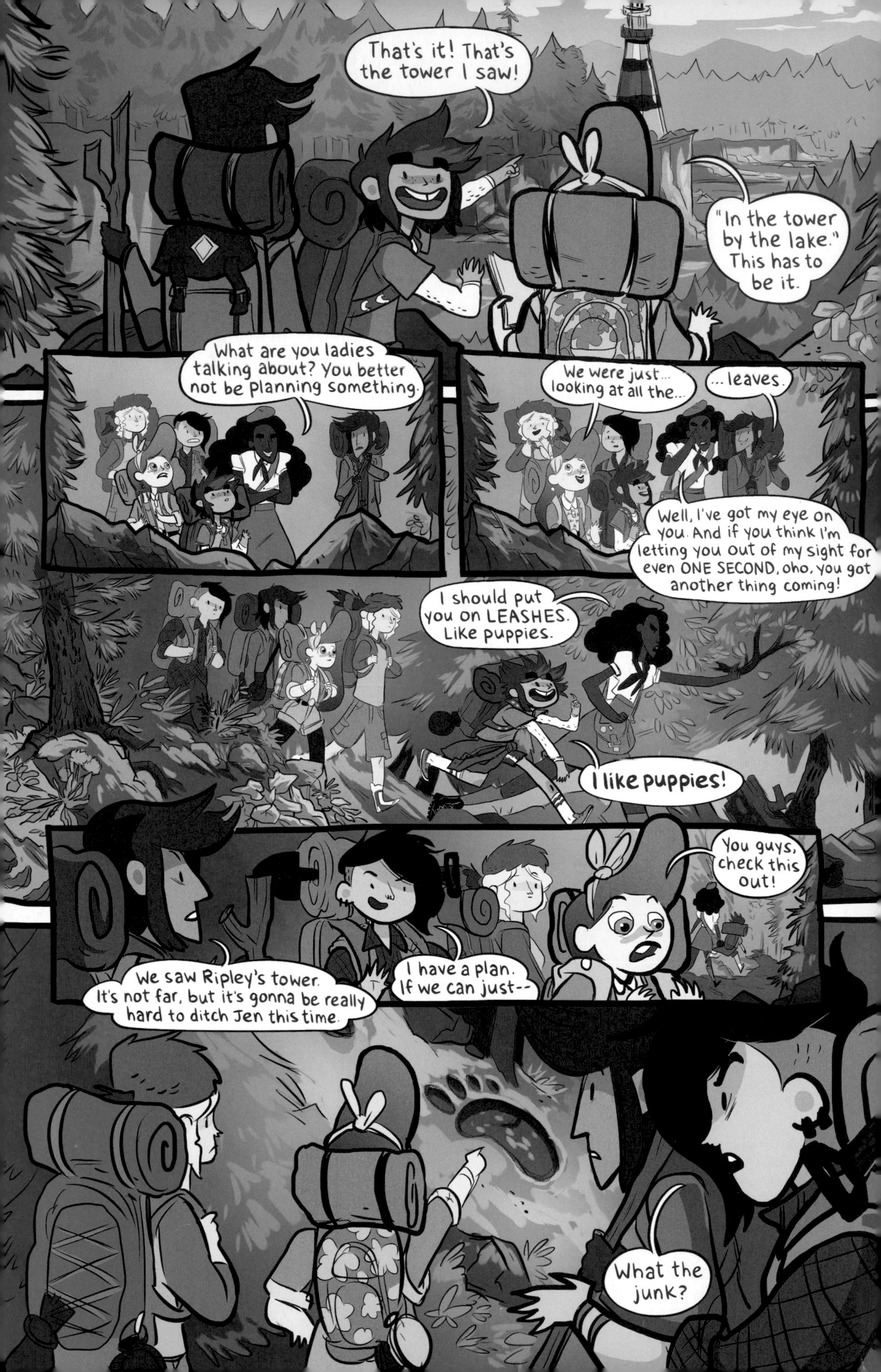
That's it! That's the tower I saw!
"In the tower by the lake." This has to be it.
What are you ladies talking about? You better not be planning something.
We were just... looking at all the...
...leaves.
Well, I've got my eye on you. And if you think I'm letting you out of my sight for even ONE SECOND, oho, you got another thing coming!
I should put you on LEASHES. Like puppies.
I like puppies!
We saw Ripley's tower. It's not far, but it's gonna be really hard to ditch Jen this time.
I have a plan. If we can just--
You guys, check this out!
What the junk?

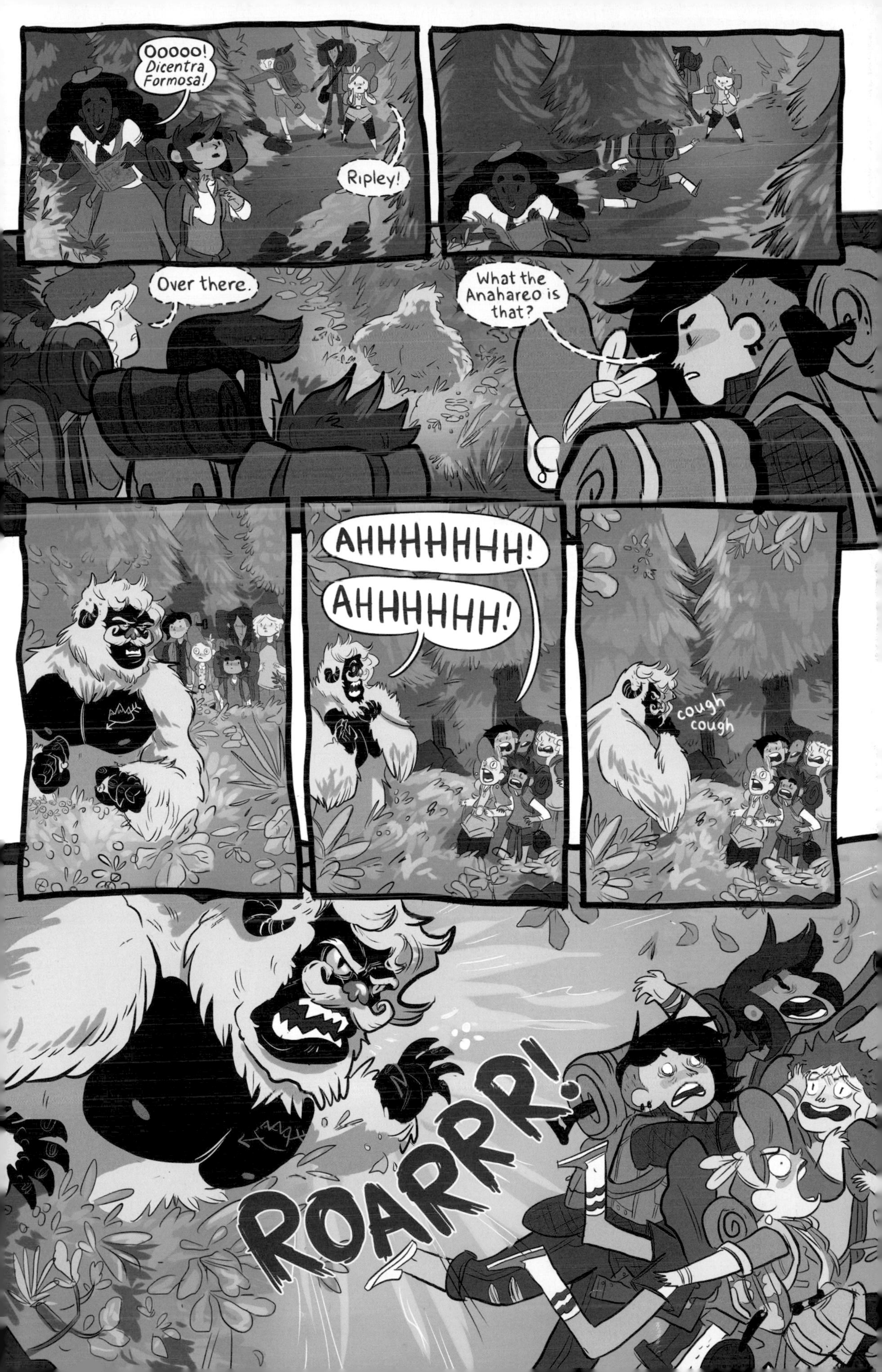
Ooooo! Dicentra Formosa!
Ripley!
Over there.
What the Anahareo is that?
AHHHHHHH!
AHHHHHH!
cough cough
ROARRR!

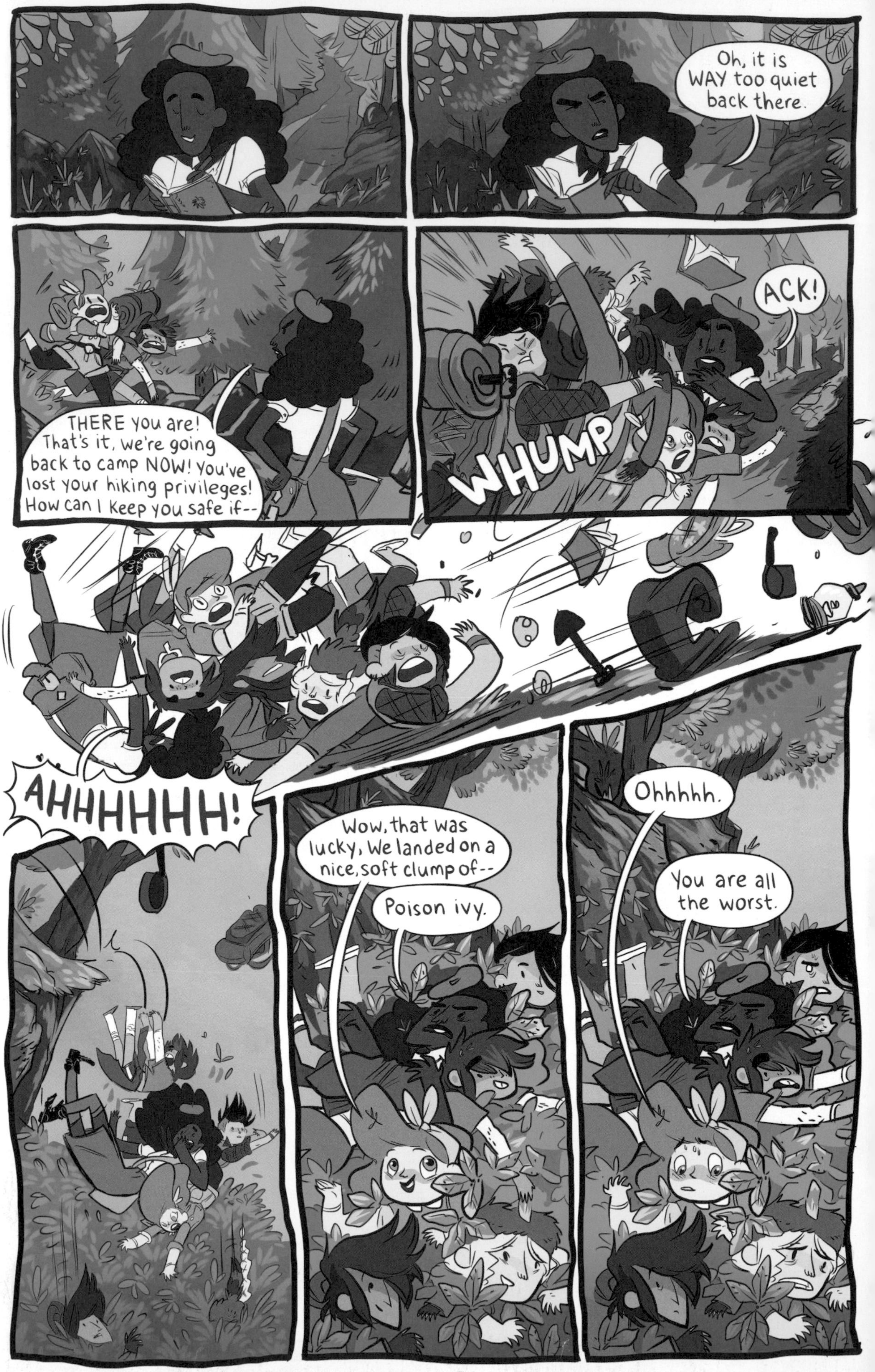
Oh, it is WAY too quiet back there.
THERE you are! That's it, we're going back to camp NOW! You've lost your hiking privileges! How can I keep you safe if--
ACK!
WHUMP
AHHHHHH!
Wow, that was lucky, We landed on a nice, soft clump of--
Poison ivy.
Ohhhhh.
You are all the worst.

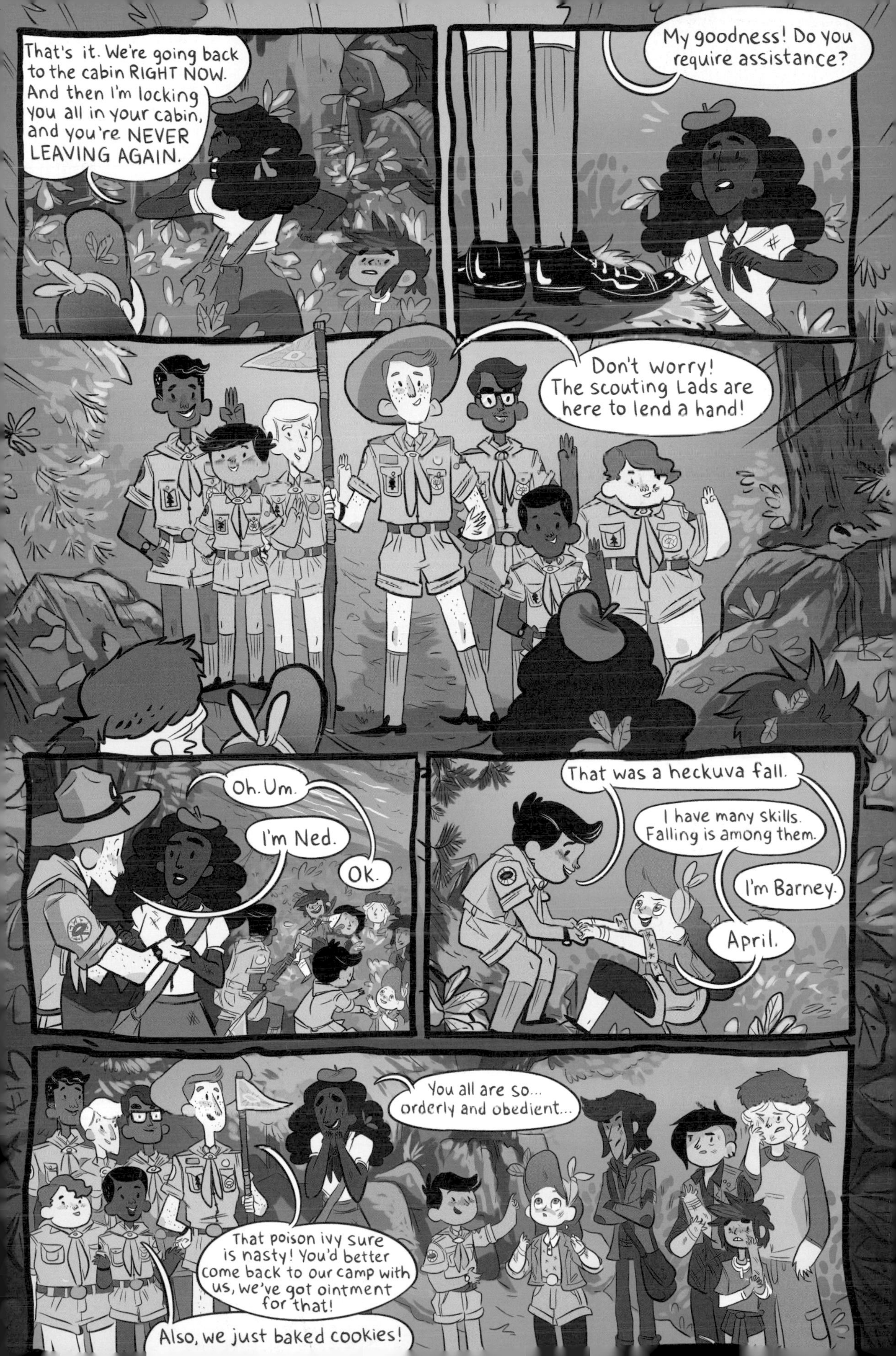
That's it. We're going back to the cabin RIGHT NOW. And then I'm locking you all in your cabin, and you're NEVER LEAVING AGAIN.
My goodness! Do you require assistance?
Don't worry! The scouting Lads are here to lend a hand!
Oh. Um.
I'm Ned.
OK.
That was a heckuva fall.
I have many skills. Falling is among them.
I'm Barney.
April.
You all are so... orderly and obedient...
That poison ivy sure is nasty! You'd better come back to our camp with us, we've got ointment for that!
Also, we just baked cookies!

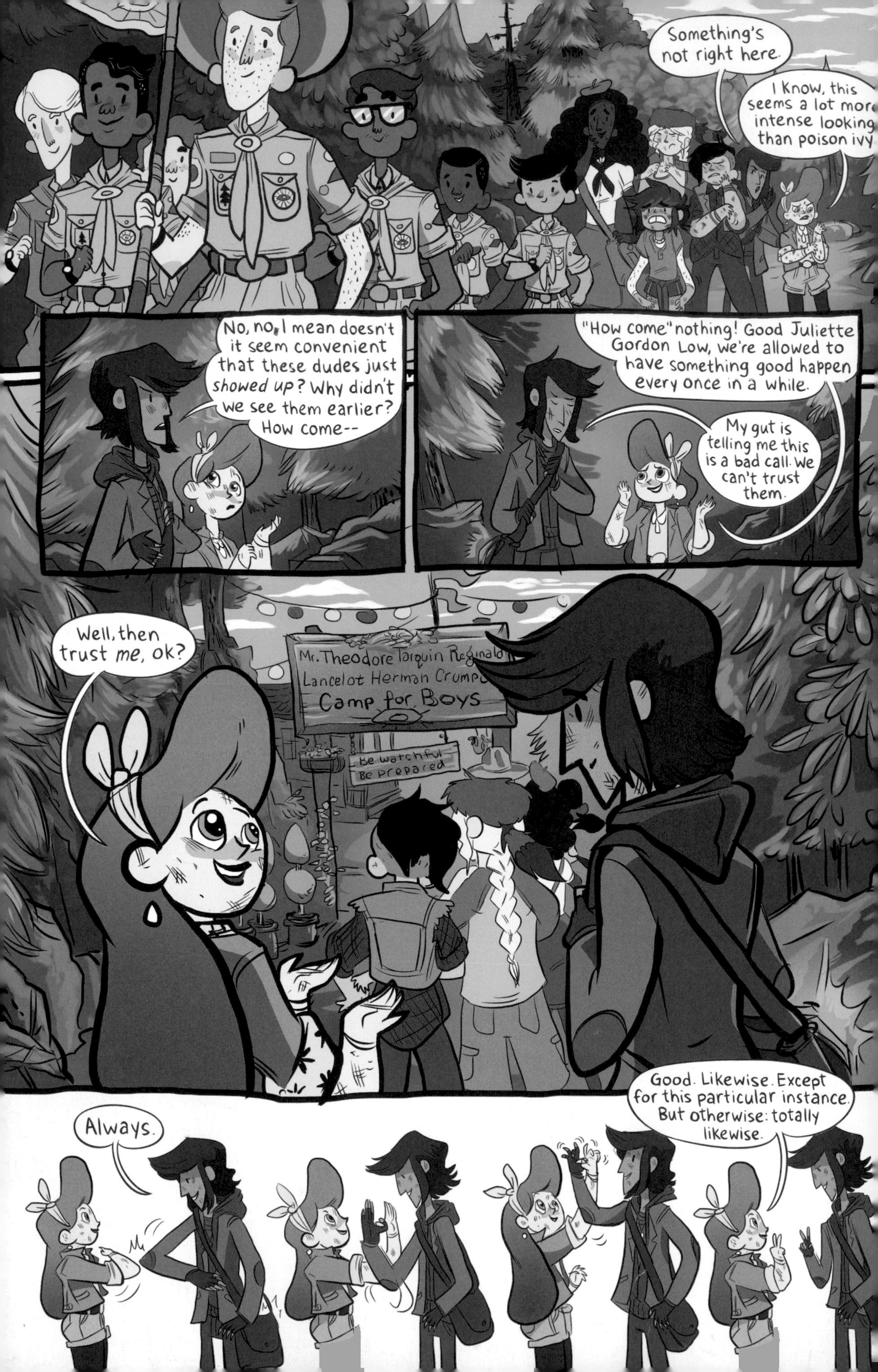
Something's not right here.
I know, this seems a lot more intense looking than poison ivy.
No, no, I mean doesn't it seem convenient that these dudes just showed up? Why didn't we see them earlier? How come--
"How come" nothing! Good Juliette Gordon Low, we're allowed to have something good happen every once in a while.
My gut is telling me this is a bad call. We can't trust them.
Well, then trust me, ok?
Mr. Theodore Torquin Reginald Lancelot Herman Crumpo Camp for Boys
Be watchful Be prepared
Always.
Good. Likewise. Except for this particular instance. But otherwise: totally likewise.

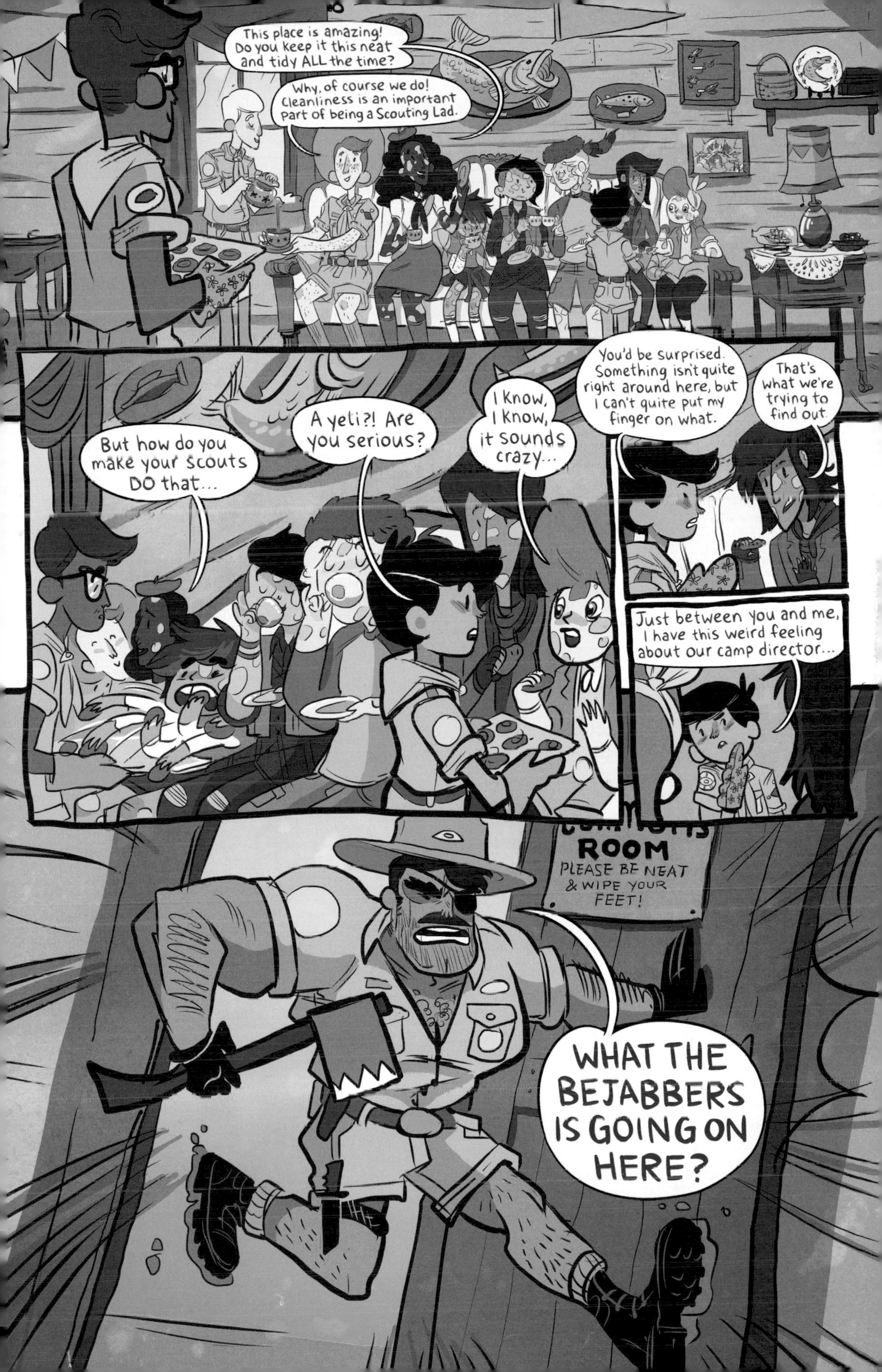
This place is amazing! Do you keep it this neat and tidy ALL the time?
Why, of course we do! Cleanliness is an important part of being a Scouting Lad.
But how do you make your scouts DO that...
A yeti?! Are you serious?
I know, I know, it sounds crazy...
You'd be surprised. Something isn't quite right around here, but I can't quite put my finger on what.
That's what we're trying to find out.
Just between you and me, I have this weird feeling about our camp director...
ROOM
PLEASE BE NEAT & WIPE YOUR FEET!
WHAT THE BEJABBERS IS GOING ON HERE?

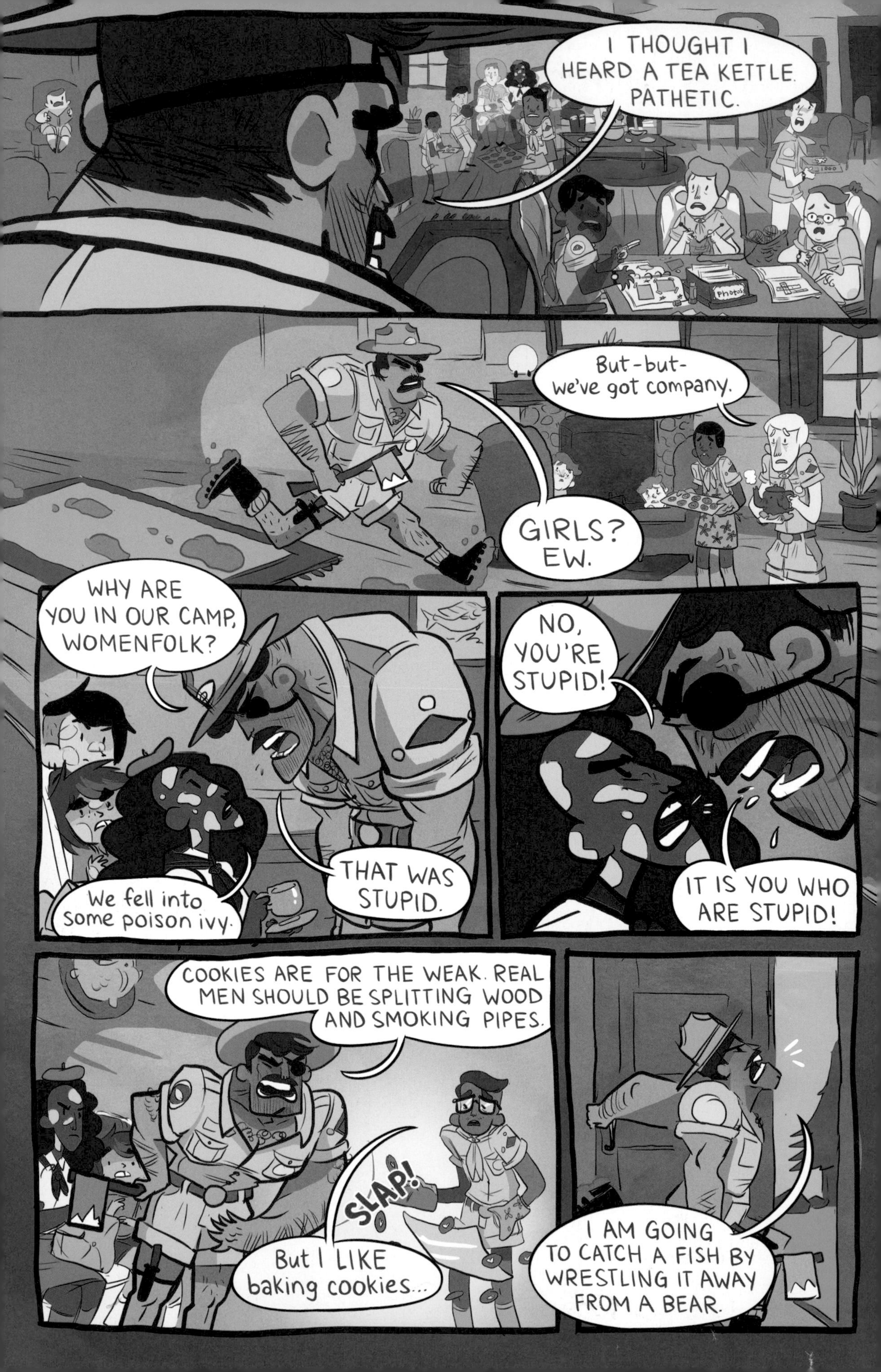
I THOUGHT I HEARD A TEA KETTLE. PATHETIC.
Photos
But-but- we've got company.
GIRLS? EW.
WHY ARE YOU IN OUR CAMP, WOMENFOLK?
We fell into some poison ivy.
THAT WAS STUPID.
NO, YOU'RE STUPID!
IT IS YOU WHO ARE STUPID!
COOKIES ARE FOR THE WEAK. REAL MEN SHOULD BE SPLITTING WOOD AND SMOKING PIPES.
SLAP!
But I LIKE baking cookies...
I AM GOING TO CATCH A FISH BY WRESTLING IT AWAY FROM A BEAR.

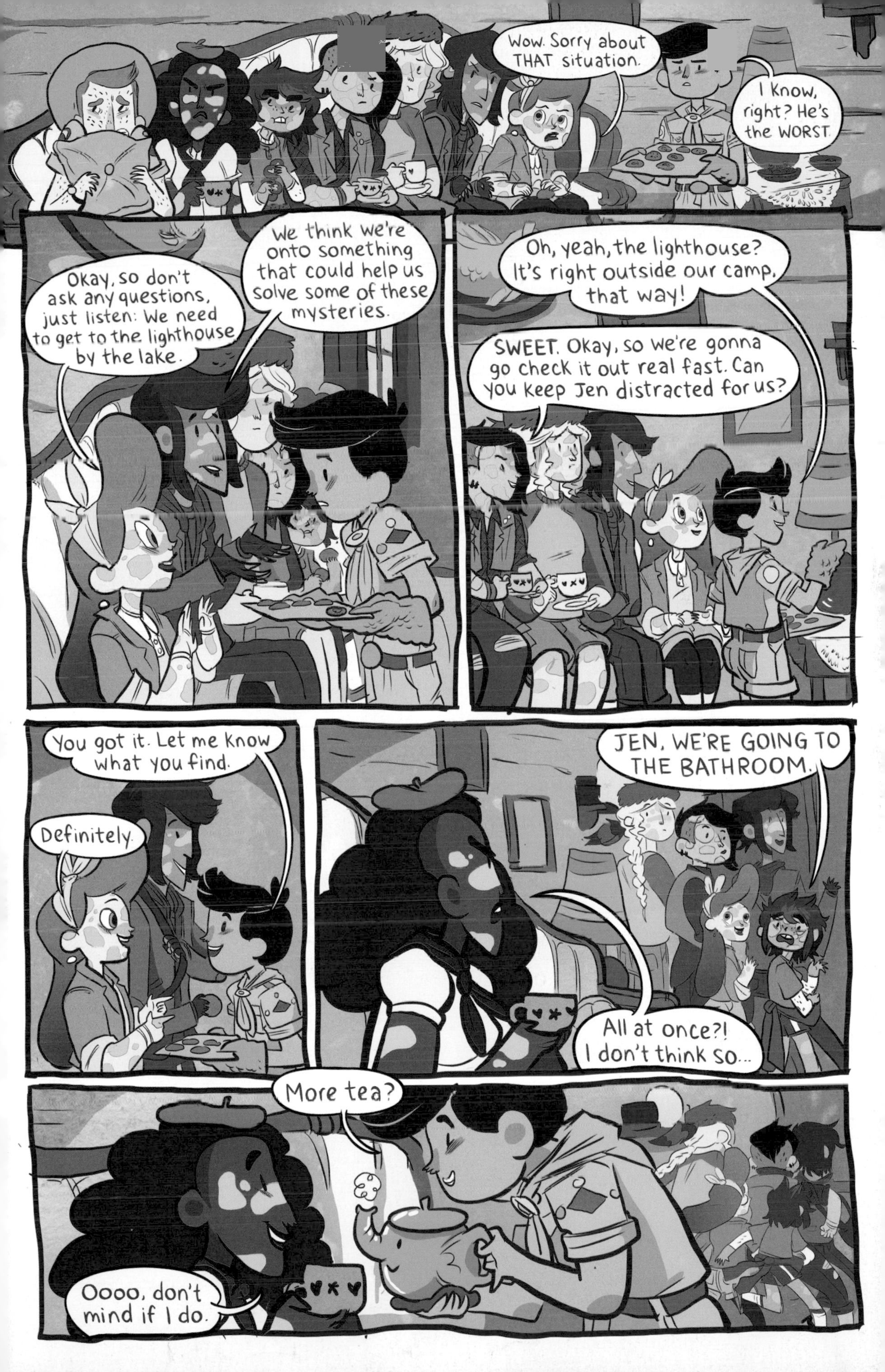
Wow. Sorry about THAT situation.
I know, right? He's the WORST.
Okay, so don't ask any questions, just listen: We need to get to the lighthouse by the lake.
We think we're onto something that could help us solve some of these mysteries.
Oh, yeah, the lighthouse? It's right outside our camp, that way!
SWEET. Okay, so we're gonna go check it out real fast. Can you keep Jen distracted for us?
You got it. Let me know what you find.
Definitely.
JEN, WE'RE GOING TO THE BATHROOM.
All at once?! I don't think so...
More tea?
Oooo, don't mind if I do.

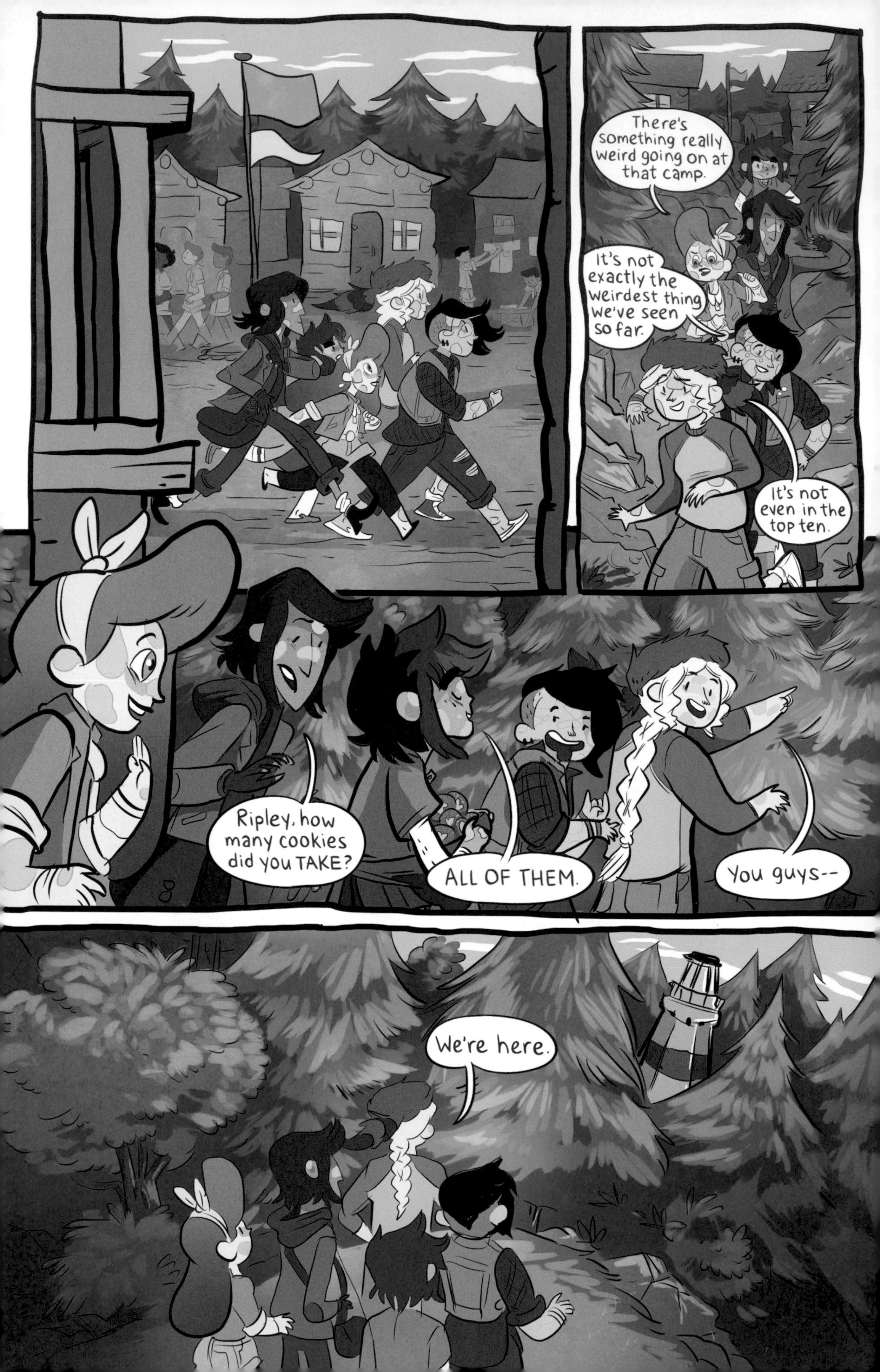
There's something really weird going on at that camp.
It's not exactly the weirdest thing we've seen so far.
It's not even in the top ten.
Ripley, how many cookies did you TAKE?
ALL OF THEM.
You guys--
We're here.

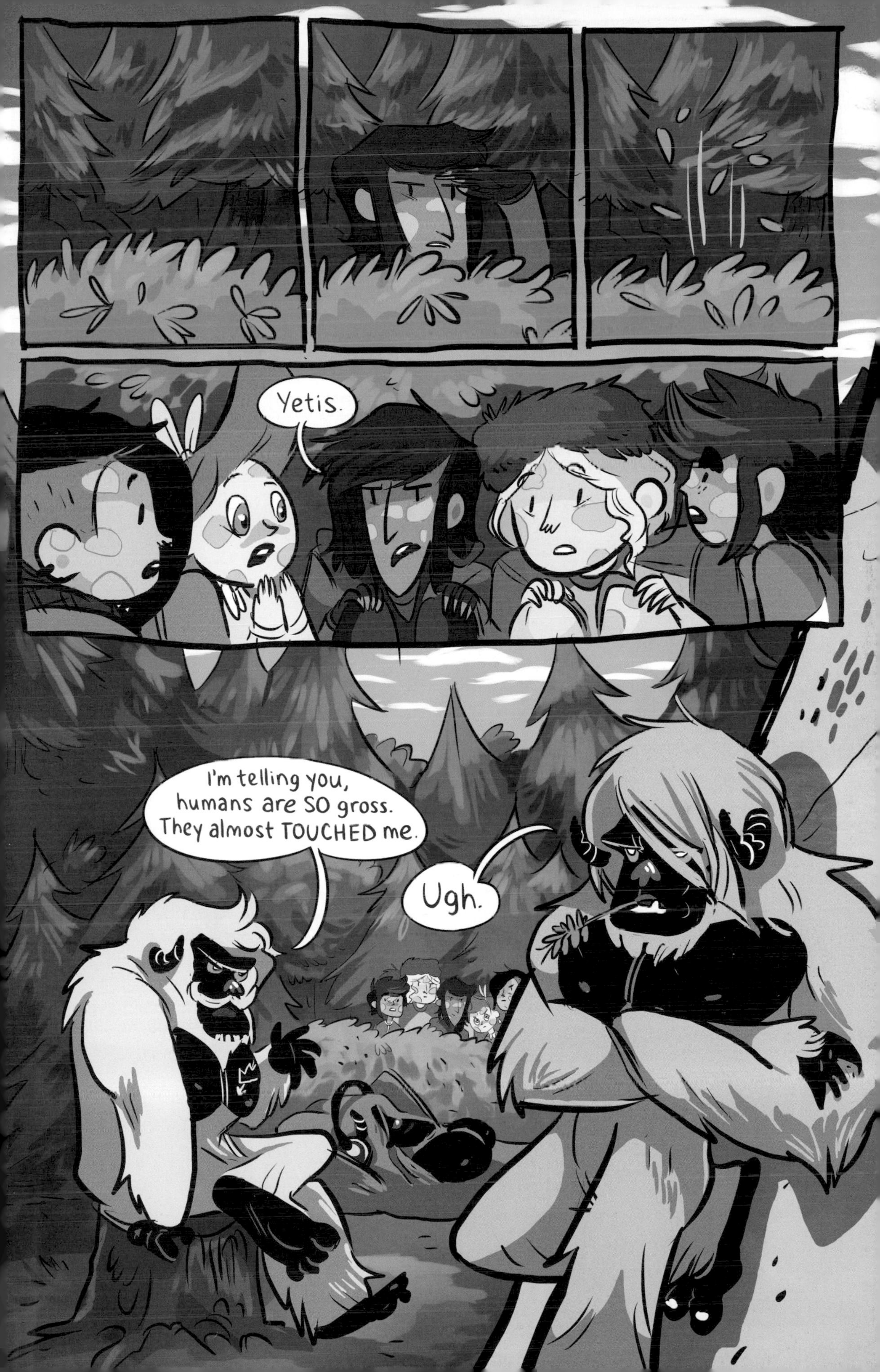
Yetis.
I'm telling you, humans are SO gross. They almost TOUCHED me.
Ugh.

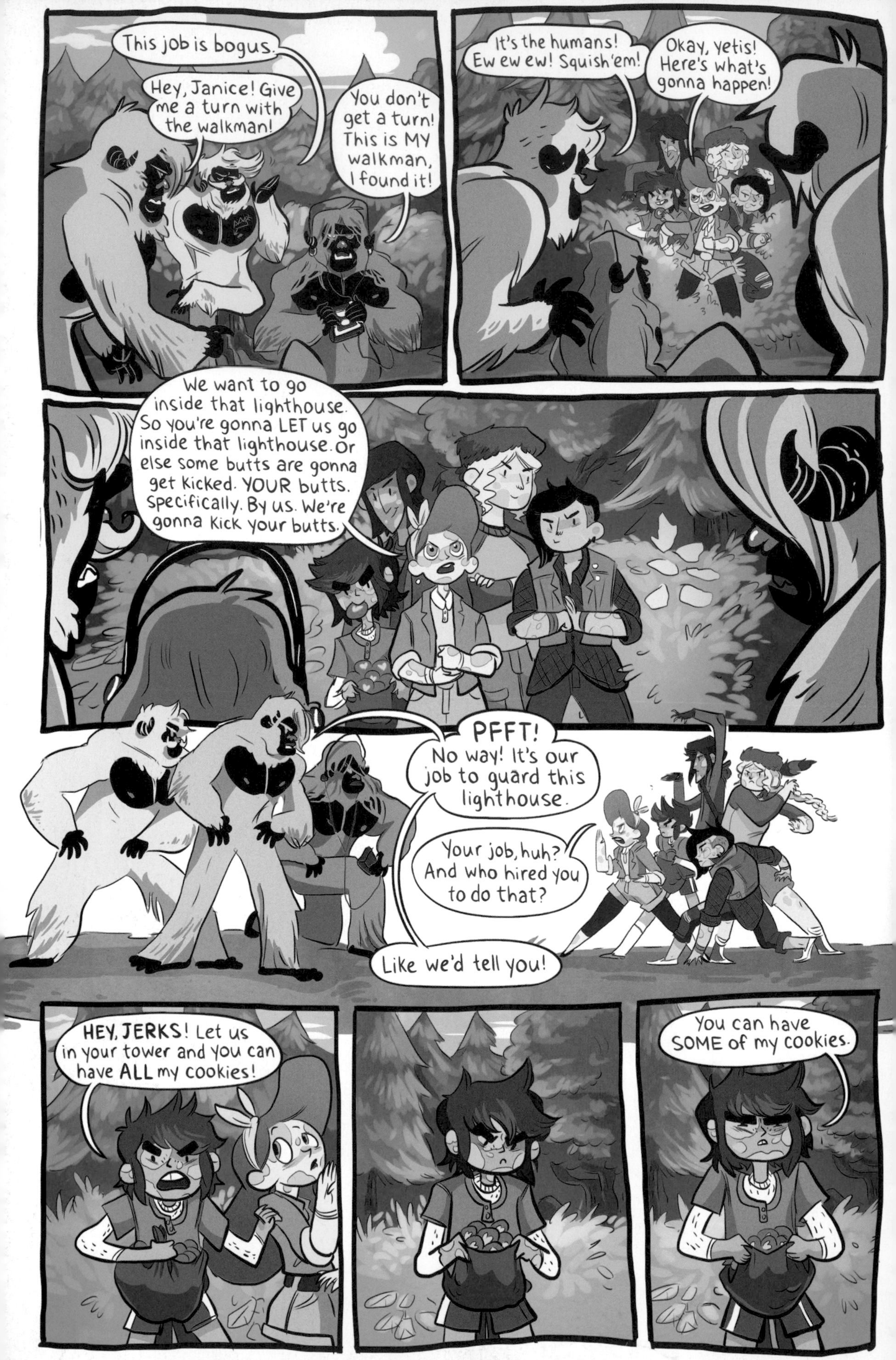
This job is bogus.
Hey, Janice! Give me a turn with the walkman!
You don't get a turn! This is MY walkman, I found it!
It's the humans! Ew ew ew! Squish 'em!
Okay, yetis! Here's what's gonna happen!
We want to go inside that lighthouse. So you're gonna LET us go inside that lighthouse. Or else some butts are gonna get kicked. YOUR butts. Specifically. By us. We're gonna kick your butts.
PFFT! No way! It's our job to guard this lighthouse.
Your job, huh? And who hired you to do that?
Like we'd tell you!
HEY, JERKS! Let us in your tower and you can have ALL my cookies!
You can have SOME of my cookies.

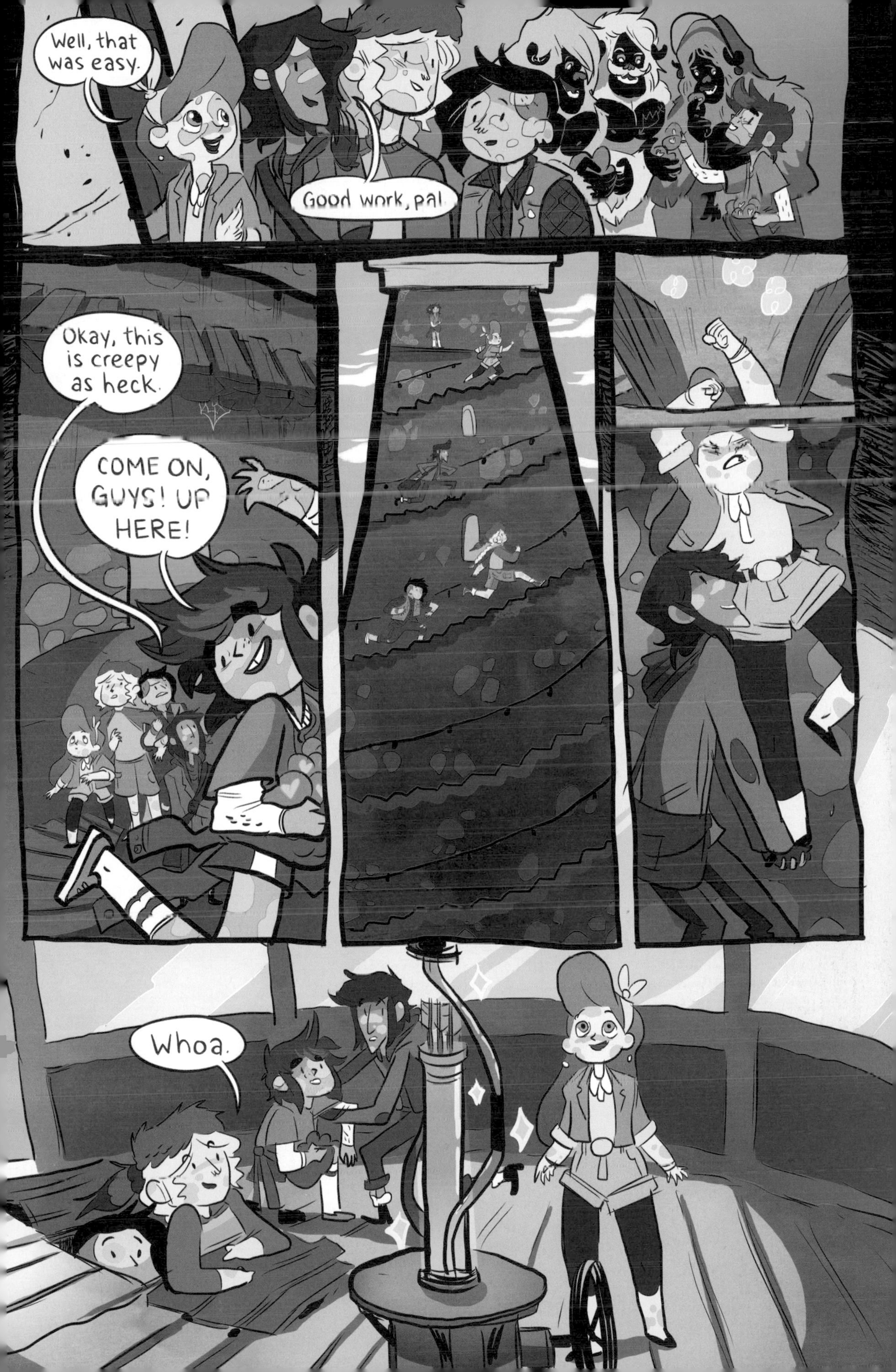
Well, that was easy.
Good work, pal.
Okay, this is creepy as heck.
COME ON, GUYS! UP HERE!
Whoa.

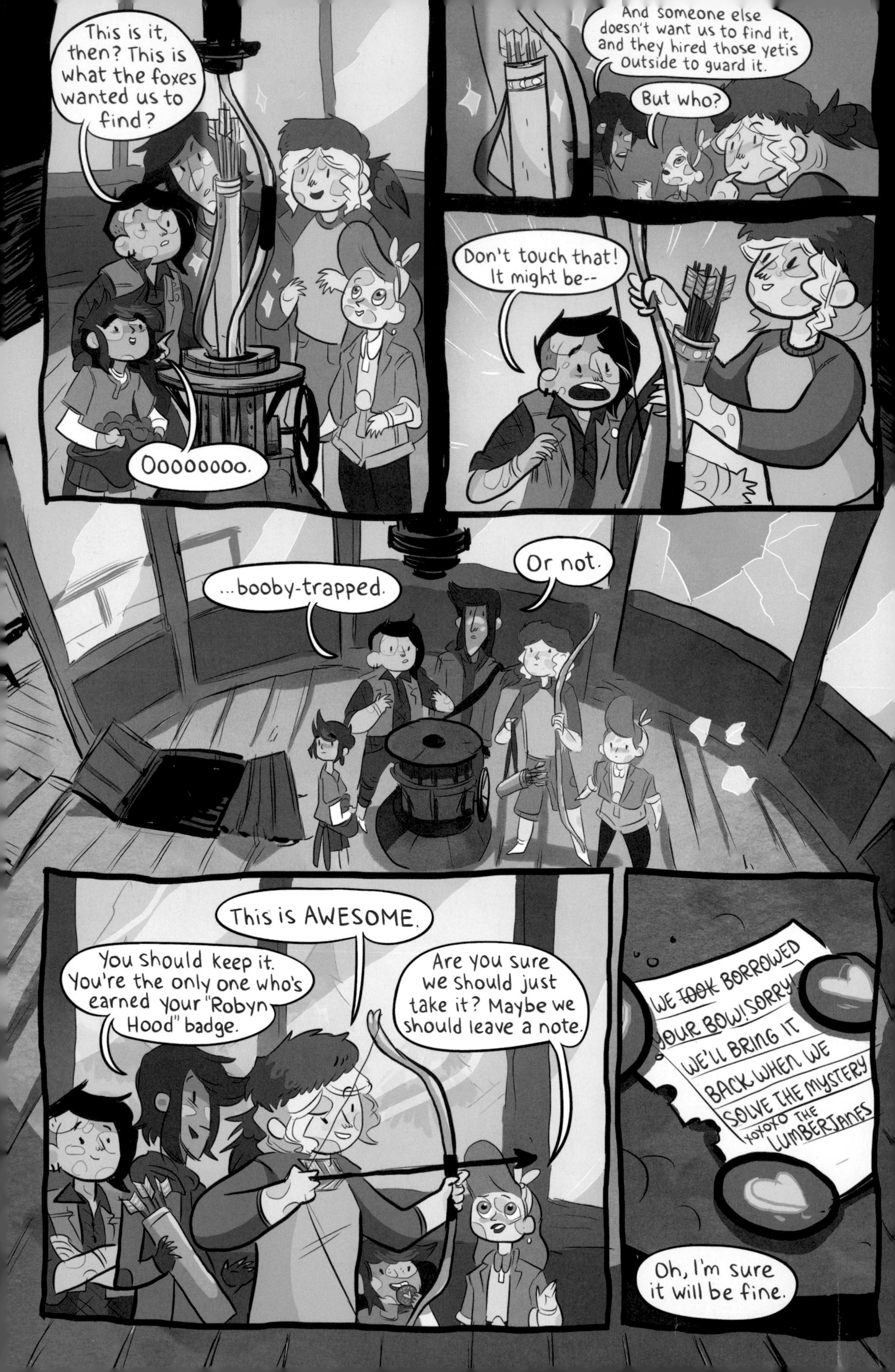

This is it, then? This is what the foxes wanted us to find?
Ooooooooo.
And someone else doesn't want us to find it, and they hired those yetis outside to guard it.
But who?
Don't touch that! It might be--
...booby-trapped.
Or not.
This is AWESOME.
You should keep it. You're the only one who's earned your "Robyn Hood" badge.
Are you sure we should just take it? Maybe we should leave a note.
WE ~~TOOK~~ BORROWED YOUR BOW! SORRY! WE'LL BRING IT BACK WHEN WE SOLVE THE MYSTERY
XOXOXO THE LUMBERJANES
Oh, I'm sure it will be fine.

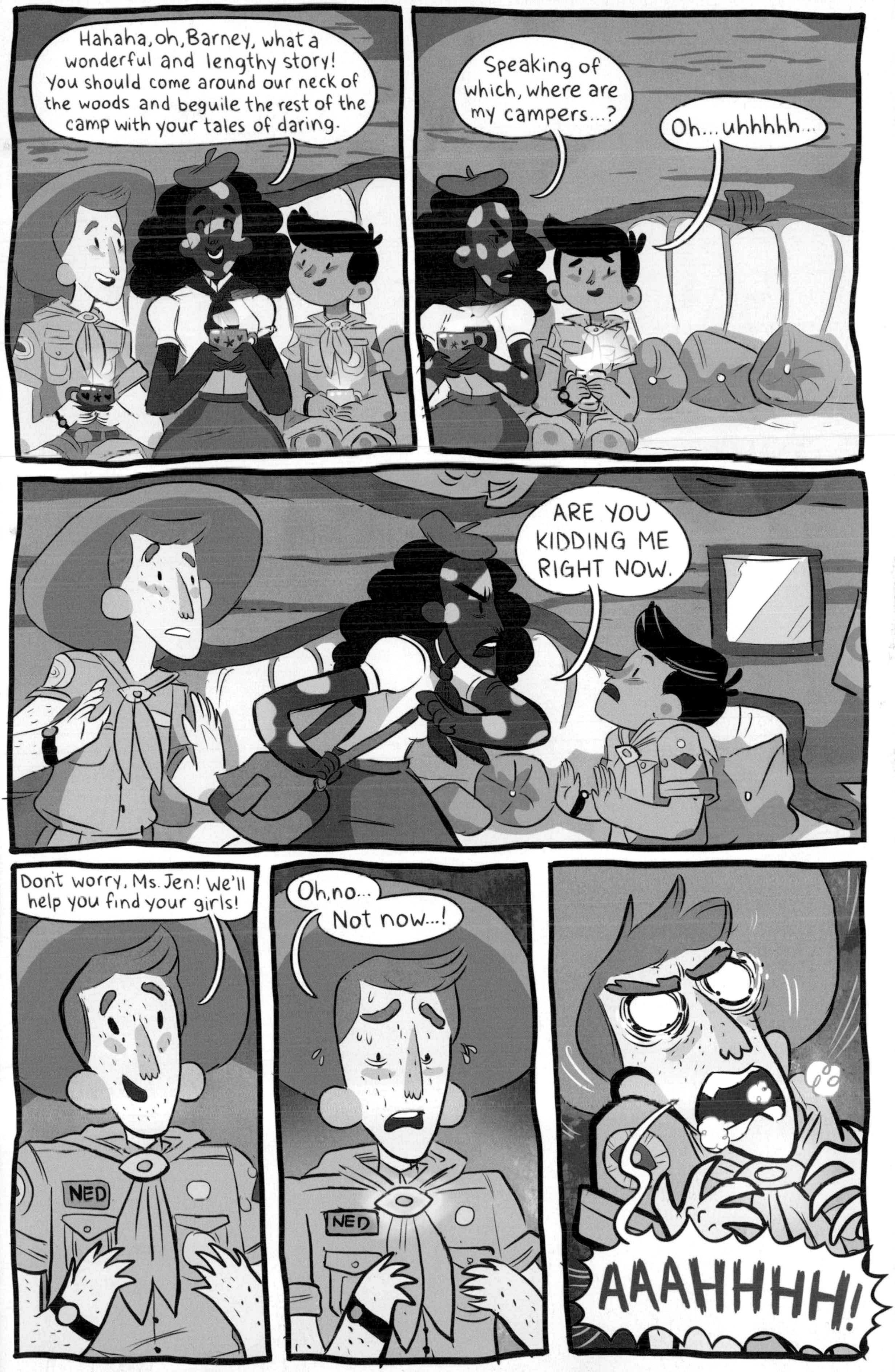
Hahaha, oh, Barney, what a wonderful and lengthy story! You should come around our neck of the woods and beguile the rest of the camp with your tales of daring.
Speaking of which, where are my campers...?
Oh... uhhhhh...
ARE YOU KIDDING ME RIGHT NOW.
Don't worry, Ms. Jen! We'll help you find your girls!
NED
Oh, no...
Not now...!
NED
AAAHHHH!

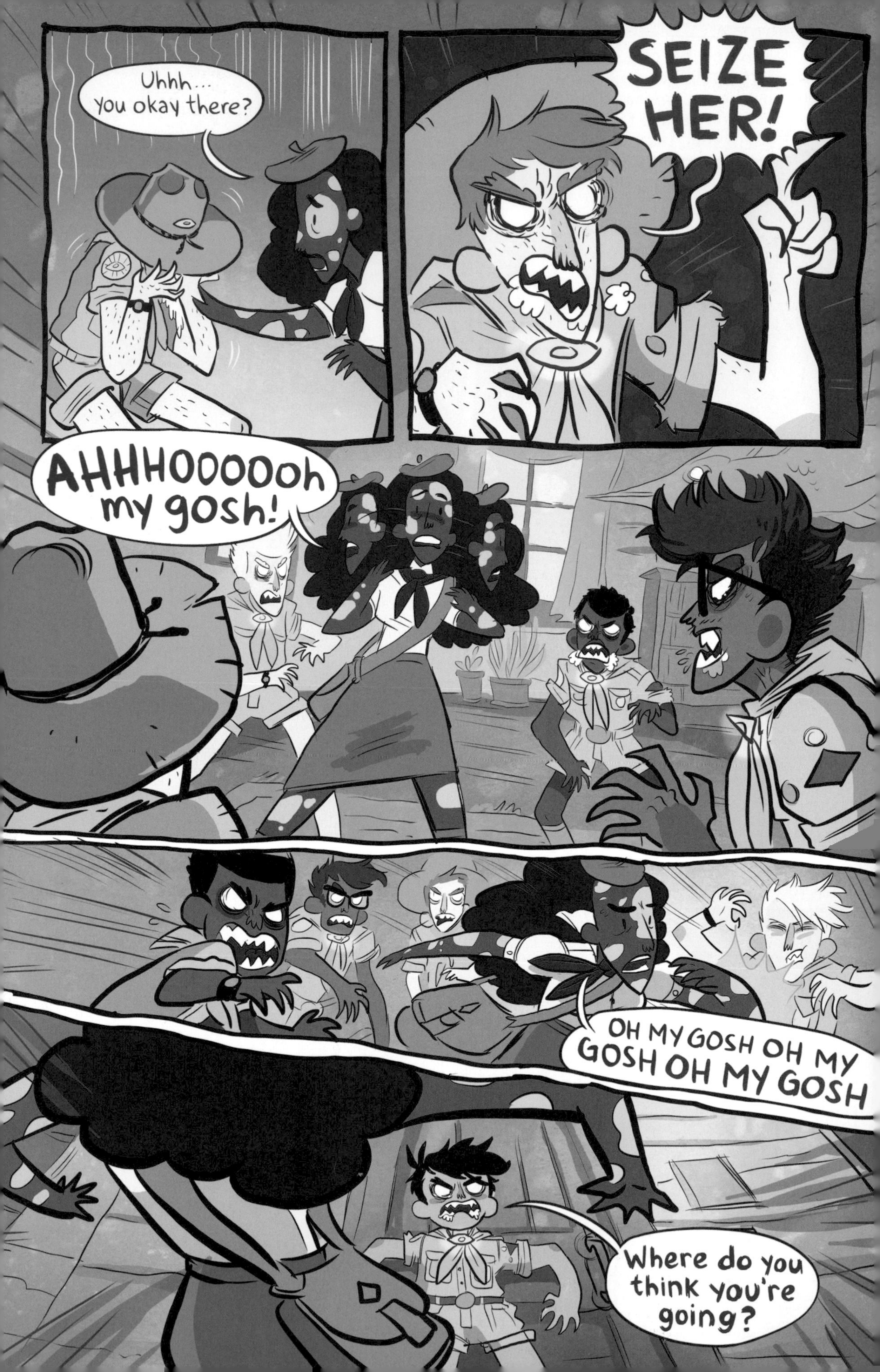
Uhhh...
you okay there?
SEIZE HER!
AHHHOOOOOh my gosh!
OH MY GOSH OH MY GOSH OH MY GOSH
Where do you think you're going?

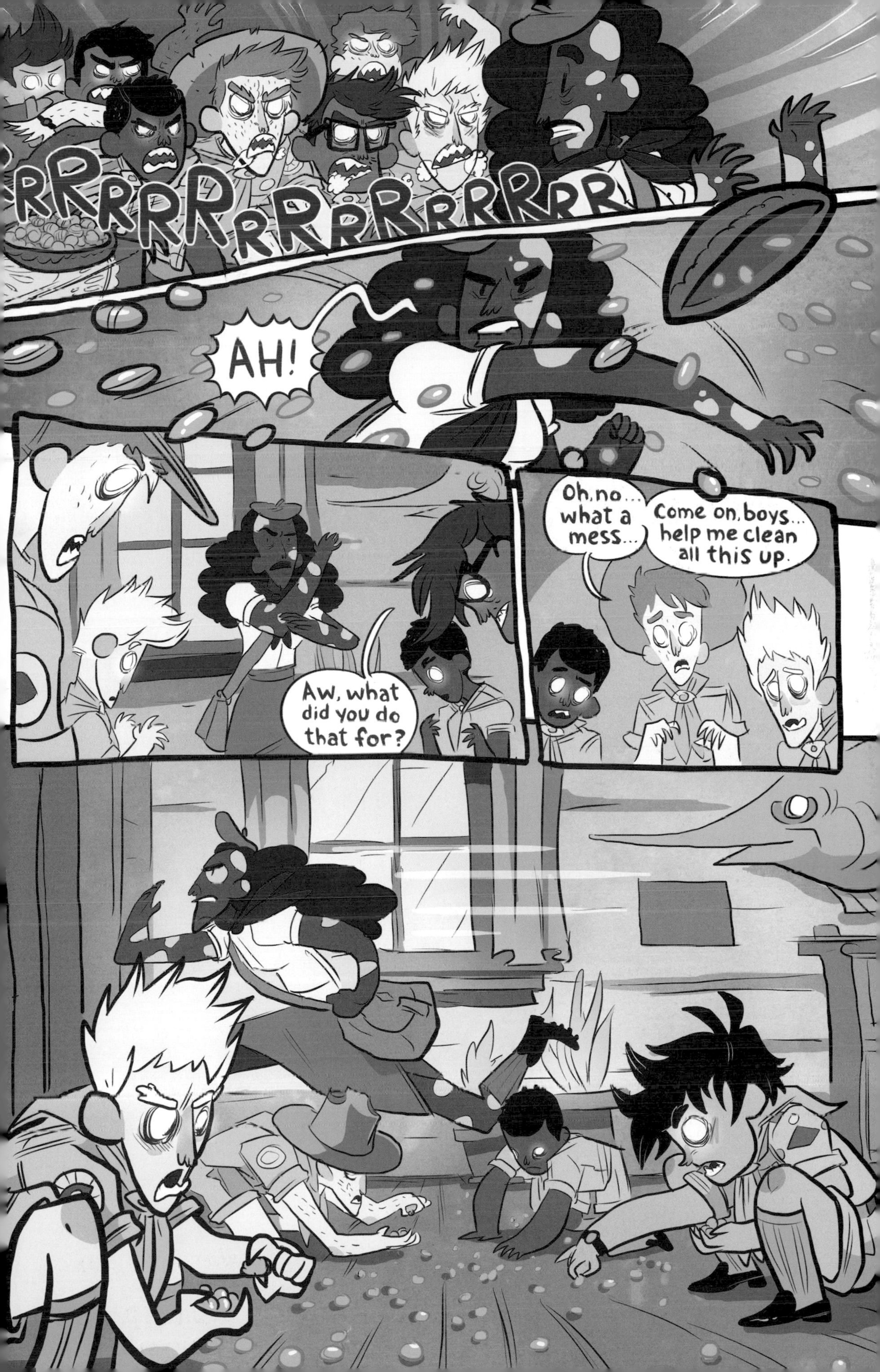
RRRRRRRRRRRRR
AH!
Aw, what did you do that for?
Oh, no... what a mess...
Come on, boys... help me clean all this up.

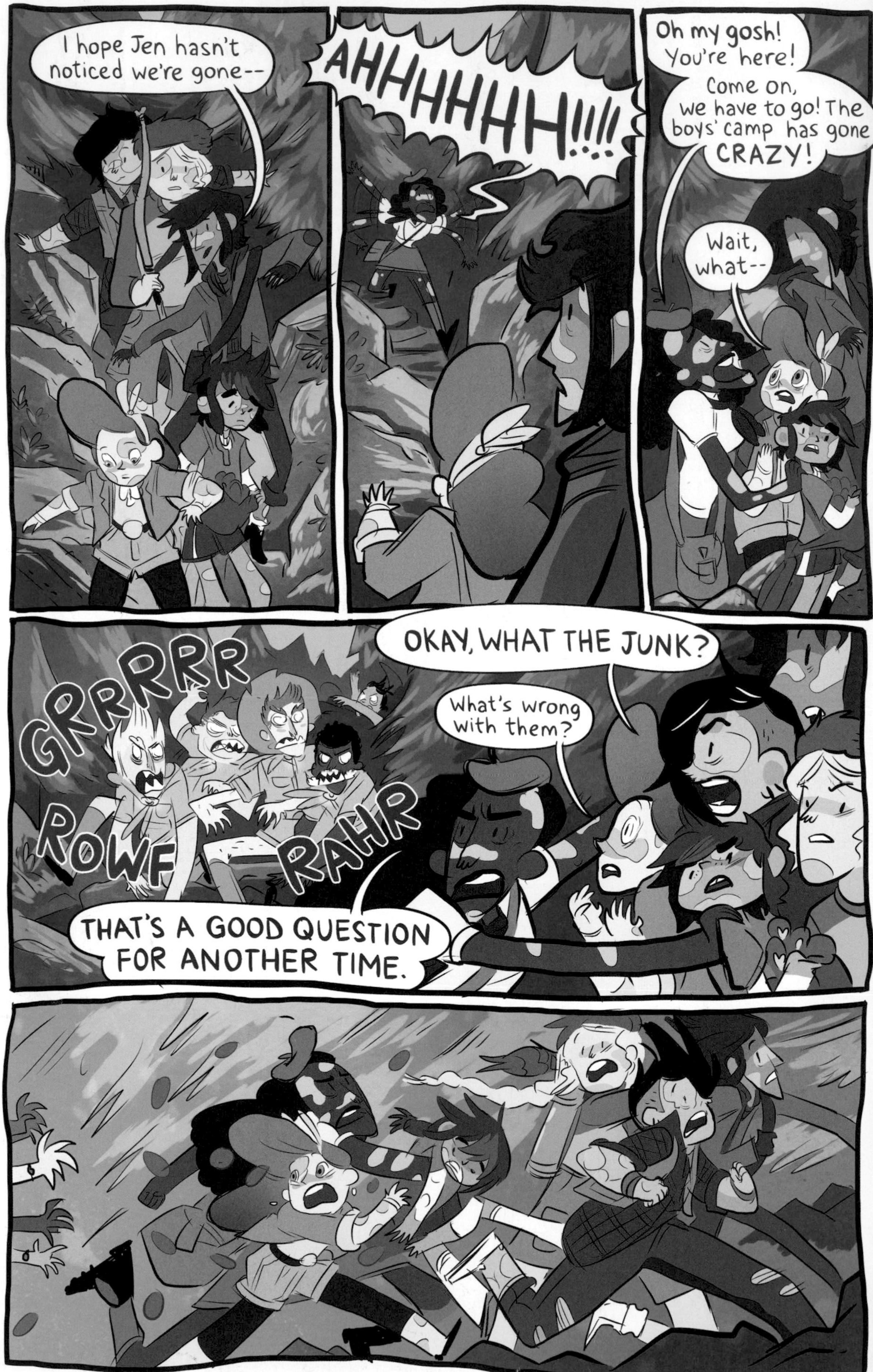
I hope Jen hasn't noticed we're gone--
AHHHHHHH!!!!!
Oh my gosh! You're here!
Come on, we have to go! The boys' camp has gone CRAZY!
Wait, what--
GRRRRRR
ROWF
RAHR
OKAY, WHAT THE JUNK?
What's wrong with them?
THAT'S A GOOD QUESTION FOR ANOTHER TIME.

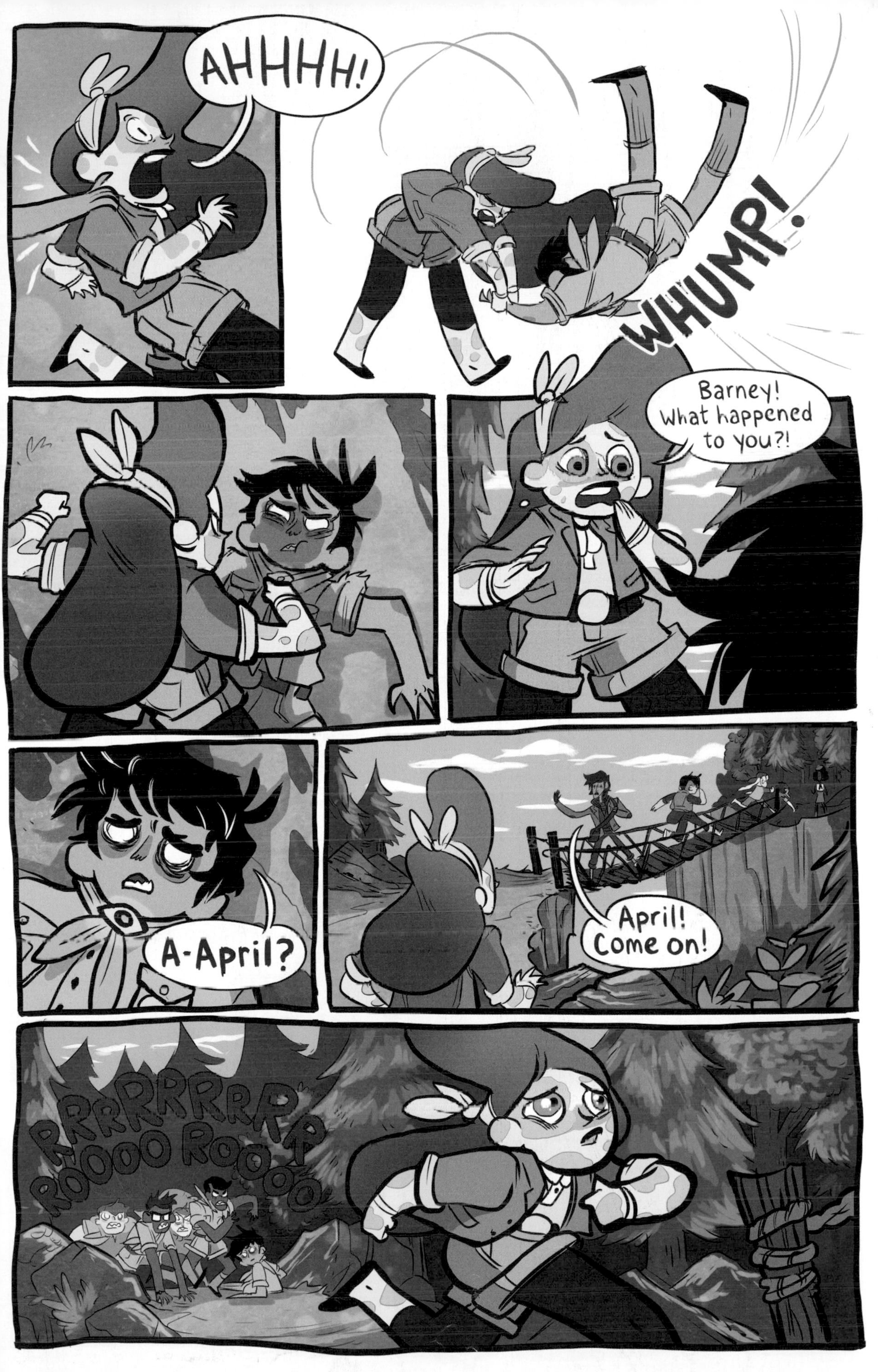
AHHHH!
WHUMP!
Barney! What happened to you?!
A-April?
April! Come on!
RRRRRRRRPP ROOOO ROOOOO

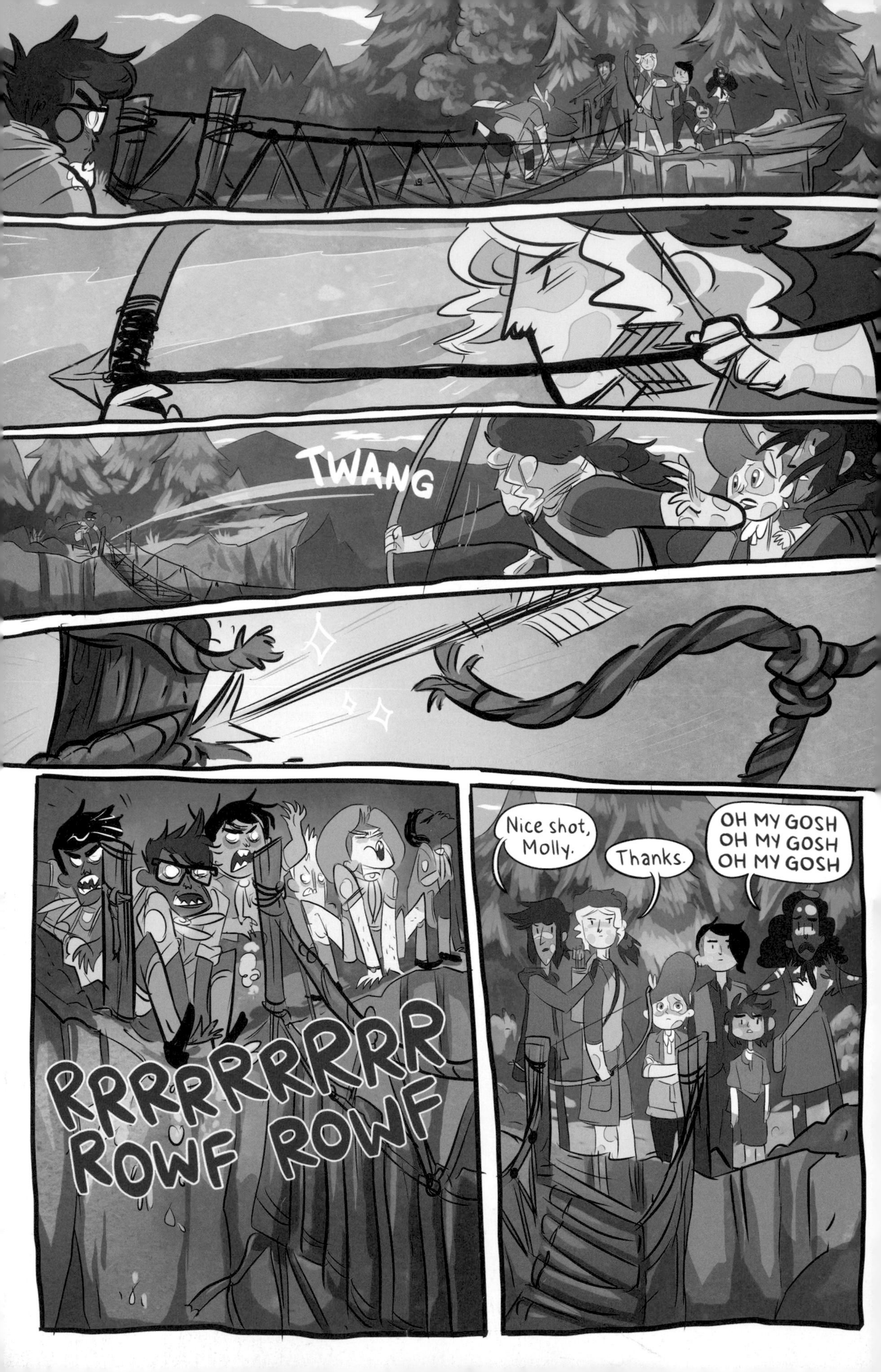
TWANG
RRRRRRRRR
ROWF ROWF
Nice shot, Molly.
Thanks.
OH MY GOSH
OH MY GOSH
OH MY GOSH

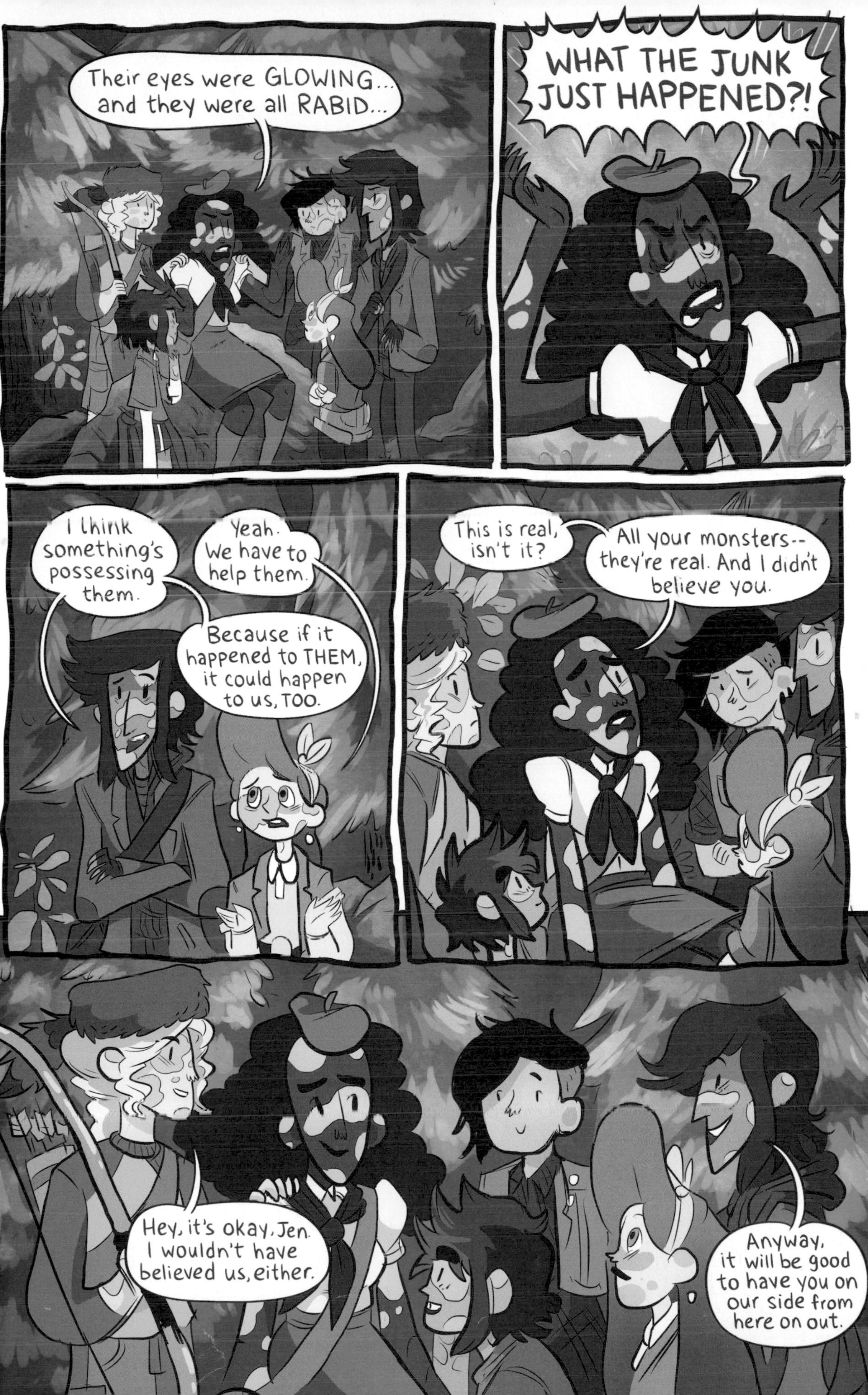
Their eyes were GLOWING... and they were all RABID...
WHAT THE JUNK JUST HAPPENED?!
I think something's possessing them.
Yeah. We have to help them.
Because if it happened to THEM, it could happen to us, TOO.
This is real, isn't it?
All your monsters-- they're real. And I didn't believe you.
Hey, it's okay, Jen. I wouldn't have believed us, either.
Anyway, it will be good to have you on our side from here on out.

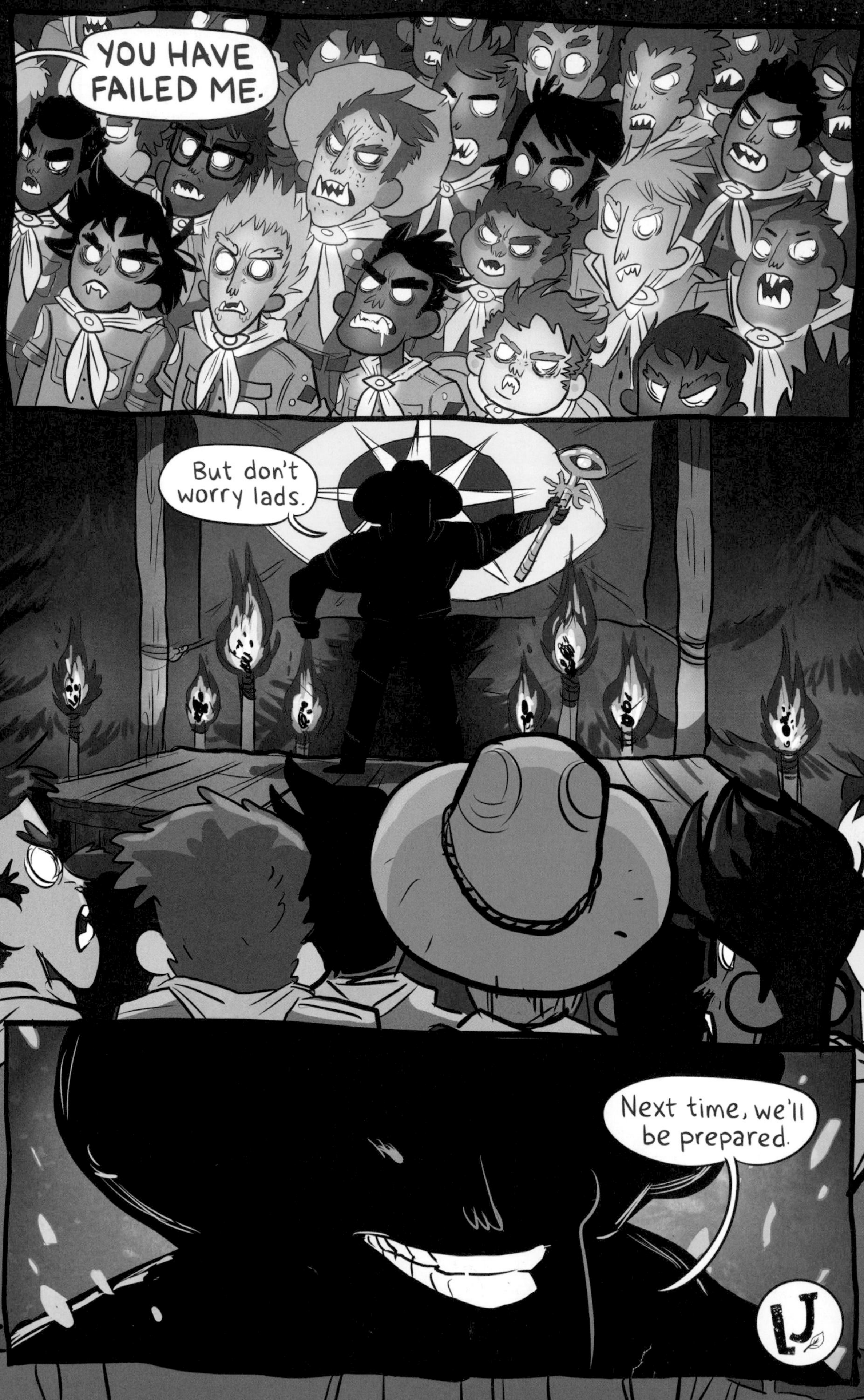
YOU HAVE FAILED ME.
But don't worry lads.
Next time, we'll be prepared.
LJ

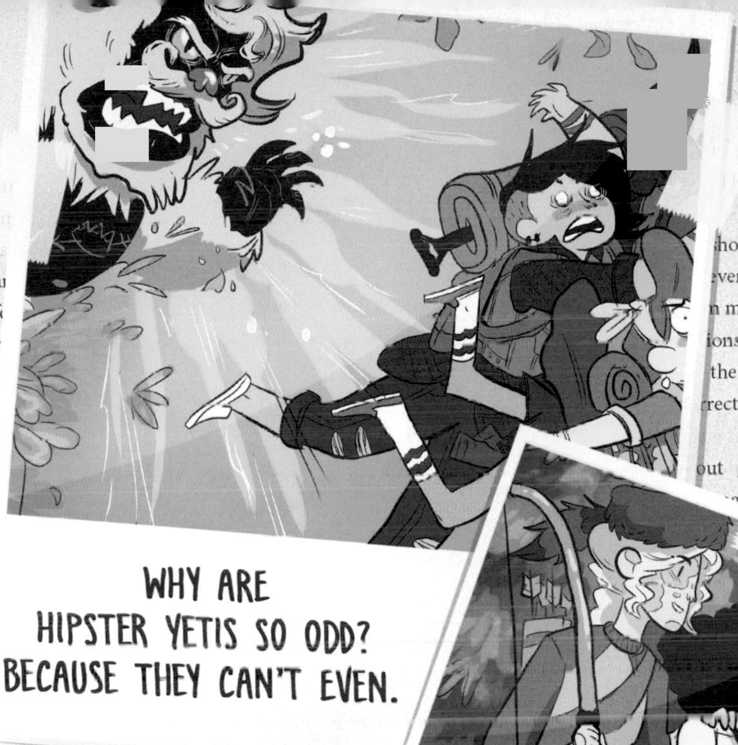
WHY ARE
HIPSTER YETIS SO ODD?
BECAUSE THEY CAN'T EVEN.

will co…

Th… It help… appeara… dress f… Further… Lumbe… to hav… part in… Thiskw… Hard… have … them…

…HE UNIFORM

…should be worn at camp …events when Lumberjanes …n may also be worn at other …ions. It should be worn as a … the uniform dress with …rrect shoes, and stocking or …

… out grows her uniform or … other Lumberjane. …ia she has … her … her

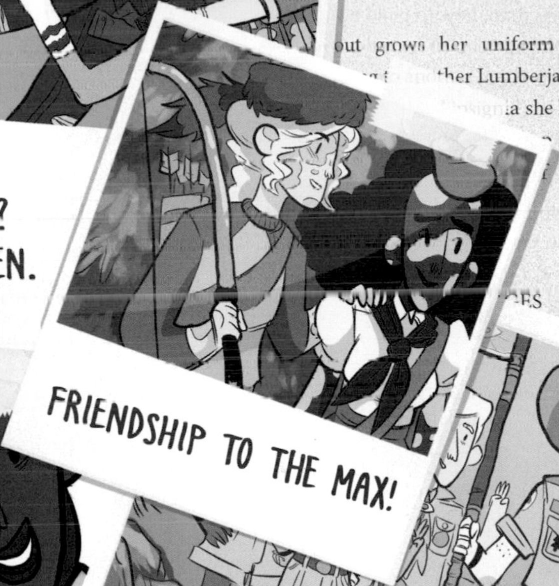
FRIENDSHIP TO THE MAX!

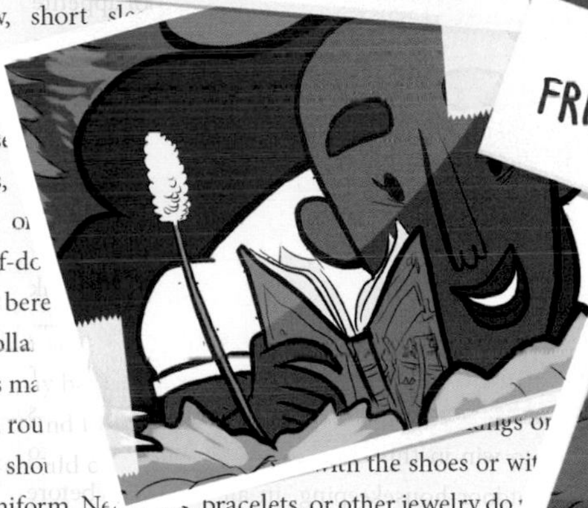

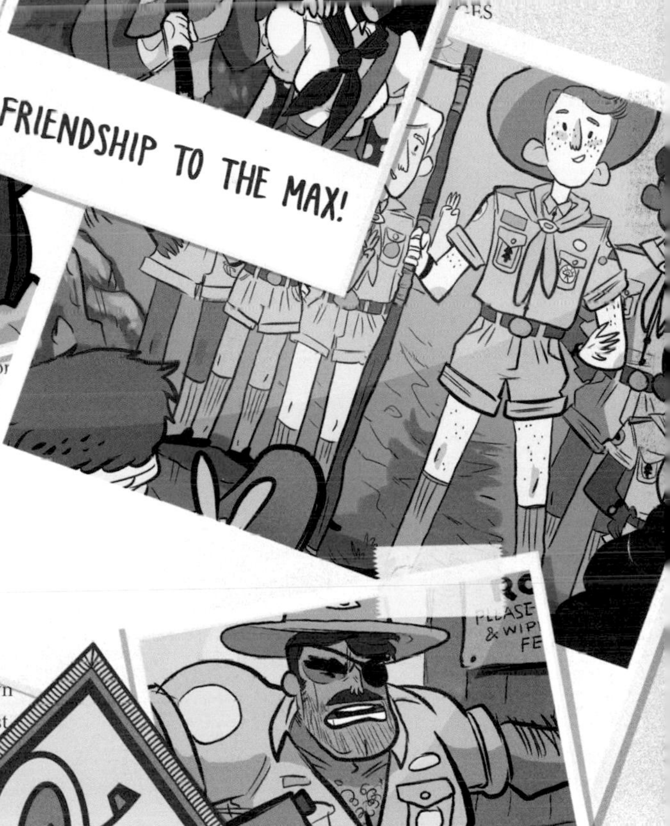

The… yellow, short sl… emb… the w… choose… slacks, made o… out-of-do… green bere… the colla… Shoes ma… heels, rou… …ings or socks shou… …with the shoes or wi… the uniform. Ne… …es, bracelets, or other jewelry do… belong with a Lumberjane uniform.

HOW TO WEAR THE UNIFORM

To look well in a uniform demands first of … uniform be kept in good condition—clean … pressed. See that the skirt is the right length for your own height and build, that the belt is adjusted to your waist … that your shoes and stockings are in keeping with … uniform, that you watch your posture and carry … with dignity and grace. If the beret is remov… be sure that your hair is neat and kept in pla… inconspicuous clip or ribbon. When you … Lumberjane uniform you are identified as a mem… this organization and you should be doubly careful… conduct yourself in a way that will show everyone tha… courtesy and thoughtfulness are part of being a Lumberjane. People are likely to judge a whole nation by the selfishness of a few individuals, to criticize a whole family because of the misconduct of one member, and to feel unkindly toward an organization because of the

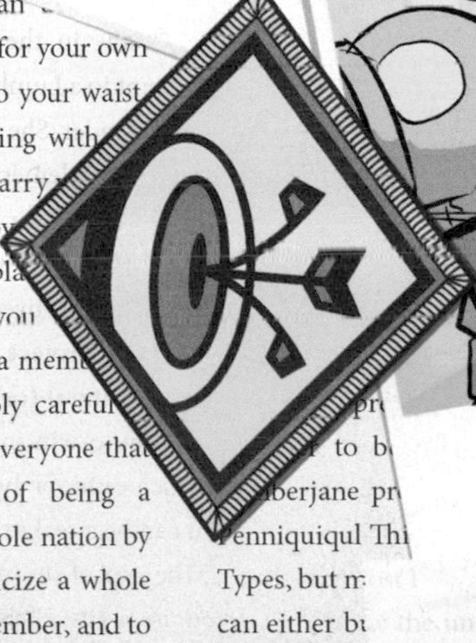

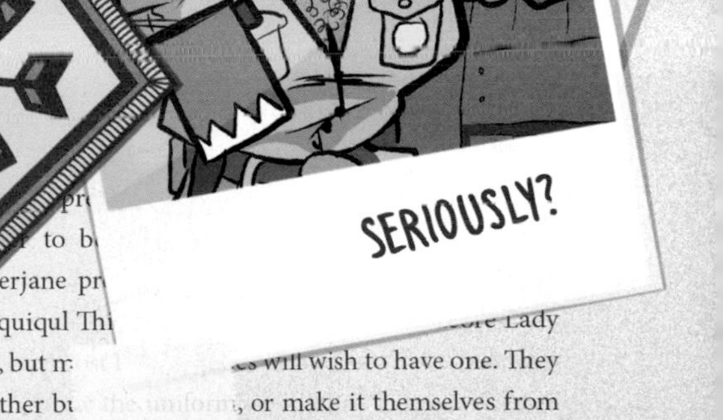
SERIOUSLY?

…pr… …r to b… …berjane pr… Penniquiqul Thi… …ore Lady Types, but m… …es will wish to have one. They can either bu… …uniform, or make it themselves from materials available at the trading post.

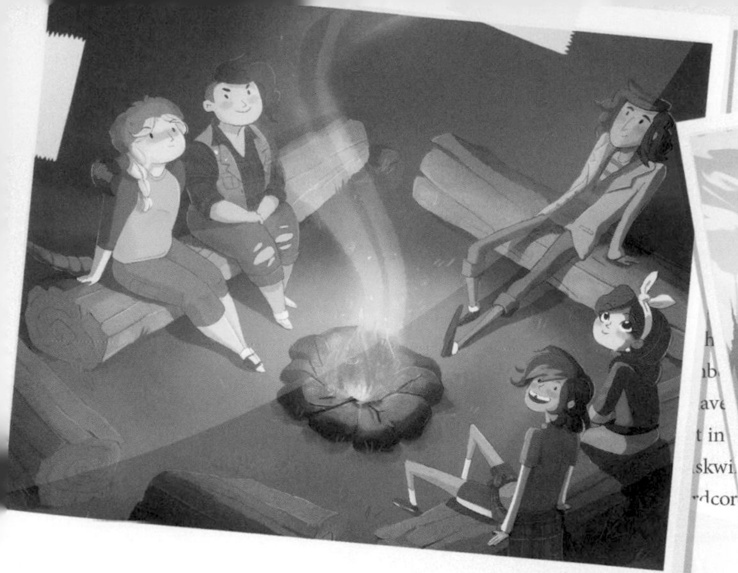

A LITTLE TIME AROUND THE FIRE

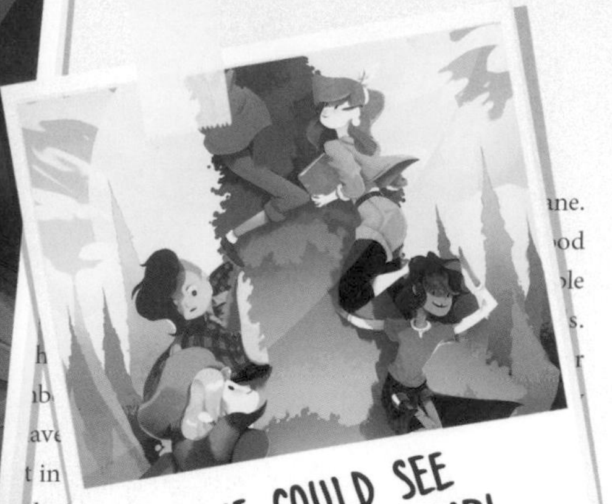

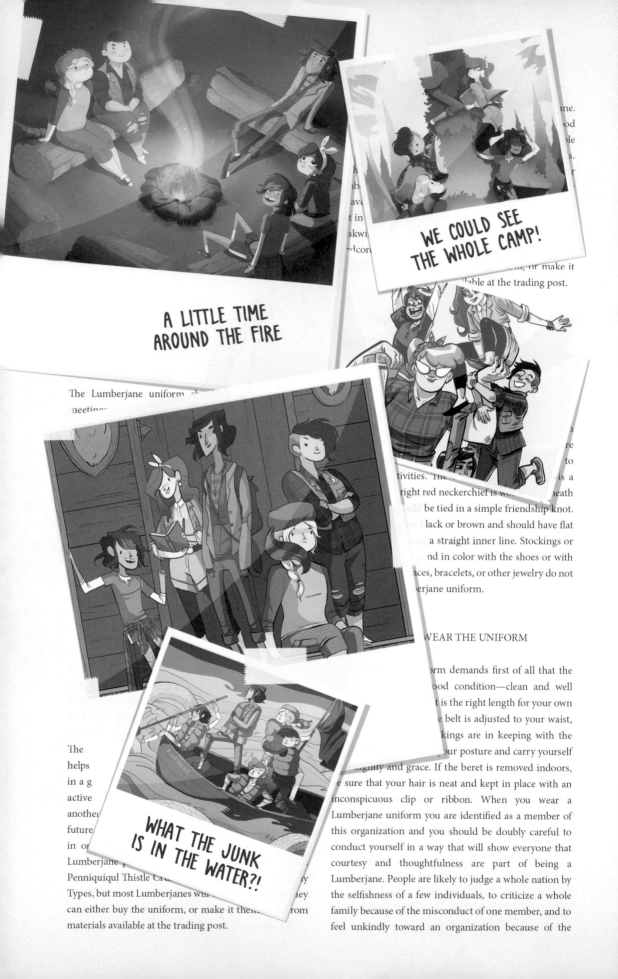

WE COULD SEE THE WHOLE CAMP!

ane.
ood
ple
s.
r
h
nb
ave
t in
skwi
rdcor

, or make it
ilable at the trading post.

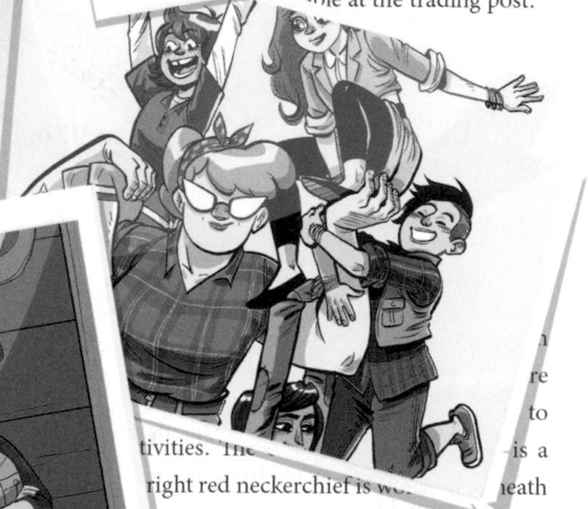

The Lumberjane uniform sh
meetings

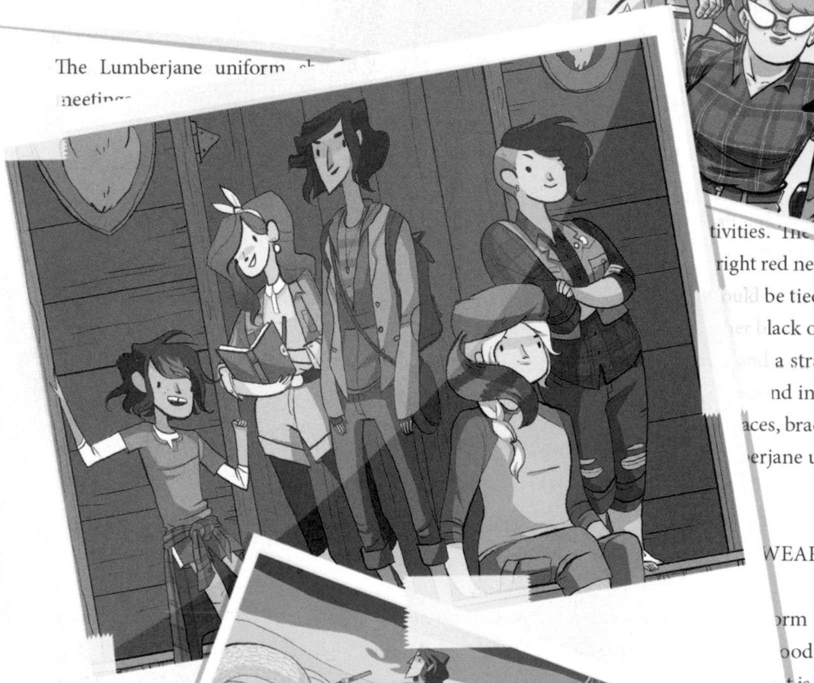

n
re
to
tivities. The — is a
right red neckerchief is wo — neath
ould be tied in a simple friendship knot.
her black or brown and should have flat
and a straight inner line. Stockings or
nd in color with the shoes or with
aces, bracelets, or other jewelry do not
erjane uniform.

WEAR THE UNIFORM

orm demands first of all that the ood condition—clean and well t is the right length for your own e belt is adjusted to your waist, kings are in keeping with the our posture and carry yourself dignity and grace. If the beret is removed indoors, e sure that your hair is neat and kept in place with an inconspicuous clip or ribbon. When you wear a Lumberjane uniform you are identified as a member of this organization and you should be doubly careful to conduct yourself in a way that will show everyone that courtesy and thoughtfulness are part of being a Lumberjane. People are likely to judge a whole nation by the selfishness of a few individuals, to criticize a whole family because of the misconduct of one member, and to feel unkindly toward an organization because of the

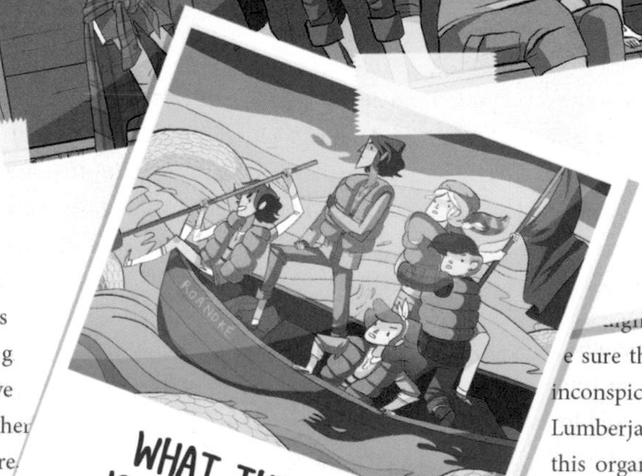

WHAT THE JUNK IS IN THE WATER?!

The
helps
in a g
active
another
future.
in or
Lumberjane p
Penniquiqul Thistle Cr — y
Types, but most Lumberjanes wi — ey
can either buy the uniform, or make it the — rom
materials available at the trading post.

COVER GALLERY

Lumberjanes "Out-of-Doors" Program Field

PUNGEON MASTER BADGE

"The best kind of punishment."

The pun conundrum is that most view it as the lowest form of word-play, but we Lumberjanes say, if it was good enough for Shakespeare and Plautus, then it is definitely good enough of our camp literary masters. The original purpose of a pun seems to be as diverse as the circumstances in how they first appeared in modern culture, and can be seen as more than a mere linguistic fillip. Lumberjanes recognize the value of a good pun and its cleverly worded effect on those around us and the future of civilization. A Lumberjane not only enjoys the creativity behind a pun but the importance of how it can bring a group together.

Wordplay is a great technique that Lumberjanes will continue to pursue with the fervor of every other skill they will learn at camp, and while this badge is the most popular, a Lumberjane knows the importances of not rushing head first into this lesson. A pun is meant for a perfect moment in time and the *Pungeon Master* badge teaches all Lumberjanes the importance of not only playing close attention to their current situation and their surroundings, but how to stay on their toes with their wit so always be available to improve the conversation around them.

To obtain the *Pungeon Master* badge, a Lumberjane must have a knowledge of the game laws of the state in which she lives. Great care must be taken to determine if it is the appropriate time or place for clever wordplay as a Lumberjane may also risk her pun being misconstrued. It is important to find not only the the right audience, but time and place in order to ensure that a pun will not be missed. She must preserve the importance of the pun and truly understand the strength of the words she is using. A Lumberjane understands the importance of a pun and the power that comes with it.

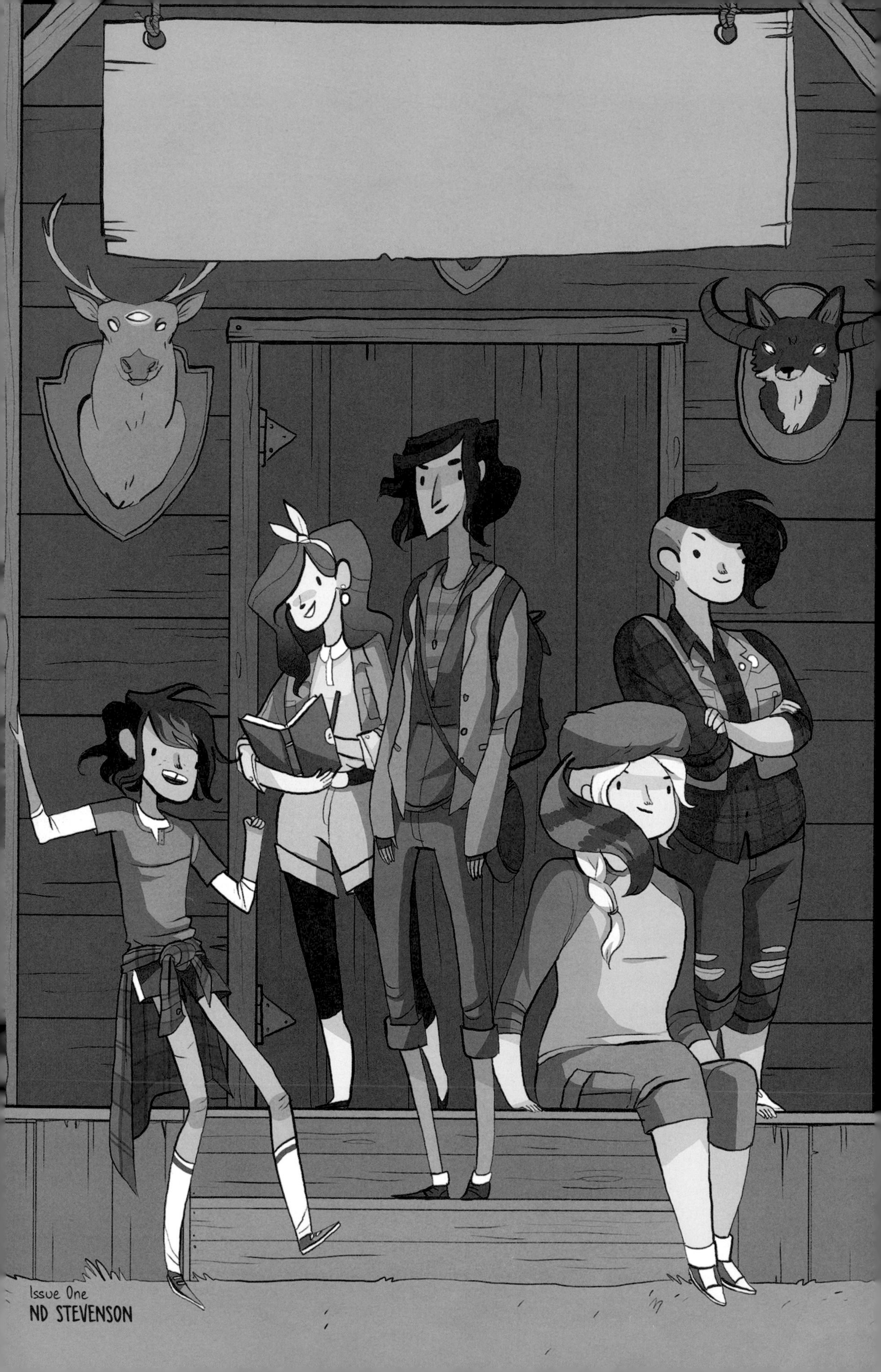
Issue One
ND STEVENSON

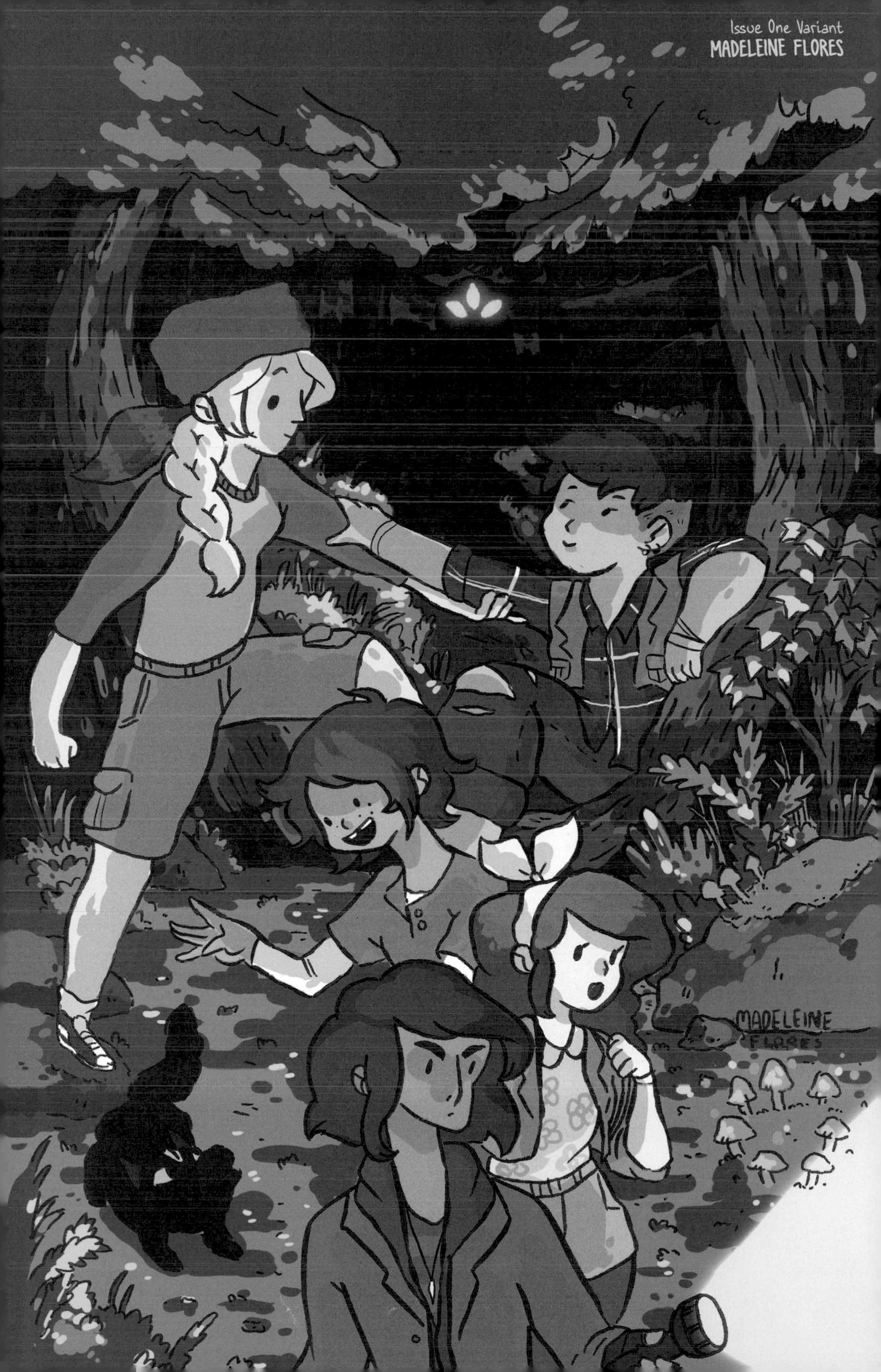
Issue One Variant
MADELEINE FLORES
MADELEINE FLORES

Issue One Variant
ZUKE

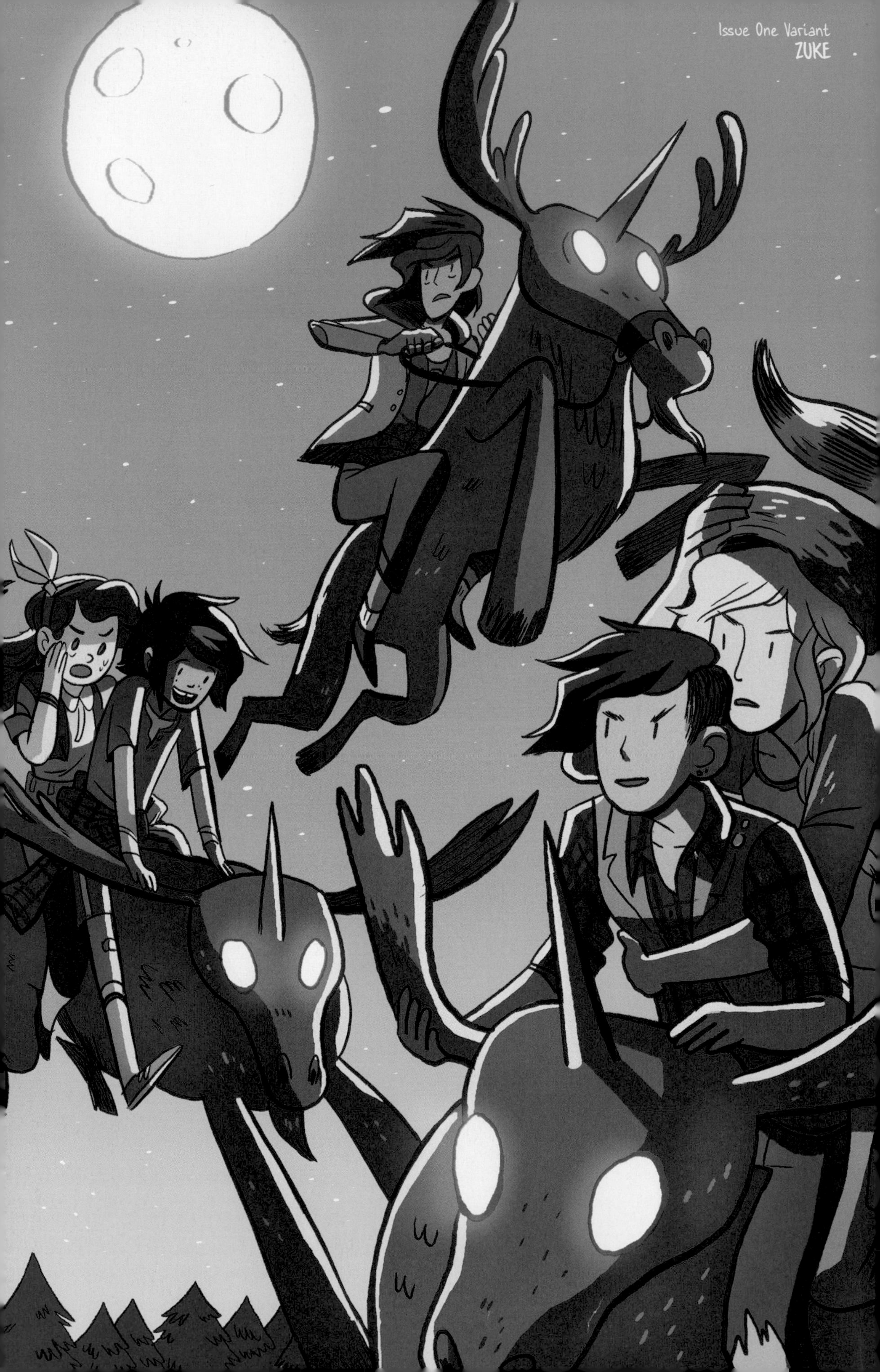

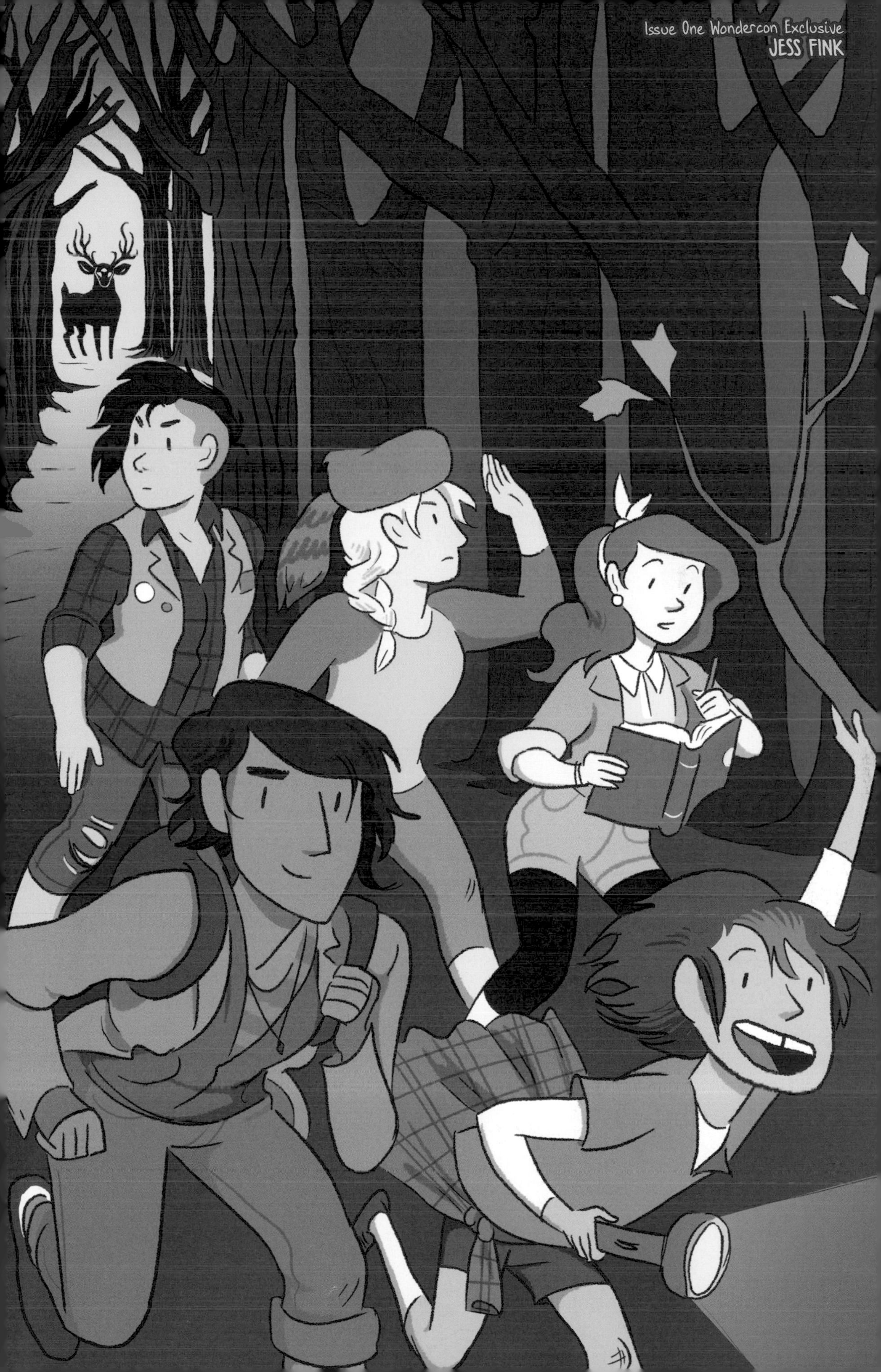
Issue One Wondercon Exclusive
JESS FINK

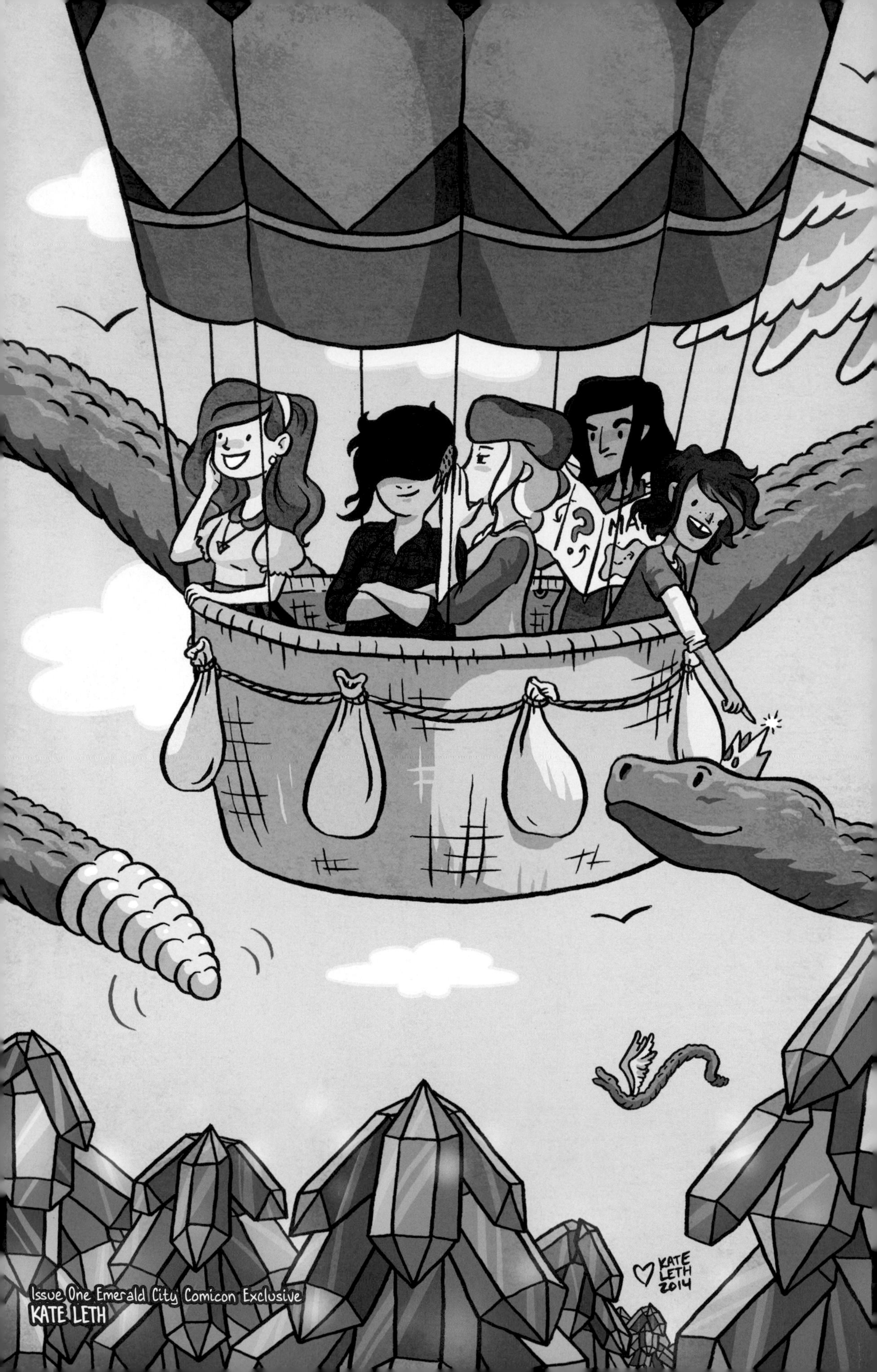
KATE LETH 2014
Issue One Emerald City Comicon Exclusive
KATE LETH

Issue One Collector's Paradise Exclusive
AIMEE FLECK

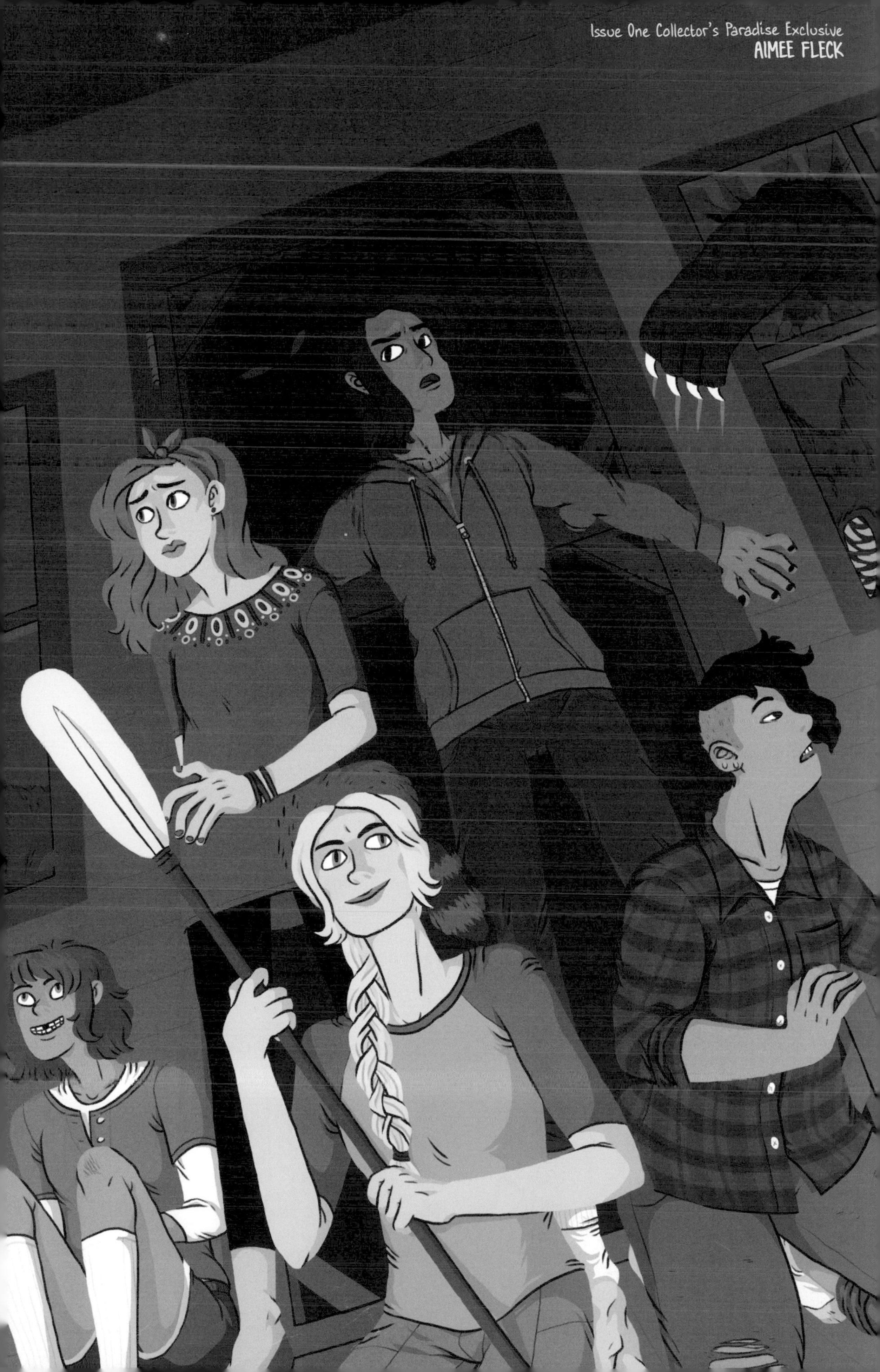

Original LumberJanes designs by GUS A.

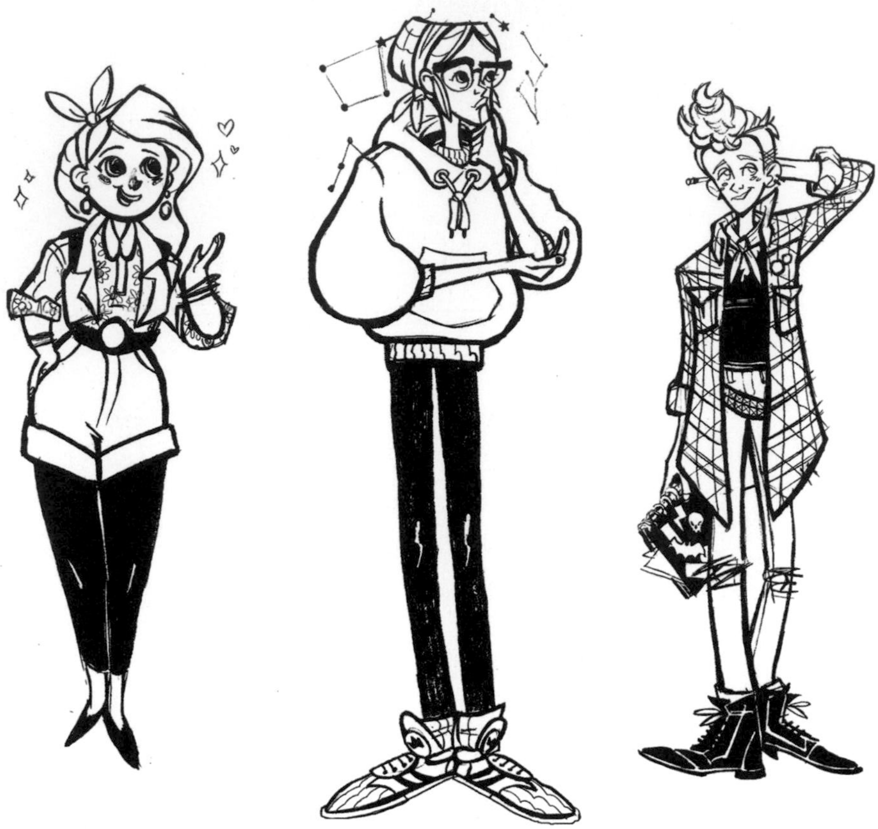

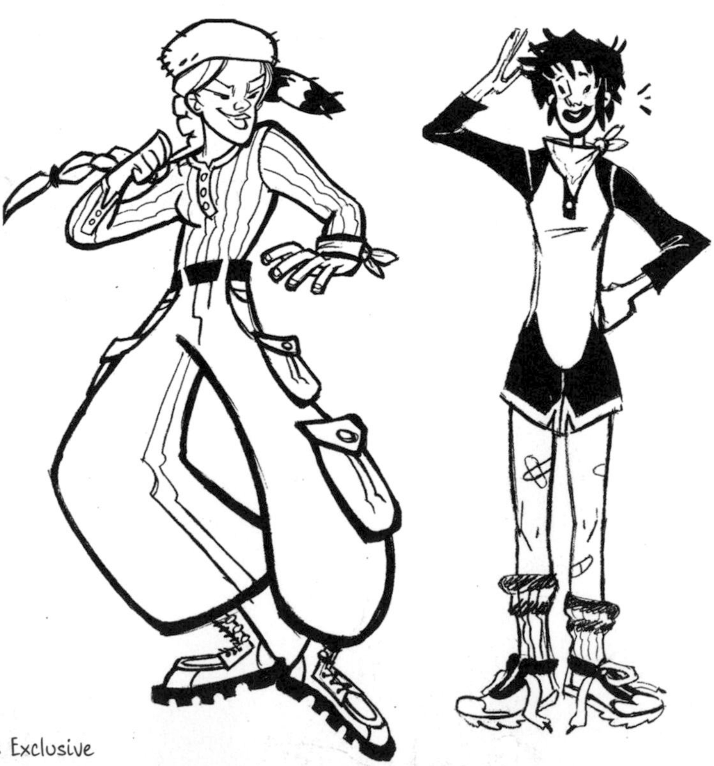

Issue One BOOM! Studios Exclusive
GUS ALLEN

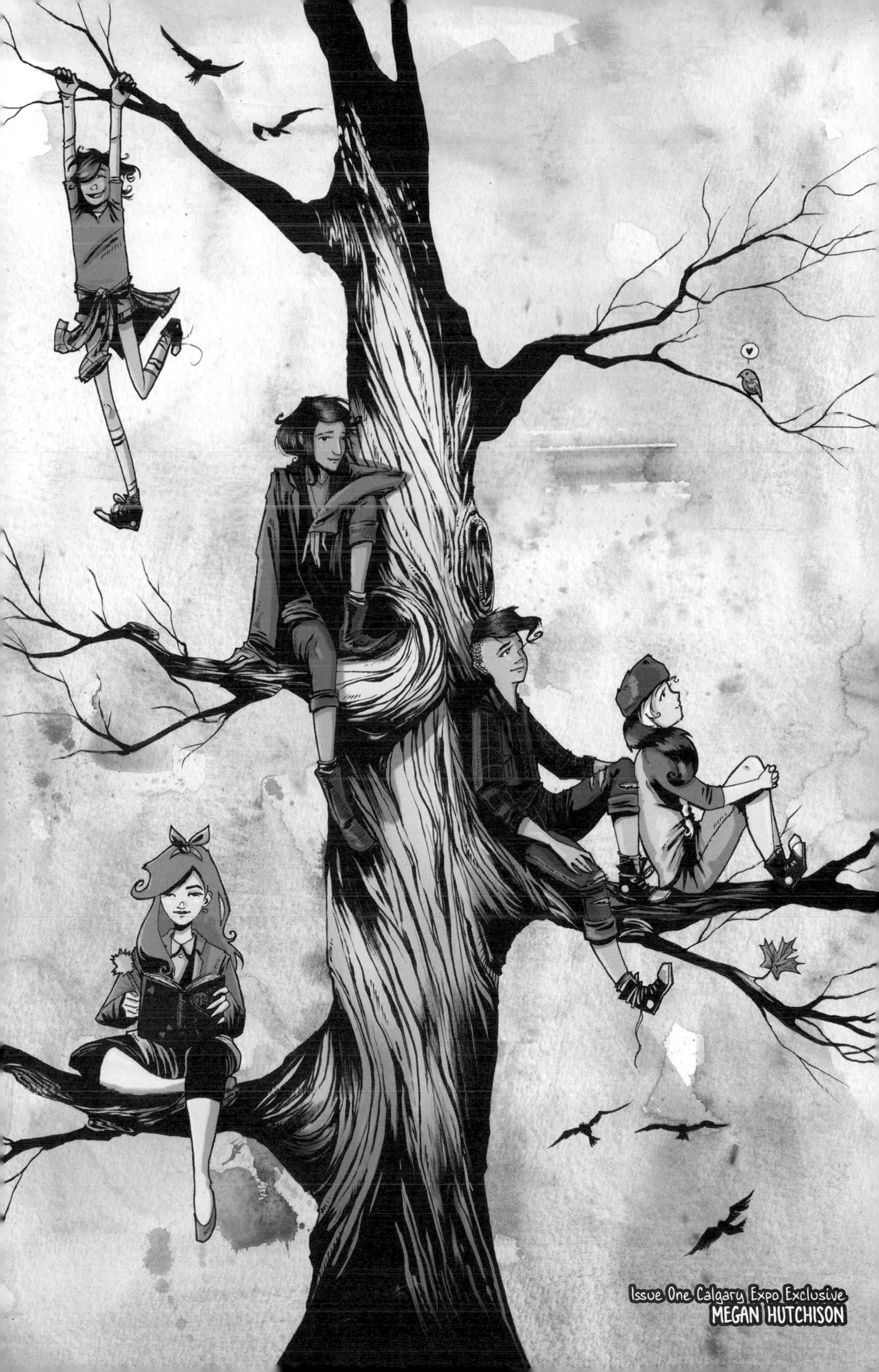
Issue One Calgary Expo Exclusive
MEGAN HUTCHISON

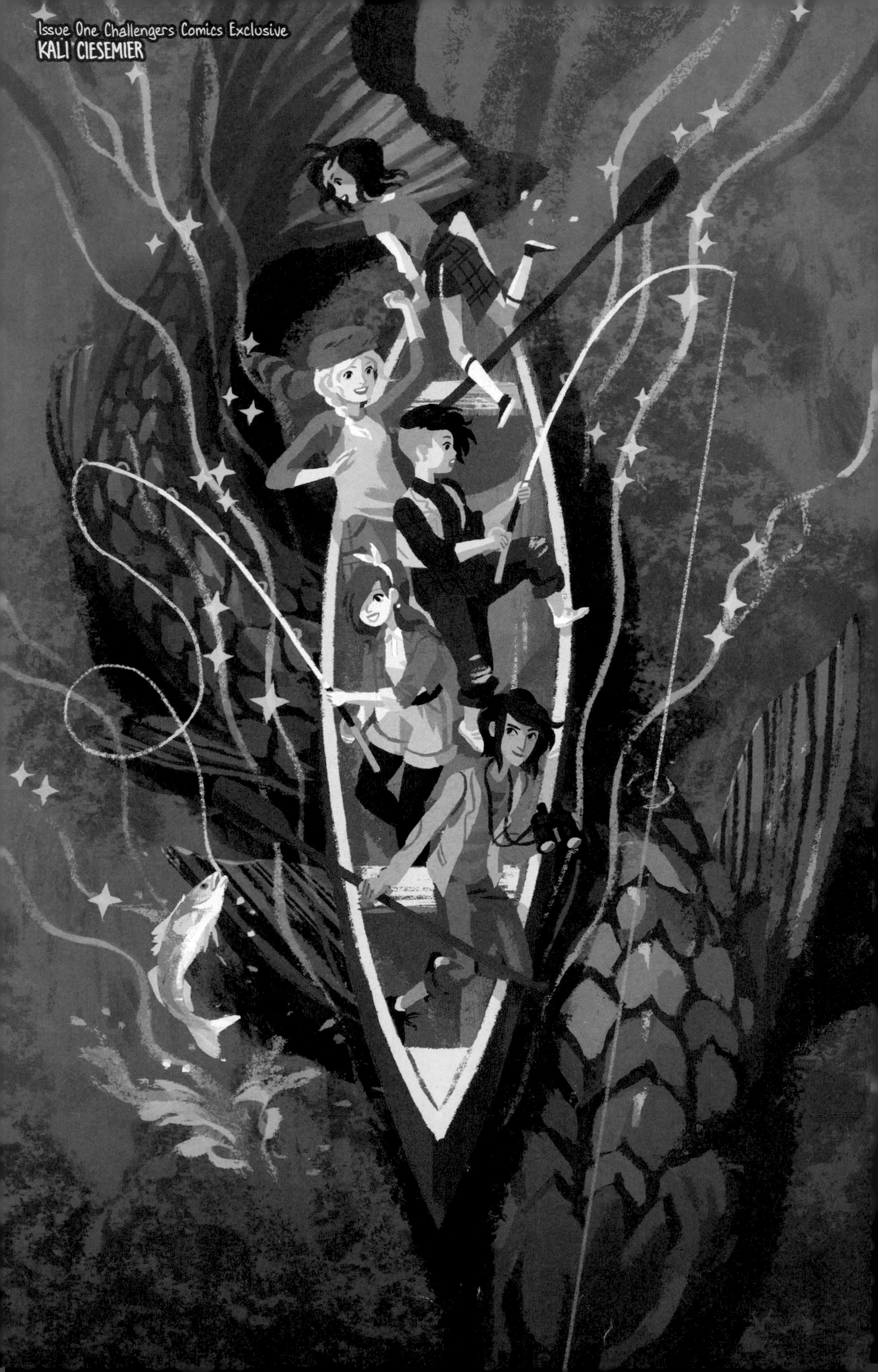
Issue One Challengers Comics Exclusive
KALI CIESEMIER

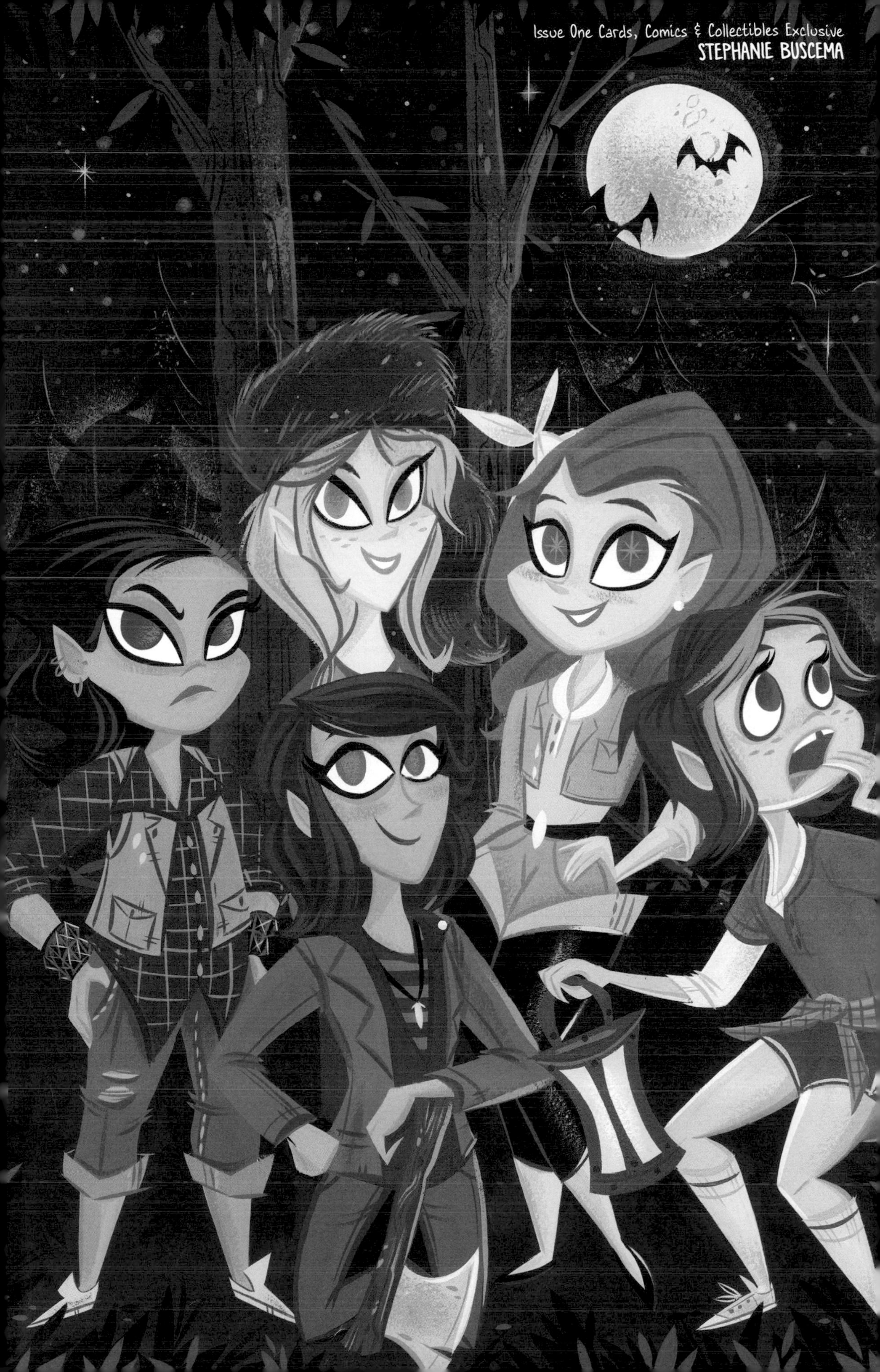
Issue One Cards, Comics & Collectibles Exclusive
STEPHANIE BUSCEMA

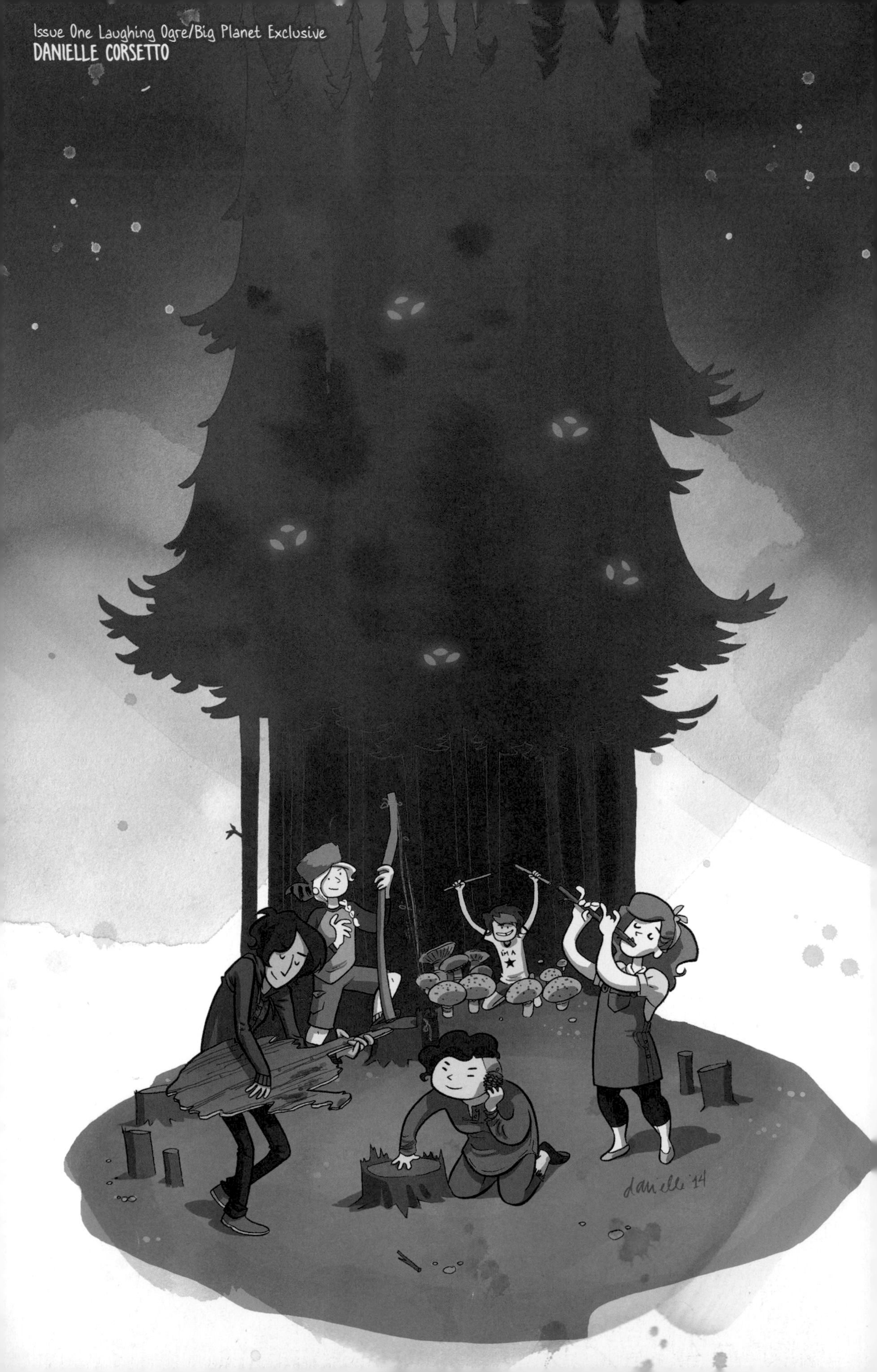
danielle '14

Issue One Laughing Ogre/Big Planet Exclusive
DANIELLE CORSETTO

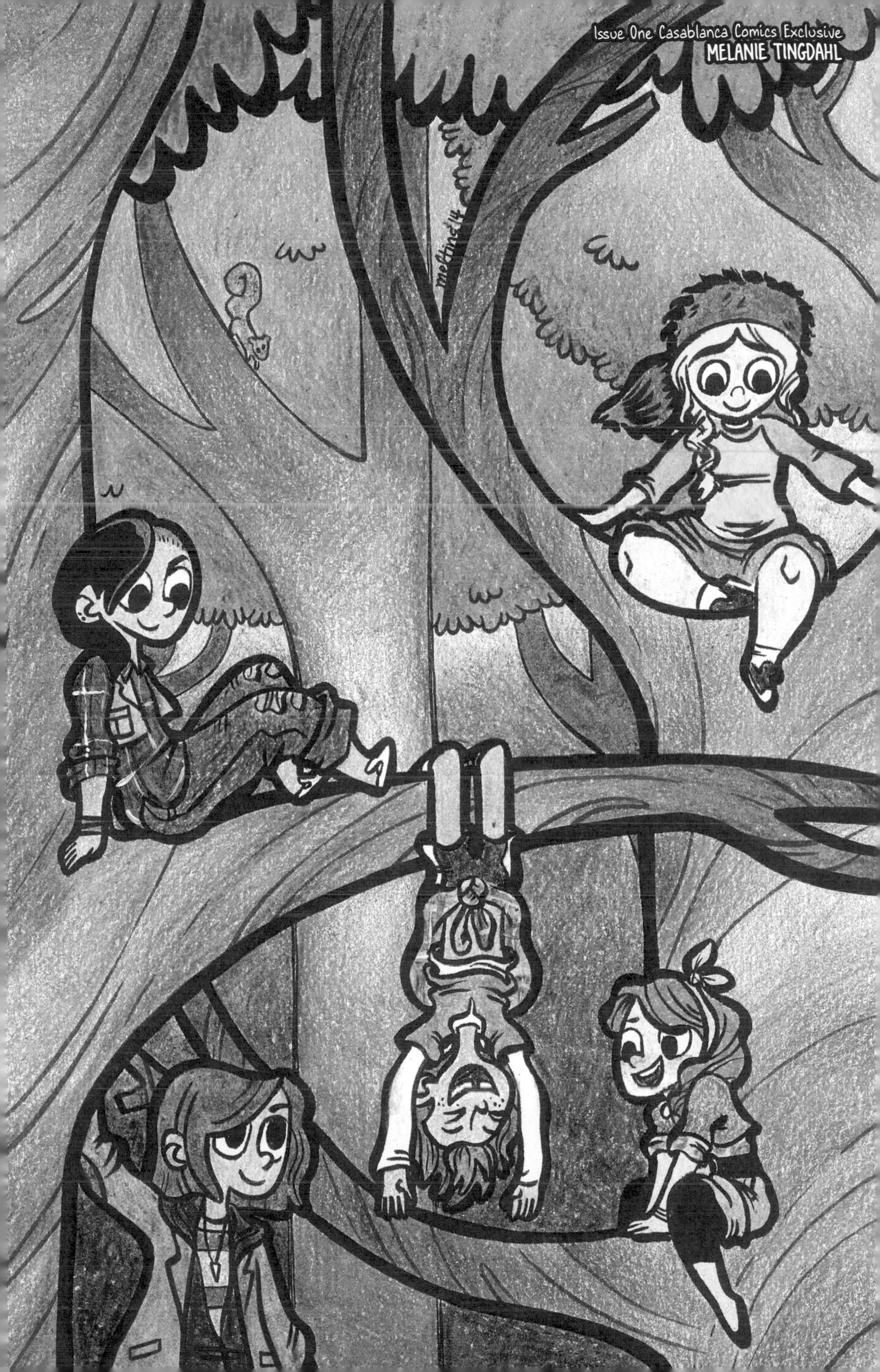
Issue One Casablanca Comics Exclusive
MELANIE TINGDAHL

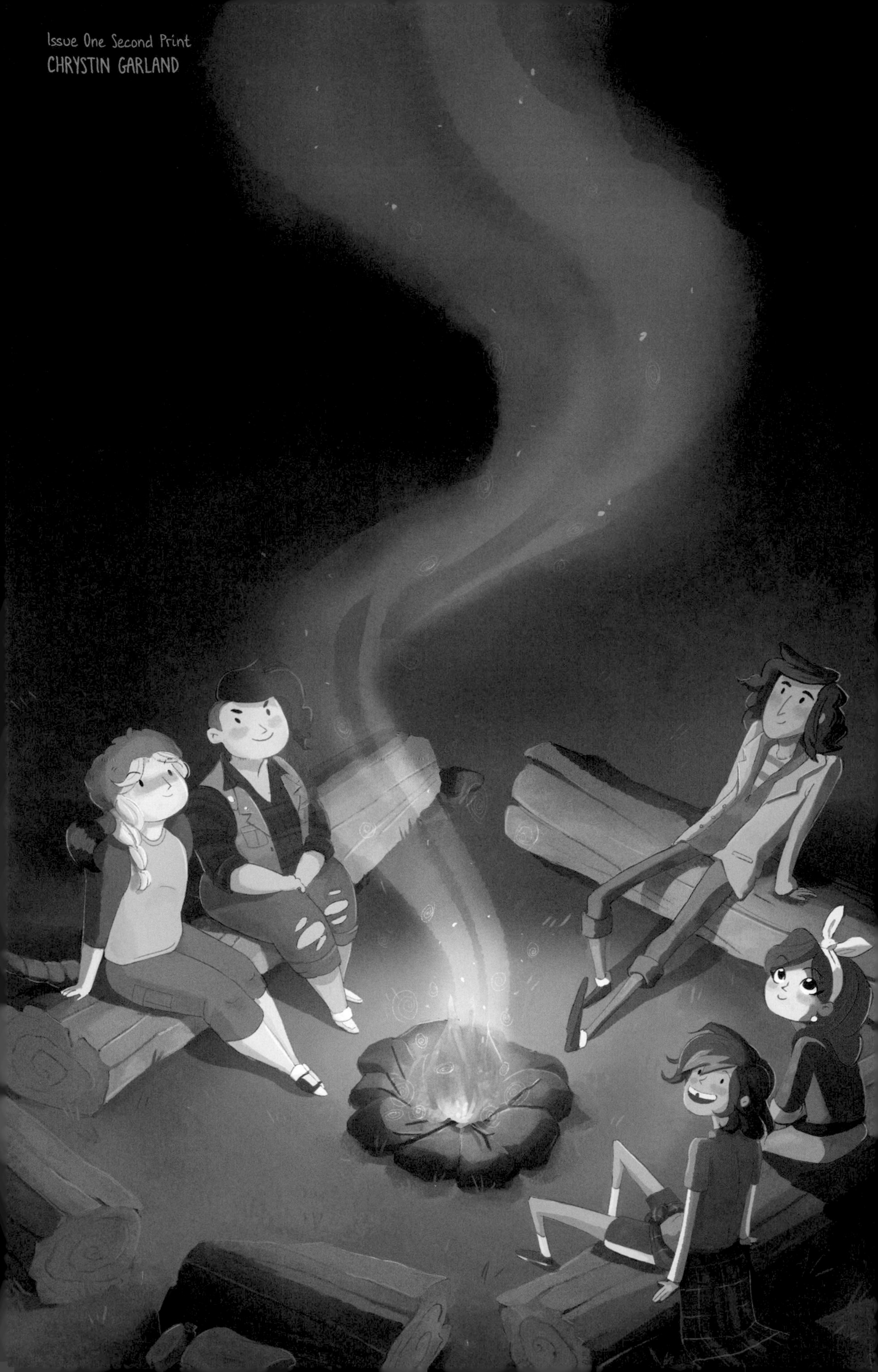
Issue One Second Print
CHRYSTIN GARLAND

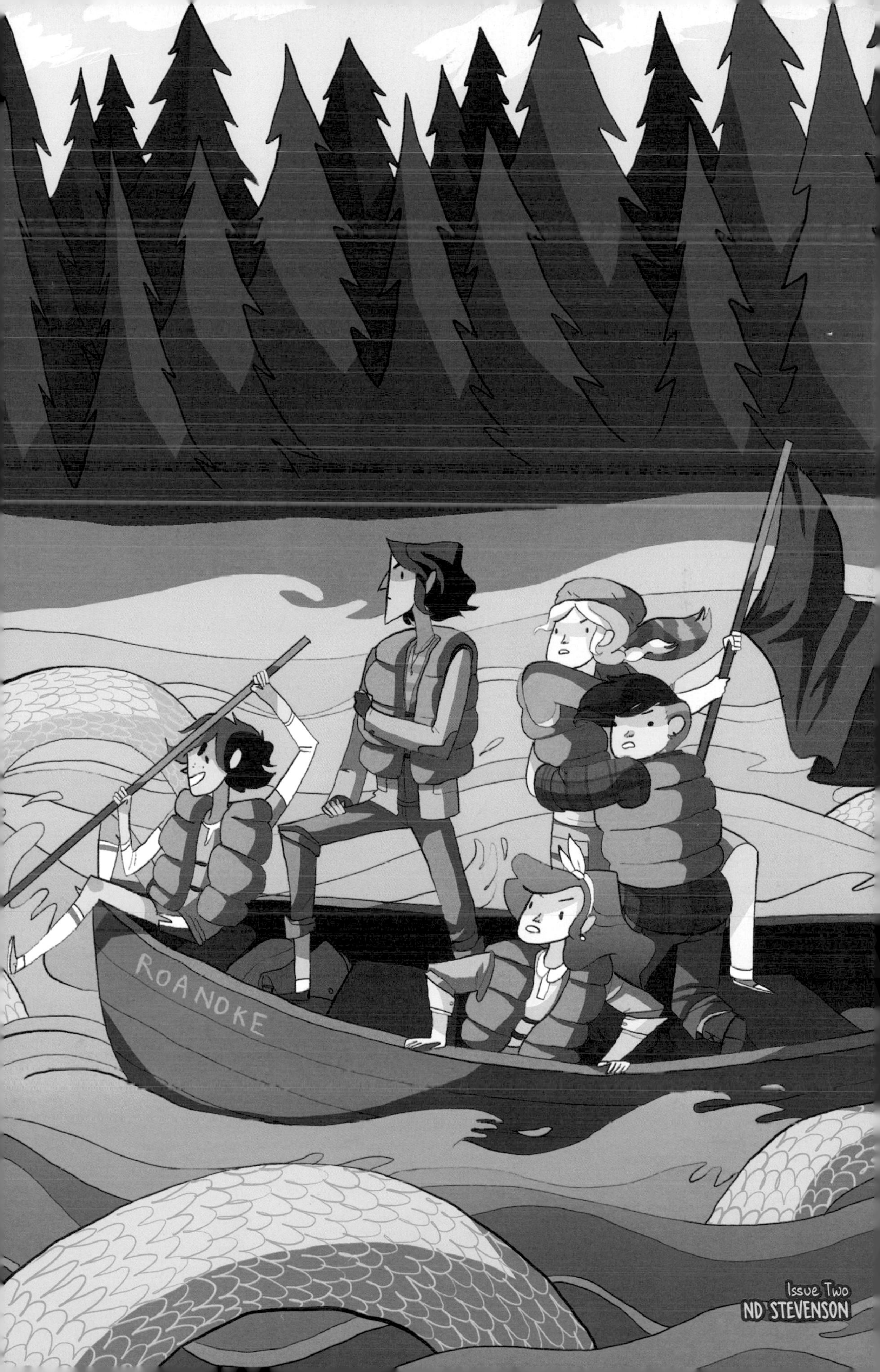
ROANOKE
Issue Two
ND STEVENSON

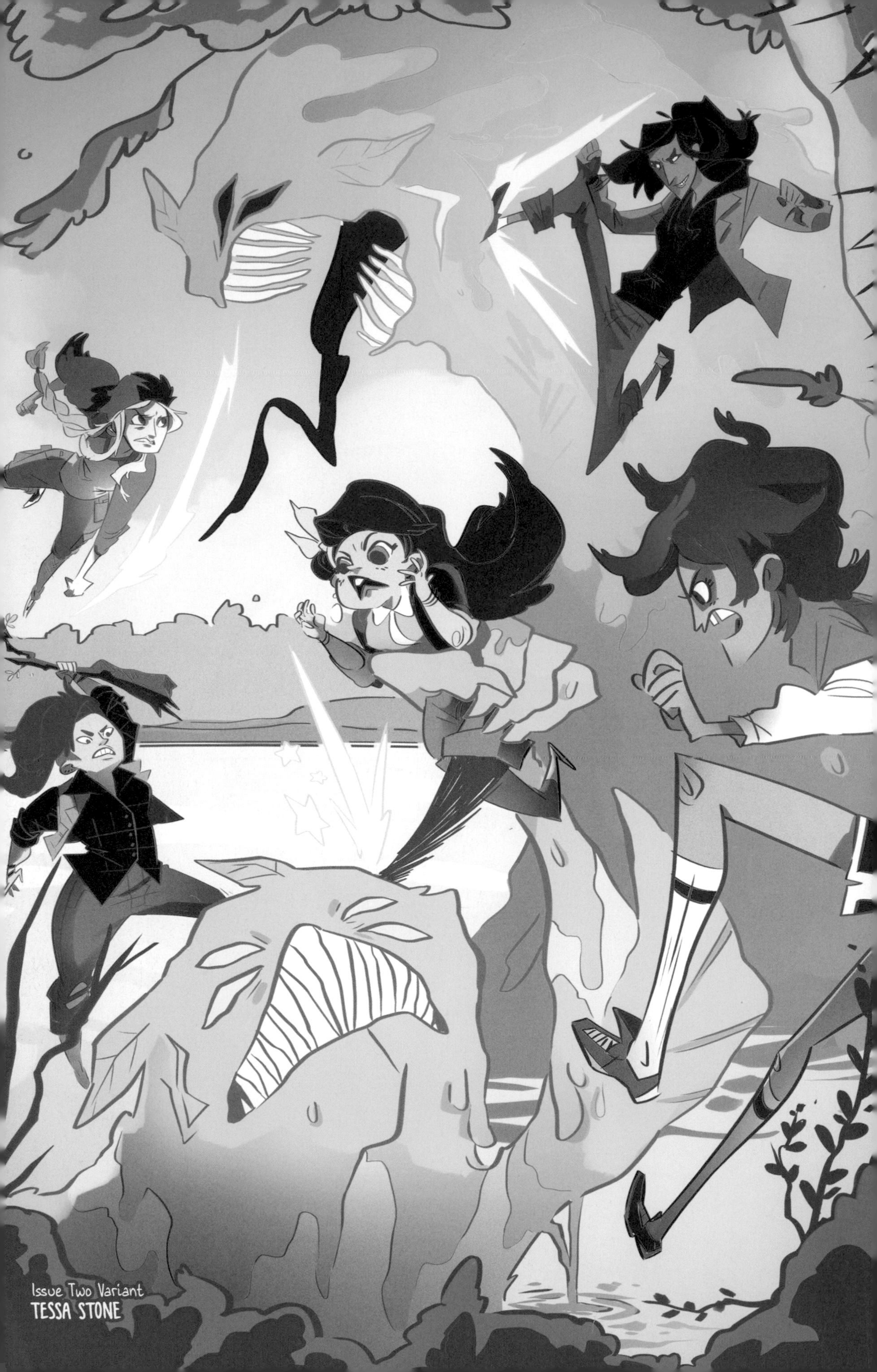
Issue Two Variant
TESSA STONE

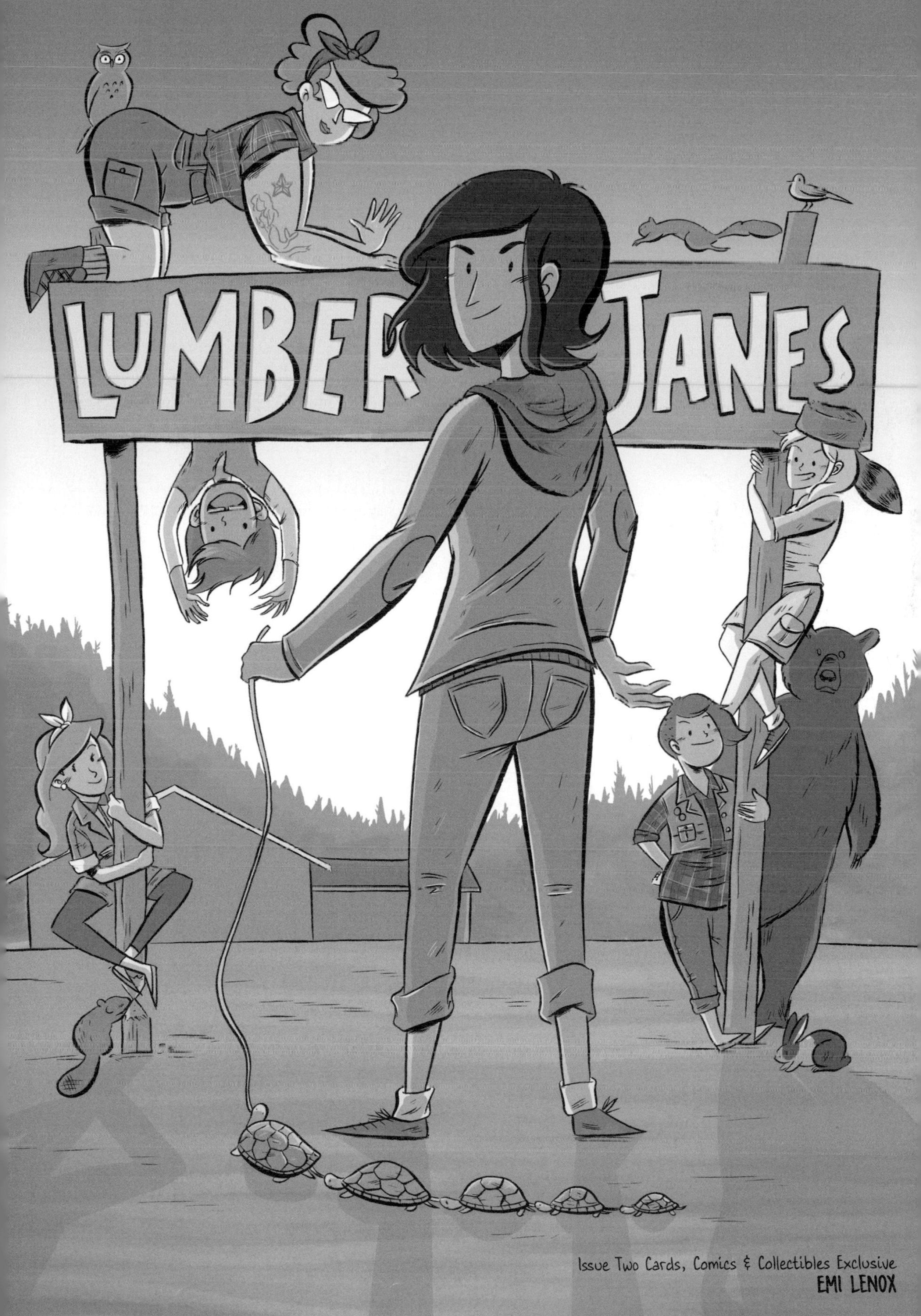
LUMBER JANES

Issue Two Cards, Comics & Collectibles Exclusive
EMI LENOX

Issue Two Second Print
PERRY MAPLE

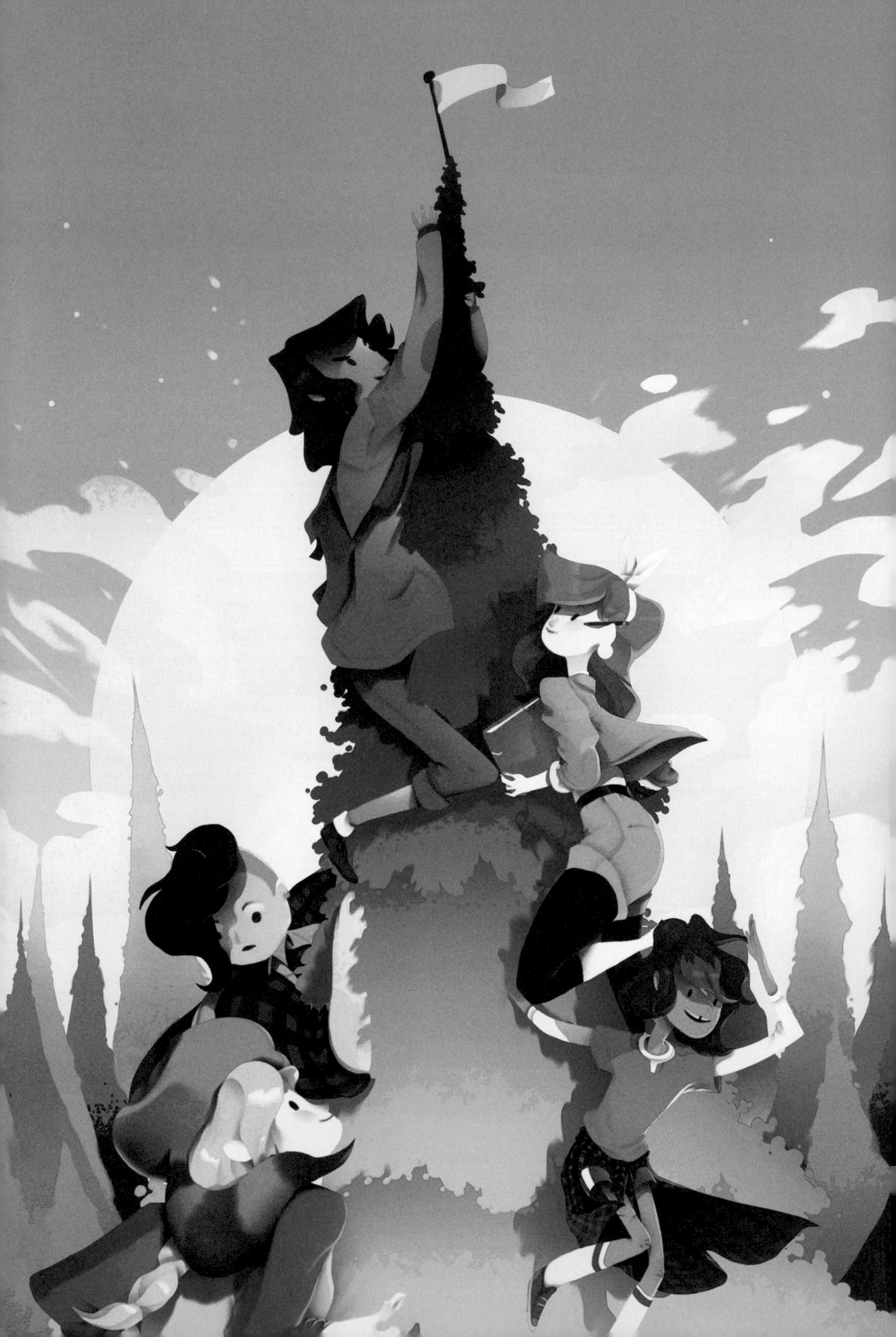

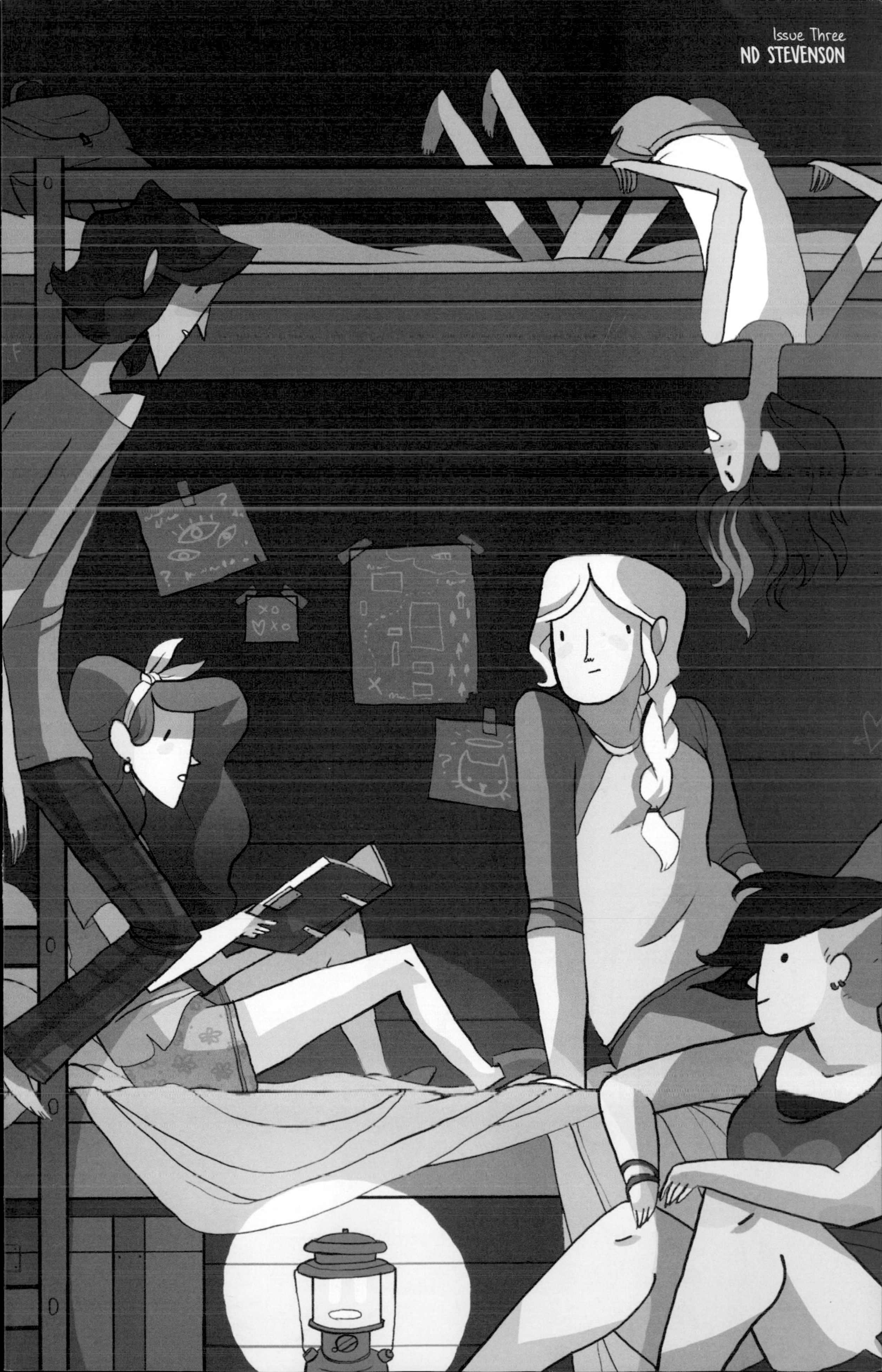
Issue Three
ND STEVENSON

Issue Three Variant
FAITH ERIN HICKS

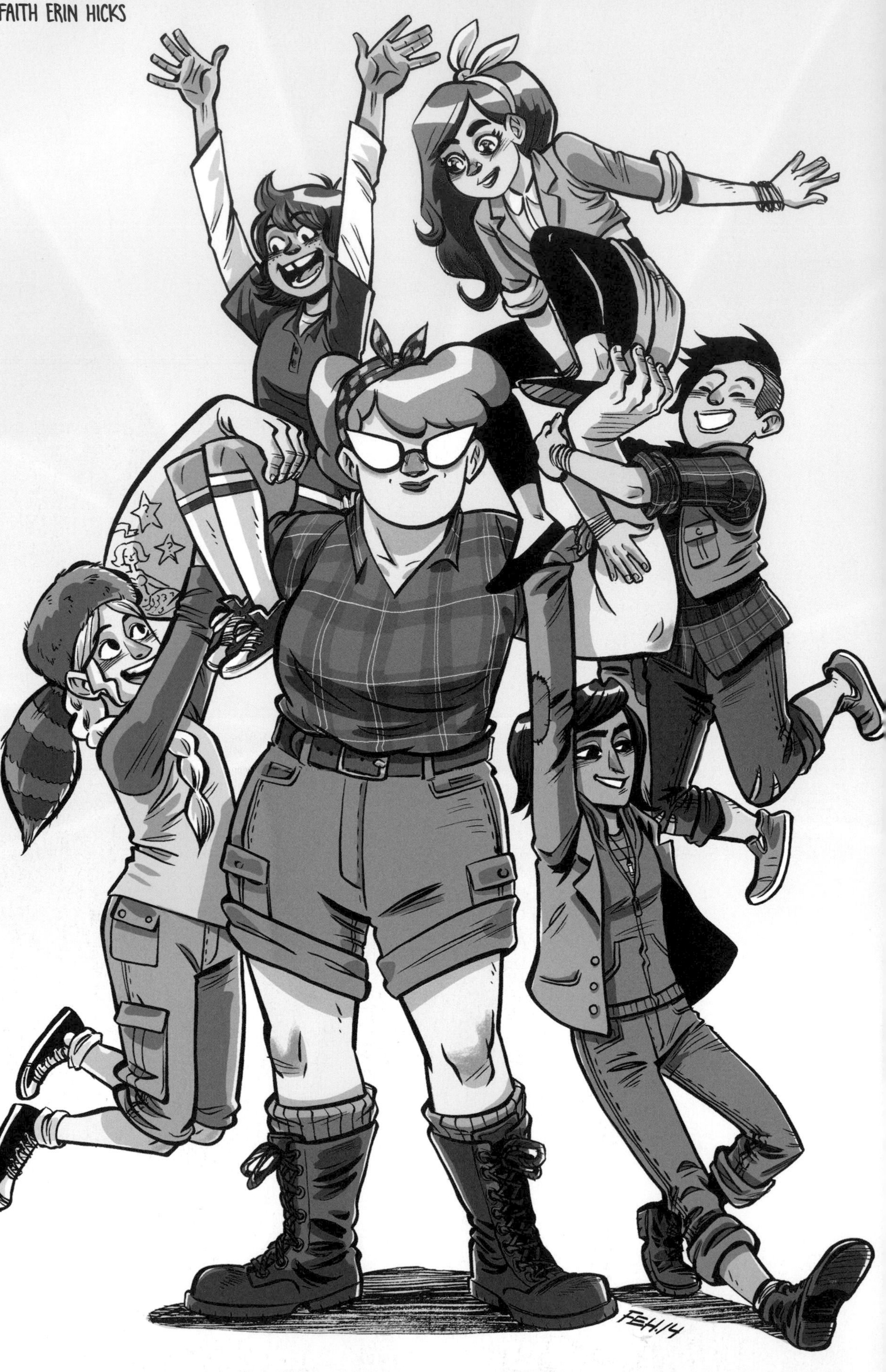
FEH.14

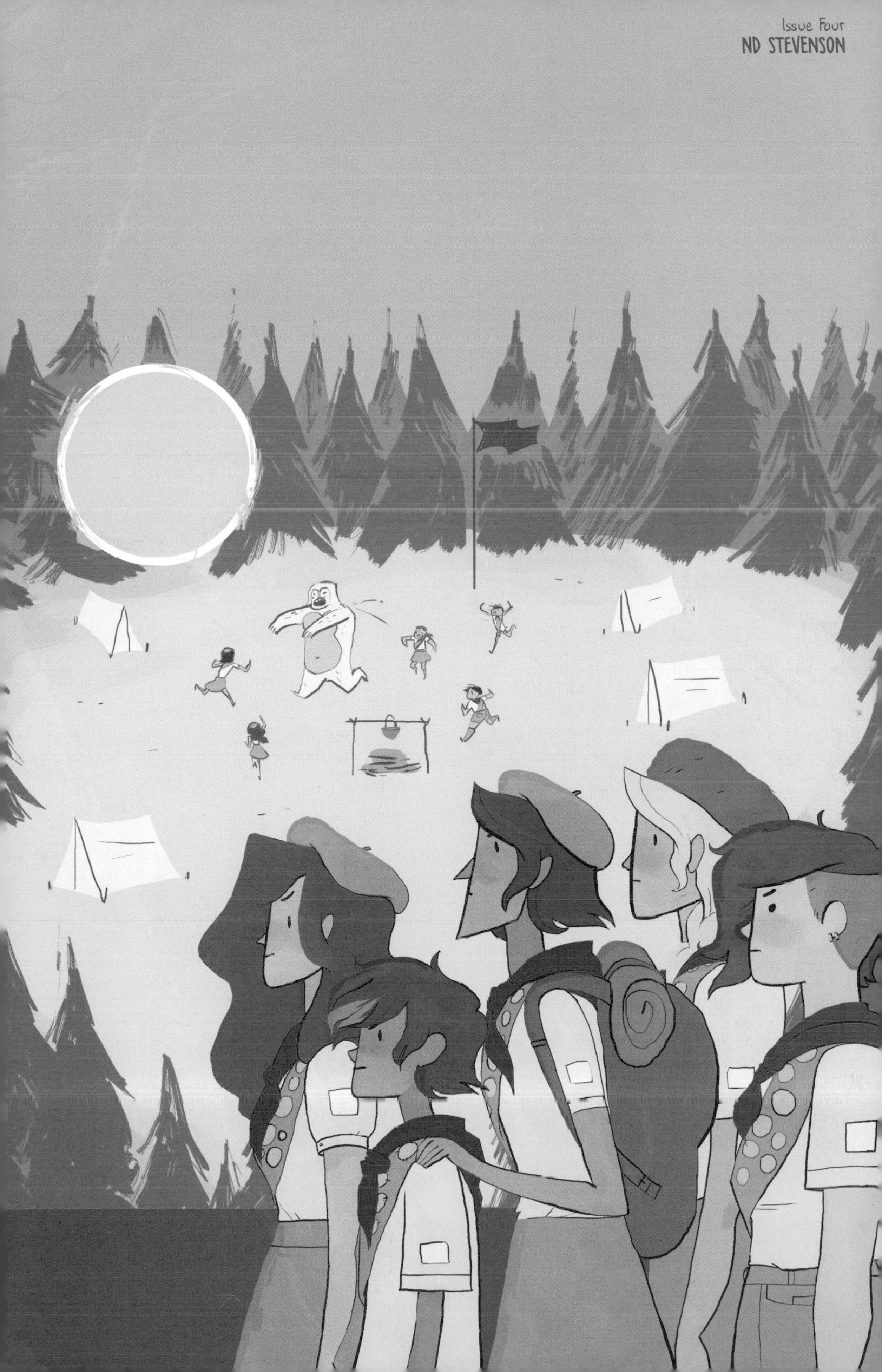
Issue Four
ND STEVENSON

Issue Four Variant
KRIS ANKA

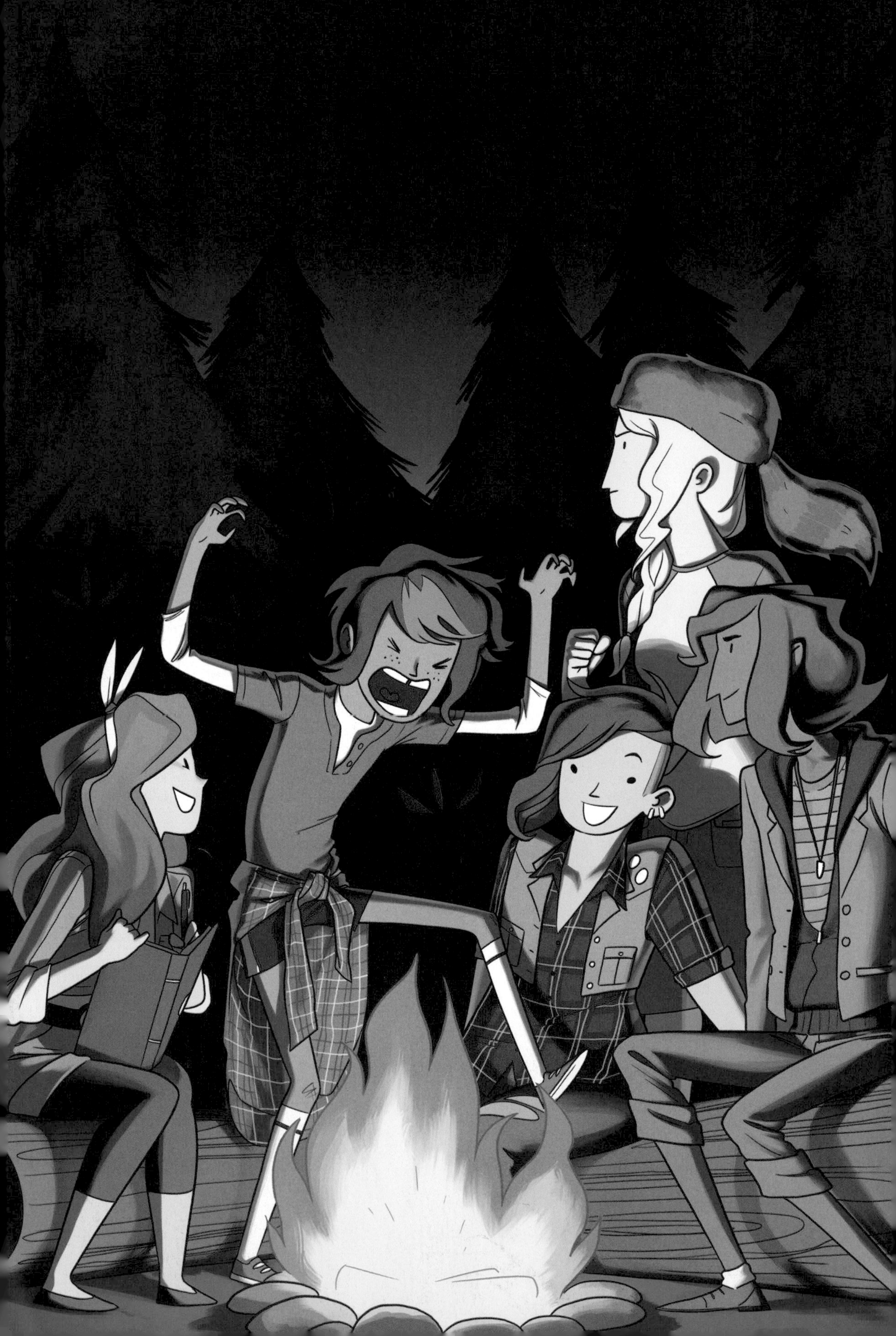

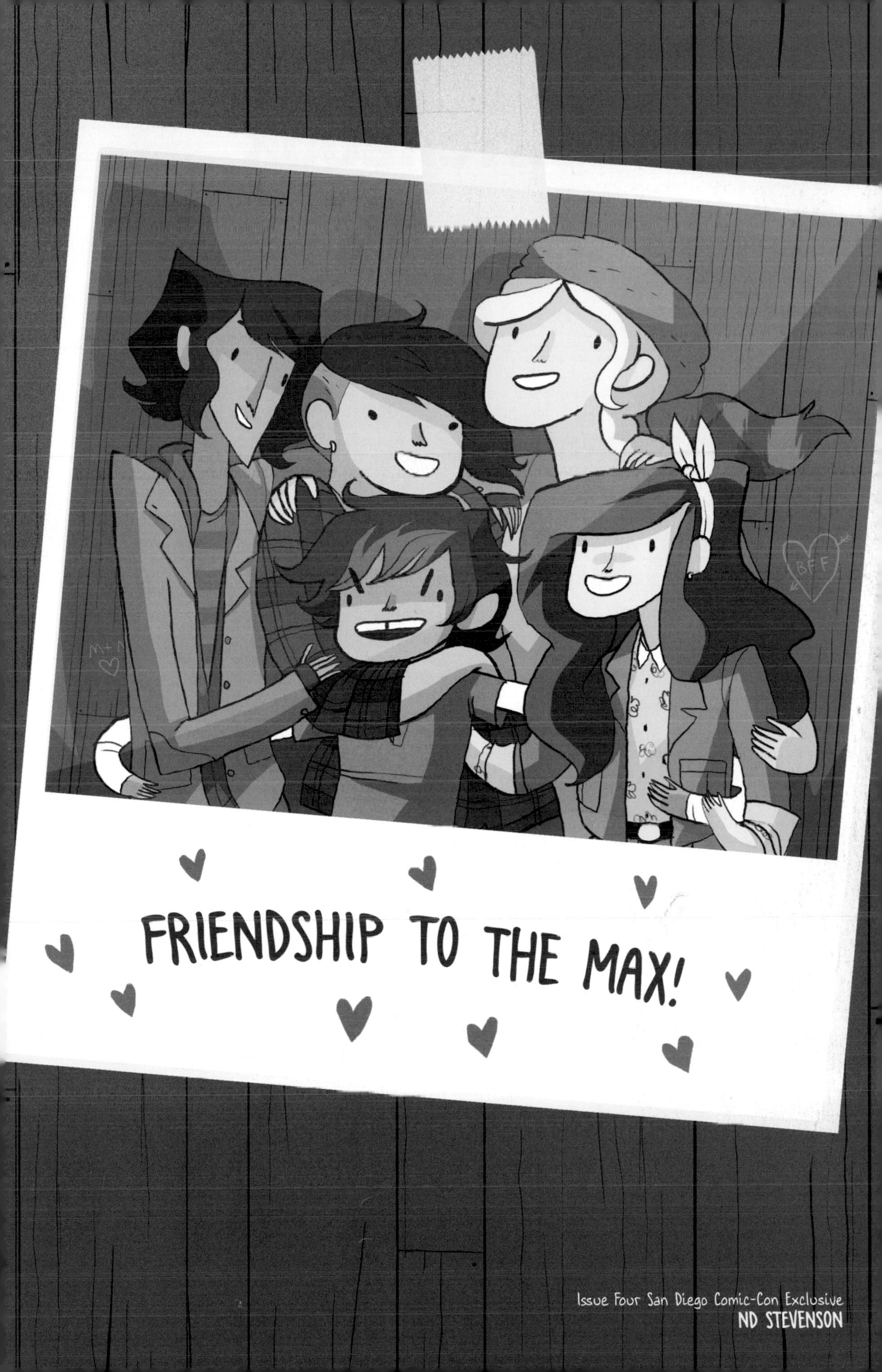
BFF
FRIENDSHIP TO THE MAX!

Issue Four San Diego Comic-Con Exclusive
ND STEVENSON

LUMBERJANES FIELD MANUAL

SKETCHBOOK

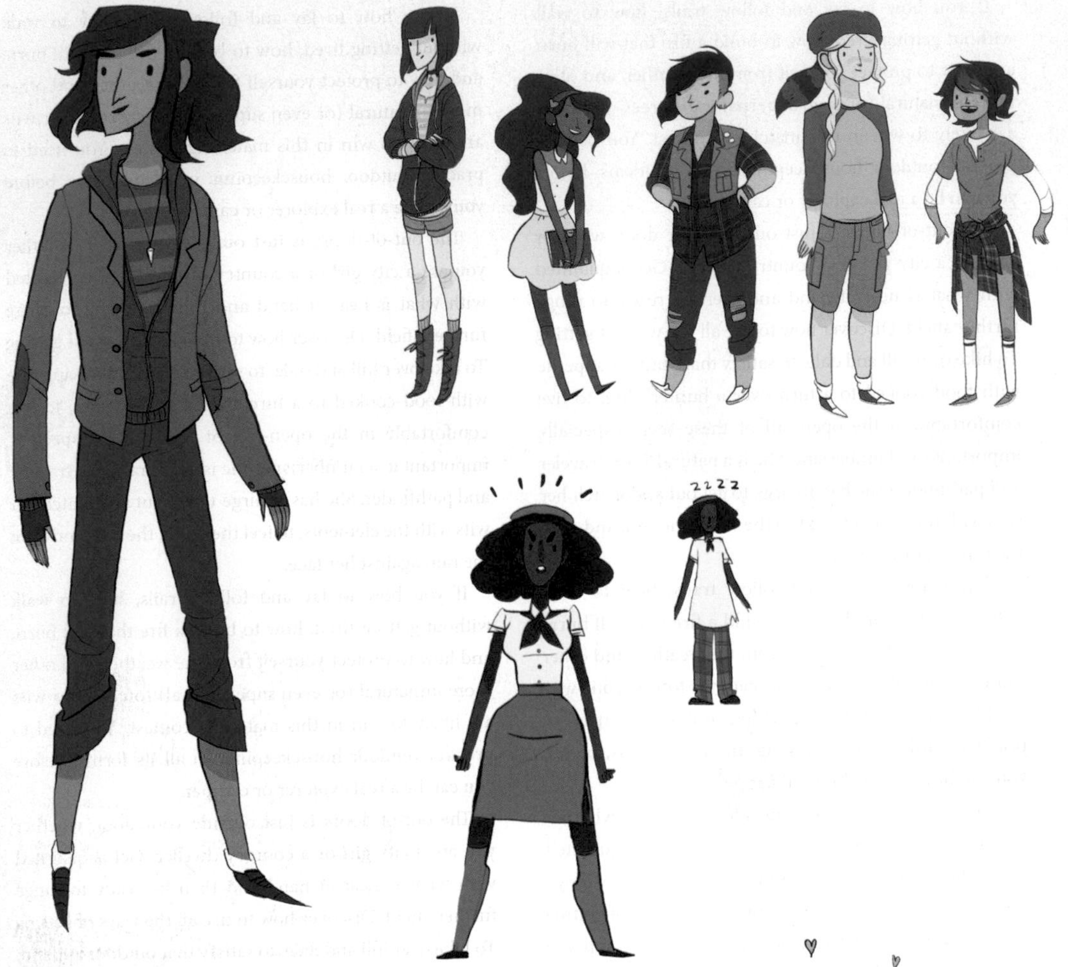
ZZZZ

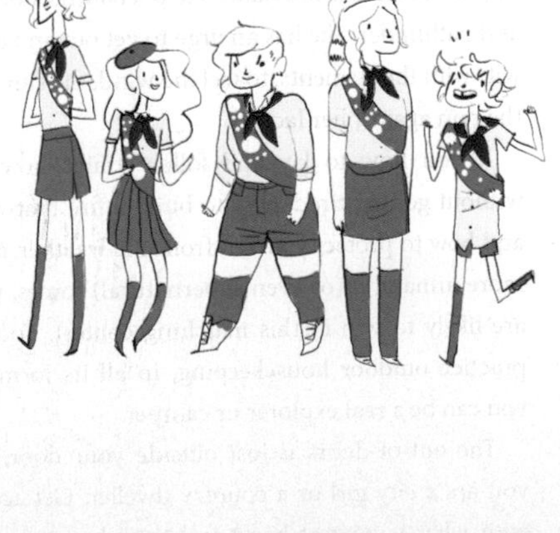

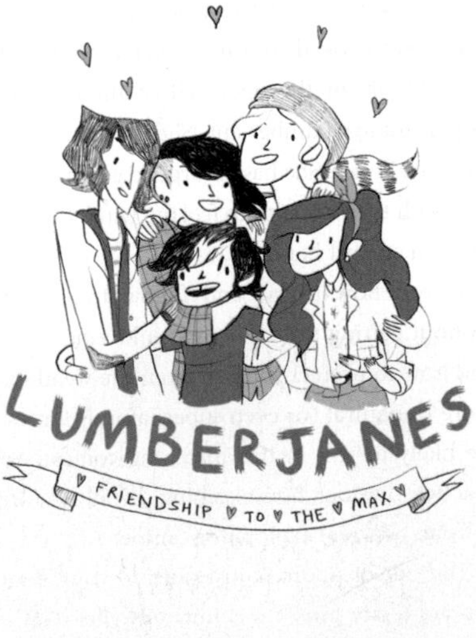
LUMBERJANES
FRIENDSHIP TO THE MAX

CHARACTER DESIGNS BY ND STEVENSON

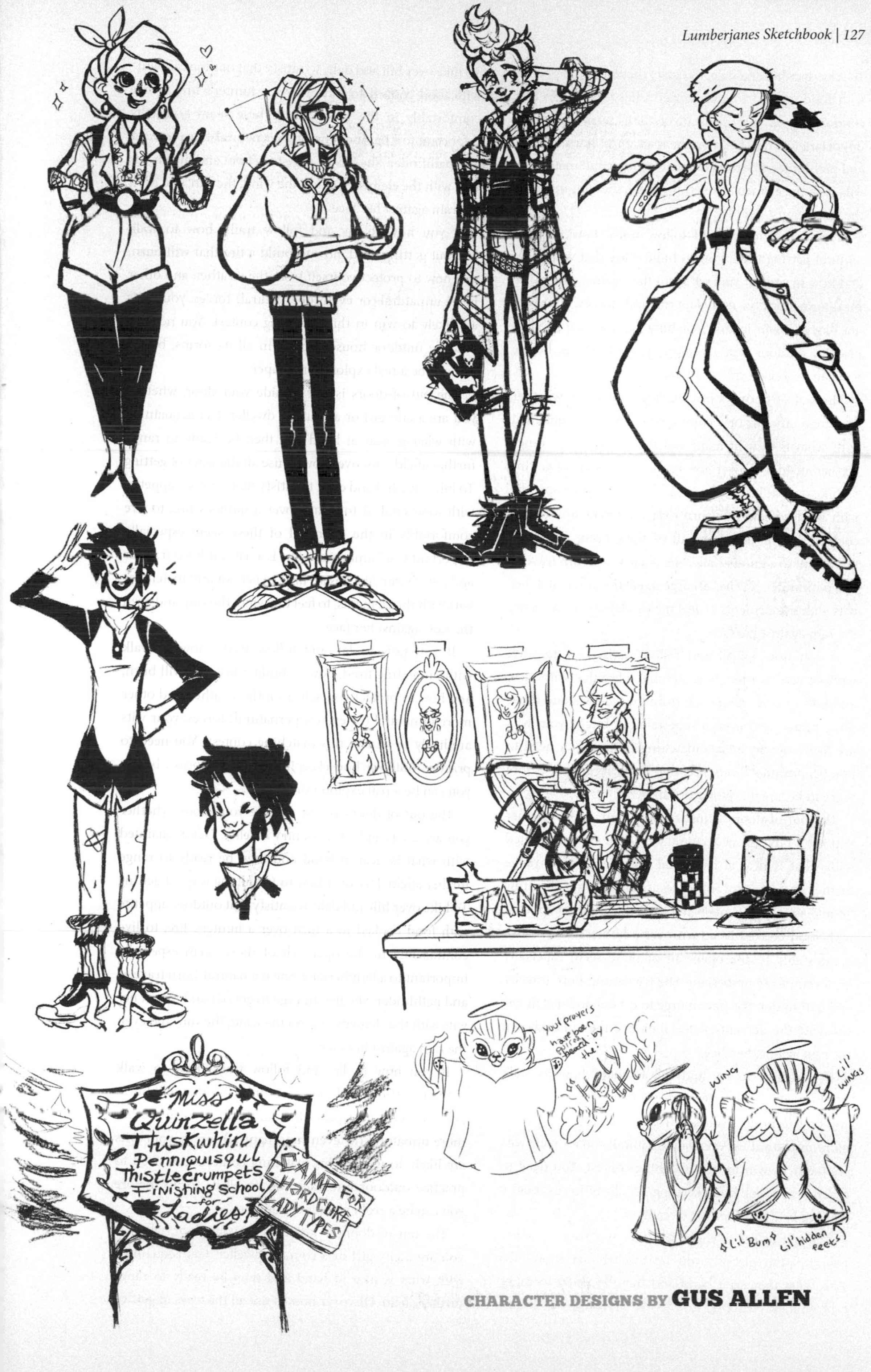
JANE
Miss
Quinzella
Thiskwhin
Penniquisqul
Thistlecrumpets
Finishing School
for
Ladies!
CAMP FOR
HARDCORE
LADY TYPES
Your prayers have been heard by the:
Holy Kitten!
WING
Cil' WINGS
Lil' Bum
Cil' hidden feets

CHARACTER DESIGNS BY **GUS ALLEN**

DISCOVER
ALL THE HITS

STEVENSON • ELLIS • WATTERS • ALLEN
LUMBERJANES
BEWARE THE KITTEN HOLY
NEW YORK TIMES BESTSELLING SERIES

Allison + Treiman + Cogar
GIANT DAYS
VOLUME ONE

From a writer of Disney's Moana
RIBON • FISH • PEER
SLAM!
VOLUME ONE

Hope Larson • Brittney Williams • Sarah Stern
GOLDIE VANCE
"Scoot over Nancy Drew..."
—Los Angeles Times
Volume One

JAMES TYNION IV • RIAN SYGH • WALTER BAIAMONTE
THE BACKSTAGERS

TYSON HESSE'S
DIESEL
IGNITION

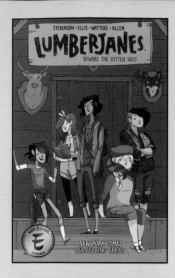

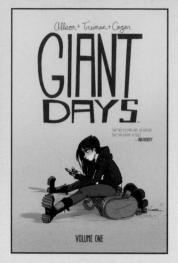

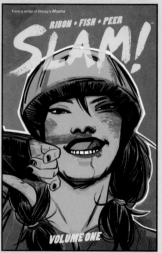

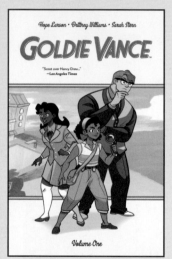

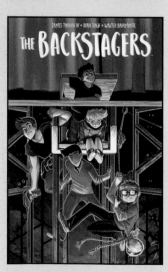

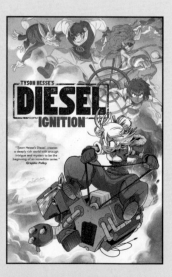

Lumberjanes
ND Stevenson, Shannon Watters, Grace Ellis, Gus Allen, and Others

Volume 1: Beware the Kitten Holy
ISBN: 978-1-60886-687-8 | $14.99 US
Volume 2: Friendship to the Max
ISBN: 978-1-60886-737-0 | $14.99 US
Volume 3: A Terrible Plan
ISBN: 978-1-60886-803-2 | $14.99 US
Volume 4: Out of Time
ISBN: 978-1-60886-860-5 | $14.99 US
Volume 5: Band Together
ISBN: 978-1-60886-919-0 | $14.99 US

Giant Days
John Allison, Lissa Treiman, Max Sarin

Volume 1
ISBN: 978-1-60886-789-9 | $9.99 US
Volume 2
ISBN: 978-1-60886-804-9 | $14.99 US
Volume 3
ISBN: 978-1-60886-851-3 | $14.99 US

Jonesy
Sam Humphries, Caitlin Rose Boyle

Volume 1
ISBN: 978-1-60886-883-4 | $9.99 US
Volume 2
ISBN: 978-1-60886-999-2 | $14.99 US

Slam!
Pamela Ribon, Veronica Fish, Brittany Peer

Volume 1
ISBN: 978-1-68415-004-5 | $14.99 US

Goldie Vance
Hope Larson, Brittney Williams

Volume 1
ISBN: 978-1-60886-898-8 | $9.99 US
Volume 2
ISBN: 978-1-60886-974-9 | $14.99 US

The Backstagers
James Tynion IV, Rian Sygh

Volume 1
ISBN: 978-1-60886-993-0 | $14.99 US

Tyson Hesse's Diesel: Ignition
Tyson Hesse

ISBN: 978-1-60886-907-7 | $14.99 US

Coady & The Creepies
Liz Prince, Amanda Kirk, Hannah Fisher

ISBN: 978-1-68415-029-8 | $14.99 US

BOOM! BOX

AVAILABLE AT YOUR LOCAL COMICS SHOP AND BOOKSTORE

To find a comics shop in your area, visit www.comicshoplocator.com

WWW.**BOOM-STUDIOS**.COM

To Gail Turner, our administrative secretary

who helps us keep it all together,

and our students of all ages

from whom we've learned